More Than You Know

More Than You Know

Rosalyn Story

Chicago

"That Sunday That Summer," by George David Weiss and Joe Sherman
© 1963, Renewed Abilene Music and Erasmus Music
Permission secured. All rights reserved.

"More Than You Know"
Words by William Rose and Edward Eliscu. Music by Vincent Youmans.
© 1929 Miller Music Corp. & Vincent Youmans, Inc. (Renewed)
Rights for the Extended Renewal Term in the U.S. Controlled by
WB Music Corp., Chappell & Co. and LSQ Music Co.
All Rights outside the U.S. Administered by EMI Miller Catalog Inc. (Publishing)
and Warner Bros. Publications U.S. Inc. (Print)
All Rights Reserved. Used by Permission of Warner Bros. Publications

Printed in Canada.

Library of Congress Cataloging-in-Publication Data

Story, Rosalyn M.
    More than you know / by Rosalyn Story.
        p.   cm.
    ISBN 0-9724562-8-7 (hardcover)
    1. Street musicians—Fiction. 2. Separated people—Fiction. 3. New York (N.Y.)—
Fiction. 4. Women singers—Fiction. 5. Saxophonists—Fiction. 6. Secrecy—Fiction.
    I. Title.

PS3619.T694M67 2004
813'.6—dc22
                                                                    2004012184

10 9 8 7 6 5 4 3 2 1

Agate books are available in bulk at discount prices.
For more information, go to agatepublishing.com.

Again, to my dad, Algrim Story,
and my mom, Mable Story 1925–2001

Acknowledgments

THROUGHOUT THE COMPLEX and arduous process of writing this book, I have been reminded that no worthwhile journey is completed without many gentle, supportive hands along the path. Many thanks to the following for your encouragement, your devotion, your inspiration, and your unflagging belief in this undertaking:

To Doug Seibold, my editor and publisher, thanks not only for your commitment to and faith in my story, but also for your magnanimous spirit. It's rare when one finds a working partner who is both efficient and reasonable, truthful and kind, good humored and wise. Thanks also for the courage to create something much needed—a place that truly respects and trusts the writer's sensibilities and creative vision.

Many thanks to my agent, Ann Collette of the Helen Rees Literary Agency in Boston, first, for "getting" my story and for standing by it, for your earnest hard work, and for your infectious, buoyant spirit that refused to be discouraged and therefore made it difficult for me to be.

To my second family of sisters, Linda Kay Smith and Maxine Clair (and Joyce, who completes the trio), thanks for the years of encouragement, and for understanding and appreciating the daunting task of bringing a story to life. Thanks also for your love and support through this process and throughout all the many years of our friendship.

To my writing buddies Bernestine Singley and Elisa Durrette, thanks for the many laughter-filled "working" breakfasts over raw manuscripts, and the sharp-witted, honest input that helped this story find its way. And also to Lisa Davis and Marie Brown of the Marie Brown Literary Agency, for your early encouragement and faith in my writing and in this book.

To Emma Rodgers and Ashira Tosihwe, for creating, in Black Images Book Bazaar of Dallas, Texas, not only a truly supportive haven for writers, but also one of the best bookstores of its kind anywhere.

To Jean Lacy and Nathaniel Lacy, my thanks respectively for your artistic vision and your computer knowledge where mine failed, and as always, for your friendship.

And finally, thanks to my many friends and relatives in the Boswell and Story families, to my dad, and especially to my mom, whose spirit and smile lives in my memory.

You have all helped and guided me, more than you know.

· Prologue ·

Arkansas, 1955

*L*ONG AS YOU LIVE, *the woman had told the boy. Her grief-torn eyes still glowed like twin stars in the back of his mind. She handed him the baby. Long as you live, don't you tell nobody.*

It was not yet dusk, but black clouds weighted the sky; then came the storm with locomotive force. Rogue winds blew in, danced crazily, railed and pitched their fury. Hard rains whipped shutters, shined the streets, and bullied the trees, thrashing and hollering in woman's-pain. When the rains had retreated, fully spent, washed skies were signed with rainbows and a greening world wondered what newborn life cried in their wake.

The little boy walked with his thin shoulders hunched, as the baby the woman had given him kicked its legs against his chest. His eyelids were pinched but allowed slits of the main street ahead: the grocery, the Handy Dandy Five and Dime, the Beauty Palace.

A pop of thunder shot up the boy's back like a hot spark, and forced a small cry from his throat. His shoulders shook, his eyes bucked wide; the whole world around him was cold, wet, and angry. He stepped in a puddle of water and stumbled on a broken piece of sidewalk brick.

Don't drop her, he told himself, whatever you do.

He wrapped both arms around her as if his own life were the prize for holding on. He glanced back at the woman now far behind, who had found cover under an awning. Her wet dress clung, and she crossed her shivering arms, empty where the baby used to be. She nodded, egged him on with a backward flick of her hand.

His toes squished inside muddy canvas Keds as water eddied up at doorways and curbs. But he walked faster, clutching the child, who had grown hot in his sweating hands. Rain beat his knotted hair; his head ducked over the baby's face. He wanted to look back again, but the woman would be too far away, lost to the rain. Finally he reached the door with the only light at the end of the street.

He reached up and knocked, then knocked again, louder, desperate.

A plump, kind-eyed woman answered, looked out through the rain, then down at him. Her face a startled question mark. She took the child from his arms, beckoned him inside, queried him.

Whose child is this?

Long as you live, he remembered.

He'd keep the promise, or so he thought. For how could he know what the coming years would bring?

It was warm inside, so warm and dry he wanted to stay. But he waited for her to turn, and when she did, he ran back into the rain.

I

· ONE ·

New York, late 1990s

WHILE THE LAST WEDGE OF LATE SEPTEMBER SUN lights the L-shaped sky between the highrises above the city, and buses bleat like frantic trumpets and Yellow cabs blare like choruses of big-band brass, and the cacophony swells to *forte* beneath street lamps that spotlight the theater of midtown at dusk, L.J. Tillman watches the people. He scours the to-and-fro parade in the evening rush for a rhythm in arms, legs, or feet, a beat in the sway of shoulders and hips. He nods to the straight-legged strut of the young banking women with their fitted brown suits and briefcases, the syncopated shuffle of old men's weary feet ambling toward the park, the swinging arms and busy swagger of busboys rushing to meet the time clocks of the uptown kitchens.

The whole town is pulsing to a time-worn tune. Feet planted on a busy midtown corner, L.J. licks the reed of his tenor horn, searching the city for a song.

On the other side of the sky, a quarter-moon of faded pearl rises, but he's heard there is the slightest chance of rain. Something needs to happen soon if he expects to eat. The women are the best, he figures; whether old or young, jasmine- or rose-scented, sneaker-shod or stiletto-heeled, there's always a rhythm, a melody carved into the curve of lipsticked smiles.

A young black woman in long, flowing, navy blue, hair piled high above a heart-shaped face, glides by in samba time. He blows a liquid, Latin "Summertime." She keeps walking without a glance his way.

Sometimes a good tune is all you got, boy; your best friend, your home. Climb on into it, crawl in the corners of that tune and pull down the blinds. It'll make you forget what's troubling you. Just go on inside, and the people will follow.

The old man who raised him had been good at dispensing advice that didn't work. Because, for sure, nothing is working tonight. A half-hour on this corner—searching his mind for the one tune that would make them stop, even pause, and give up a little change—and nothing. Apparently, Gershwin held no favor with these folks tonight, and for that matter, neither did the Duke. He looks up and down the street with a frustrated frown: at the hospital workers leaving the day shift, the cluster of waiters on cigarette break at Gennaro's before the dinner hour, the going-to and coming-from bustle, but nobody stopping to listen.

He plays with his sax strap, looks down at the torn velvet lining of the bruised leather case splayed open against the bank cornerstone, empty except for the crumpled dollar he'd thrown in himself.

The ching-chinging reggae beat of a Jamaican steel band a block away plays faintly on the air across the distance and L.J. envisions piles of money in the coffee cans beneath their drums. They always had a crowd. Figures—there are four of them, dreadlocks swinging, young and good looking, and a beat so infectious that even L.J. was tempted to put down his horn and listen. Maybe he should move a little further away, but no, this is where the crosstown buses and the IRT stop. On a good night in this very spot he'll collect at least enough for dinner, a morning muffin, and a cup of French roast. But some nights, like this one, the going is slow.

L.J. fingers the keys, licks the reed again, and blows air through the hollow coil of plated brass. Got to play something, they won't pay me for standing here. There's a night chill snapping the air with a promise of fall and around him the thick traffic crawls, the brake lights carnival-red sequins blinking stop-and-go against the twilight gray. The jewel-blue sky is dimming to deep purple, and a soft growl in the bottom of his stomach warns him the evening rush is slipping away.

One thing the old man did get right: *Boy, if it looks like nobody gives a hoot about your horn, just close your eyes, say the hell with it, and play.*

"The hell with it." Saying it out loud even feels good. He closes his eyes. If enough money for a hot meal falls into his case, fine. If not, so be it. Another missed meal won't kill him. He decides on "Someone to Watch Over Me."

A sweet tune, a perfect melody. And who doesn't love it? He licks the reed again, and pinches tight his eyelids to shut out the city. He warms up gently to it, starting soft and low. Then soars on the tune in the high octave. Good reed, fingers feeling good. In a minute, even with his eyes closed he can feel a presence, someone standing before him, listening.

Finally.

When he opens his eyes, a black man of about sixty (older than him, slightly built, and fairer of skin), is standing there. Dressed to kill in a pinstriped suit, shoes showing a slick shine. *A dandy, from back in the day.* Cab Calloway as Sportin' Life comes to mind. He's smiling approval, nodding to the beat.

Come on man, dig down and shell out a couple of bucks.

But the man is not reaching in his pocket, not even thinking about it. Instead he closes his eyes. His arms spread wide like eagles' wings, mouth O-shaped to the sky. A visible sucking in of night air, and out comes a sound that takes L.J. back some forty of his fifty-two years.

There's a somebody I'm longing to see...

It's a baritone as smooth and gritty as raw silk, flowing honey-thick, a perfect mix of southern cooking and northern cocktails.

There, in the middle of mad Manhattan comes the dewy heat of a juke joint in Tupelo. Or Biloxi, or Memphis. When he was a boy, L.J. and the old man often set out from one blues quarter to another—the old upright rattling out of tune in the back of the pickup truck—finding a place for the old man to play. The plank-floor jukes attracted the foot-stomping crowd, but now and then there'd be a voice like this man's, an old-style crooner who made the women swoon and the men smile their envy.

I hope that she turns out to be...
Someone who'll watch over me.

Eckstein, Prysock, Nat King Cole. Their ghosts were smiling, humming along.

L.J. keeps playing, weaving woolen threads around the silken tones, sliding to the bottom of his range to let the baritone float above. He wanders through the open spaces between each phrase. Takes deep breaths, and blows.

He ends the tune holding a lusty low C and just listens as the man riffs to the cadence like a pro, up and down and circling around and finally landing on L.J.'s pitch, vibrating like a cello in a master's hands. At the end of the tune the man nods, but neither man speaks. L.J. lifts his brows and begins "Body and Soul." And the man joins in.

I can't believe it, it's hard to conceive it, that you'd take away romance... The two stand there facing each other, music flowing back and forth between them like charged ions. And a full ten minutes pass before they even notice the swarm of people circling them in. They start another tune and another, without a word.

Money rises in heaps on the worn felt—quarters, ones, and fives. A couple of people leave tens or twenties, leaning over to make change.

They yell out their favorites. "Sunday Kind of Love," an older bearded man in a Paul Bunyan plaid shirt yells, while a woman in a suit with a briefcase calls, "My Funny Valentine."

"Autumn Leaves."

"Love for Sale."

"All of Me."

The old tunes, the standards. A young girl in a hospital smock with an opera voice sings along softly on "Autumn Leaves," and a man in a cowboy hat grabs her hand for a dance. They are young and old and middle-aged, slender and fat, black and white and every color in between. They are just getting off from or coming to work, dressed in Italian shoes or steel-toed boots, overalls or blue jeans, plain coats or expensive coats or no coats at all. Fingers snapping, shoulders working, feet tapping.

At a lickety-split pace L.J. starts "All of Me," his fingers sculpting melody while the older man scats. *Skiddle dee bop, bop, do weee, do wow.* The two men banter in melody and counter-tune, rapid exchanges, flurries of scales and licks, back and forth while the crowd, now more than thirty, hums along and eggs them on.

After an hour or so, the men, exhausted, bow to disperse the clapping and whistling and hooting crowd. When everyone has left, the man sticks out his hand to L.J., grinning. L.J.'s large hand engulfs the man's small fingers.

"Man, you are something else!" the stranger says. His smile suggests two even rows of piano keys. His dark eyes seem lantern-lit. "Whoa, man. You can play!"

L.J. smiles too, as he squats before his case, counting money. More than he's seen at one time in more than a year.

"Aw, man. That was great," he says. "You got a voice on you. Really. You got some set of pipes."

"Roscoe Covington," the older man says.

"Oh yeah, man, sorry. Tillman. L.J. Tillman. Pleased to meet you."

L.J.'s heart races as he gathers the money, counts it. He hands the man a fistful of bills and loose change. "OK, half of this is yours. Here's your share, sixty-three and some change."

Covington waves his hand dismissively. "Oh, hey, I wasn't doing it for no money, I just saw you standing here by your lonesome, playing the hell out of that horn, and I just felt like singing along."

L.J. is embarrassed. The man couldn't know how much these few dollars mean to him. Or maybe he does. There was a time when it wouldn't have mattered, but now he can't imagine somebody waving off this much money with a flick of the hand.

He shakes his head. "Man, you gotta take some of this. I was dying out here before you came along."

"Naw, it's just two is better than one. Folks like a little harmony. Folks like a show."

"Man, please. Take some. I insist."

It isn't that he doesn't need the money, he's playing on the street, after all. It's just that he believes in being fair. The man worked for it, had more than earned his share.

"Look, I tell you what. You can buy me a drink. I know a place not far from here. I got a few minutes before I got to head off."

The lantern-lit eyes seem to do the inviting. There's a shred of pain behind those pupils, but if his eyes confirm a trace of it the rest of him betrays it; the straight shoulders and full head of thick black hair, the shiny wing-tip shoes and cuffed gabardine slacks, the cufflinks blinking in the streetlamp light all bespeak a good life. L.J. is sure his own trials show in every pore and fiber of skin and garment: his oily complexion, uncombed hair, sleep-matted wool, and dusty shoes. He rubs a hand along the old stain on the sleeve of his too-short blue blazer. "Uh, I'm not dressed for any of these places around here."

"Nothing fancy. Cup of hot coffee. Say, you ever been to French's? Right over on Fifty-fourth. It's just a little old place but they got the best coffee in New York, man…hey. Let's go."

Covington even walks with a little bounce, a brisk strut.

"You coming? It's not far. Just right over here."

The night is chilly, the coffee will be hot. L.J. shrugs, then tugs again at his jacket, his horn case and satchel slinging against his hip as he lopes behind the man with the bouncy gait and the natty suit.

At French's, a tiny diner with red swivel stools along a Formica counter and faux-leather booths along the wall of plate glass looking out on the busy street, they walk toward a booth in the back.

"Hey French! Couple of coffees over here!" Covington yells to a bald, middle-aged, olive-skinned man behind the counter.

When the coffees arrive, Covington takes a sip. L.J. warms his fingers around the cup. He blows ripples across the smoking surface, empties in half a pack of sugar and a pack of cream, then takes a drink, long and slow, letting the hot nutty flavor settle on his tongue. He closes his eyes and lets the steam warm his nose. He sighs and smiles.

"You're right, man. This is the best."

"Didn't I tell you?" He pushes up his sleeve and looks at a gold-trimmed watch on his wrist. "Got a gig to get to in a little bit. Ever hear of a place called the Baby Grand? Uptown. East eighties. I been there a few years. Nice place."

L.J. nods. Who hadn't heard of the Baby Grand? "Yeah. Nice place, I hear."

"Nicest place I ever worked at, that's for sure. Back in Cleveland we didn't have nothing like that. Not for jazz, anyway. And the tips, man. On a good night…" He shakes his head and takes another sip.

L.J. listens while the older man talks about living in Cleveland where he was the singer for a downtown hotel lounge band that played together for twenty years. How he moved to New York after his wife died, just because he'd always wanted to, and she hadn't. How he had dreams of making it big, recording, the whole thing, but settled for a gig in a top-drawer club where the customers, and even the waiters and waitresses, think he hung the moon.

"That was seven years ago. I been there ever since. It's a nice little gig, you know. Pays all right. I give up on trying to make it big-time a while ago. I thought as soon as I got up here, agents would be breaking down my door. Thought I was gonna be Bobby Short. You know how that is. But I do get a couple of jingles and a TV voice-over now and then. You ever hear of Toasty Wheat Crackers?"

L.J.'s eyebrows arch up. That's where he's heard the voice. He'd even tried the crackers one time; they reminded him of salted cardboard. "You're the guy in the Toasty Wheat commercials?"

Toasty wheat, toasty wheat, when you want a tasty treat, Covington cups his hand to his ear studio-style and sings in a rich, deep bass.

"Man, that's you?"

"That's me," he says, nodding, grinning, sipping.

L.J. spoons more sugar in his coffee and stirs. "Hey, that's a good commercial. But you know, I didn't like the crackers all that much."

"Me neither, at first." Covington winks. "But after eight years, them funny tasting little crackers bought me a nice little time-share down in Florida. They taste a whole lot better, now."

They both laugh, take another sip, and lean back.

Covington looks up at L.J., his face changed now, the smile settling into a questioning look. He lowers his voice, drums his knuckles on the table, and leans forward. "What I want to know is, man, how come you playing out *here*? You're better than half the dudes I've played with in this town. Cleveland, too."

L.J. smiles wryly, shrugs, and stares down into his coffee before absently taking another sip.

The older man fills in the silence. "You read music? You do, I can tell. Why don't you come up to the club sometime, sit in? All I got's a trio behind me. Be nice to hear your horn backing me up."

L.J. studies the backs of his hands. *'I've told you my story so what's yours?'* is what he hears in the silence. And for a minute he wonders if the man doesn't know. Doesn't he, L.J., look like every other homeless brother on the street? Sure, he's cleaner than most—he keeps his hair trimmed with cheap scissors, his armpits sticky with Old Spice roll-on. Washes his clothes in pre-dawn fountains a piece at a time. But he's seen in others—not just the ones in doorways huddled up against their own madness or warming themselves by the trash-barrel flames, but also the ones who just walk the streets without aim—something dull in their eyes. This city has a way of stamping its human jetsam with an indelible brand. And if he's seen it in others, surely this man can see it in him.

L.J. leans forward, his voice low. "Man, look, I'm not even sure what I'm doing here myself."

Covington nods slowly, takes a long drink of coffee, folds his hands.

L.J. rubs his brow. He is not often given to openness; most of what he feels or thinks he simply blows through the bell of his horn. But partly out of gratitude and partly because he's never spoken it out loud before, he begins. Maybe telling it will help sort out the mess of last year—order the loose puzzle pieces scattered across his mind.

He clears his throat. "My wife," he starts. "We were married twenty-four years. And one night about a year ago, she…well…put me out."

Covington shakes his head. "Oh, man, that's tough."

L.J. nods. He hadn't expected his confession to ring with such finality. He also hadn't expected it to sound like such a boring cliché, the same old man/woman thing played out a thousand other times. But no, this is different.

It was almost a year ago, he recalls. One minute he was standing in the kitchen of his green-shuttered two-story in Kansas City, smelling mustard greens and a peach pie in the oven, getting ready for work, watching his pretty wife humming into steaming pots. The next minute, all hell broke loose.

"I…we argued. It was something I did a long time ago, it was all my fault. She got mad and told me to leave."

Told him? She'd screamed for him to leave. *Get out and don't ever come back* were her exact words, each one exploding like flint meeting flame. He could still feel the singe of their heat. Even the food recoiled; the mustard greens turned black and crisp, the pie bubbled over and smoke-blackened the oven. He had just looked at her, perfect skin flushed with anger and kitchen heat, her red-eyed stare clashing with the delicate purple in the flowers of her dress.

He'd searched for words to explain, but he knew an army of them could not defend him. Instead he opened the door quietly and the wind grabbed it and slammed it shut. He drove to the club—his gig five nights a week at Jimmy's, in the old part of Kansas City. Jimmy's was where he played his way through whatever bothered him, let the blue notes salve the wounded spirit he brought in the door. But the club was quiet, dim. Chairs on tabletops, the quartet sidemen—Ace, Conny, and Walt—sitting with elbows resting on their knees, staring at their shoes. The club was belly-up, after twelve years.

L.J. takes a long swallow, sets down the cup and stares at the table, then looks up to see Covington's shaking head, thick eyebrows furrowed in sympathy.

"I felt like I'd lost everything. My wife…" he clears his throat. He hasn't used those words in over a year, and the tear in his voice behind them is a shock to him. He massages the tightening muscle at the back of his neck. "My wife, my twelve-year gig. I didn't know what to do. I'd never been much of a drinker, but I grabbed a bottle of Jack and left. Sat in the car outside the club and drank for an hour. Just thinking about everything, feeling sorry. Then I did something really crazy, I still don't know what got into me."

He drove wildly, out of control, mind spinning, wondering how it was that a life could turn on a dime, that the life you had when you woke up that morning could vanish like a shadow beneath a cloud before the night was done. He hadn't realized his speed, and the liquor loosened his grip on the wheel. Before he knew it, he'd landed in the middle of the river, flailing for his life.

"It had been raining; the river was high," he says. "My car was going down faster than I could think. I thought I was a dead man; maybe I wanted to be, for a hot minute. But, funny how stuff like that works, no matter how much you feel like dying, when that water starts to rising around you, all you can think about is living. I mean I never been much of a praying man—oh, I went to church with my wife now and then, when I could get myself out of bed on time—but you'd a thought I was one of those TV evangelists. I got myself on top of the car, the hood, some kind of way. I don't even remember doing it. Then I flung my horn far as I could—landed on some railroad ties. Then I swam, crawled, whatever, got myself to the bank."

He rolls the coffee cup between his palms. "I sat on the bank for a while. It was cold but I was so wasted I couldn't feel a thing. Then I heard the train."

The Union Pacific. How would things have been different if it hadn't pulled into view, its noisy bulk of freight cars heaving, smoking, wailing, bugle-calling him to hop aboard and move? He hadn't thought of actually going anywhere, just getting on and moving. The heaviness of his sopping clothes and shoes hadn't stuttered his step as he sloshed through grass and mud—his wet shoes slipping on beds of stone and coal along the track—and pulled himself aboard.

With the river's roar still in his ears and without a sensible thought crossing his mind, he'd hopped another train, then at a weigh station in Pennsylvania hooked up with a trucker bound for Newark. After all that had happened, the mix of strong drink, river water and the whistle of an eastbound train were too heady for him to stay put. He'd always been curious about New York—he was a jazz man. So he rode on, high on the smell of ripe cattle and the rank odor of his river-washed clothes that dried and shrank while his mind sobered.

"By the time I got up here, I wondered what the hell I had done, felt like I had lost my mind or something. I'd never done anything that stupid in my life. I started to go right back. But I damn sure wasn't going to go back the way I came. Didn't have no money. And then I didn't know what I would say, anyway, how I would handle things. How I could make things right between us. I still don't know."

He takes a sip of coffee, then takes an empty sugar packet, wads it up and rolls it between his fingers.

"So here I am."

Covington says nothing, just looks at L.J.'s hands as the sax player rubs them together. After a moment, Covington signals to French and points two fingers at the empty coffee cups. French brings a smoking pot to the table and fills them up.

Covington blows on his coffee, sets it down and strokes his chin. "After my wife died, I felt lost," he says quietly. "It took a while, but I got it together. But one thing I learned."

"What's that?"

"Anything you got to say to somebody, say it. Say it whenever you can, don't let the time get too short before you make it right."

Sympathy softens the man's eyes. Behind the counter of the restaurant smoke rises from a greasy grill, and a queasiness rises in L.J.'s empty stomach. He doesn't know if it's the smell of frying meat that causes it or the thought of actually doing what the man suggests.

"I know," L.J. says. "A whole year up here in this crazy place, and the strangest thing about being here is not seeing her. I miss her like...I don't know. It's strange. You're with somebody every day for twenty-four years, and then you're not."

"So how come you don't call? Maybe it's not as bad as you think."

L.J. turns up his cup and finishes off the coffee. "Well. It's a long story."

Covington looks down and nods. "Ain't it always. She know you're alive?"

"What do you mean?"

"I mean if they found your car, folks might think you bought the farm that night."

L.J. is amazed that he has never thought of this. She had told him to leave, and he did. The fact that he might be considered dead in Kansas City never occurred to him.

"The car went down. I guess I never thought about anybody finding it. I'd messed up so bad, all I could think about was just getting away."

Covington shrugs. "Some cars stay down, some don't."

French arrives at their table with a fresh pot of coffee, but Covington covers his cup with his hand. "No, thanks, Frenchie. I got to run now."

"I'll take the check," L.J. says.

L.J. opens the door to the humming streets, the chilling evening air that presses against the glass door. The two men shake hands.

"Everything OK where you're staying?" Covington asks.

"Huh?"

"Where you're living. Is it decent?"

He *doesn't* know. "Oh, yeah. I'm cool. Just fine."

"All right, then," Covington says. "I'll be getting on. Sure wish you'd think about sitting in with us. It'd be a blast, man."

"Well, sometime, maybe. Hey, look. Thanks again. I sure appreciate your stopping by."

Covington's eyes glow. "My pleasure, man."

After the two men walk away in opposite directions, L.J. turns to see the sprightly gait, the bouncing step, then turns away, humming the last tune they played.

The sky is dark now, the streets quieter. No rain, good. There are even a couple of rare visible stars between the building tops as he looks over west by the river. He finds a bodega that sells microwaved lasagna for $2.95, and downs half a loaf of bread, sitting on the stoop of a West End brownstone. He walks an hour or more before he finds a bench in Riverside Park not already occupied. He stretches out on it, his jacket draped over his head, the horn case and his vinyl knapsack under his head and money bulging in his socks.

Tomorrow, he'll have to deal with it. Find out for sure.

The bench is rock-hard. But he's spent the whole day playing his horn and walking against the wind, so he sleeps like the dead man she probably believes he is.

TWO

MORNING LIGHT FLOATS IN WITH A STRONG WIND whipping off the river. The park bench leaves L.J.'s body full of dents and twists and bends that take a minute to loosen and unwind, and with a slight misting of dew on the grass, the sun shines brightly through the bracing November air. He finds a men's room at the Café Delisa close to the Museum of Natural History to wash his face and brush his teeth.

He arrives at the Forty-second Street library only a couple of minutes after it opens for the day and heads straight to the section of magazines and periodicals.

The brown-skinned middle-aged woman wears what seems like inches of makeup, and her hair is piled in a bun slightly darker than the rest of her hair. Her half-glasses sit perched on the edge of her nose.

"The *Kansas City Star*? We have it on microfiche. Right over this way."

L.J. follows her to a section of cabinets and watches while she opens a drawer. "October, did you say? Last year? Let me see, ah, yes, here it is."

He thanks her and looks puzzled at the box before she says, "Have you not used these before? Here, let me show you."

She finds an unoccupied projector, flicks a button to light up the screen, places the thin celluloid sheet under the glass, and clamps it shut.

"There. Use this knob to advance it, and this one for reverse. That'll get you started. If you need help, I'll be at the desk."

"Thank you," he says.

Just reading the hometown paper is a comfort, like sneaking back and peering through a giant keyhole to a room where he'd once lived. The Chiefs lost to Denver in overtime, the bond issue passed. Some school administrator embezzled money from the Board of Education, and a flash flood on the Plaza damaged the tennis courts. He has been reading for an hour before something in his stomach does a backflip, as if he's seen his own ghost.

A picture of himself stares from the page, and beneath it an article dated October 12, a few days after the accident.

Local Musician Believed Drowned

A 1991 Ford Mercury registered to local jazz musician Louis James Tillman was found Friday night floating in shallow waters near the northeast bank of the Missouri River, two miles north of downtown. Tillman was last seen earlier in the evening at Jimmy's, a once-popular jazz club in the historic Vine Street district.

Police say Tillman apparently lost control of his vehicle and crashed into a tree. The car then likely careened over loose railings and into the river. Officers at the scene found no sign of Tillman, and believe him to have drowned in the river's strong current.

Sgt. Delvin DeMarque who investigated the accident said chances of Tillman's survival are "slim to none."

"It looked like he managed to get out, but the current was too strong," said DeMarque. "It probably just swept him away."

James Oliver Bell, owner of the club where the popular, 51-year-old saxophonist worked for twelve years, said Tillman was distraught over the closing of the club and may have been drinking heavily. "He wasn't a drinking man," said Bell. "L.J. was straight as an arrow, solid as a rock. But we all were pretty depressed that night."

Bell said dwindling attendance forced him to close the night spot after twelve years.

The saxophonist's wife, beauty-salon owner Olivia Benton Tillman, said her husband did possess some skill as a swimmer and may have escaped, though police investigators were not hopeful. "As long as there is a chance," she said, "I believe he might still be alive."

L.J. feels his heart pound inside his chest. So they had found the car. They'd found his car and written him off as dead.

Except Olivia. He reads the last sentence again. "As long as there is a chance, I believe he might still be alive."

Chance? Believe? Could that mean hope? Of course she wouldn't have *wished* him dead; what kind of person would, even after what he'd done? But could the words mean she wanted to see him, wanted him to come back?

He sits back in the oak chair and massages the bridge of his nose. He remembers the church secretary had taken the picture of the two of them, and of Olivia's half, cut away by someone, only the curled ends of her hair against his shoulder remained.

It had been taken four years ago at the Founder's Day picnic. The July sun blazing hot, the park crowded with church folk. He was sweating, walking back from a softball game with the stewards when he saw her at the other end of the park, dressed in bright yellow, smiling with her girlfriend Maxine Tuttles as they arranged rows of pies on a card table. Suddenly, the table collapsed and pies flew, the two women splashed with pie filling and broken crusts. The culprits—three little boys chasing each other in reckless flight. L.J. recognized them as the Stevenson boys, recently orphaned by a terrible car accident. Olivia reached down and picked up two pies that had miraculously landed right side up, while Maxine reset the table on its hinges.

Two of the boys made clumsy helping-out moves, and one began to cry. But Olivia smiled as if the deep red cherry on her yellow hem was water, and carefully cut three extra-wide slices of apple pie. She reached down to dry tears, buss cheeks, hug each one. The boys grinned bashfully and danced off—faces smudged with lipstick and pie filling. L.J. had never watched her like this, spying from a distance. She was still smiling as she dabbed a tissue at the red splotch on her dress, bought the day before for the picnic. Whether or not it was precognition of what was to come, he had wondered then whether she could forgive *him*—anything? Wondered if someday something he did might test the range of her heart.

Someday had come. But he was no mischievous boy. And the cart he'd upset could not so easily be set aright.

A thick-handed clock on the west wall chimes the hour. She's at work now. Tonight will be a long stint of what he called her "faith-healing" miracles. It was his favorite joke. Honestly, he told her, some of those women would waltz into her shop looking like whatever it was that made banshees scream and would step out looking like queens. Even if Jesus *could* turn water to wine, some of those rougher-looking heads could only be saved by deep prayer and Olivia Tillman's hands. She laughed. The joke was a gift; later, as her evenings dissolved into aching feet and tightening wrists, she'd remember and smile. On Fridays, standing at the door before leaving for three sets at the club, he would nod at the kitchen. "Pot's on the stove." The sweet stew sea-soned with garlic and bay leaves and good red wine was the only dish he knew how to make, but it was good. He'd wink, slyly. "Later, you and me," he'd say. She'd wink back. "I'll be up."

Somewhere in their twenty-four years, their lives took on a rhythm, vamping along in a harmonious hum, the marriage cooling into an unconscious bliss borne out in subtle signs: a stray hand ab-sently caressing a shoulder or wrist, glances over breakfast or dinner, private jokes shared in public through a wink or smile. They seemed to move and grow in common time. Olivia had her faults—always running late, needing a little too much attention, and her clothes messily consuming his side of the closet (she never threw anything out, except once in a rare fit of housecleaning when she'd accidentally discarded the precious *Downbeat* magazines he'd collected for twenty years, leaving him in a speechless funk for a whole day), but there was the way that the chicken soup she'd made for him one winter night warmed his infected throat. The way she tiptoed around him on the couch when he'd come home from a late gig too dog-tired to climb the stairs. The way the thick cotton quilt she'd tucked around him smelled of her lavender perfume.

He breathes deeply, eyes glazed and staring at the screen.

The library clerk walks over when he catches her eye. "I'd like to make a copy," he says.

"Oh, certainly. These machines make it for you. Do you have a quarter?"

He digs in his pocket for one and she puts it into the slot.

"Now. What page? This one?" She looks at the article on the screen, sees the picture of him. She adjusts the focus and looks at him, a lingering look, then back at the screen.

He lowers his eyes.

"It'll be just a second." And the article and picture slide out.

"Thank you, miss."

"No trouble," she says, and after a pause, "And good luck to you."

He folds it, and tucks it into the inside pocket of his jacket, and pats it with his hand.

He steps outside into the afternoon air—a sunshine-filled day with few clouds—and walks a wide circle around the library building before going back in. He finds a bank of pay phones and begins to dial.

Hi honey, I'm homeless. Living up here on the street.

Words he can't say. He puts the phone back into the receiver. He'll have to tell her sometime, but not now, not today.

Days pass, and survival is the usual seat-of-his-pants affair of beans and crackers in soup-kitchen lines, of Spam and cheese and week-old bread from church pantries, of waking to the scuttle of pigeons or the ruckus of drunken fights, of dodging skidding cars and braking buses, of aimless, endless walking, and the long stares of cops. When the weather is good he sleeps in the open, but when the street's sharp edges cut too deeply, there's shelter at the Bowery, or better, the old Rescue Mission down on Cooper Square. Not the Ritz, but the humiliation of walking through those doors is small enough price for a room and a decent wash-up. The first time in he nearly gagged, swallowing the stale air chased with a heavy dose of pride. But at least the Christian brethren who kept the place were kind, never making their "transient guests" feel like the hapless losers they were.

Being in this city, however, has its moments. One summer Sunday in the park he stumbled on a concert—Pavarotti with an orchestra, singing slow in Italian (o mio something)—and wept as the last high note floated into the trees. And sometimes there's a sweet something in the pleasure of a well-played tune, a stranger's smile or nod, a cup of hot brew warming his hands while he looks out through a foggy diner window at an afternoon rain.

But there's another side to it. Kansas City was a city, true enough, but this one, with its arc of bridges and skyward sweep of steel, blasts of acrid fumes and drones of machinery and human life, takes his breath away. Every ante is upped, the daily boil of life and death playing out in wild extremes, like the sizzle and pop and swirl and glide of jazz. Homeless or not, a man could feel truly alive, and L.J. can't help but think, "Man, I'm right here. I'm right here in it."

Today, he woke early (cold and stiff as usual from the park bench), to begin his routine. Clean up. Find food. Walk. Play. A warm, October sun sweetened the prospect of walking, and at the corner of Seventy-second Street a window displays a bounty of pastries and breads. The éclairs look good today, and he thinks of making it his breakfast along with some of that good coffee from French's. The window throws back his own image and he sees himself in full view as if on a stage—New York as the curtained backdrop.

Clean, mirroring windows are rare, so the thinness of his reflection surprises him. At six-two with an athlete's build, he's always taken his strength for granted. But the extra girth he arrived with had fueled his battle with the daily assault of the street until the extra pounds disappeared. He could do with a little protein, and seeing the shine in his skin, some water too. Stepping inside the bakery, he vows a decent meal later in the day.

L.J. slaps down two bills on the counter for the éclair ("The one on the right, that's right, the big one, please") and decides against the coffee at French's; the bakery coffee smells great and only costs a dollar.

Standing in generous sunlight in front of the bakery, he eats the éclair as messily as a kid and gulps the coffee down in four swallows. He tosses the wrap in the trash and wipes his face and hands with a napkin before continuing on his way. Along Broadway, two white-haired men in thin jackets of frayed wool sit on folding chairs by the newsstand. He drops a dollar in their empty coffee can. Invisible, he thinks. Invisible as ghosts. When he passes the homeless ones, he offers a fraternal nod (in exchange for a cold, blank stare), then counts them; today so far he's seen sixteen.

At the corner of Sixty-sixth, he pauses; an attractive black woman in a red-striped running suit has stopped her jog and bends over to tie her sneaker. It isn't that she looks so much like Olivia, but she is around her age, shares the loose cut of hair, the deep slope of shoulder, the ginger tone of skin. Now and then, when some part of Olivia—her shoulders or longish legs or rhythm of walk—appears in front of a deli or steps off a bus, something flips over in his chest. The jogging woman takes off in a quick run, and in the place where she stood he sees the shop window for the first time.

A dress of deep purple, silk maybe, hangs on the window mannequin. The skirt is full the way he likes it; the elegant swoop of neckline and fitted waist would show her figure, which, the last time he had seen her, had lost none of its youthful taper.

The resistance of the heavy glass door of the shop should have warned him, but once inside, amid faint violin music and a waft of cinnamon and cloves, the dress hangs on a rack like the figment of a dream. Without thinking, he reaches out to touch its skirt, twirling the cool silk between his fingers.

Behind him, too close, is the fragrant breath of mint, gardenias, and hair spray. He turns. Bow-shaped, strawberry-colored lips speak in a low tone. "That's $875," the clerk says. "Pure imported silk. From Italy."

He takes a step back, his hands finding both pockets, his words stumbling. "OK. Well. Thanks."

She may as well have spoken the words they both understood. Outside, he gives his head a quick shake, as if to snap back into place the sanity that had temporarily fled his grip. Why did he go in? He never bought her expensive dresses anyway—flowers and the prime rib special at Max's were what he could afford. And now, homeless and broke, a dress for a queen drapes across his mind. But he was thinking of her, and for that moment wanted that soft silk touch on his skin.

A dumb thing to do. He adjusts the knapsack strap higher on his shoulder, looks both ways and crosses the street, heading south. At Fifty-ninth, he stops, takes out his horn. *Time to work. No good thinking about all this other stuff now.* He considers a different intro to "I Can't Get Started," but pauses when a thought invades; he's never felt farther from home. With so much time and distance between them, she seems a whole world away. And he couldn't be farther from standing in front of Olivia with a beautiful new dress in hand than if he were living on the moon.

For the next few days, with good weather bringing out pedestrians in throngs, he plays like a fiend. Jazz standards, showtunes, even polkas, whatever the crowd inspires. "Havah Nagila" for a pair of Hasidic Jews walking by, "Moonlight in Vermont" for an elderly tourist couple holding hands, Motown medleys for a trio of middle-aged black women who smile at him and empty their change purses into his case.

A few purchases keep him groomed and fed: some Dove soap, Schick blades, a bottle of roll-on, and sax reeds. A good late lunch. In two weeks he's saved almost two hundred. A good start toward a new change of clothes and some decent shoes, and maybe even a one-way ticket on a bus.

Then, on the next Friday evening, L.J. is playing "Someone to Watch Over Me" when he hears a full-throated baritone behind him.

There's a somebody I'm longing to see...

Roscoe Covington grins, eyes flashing above those perfect rows of piano keys.

L.J.'s eyebrows arch up above his smiling eyes. He keeps playing.

It's like magic. In the past couple of weeks, he's done all right. But with Covington showing up again, it's as if two stars are making a return engagement before a crowd of loyal fans. People do not gather, they flock like starving birds to a spill of crumbs. A ring, then a double ring, and then a third wide ring of people stand, sit, or lean in doorways to hear the music that makes even the too-young ones think of long-ago loves, blue lights in basements, and dancing in the dark. Tight jaws slacken, aching feet tap, and stressed shoulders shimmy and shake. The crowd consumes half a block; anyone who wants to pass has to cross the street.

They play for an hour and a half and only stop because a policeman wants to see what the commotion is, and after humming for a couple of minutes decides to break up the crowd and scurry the people along.

When the last chord of the last song settles around their shoulders like a low-sitting fog, L.J. grabs Covington's hand to shake it. Both men grin and slap each other's backs.

"Hey-y-y, stranger!" L.J. says. "How've you been, man?"

"Going good, going good," Covington beams. "Man, you're sounding as fierce as ever."

"You the one," L.J. says. "I could hardly play for listening."

"I was checking out them monster licks coming outta that horn."

"Hey, just trying to keep up with you."

"Shoot, you doin' more than keepin' up."

L.J.'s gaze keeps floating over to the mound of money spilling in and around his case.

"Man, check out this pile. You gotta take some."

Covington holds up both palms, turns his head. "It's your show man, your corner."

L.J. kneels to arrange the money, mostly bills. He's a little self-conscious at his excitement, seeing so much green. He's surprised at the number of large bills, tens, even a couple of twenties. When he finishes, he has to suppress a gasp.

One hundred and eighty-four dollars. Did he miscount? He counts the larger bills again. No, he's counted right.

He stands to his feet as if he's rising from a hole in the earth and is seeing the sun for the first time in a year. Covington smiles his wide piano-key smile.

L.J. whispers around the break in his voice. "Man, I don't know how to thank you."

"Don't thank me. Just come over to the club and sit in for a while. Tonight's my last night."

"Say what?"

"Yeah, you know I'm moving back to Cleveland next week. I been thinking about it a while. My son and daughter-in-law, they live there, they been after me to come back. They think I'm getting too old for this New York foolishness. And what with my being alone and everything. Anyway, they just bought a new house, and they got space for me."

Well. A friend, finally, and already he's gone. "Well, that's too bad. I mean, good. Good you got family that wants you to come back. I'll just be sorry to see you go, is all."

"Yeah, well. They giving me a little send-off down at the club. They think they surprising me but I seen a case of champagne in the back, heard the waiters talking. I figure I'll fake it so they can't tell I know. Anyway, it's my night and I can do what I want. So you come on down and play."

Hating to dim the gleam in the man's eyes, L.J. hangs onto the residue of a smile that has nothing to do with what he's thinking now. Him at the Baby Grand? On the stage? No way. He scratches his rough chin, runs a hand over his hair, short, but unwashed in three months. Sure, he looked better than some. But he'd walked by a couple of times and seen the coifed and decked-out after-theater crowd huddled at the door with fur-draped shoulders and pearl-trimmed necks, polished skin and hair and shining teeth. Looking like fortune's favorites.

"Well, what do you say?"

Was the man *trying* to embarrass him? "Well, uh, I'm not dressed right for that place."

Covington glances down at L.J.'s jacket, the smile not leaving his face. "Listen, I know what you're saying, but all you gotta do is run home and put on something black. Black jacket or shirt or something, and some slacks, that always works. They do have a little dress code, tie and all, but you're my guest. Go change and come on when you can."

L.J. smiles weakly. "OK. I might see you up there later. Maybe."

"Just tell 'em Cov sent you."

"OK, man."

"All right then. I gotta get on over there. You try and get by if you can. It'll be a blast, I promise you."

They shake hands again, and L.J. is losing the grip on the smile.

No way will he go to a club like the Baby Grand in his shrunken suit, his face stubbly, his hair unkempt. The men part company, Covington strutting away towards the uptown IRT, and L.J. rocking on his feet on his corner, counting the money in his hands, arranging the faces of the presidents over and over again.

At least he's got some money, now. Four hundred could mean something. Something big. A suit, a room, even a ticket on a bus. He doesn't know what just yet, he'll have to think. But something. Something big. He sucks in air, purses his lips, and blows. Oh, yes. Yes, yes. Lady Luck is batting her eyes. He pats his pocket, and smiles.

· THREE ·

FEELING GENEROUS AND EASY-MINDED, he settles on Gennaro's, an Italian diner a block from Lincoln Center, the place he's saved for the time when a healthy appetite, good mood, and bulging pockets appeared all at once. The bespectacled waiter brings a plate of linguini swimming in a steaming marinara to the checked tablecloth, with a huge Greek salad and basket of olive bread and garlic butter. The savory perfection of the sauce brings a thankful prayer to his lips.

Forty minutes later, with a full stomach and rested feet, he steps out of the restaurant to the gathering of thick, dark clouds. In less than a minute come small, fine scattered drops of rain. *This changes things. Gotta find cover from the rain.* He could take the subway down to the Rescue Mission, or a shorter jaunt to Grand Central Station. Rumbling trains coming and going, waiting room bustle, the clamor of passengers hurrying out to tracks, the staticky announcements of arrivals and delays offer him, oddly, comfort. Trains have been good to him. And he'd just recently learned that with a horn case and a satchel and trimmed hair and clean clothes, he can nap discreetly on the bench like a stranded passenger while the cops around him roust the unkempt homeless from benches and turn them out to the street.

Plus, he can check out the price of a train ride home.

And then a thought occurs: would he go home tonight if the price were right? No, not like this, not looking this way, and with no extra cash to speak of. But he could at least put the idea in motion.

The rain thickens into prickly needles. Wet streets glassy and slicked, the traffic singing a slurred hiss of rolling tires on watery road. *Come on rain, let up a little. Give a man a break.* This rain is definitely bad luck. The last time he'd gotten caught, he was sick in a shelter for six days. Didn't make a dime that week. For some reason, he thinks of his old man, dead now thirty years. Purvis was bad luck walking on two legs. But he wouldn't have been discouraged by a few drops of rain; he'd just shrug his narrow shoulders, cluck his teeth, and go on. That man could change his course quicker than anyone L.J. knew, and no looking back.

Like that night long ago. He, L.J., was just a boy. The moon had been up so long it had begun to slip in the western sky when the old man's rough hands, smelling of Wild Turkey, had gathered him up from his bed in mid-dream to put him on the passenger seat of the truck. He didn't hear an explanation of why there was such a rush to leave. But it was understood that when a colored man stood his ground to a white man in the public square of Wynette, Georgia (even if the colored man calling him a lie had stolen nothing, as the white man claimed), there was danger in letting another moon rise before you made up your mind to leave. You were as good as gone, no questions asked.

And since this piano-playing, hard-drinking great uncle he'd lived with since birth was his only kin, and there was no one either of them needed to say goodbye to (save a few of Purvis's women), the truck had been piled high with all it could hold, and made its way bounding past the creek and the copse of tall pecans. No noise in the night but the rattle of rubber on road and the plink-plink of piano keys.

Purvis had always said he didn't need to see his way around the corner, down the road was far enough. *'Cause when you reach that corner, there'll be a whole 'nother view.* So it didn't matter that while night bugs jittered in headlight shine there had been precious little road ahead to see, even if L.J. had been awake enough to see it or old enough to care.

And it didn't matter that the old man had struck out in the darkness without a plan greater than just getting away.

Now as L.J. walks along the broad avenues that slim into smaller, older streets, the fog is sitting low, the rain has slowed, and there is little clear path ahead to see. But there is enough for him to know that he has been walking the wrong way. He has been walking for twenty minutes and by now he should be passing the cathedral, but instead he has reached a basketball court of broken asphalt, strewn shards of glass, and sagging hoops surrounded by a chain link fence. He has been walking west instead of east.

It was the trash along the street that had clued him even before the warped chain link fence. One block the wrong way in this city and you've crossed a border into another world. He stops and turns to double back, muttering under his breath, shifting the weight of the horn case, the satchel, easing the grip of both and changing their balance a little.

He walks faster, whistles to occupy his mind. He's thinking of long-ago nights in Purvis's kitchen, the old man pounding the piano and the smell of hulled peanuts roasting on the stove top, when he hears the footsteps behind him.

Even after the whine of a passing ambulance recedes into nothing, there is still the shssh, shssh of footfalls, quickening now. They are not the footsteps that accelerate and pass or veer off to another direction, but the ones that trail and stalk. Steady, steady, like stealth. Steps that make the hands grip tighter whatever they are holding.

Just keep walking pal, mind your own business. Except for one shelter night of a flashing knife and crazed eyes, and another time when he felt a hand on his pocket as he lay sleeping against a Dumpster behind a Thrifty Mart, he hasn't had much trouble in this town. But there is something in the shuffle against the wet cement that makes L.J. hurry his steps.

But the steps that follow are hurrying, too. L.J. shifts the satchel strap to his shoulder to free up a fist, just in case. Now he smells wet leather, cheap wine. Hears breathing. He looks ahead for safety, some well-lit doorway, an open bar or restaurant or laundromat, a group of people to walk toward. Something.

As the footsteps increase, he realizes there is nothing ahead, nobody to hear him if he yells. A chain-link fence around the basketball court stretches far ahead of him. Across the street, only dead buildings of red brick and shattered glass. No sign of life, no chance of rescue.

He gathers himself. *OK, just deal with it. The showdown coming might as well be now.* He stops and turns.

"Can I help you?"

Dark-skinned, tall, lanky. The boy sports blue jeans bagging below his waist, a shaved head, a menacing smile. Narrow shoulders slope beneath a jacket of cheap black leather.

"Bet you could reach in them pockets and find something to help me." He raises his shirt to show a gun stuck in his belt.

L.J. levels his gaze at the boy's eyes. This kid couldn't be more than fifteen. But where eyes should be, there are bloodless voids.

"Come on, pops. Give it up."

His heart pounds. L.J. reaches into his pocket. Groans when he realizes he's forgotten to tuck most of his money in his socks. All of his money is in his pocket, more than four hundred.

He pulls out a wad of money and hands it to the boy. The boy's eyes light up. He pushes the bills down into a baggy pocket.

"That's more like it. Now. The other one."

"What?"

"The other pocket."

L.J. huffs a sigh, then reaches into the other pocket and pulls out a smaller wad.

"OK, that's good. Now empty 'em. I know you got change. I can hear it."

L.J. reaches again, empties two fistfuls of change into the boy's hand.

"All right, now we talking. What you got in that case?"

A small sound erupts from L.J.'s throat. *Hell, no. No you won't. Not my horn.* Bile rises in his throat. Money, he could get more of. But his horn, his prized Selmer. No way.

L.J. stares, too long for the boy. He takes the gun from his belt and points it at L.J.'s stomach.

L.J.'s head feels hot. *Think, think of what to do.* The boy is thin, couldn't be that strong. Maybe if he is quick enough…

A shot crackles in the silence.

For a moment, L.J. believes he has been hit. But another shot fires, and the sound comes from a half-block away.

"Police officers! Freeze!"

The menacing smile falls like a brick. The boy turns and reaches for the fence, grabs wire and hoists himself up and over the top. He jumps to the asphalt on the other side and runs like a wild deer.

Within seconds, two uniformed police officers are standing next to L.J.

The short one is black with a thick mustache. "You OK? We've been watching him since he stopped you. We saw him pull the gun. You're lucky we came along."

"Yeah." L.J. is breathless. "He didn't get my horn. I wouldn't let him have it. But he got my money. I guess I shoulda yelled or something. He got all my money, 'cept a little change. He took off that way, across the court. Can you get him?"

The black officer talks into a two-way radio. The white one, tall and broad shouldered with thinning hair, shrugs. "Not much we can do now. Sorry. We'll report it, but there's not much chance of finding him now. He's got too much time on us."

The black officer turns to L.J. "We got a car headed toward here. Describe him for us."

L.J. gives him a rough description. Black, young, tall, thin. Big shirt, baggy pants, dressed the way they all dress. The officer talks into the radio again.

"OK," he tells L.J. "They're looking for him. But I gotta tell you, there's not a whole lotta chance of finding this boy. Hundred kids out here look just like that. Best thing is you come down to the station and look at some pictures. Maybe you can pick him out. Then we'll take you home."

Home. L.J. shakes his head. "No, it's OK. I'll just go on. Like you said, not much chance."

"You sure? Won't take but a few minutes. There'll be a car here pretty soon."

"Naw. I just as soon not. It's OK."

"Well. OK. Sure you're all right?"

"Yeah."

"Be careful. Best not to carry your cash around like that. Leave at home what you don't need."

"I'll remember that."

"Sorry about your luck," the other says. Both policemen turn and walk away.

The rain has stopped, the streets shine like polished metal. L.J. looks up and down the street; left, then right.

A year, and it has all come back.

Back then, on that night of the burned pie, the swallowing river, and the singing train, he felt that every nerve, muscle, fiber in the world had congealed into a giant fist that raised up to knock him to the ground. And then the fist turned itself into a laughing face. Worse than bad luck: hard, slapping, heavy-handed luck. And damn it if he's not here again, knocked down and stripped clean. Every foul word he can think of wrestles under his breath. He reaches deep in his pockets, searching every lint-filled fold. There is some change. He counts it. Forty-eight cents.

He doesn't know what it is that makes him look down at this moment, before walking away. Maybe the ache of his corns, or the jellied feeling in his knees. Or maybe just the weight of his head, too heavy now to hold up. But later, when he remembers this night, he'll remember that everything changed when he looked down.

It isn't much of a gun, as guns go, lying there, two yards away from his feet. A snub-nosed revolver, .38, like the one Jimmy had kept behind the cash register at the bar. Part of the handle broken off. But a gun, still. Small. Easy to hide, fitting nicely into a palm, or a pocket.

Was this luck? he wonders as he reaches down for it, turns it in his hand. Slick with rain, and cool. Heavier than it looks. The kid, stripped of his piece, his manhood. Wherever he is, he's standing a little shorter now.

The last time he was this close to a gun he was a small boy, and a woman dressed in blue had used it, the odor of powder so strong he could taste it on his tongue. But a man doesn't have to use a gun just because he has one. He can show it, point to it, exhibit it with nothing said. Just like the kid had done raising his shirt, a message sent in the shine of steel.

And what could it bring? Money, things to be sold for money. Rent, food, hot running water, bed, pillows. Cool sheets and radiator heat.

He understands something now. This is how it happens. How people go from right-living to wrong. How, when you've hung on to the man you think you are for as long as you can, the rope snaps and then down you go. He wonders how many men can point to the minute, the hour, when they slid down that hole, turned down that different street.

A whole year living like this, and he's never stolen a dime. This is how it changes.

He walks now, looking neither left, nor right.

It takes him an hour of walking and thirty minutes of circling the block around the place. The swirls of neon blue curving into the shape of a piano and the tubes of glass swirling above form the words, THE BABY GRAND.

He pauses as people from the club open the door to leave, men dressed in suits and women wearing the wraps of easeful lives. Inside, he squints at the incandescent glare of hooded lamps, the winks of glinting brass. Suddenly, painfully, he's aware of his appearance, and he feels wet, hot, dirty. He feels for the gun.

Covington's last set, he knows, ended at midnight. He is sure that he left hours ago, and this is the later, theater-going crowd. A rich crowd, fancy purses, jeweled fingers and wrists and pearled necks catch his eye. *Just this one time. Only once is all I need. Then never again.*

He clutches the gun deep in his pocket. He scans the last-call scene, elbows hunched on tabletops and bar railings. Plenty of people still left, but the group looks as leftover as the last swallow at the bottom of a forgotten glass of wine.

A young black woman in a short, black dress with pixie hair smoothed neatly against her soft face approaches him as he stands awkwardly near the bar. His gun-holding hand feels wet and limp.

"May I help you?"

Pretty young black girl. Sweet-faced with a disarming smile.

"I...," he begins. A boulder lodged in his throat leaves no room for words to pass. His heart pounds against the wall of his chest as he tries to speak again. Nothing. Why has his voice deserted him now?

Yes?" says the woman.

He releases the gun and lets it drop into the well of his pocket.

"Uh, I...I'm looking for work."

He was always good at improvising.

Relief brightens the woman's smile. "Oh, you're a musician. We're about to close now, but I'll let you take that up with the manager."

Her heels click against the hardwood as she walks away, then reappears with a tall white man with narrow shoulders and long arms. His thick black-rimmed glasses highlight the narrowness of his eyes.

"I'm afraid we're closing now," the man says, managing a wan smile. "You'll have to come back when we're open, after eleven a.m."

"Ah... my name's Tillman. A friend of Covington's."

"Mr. Covington? Oh, yes, he left hours ago. I'm afraid this was his last night. In fact, we gave a little party for him."

"I...I just thought you might be needing a musician now."

The man gives him a scanning look, down to his wet shoes, then up again, but not as far as his eyes. "Well, that's true, we're looking for someone to replace him to fill out the quartet. But, uh, we've got a few people in mind already. If you want to audition, call early next week, during the day..."

But L.J. looks around the room, takes in the gentle clink of crystal, the soft buzz of genteel conversation. All quiet manners and polished smiles. He leans over, takes his horn out of the case, hooking it to his strap. The man and the woman pass nervous looks between them. "No, hey, wait," the man says. "If you'll just come back..."

Eyeing the empty bandstand, he steps up on the carpeted stage, dripping water. *Hell with it. The hell with all of it.* The thin man looks edgy, glancing over his shoulder at patrons leaning curiously over their drinks, and extends one of his long arms toward L.J. in a quieting gesture.

Sometimes, there's nothing to say, nothing a man can do but play. Defiantly, L.J. steps back, cocks his head, and lifts his horn. Buckles both knees, then arches his back. His fingers are cold—stiff as reeds—but the air around him is charged and hot. Eyes closed, he tongues the cane until he tastes a tune. The metal is so cold he has to squeeze out the sound, which seems not to come from his horn but from something else, someplace else. A chorus of voices—'bones, trumpets, drums, and bass—rings in his head, and in seconds he's lost in a rapture so powerful he has to steel the tremor in his thighs.

He plays on, the horn buzzing, braying, crying, sighing like the wind. Note-flurries bounce from the bell and thread into tunes that tell his tale: from rag-tag times in boondock towns to his first slow-dance with a silver-throated woman, to nights of howling trains and deep rivers. Wave after wave of memory crashing against some inland shore.

Somewhere in the middle of it, the blood-hot music rises to his head, and one thing dawns on him: he's still got *something*. Like his life, the music wasn't pretty, wasn't clean; it was more jumbled than ordered, had more bite than beauty. But it was good, and it was his. They could take anything they wanted from him, but not this. Even if he's lost everything, he still has this moment, this music, this one inexhaustible song.

When the memories fold, the rapture cools, and a perfect final phrase composes itself in his head and unrolls like fine, finished silk. He lets the silence surround him before he opens his eyes.

The applause is thin at first, like the shy patter of gloved hands at afternoon tea. But it moves like roof-top flames from table to table, and in little time there are shouts and knives clinking glasses and whistles and stomping feet. The polished smiles shine through the smoky, gin-laced air.

The thin man nods nervously. His voice is low, almost whispering. "Let's talk over here." He leads L.J. aside to a corner of the bar. "OK. You've obviously got some talent. If you will just come back, let's say next week..."

"No, listen." A new insistence booms in L.J.'s voice. "I'm new in town. I just got robbed. I've got nowhere to go and no money and I need you to tell me now if I can work here."

"I'm sorry about your bad luck. Frankly, we were hoping to find another singer. But you at least need to come back for an audition with the group. That's the way we do it here." The man's brow twitches.

He must think I'm crazy, L.J. thinks. And what a sight he must be. His eyes are large. His face glistens with rain that trails down cheeks slick with sweat. His hair, wet and thickly matted, is grooved with finger strokes.

But he leans forward, centering his gaze deep within the man's thick glasses to look him squarely in the eyes. "Look," he says, his voice croaking with the exhaustion that fans from his feet to every part of his body. "I won't play any better next week. You need a good player," he thumps his chest with his palm, "you're seeing one right here. You're not going to find a better one. And as a man I give my word that I'll do what I say I'm going to do. You don't like me, you can fire me just as quick as you took me on."

L.J. can feel his own eyes pleading. He nearly holds his breath as the man lowers his head and frowns through a lengthy pause. Then he looks up, eyes first.

"The job pays four hundred and seventy-eight a week for five nights, two shows a night. You can play Saturday, that's our big night. If the guys in the trio like you, that's *if* they like you, we could hire you for a month, with an option for another two. That's it. That's the deal."

L.J. can't believe what he is hearing, but the next words out of his own mouth are even harder to believe.

"I need an advance."

"You what?" says the man.

"I've been robbed. I need to get something to wear. The clothes I have on are all I got. I can't play looking like this."

The man scratches the shadowy stubble of his beard. "OK, OK. Covington did mention he had a friend who might be coming down here, said to look out for you, said you been through some rough times. If you know Cov, I guess you're good for your word."

He looks L.J. in the eyes. "Swear to God, I never done nothing like this before. Tell you what, Tilton."

"Tillman."

"Right." He reaches into his pocket and pulls out a thick roll of bills. A slight lick of his thumb, and he counts out money from the wad. "Leave that horn with me, what is it, a Selmer?"

"Selmer Mark Six. Best one they ever made."

"Right. Leave the horn here and come back on Saturday, nine o'clock sharp, and I'll lend you this against your paycheck."

L.J. looks down at the bills. He's never even hocked his horn for money, let alone left it with a stranger. But he smiles, takes the money, and folds it into his pocket.

"OK, man."

"You don't show, the horn's mine, right? Matter of fact, you show up late, it's mine, got it? Ten minutes, fifteen after nine, don't even think about trying to claim this horn."

"Not to worry. I'll *be* here."

He turns to walk away, then stops. "Got any change? Trade you one of these bills here for some quarters. I need to use the phone."

This time the woman, smiling still, fishes in a small purse and hands him several coins. He offers her two dollars in exchange and she waves them off. "The phone's back next to the men's room," she says.

L.J. walks toward the men's room, feeling the weight of staring eyes. He picks up the phone and dials a number.

She might be upset, getting a call so late. The phone rings. A soft voice answers.

"Hello?"

Sometimes just the sound of her voice, sleepy like a child's, would jerk his mind back some forty years. And always the memory came unbidden, as now. He was all of nine years old, carrying the child who would become his wife in his arms through a summer storm. A scared boy ferrying a baby from one woman's door to another's; one whose

36

grief-torn eyes swore him to hold secret the one thing that the other's implored him to surrender.

Whose child is this?

L.J. pauses. A year gone by, it's the middle of the night, and still this is the one voice that's never wavered from the perfect key. "Olivia?" he says. "It's me."

II

· FOUR ·

WIDE BANDS OF LUMINOUS GOLD SUN spread across the wedding-ring quilt on the brass bed in the upstairs bedroom. An assortment of clothes was beginning to pile up. A short-skirted suit of royal blue silk. A two-piece dress of sherbet green linen. A long white cotton chemise with yellow and blue orchids clustered at the skirt tail. A matching cropped jacket with a Peter Pan collar. Olivia considered the royal blue silk, held it up to the mirror. A good weight for Indian-summer-into-fall. But the unlined skirt needed a half slip. She reached in the bottom bureau drawer, found one, and tossed it across the bed.

She hummed as she moved around the room, finding shoes, pantyhose. On the closet floor, the black patent leather slings, for comfort. In the dresser drawer, L'eggs (jet brown), a lacy black bra, and black silk camisole. What else? Earrings, the gold ones. A hat? No, no hat. She looked at her hair in the small mirror atop the dresser and finger-fluffed the curls, thankful for hair that still bounced after restless sleep. Still looking, she hummed louder, then opened up to a full voiced warmup. *Ahh-ooo-eeee-ohhh.* It was early yet for singing—9:38, according to the digital clock radio on the dresser. She turned it on, found the Sunday morning gospel station. But when she heard a chorus of "Take Me to the Water" her heart did a jump and turned, and when she changed to the classical station—an old Marian Anderson version of "Deep River"—it did a full pirouette.

No, Lord no. No rivers, not today.

She turned the radio off.

She was dressing in front of the mirror when the phone rang.

The familiar, high-pitched voice spoke in a nervous rush. "I'll be

41

a little late, now I know what you going to say, but I promise I'll be there."

Olivia placed a hand to her chest. This was your idea, she wanted to say. But instead said, "Winona, you promised. You won't let me down?"

"Promise."

Olivia blew out a breath of relief, and sat on the bed. "I just turned on the radio, and guess what they were playing? 'Take Me to the Water.' And then 'Deep River.'"

First silence, then an audible breath before Winona said, "Nobody's going to make you go down there if you don't want to."

"I know. I just thought it was a little ironic."

"Might you be a little nervous?"

Olivia's face changed with a small wry smile. "Nervous? Let's see. I haven't sung in twenty-some years. I barely know the song. Everybody in church will be giving me those pitiful looks. Then I turn on the radio and they're singing about rivers. What do you think?"

"Olivia, forget everything and sing the song, OK? Just sing the way you know how. It'll be beautiful."

What it would be was over, and not a minute too soon. She nodded, as if they were in the room together. "OK. I'll see you there."

Quiet has many sounds, Olivia thought as she put down the phone and listened to the silence ring like a clapper against hollow steel in the bedroom. Sometimes it sounded pure, like peace itself. But now and then the quiet in her bedroom was awful, disturbing, cacophonous. Sometimes the whole house vibrated with the unmistakable presence of his absence, and sometimes it swelled around her ears and made her whole being ache. An underwater sound, she thought, maybe like drowning.

She shook her head. No, she had not been down to that river. She didn't care what everyone said she should do to ease the pain, to close it out, to reckon with it. She hadn't been there in all these months, and she wasn't going now. But she was going to church; that, she couldn't get out of.

The mirror stared at her and approved. Gold earrings on, makeup just right. Lipstick sharp around the edges of her lips. She shifted the skirt around her small waist. What had she forgotten? She looked at her watch. Time to go.

In the kitchen, going over the song in her head, she watched squirrels at play in the walnut tree through the window while she ate a quick breakfast of toast and marmalade.

At the door, one last time, Olivia closed her eyes, and moved her lips, singing.

I was glad when they said unto me..., let us go into the house of the Lord...

Sitting in the back row of wooden pews, the center aisle, Olivia realized she had forgotten to take a long drink of water to wet her throat before she'd come into the sanctuary. And the lace-edged half-slip still lay across the bed, she'd remembered a block from the church. She would have to walk down the aisle scissoring her legs or risk everyone seeing the silhouette of her skinny thighs through the sheer skirt.

She reached in her purse and pulled out a honey-lemon cough drop. She untwisted its wrapper quietly, put it in her mouth, and rolled it around her tongue. That was better. As a child, sitting and waiting, she would have twitched with unease, clicked the heels of her dangling patent leathers, pulled at her skirt and twirled hair in her fingers, like when Big Mama first volunteered her to sing "Jesus Loves the Little Children" at Sweet Rock Revival C. M. E. in Handy, Arkansas, the little wooden clapboard buried deep in the piney woods.

"You singing all the time, child. You might as well stand up and sing in the church."

Now, as then, the possibility of failure rattled her. But if she felt comfort anywhere, it was here in New Hope and Redemption, the oldest black church in the east end of Kansas City. The grunts of the solemn stewards, the children twitching, the women fanning themselves, nodding, their bodies rocking with their resolute faith, reminded her of home. And now as she sat waiting to sing on the row closest to the amen-ing stewards, the warm glow of the autumn morning sun on her shoulder through stained glass felt like the palm of the hand of God.

We at New Hope wish to welcome all of our visitors today. You are welcome once, you are welcome twice, you are welcome, welcome, welcome…

Altar call now. Then the offering. The choir's "B" selection, the scripture reading, the sermon, then her. Reverend Eames was cleaning his wire-rimmed glasses with the sleeve of his black robe while the small altar of darkly stained oak filled up with the first few pews of the most devout. With all the attention that had come her way in the last year, these days she preferred to pray in her seat.

She prayed for easy nerves, a calm ascension to the B-flat above the staff, and a solid pitch on the final G.

"Excuse me, could you scoot over a little?"

Olivia looked up. An usher was extending a hand toward her aisle and then a finger at the space next to her. The woman in orange at the end of the pew was angling her knees making room for someone.

Olivia smiled. Good, Winona was here.

Winona Lovejoy was a busy bustle of crimson silk, black-feathered hat, Revlon scented powder, black satin coat over one arm with a jangle of gold bracelets, and a full-faced smile that gushed without words. She sat down next to Olivia—the row of members now tight with shoulders nudging shoulders—and arranged herself.

She put a hand on her friend's arm and squeezed a little. "Sorry I'm late," she whispered. "I sure didn't want to miss this."

Olivia acknowledged with a smile and a small relieved sigh. "I knew you'd get here."

Now, things would surely go well. Winona was in place. And despite not having sung for longer than she could remember—or maybe because of it, since resting the throat was good—she was in good voice. This morning, singing in her kitchen to the squirrels climbing the backyard walnut tree, she had to admit, there was something still there; yes, after all these years, and after all that had happened, the music hadn't gone.

Please turn in your hymnbooks to number 253, Pass me not, oh gentle savior…

She reached for *The Good Shepherd Hymnal*, but put it back. She needed water, for real, and to check her skirt. She looked at the program. Ten minutes at least. There was time.

When the congregation stood, she raised an apologetic index finger and tiptoed out of the sanctuary, heels clicking lightly against hardwood, her patent leather clutch tucked under her arm. At the bottom of a swirl of wooden steps, the ladies' room, its cool plaster walls layered in pastel pink, smelled of dank basement odors and floral talcum powder. An oval walnut-stained floor mirror stood slanted in the corner next to a few scarred French Provincial style coffee and end tables, and some plastic covered lamps—and she looked at herself.

The rippled mirror made her look wider than she was, which she liked. Skinny thighs that refused to meet, tiny shoulders. She looked to see if light shone through between her legs. She pressed her thighs together. There was nothing she could do now about a missing slip and a transparent skirt.

She checked her makeup—she didn't look all that old with the new Iman shades of foundation and lipstick. She didn't think so, anyway. And forty-three wasn't all that old, was it? When she'd gotten married, at nineteen, forty-three had seemed beyond old. Time sped like a train—forty-three years pressed tightly into the space between two blinks of an eye.

She heard a toilet flush, the bustling of skirts and underthings, and running water through old pipes.

"Morning, Olivia. Ain't you singing today, honey?"

"Yes, ma'am." Miss Ondine Walcott, going on eighty, still had a straight back and a smooth neck. She was washing her hands. A pretty woman, still. Olivia was feeling younger now.

"You look so pretty today, darlin'."

"I was just thinking that about you. Thank you. But I forgot my slip. Do you think my skirt's OK?"

Miss Walcott stood back, put a curved index finger to her chin and frowned. "Well, I can see a little."

Then, in a one movement flourish, she reached beneath her gray wool skirt, pulled down a black nylon half-slip, stepped out of it, and handed it to Olivia.

Olivia looked at her. "I….I couldn't."

"Child, you want to sing with nothing on your mind but singing."

Olivia blushed, but took the slip and stepped into it.

"Good," Miss Walcott said. "Now don't worry about getting it back to me. My skirt has a lining. And I got a dozen more at home." And before Olivia could talk again, she was up the stairs.

In the mirror, Olivia smoothed the front of her skirt, and finger-combed her hair. And how would she look at eighty? Would her spine be straight and her mind right? Would younger women look at her and think, "pretty"? Life is not short, she thought. It's just *fast*. How long had he been gone? Days. Or so the whole year had seemed. It seemed just a year or two ago that she was eighteen, slinging a heavy green Samsonite Pullman onto a Greyhound bus headed north to Kansas City, where she would meet the man with whom she would spend the next twenty-four years.

It would have been twenty-five. A blur of events, a compression of years to days, from bride to widow. Another eye-blink, and she was alone again.

Psalm 36, verses 1–8. May the Lord bless the reading of his word…

Back in her seat, Olivia pinched her eyes shut to sharpen the vision shaping behind her lids. That last night, she had screamed at him, *Get out and don't ever come back,* her words exploding in an aria of anger. And as soon as he had vanished behind the slammed door, the words pooled like spilled blood, spreading around her.

The elders rocked their heads back and forth, their amens punctuating the reverend's sermon on "The Woman at the Well." The choir sang a rollicking gospel and the church reeled and rolled to the pedaled beats of organ bass. Dry-mouthed again, Olivia fumbled in her purse for another cough drop.

Even before the policemen showed up at her door, there had been the gnaw of regret. Then, "Your husband's car's been found at the bottom of the river. Accident, looks like. Car bounced off a tree, then straight in. But no trace of him; he evidently floated out, and drowned." Boiling pain had shot up her back, no, no, she had not wished him dead, just away, and not forever, but for a time. She'd needed time, and suddenly there was none.

But he could swim, couldn't he? So he'd always said. So ads in the *Star*, as well as the local black weekly and the musicians' trade paper, surely would make him surface. His picture, the word "missing" underneath. A whole year and still nothing.

Two prim, white-gloved young ushers with low-heeled black pumps and patent-leather hair approached her aisle. Olivia smiled at Pauline Jacks sitting to her right, as she extended the collection plate, and Olivia dropped in her tithe stuffed in the white envelope. Pauline smiled at her through the beige veil of a saucer-shaped hat of brown felt and pointed a manicured fingernail at Olivia's name in the church program opened in her lap.

"Can't wait to hear you sing!" she gushed in a loud whisper.

Olivia smiled back and nodded, and arched her back against the pew, her heart beating like pounding surf, so wildly that she wondered if Pauline and Winona could see the rise in her chest.

Whose idea was this?

Her best friend had been ready with timely counsel. "You need closure," Winona Lovejoy had said two weeks ago as they sat over Kansas City strips at Jimmy and Mary's Steakhouse on Main Street. "You didn't want a memorial. I understood that, what with the way it happened. And you wouldn't go to the river. But you need to do something to close it out. It'll help you get on with your life."

But what if he's still alive? What then?

"Honey, look. If he was alive, and wanted to come back, he would have." Winona had said, a hand on Olivia's arm, peering over the tortoise shell rims of her glasses.

But how do you put it all to rest, bury a man without his body? How do you do it without the ceremony of freshly turned earth, gentle words and flowers, without the unmistakable finality of confirmation?

"You just do it," Winona had said, sadness muting her words. She had poured more Beaujolais into Olivia's glass, as if to numb the sting of blunt-toothed truth.

Olivia had toyed with her steak and listened sadly, nodding. Got to go on, got to. He wasn't coming back. So this was it, closure, they called it. A musical tribute, an earth-turning ceremony in song. She would bury him beneath the final B-flat major chord, and there he would rest, in peace. She had asked the Reverend and the Reverend had said, yes, of course, Mrs. Tillman, and may God be merciful to you. And the church secretary had put her name on the program, and this would do it surely, a final act, an owning up. *And now Sister Olivia Tillman, whose husband, God rest his soul, was drowned in the North River last year, will favor us with a selection dedicated to his memory.*

"Amens" rumbled from pew to pew. Olivia gathered herself to rise, walked past the elders' pew, past the stained glass windows of the twelve apostles that permitted the diffused light of October sun, and up to the altar where the grand piano stood. She touched a nervous finger to her forehead; it was moist. She closed her eyes and quietly cleared her throat.

She looked through the haze of sunlight from the row of windows along the back of the church, and blinked.

"This last year has been difficult for me," she began. "But so many of you were so kind to me during my most difficult days."

Her eyes scanned the room. Anne Sloane and Martha Hedley, both fanning themselves in the far pews, had rushed over with hot tea when they heard the news. Peter and Cynthia Curry, sitting near the row of ushers, cleaned her house for the onslaught of company the next day. That day, the normal laws of time lost all meaning. Hours flew by, reduced to flashes of blurred motion, and in seconds, church members had descended on her house like a flock of roosting birds. In minutes, the rooms were filled with warm-handed women with praying lips and arms laden with pots of food, their men at their sides, sad-eyed and wordless.

They all nodded and smiled at her now as she stood in front of them.

"I thank you all for your prayers, and your acts of kindness," she said. The pianist played broken chords in B-flat, and she closed her eyes.

"I trust in God, I know he cares for me..."

Sing, child. Sing your song. Gifted little thing. She could almost hear them, the women, see them through the closed-eyes view into backward-looking windows. She was ten again, or eight maybe. And there was the sound of sweet old-woman chatter, approving, loving noises, Sing your song, child. The first note felt like she'd hoped—pure as water, unrestrained. The second note came from somewhere inside the girl-child she'd been, and after that, she settled into the music as if, through all the years of silence, it had never stopped.

When she finished, applause rose in generous waves from the front pew back to the hand-carved maple doors leading to the vestibule. Olivia floated back to her seat on a tide of murmured love, nodding eyes, and soft, sympathetic grunts. She settled back and pushed a long stream of air through her pursed lips; Winona squeezed her hand. Olivia placed her other hand on her chest, a half-smile fighting its way out from behind her eyes. And the sun streamed in and warmed her shoulder. It's done, she thought. It's over.

And she had to admit it wasn't so bad. It wasn't just pity washing over her; they'd liked her. She'd made a beautiful sound.

· FIVE ·

WHERE HAD THAT SWEET VOICE COME FROM? Nobody knew, since nobody knew where she'd come from. Olivia Benton Tillman had not been brought up like other girls. Five "parents" to raise her (none of them her own) and three houses to shuttle back and forth between. Ten hands for cuddling or spanking, five laps for sitting and sleeping. It had seemed to her the most natural thing in the world. And for a while she'd thought all little babies had been delivered to their mama's and daddy's door by a young boy barely old enough to comb his own hair.

When Big Mama and the others had finally told her the whole story after one of Big Mama's Sunday fried chicken dinners, the five of them—Big Mama and her husband Uncle Joon, her sister Clo T., and their cousins Glodean and Country—made the story of a mother's abandonment and a doorstep delivery by a rain-soaked little boy seem like the grandest event in the world.

"You were a present to us, a gift from God," Big Mama had said. The storm that railed and pitched that afternoon had cooled the air and shaded it to a deep evening gray. Big Mama and Clo T. were just closing the shop and almost didn't answer the door; the rap of nine-year-old knuckles was almost inaudible. The little boy stood beneath the awning soaked in rain, the small quilt bundled around the wriggling infant. "Lady told me to give you this," he'd said, holding the baby tightly against his chest. His eyes were bright and his shoulders tense and arched with effort and responsibility. Water beaded in his uncombed, knotted hair. Big Mama had looked behind him across the street and no one was there. Baby and blanket were dirty, smelling of stale diapers and formula spittle. Big Mama had taken the child in her arms. "What's this? Who's this child's mama?" she insisted.

But the boy would not say. Only that a woman he swore he did not know had given him a baby, a note, and a two-dollar bill for his trouble.

"Take this baby down the street and give it to whoever answers the door," the woman had said. "And don't tell nobody, for the rest of your life, who gave it to you."

Big Mama had unfolded the note with fingers still wrinkled from scorching water and smelling of Queen Helene shampoo and Hair-Rep pressing oil.

"She don't like no strained carrots or whole milk." Big Mama read the note scrawled on Big Chief tablet paper.

Big Mama looked down at the bundle of wriggling limbs and the wide, dark eyes and thought she would offer the boy another two-dollar bill to tell her who had given him the baby. But before she could question him, he had disappeared behind the thick curtain of rain.

She brought the baby inside. Clo T. was washing her hands at the sink.

"Who's delivering supplies this time of day, in this rain?" She shook her hands and reached for a towel on the counter.

Big Mama was speechless, just turned with the child in her arms and faced Clo T., bewilderment masking her face.

"Lord have mercy," Clo T. said. "A baby? What in God's name?"

"Call Joon," said Big Mama, rocking the baby in her ample arms.

But the storm had knocked out the phone lines. When service was restored an hour later, Clo T. and Big Mama summoned Uncle Joon from a poker game at High Willie's, and called over their cousins Glodean and Country, who were fitting Helen Crawford for a bridal gown at their house across the street. Uncle Joon complained at leaving the straight flush he'd been working on, and Glodean and Country, owners of their own dressmaking business, had left Helen locked inside an unfinished wedding gown festooned with straight pins.

The sight of the bright-eyed, cooing baby, however, silenced all complaints. Their alarm at the unexpected delivery was soon over-shadowed by something else: pure joy. Five fascinated smiles and baby talk and big fingers locked in gripping little hands postponed the worry, the wonder of whatever sorry-excuse-for-a-mother did this awful thing.

"Shame on her, whoever she is, right, precious little dumplin?"

"Shame is right. And her is a sweet little thing, yes her is!"

"Must of done lost her mind, ain't that right, little baby doll?"

When they had spent themselves smiling and oogling, they sat down to decide. Secretly, they all wanted her, each one of the five childless and past the age of childbearing. Big Mama and Uncle Joon had long ago stopped trying. Clo T. and Glodean had never married and no longer expected to. And Country's third husband had left her, childless, long ago.

By the time the storm ended, Big Mama and Uncle Joon, Clo T., Glodean, and Country had decided to keep the baby they called Olivia and raise her, equally, as their own.

But word got around that a baby had just appeared one day and was living inside of a cardboard crate at Big Mama's Beauty Palace. The sheriff showed up, and so did the chief of police, demanding answers, threatening to turn the baby over to child welfare authorities. But Big Mama pointed out that she had midwifed at the birth of the sheriff's two children (and had saved one's life by forcing her own breath into its tiny lungs), and had loaned the chief of police money to buy his first house.

Big Mama, who was neither big nor anybody's mama, got her name from the size of her spirit, the breadth of her generosity, and the ring of her authority, which echoed throughout Handy. Everybody went to her with their troubles, and if Big Mama didn't have a solution, none was needed or none was possible. She knew that prodding the men to feel properly beholden to her for these favors (and others) should be enough, but for extra measure she reminded the sheriff of a not-so-small one—did he really think he would have gotten reelected without her help? And to the chief of police she said, "Wasn't that Martha Flacks from over in Cross County I saw you coming out of the picture show with last week? By the way, my best to your *wife* Mildred. Tell her I got some pecan pie I been saving for her in the freezer. She just loves my pecan pie."

That was enough. Both men turned to each other, then to the door. The sheriff muttered on his way, "Better take her over to Doc Robicheaux's before too long. Make sure the child gets her shots."

And so Olivia had grown up with a passel of parents, and from each one she plucked little bits of living. From Big Mama she learned how to wash, hot comb, and curl hair. From Uncle Joon, who took her when he made his plumbing rounds, she learned to unstop toilets, to pack homemade sausages in their casings for his on-the-side barbecue business, and to love jazz. Clo T. and Glodean taught her how to sew straight seams and fry chicken and make hot-water cornbread, and from Country she learned how to match solids with plaids and walk straight-kneed in high-heeled shoes.

For whatever concerns might arise, she had the luxury of choice. When she needed spare change for a Moon Pie or an all-day sucker, Uncle Joon was a soft touch, and when she wanted permission to change her hair from braids to chin-length curls, she knew to go to Clo T. The town of Handy came to see Olivia as the girl "with all them people taking care of her." And when her school held open house day, any two of the five people claiming to be her parents might show up to meet the confused teacher.

Olivia had been happy and wanted for nothing. As a little one she crawled in and out of a cardboard Standard Oil carton set up next to the row of dryers in the middle of the Beauty Palace and lined with the blue-green quilt the boy had delivered her in, and toddled between the legs of Big Mama and Clo T.'s customers. On Saturday mornings with the shop full of women, she sat cross-legged on her Romper Room rug in a corner on the pine floor with a box of Crayola crayons, or humming to the Betsy Wetsy Uncle Joon had bought at a Fourth of July sale at Woolworth's. "Ain't she cute," the customers would say above the electric hum of hair dryers. And then would follow the ongoing speculation about her parentage.

"Got to be that Marshall girl's child. She fast as greased lightning."

"Why anybody want to mess with her? Ugly and skinny as she is?"

"Man got a itch in his pants, he don't care who he get to scratch it."

"Child must have a little Blackfoot in her. Look at those eyes."

"No she ain't. Look to me like she part white. That hair too straight for her not to be mixed with something."

"She ain't got no white in her at all. Look at her color. Too brown-skinned. Them cheekbones is Cherokee sure enough."

Then Big Mama, angling a freshly washed head down toward the sink, spoke.

"Y'all listen here," she started. The wet-haired customer's head jerked back and forth in Big Mama's strong hands as she talked through clenched teeth, giving the head an extra jerk on emphasized syllables. "Ain't got *no* Blackfoot in her, and no more white than you and me. She's a *colored* girl. That's all there is to it. As far as who her people is, that's me, Clo T. over here, my husband, Glodean, and Country. We her mamas and daddy, and that's *that*."

Big Mama's words quieted the shop, reducing the noise to the sound of hot running water, the click-click-click of curling irons, and little Olivia humming along with Clo T.'s Motorola radio. The singing had come naturally with Olivia; at four the tiny sound was pure and sweet as Ozark honey, by seven it vibrated like a violin. By nine it had unfurled like a spring rain's new rose and bloomed to a fresh, high-glossed sheen. And when the voices of Etta James or Dinah Washington rang from the broadcast of the blues stations in Little Rock or Memphis or Shreveport, Olivia sang along for the customers:

"What a difference a day makes, twenty-four little hours, there are sunshine and flowers, where there used to be rain."

She swirled and danced as she spun around the room, using Big Mama's spare hot comb for a microphone, and ended with a curtsy. Applause would explode, producing a wide-toothed grin on Olivia's face.

But the singing stopped almost as quickly as it had begun. At ten years old, singled out at school to sing "Home on the Range" or "The Star-Spangled Banner" while a beaming teacher accompanied her on an aged spinet, Olivia became the target of merciless teasing. Classmates, two in particular named May and Mary Frances, would follow her home, mocking Olivia's beautifully spun vibrato and silvery tone. Giggles turned to guffaws, the little girls doubled over in mean laughter.

That might have been all right, had not the words, "Your mama's a ho," stunned Olivia like a hard slap across her face.

The two girls waited for her reply. Hearing nothing, they continued. "Yeah, and my mama said that she sang at that place called Ray's, long time ago. She sang and went off with a bunch of different men."

Then, "And she shot a man, too. Shot him dead."

And then, "That's who you got all that singing from, my mama said."

What were they talking about? Olivia whirled around, fists balled, stomach tight, and a hair-snatching, ear-pulling fight left her on the ground with a bloody, inverted V where her two front teeth once had been.

Exhausted, and realizing the futility of two against one, Olivia got up, brushed blood from her knee, and ran, leaving her fifth-grade geography book on the cobblestone.

At home (this week belonged to Glodean and Country), the two "mothers" stood at the door gape-mouthed at Olivia's torn dress and bleeding lip. "What's wrong?" they asked. But Olivia, sobbing through violent hiccups, wouldn't say. "Who is my mama?" finally spat from her swollen lips.

Glodean and Country looked at each other, then Country nodded to her sister. Glodean disappeared behind the bedroom door of the tiny shotgun house, and re-appeared carrying a brown paper bag.

From it she pulled, a yellowed, folded sheet of Big Chief tablet paper, a pacifier, baby underpants, and a small, blue-and-green quilt. She spread the contents on the oak kitchen table, and patted the chair next to her. Olivia sat, and wiped her eyes with the back of her hand.

"Baby Doll," Glodean said, "We just don't know who she is. The little boy ran away before we could find out. But look at these things.

Your mama cared a awful lot about you." She unfolded the blue-green quilt and held it up. It was hand-stitched and bright-colored, shot through with tiny squares of orange and red in its center.

"Your mama must have made this quilt when she knew you were coming. Just look at it. Ain't it pretty? Just for you. And look at this."

She handed Olivia the square of Big Chief tablet paper, frayed and yellowed, inscribed with angular, slanted handwriting.

Olivia read: "She don't like strained carrots, and no whole milk."

Glodean sat next to Olivia and stroked her hair, pushed a stray wisp behind her ear. "You see? She didn't want you to have anything you didn't like. And this quilt. She wanted you to be warm. And this pacifier. She wanted you to be satisfied. And then she took you to Big Mama's, where she knew you'd get the best kind of care, the kind she couldn't give you herself. She loved you enough to give you up to us."

Olivia took the quilt and rubbed it against her cheek. A baby quilt. It *was* pretty, she thought. "But who is she? Whose daughter am I?"

Glodean looked at Country, then at Olivia. She leaned forward and put her hand on Olivia's. "Ours, Baby Doll," she said.

Olivia didn't sing the rest of the school year. When Mrs. Squires called on her to sing "Silent Night" at Christmas time for the annual pageant, she said she had a cold, to Mary Frances's and May's delight. Whenever she felt the urge to sing or laugh, a hand flew up to her face to hide the broken smile.

Years later, in high school, her teeth neatly capped but her singing voice still mute, Big Mama, Uncle Joon, Clo T., Glodean, and Country met in the Beauty Palace one night after closing to discuss her schooling.

Olivia sat in a back bedroom behind the shop, knees tucked to her chin, listening, hearing muffled tones of her life in planning. Something about "a good singing school, up north," and Uncle Joon coming back with, "But she done stopped singing," and later Big Mama saying, "I got a idea about where she could go to school."

Olivia got up from her bed to close the door. Sing for a living?

Never. Never give anyone a chance to place her with that woman, no matter how much she loved the sound of her own voice. Hairdressing seemed as good a job as any. There were worse things to do than make women look pretty.

The woman couldn't be her mother, anyway. Years had passed since she heard the rumor, and somebody would have said something by now. Country knew all the gossip. She would have told her if it were true. One of them would have told her. If it were true.

But Olivia couldn't sleep. The sleep-time images she used to conjure, herself on a stage under pastel lights singing like Dinah or Etta, had long since been shelved like the dolls she'd loved to hairlessness, replaced by a blankness on her dream palette that kept her awake into the night. Now she only stared at the dark space behind her eyes until sleep came.

Mother or not, the woman had stolen her song. And if the woman was not her mother, then who was?

And who, anyway, was *she*?

Eighteen years old. The green Samsonite suitcase chafed her stockinged legs as she climbed aboard a Greyhound headed north to Kansas City. In a leather satchel (a present from Uncle Joon and Big Mama) she carried letters of introduction to Idabelle Washington's School of Cosmetology and the Mayfair Boarding House for Single Women on Fourteenth Street. But she was so anxious to see the city where she would be living, smell the earthy city scents of its chimneys and buses, stroll down an actual boulevard, that she got off the bus too soon.

When it had departed and left her standing in front of a small, red-bricked station, smaller than Moore's Funeral Home in Handy, she realized she was not in Kansas City at all but Joplin, three hours south of town. For a moment she stood in front of the station dumbfounded. She went inside and asked at the ticket window when the next bus to Kansas City would come.

A woman in her fifties with stringy hair the color of corn husks popped her gum as she chewed, leaning across the ticket window counter. "What'd you get off the bus for if you wanted to go to Kansas City?" she asked.

Olivia shifted her weight to another foot. "Um, well, I thought I heard the bus driver say next stop Kansas City, and I thought this was it."

The woman smirked. "You thought this was Kansas City? You ever *been* to Kansas City, honey?"

"No ma'am."

"Figures." The woman sucked her teeth and looked down at the bus schedule. "You got a long wait, honey. Next bus to K.C. is at 9:00. Gets in at midnight."

Olivia looked down at her birthday watch, a waterproof Timex from Clo T. and Glodean. It read 6:05.

"Thank you," she said, and turned away.

"There's a diner next door where you can pass the time if you got a long wait."

This was a new voice, coming from behind her shoulder. It was softly masculine and young sounding. She turned to see a young man in a gray tweed coat, a partial smile softening his face.

He had scared her half to death. Olivia tried to regain her composure enough to be polite. "Thank you, but I think I'll just wait in here," she managed to say through a forced smile.

"Suit yourself," the young man said, straightening the brim of his hat.

She didn't see him again until she finally walked the short distance to the diner, after the wooden benches in the bus station began to harden against her behind. It was deserted except for three customers, a waitress, and a cook. He was sitting there on a barstool sipping coffee, long legs crossed beneath the bar's countertop.

She took a seat in the corner booth, heaving the suitcase onto the seat next to her. She was tired now, and so angry at herself that she wanted to cry. She'd begged them to let her take the bus on her own (no need for Uncle Joon to drive her because after all she was eighteen now and grown), and look what happened? Stupid. Now her head ached too, and here she sat in a dive in, what city was it? Joplin? Someplace she never heard of, waiting three hours in a greasy spoon for a bus that would get her into town so late that no one would care about her new perm that Uncle Joon said made her look just like one of those sophisticated girls from the city, or her navy blue pumps from Davidson's clearance rack that Country said set off the nice muscles in her calves.

She would come in late and looking a mess. She stuck her hand under the table, took off her shoe, and rubbed her foot. These damn shoes were killing her. Even Country had told her nobody wears three-inch heels on a bus ride, but she wouldn't listen. She touched the ends of her hair, already getting a little frizzy from the moist night air. Maybe she could touch it up a little with a light combing and a spray of the Oil Sheen Big Mama had packed for her. She'd looked in the direction of the young man with an oh-so-casual turn of the head that she'd intended to express a certain indifference. But he had the audacity not to be looking her way, not to be looking anywhere near her. In fact, he seemed to have struck up a conversation with another customer at the counter.

"What'll you have, Miss?" asked a woman with a red-checked apron, her blond hair netted in a beehive hairdo. "Coffee?"

"Tea," Olivia said. "A hamburger, and, um, a piece of pound cake, please."

The waitress looked toward the counter. "That piece of cake is been sittin' out since last night. Why don't you try the berry cobbler instead? It's real good today. Fresh."

"OK," Olivia said, "Thank you. I'll try it."

"I sure hated missing that bus. Ran all the way up here, and then missed by just a couple of minutes."

The young man was talking to her from the lunch counter. She looked to find him smiling at her with beautiful, even teeth. "This your first time going up to K.C.?" he said.

"Yeah," she said flatly, and turned her head back to look at the wall in front of her. She didn't like talking across a room to a stranger, even if his skin was burnt-butter brown and blemish free, his lips rimmed with the shadow of budding growth, and his face divided into two perfectly symmetrical halves by a straight nose and a deep chin cleft.

He was tall and thin, and older, late twenties, maybe.

"Yeah? I live there myself. Nice place. You'll like it."

"Umm-hmm," she said. A small run in her hose tickled its way up her thigh and she tried to cover it with her hand. She wished that he would stop talking to her, making her speak louder than was comfortable for her. Suddenly she was afraid he might try to sit next to her on the bus. Uncle Joon had warned her about men traveling alone and people who might try to start up conversations. Her pulse quickened at the thought of this man trying to latch on to her. She decided she would get on the bus first and sit next to the first person she saw. And if there was nobody on the bus, she'd put her coat on the seat next to her, put a book over her face, and pretend to sleep.

"'Course there won't be much to see tonight, getting in so late," he said. "Not much happening at midnight during the week."

The beehived woman brought her tea and a hamburger, and sat the cup and plate in front of her.

"Thank you," Olivia said, and drank from her cup of tea. Small talker. She gave him a look long enough to pass for politeness but short enough to project blasé disinterest. But in that time she met his eyes. They were wide and round and dark. They made her uncomfortable, the way they seemed to see more of her than she wanted seen. He was staring at her as if he knew her, but she knew she had never seen him before. She would have remembered him. And yet, there was in his look a definite sense of recognition.

Or maybe it was just that by looking he could see the truth of her: young, shy, striking out on her own, a little girl taking high-heeled steps in the world and faltering on buckled knees. But he wasn't laughing at her inside, she saw that. If he could tell by looking at her that she was a young country thing trying her best to look grown-up and cityfied, he didn't seem to care.

She finished her hamburger, took forkfuls of her cobbler, pulled a paperback copy of Raymond Chandler's *The Big Sleep* from her suitcase, and began to read. She stretched her feet out under the table and propped them up on the seat in front of her. She didn't realize how quickly the time had passed until the waitress told her, "Hon, if you're wanting that Kansas City bus, it just pulled in."

"Oh, thank you," Olivia said, and jumped up from her seat. She looked at the counter and the man was gone. When she got to the station, passengers were loading onto the bus. She stepped on and walked down the aisle, found an empty seat among the travel-weary group of passengers. Good. She hadn't seen him. Maybe he decided to spend the night in Joplin, or got a ride with somebody. A long sigh gushed from her, and she sat back and closed her eyes.

She awakened hours later to the smell of diesel fumes and the murmur of motor hum. The bus had pulled up to the brightly lit station, and three other buses had pulled up behind hers, emptying themselves of passengers. She got off the bus, got her suitcase, and walked to the curb. She felt a tingle of excitement as she looked up and around at the red-brick and stone buildings of downtown Kansas City.

The Mayfair had been expecting her at nine and now it was after midnight. The car that was sent to pick her up had surely gone hours ago. The sky was pitch black and there was a slight chill in the air. Passengers disappeared one by one into waiting cars or just walked away, knowing exactly where they were going and who they were meeting.

Surely there would be a taxi, but no, she looked around and there were none. And where was the boarding house? Not far from downtown, they had said, but where? She picked her bag off the curb and headed into the bus station.

"Need some help?"

She turned expecting to find the young man, but this man was old. Matted hair like a robin's nest; loose teeth dangled like yellow icicles in his mouth, and the air around him was ripe with the odors of unwashed skin and beer.

The man reeled on his feet like a bowling pin not quite ready to fall. "Let me grab that bag for ya, missy. Look like ya could use a little help."

Olivia reached for her bag, her heart racing. "Uh, no thank you..."

"Naw naw. Let me carry that there bag for ya. Where ya goin'?"

"No really, I can manage…"

They were tussling now, Olivia clutching the suitcase handle, and the old man, stooped and unsteady, grabbing its corners with both hands.

"'Scuse me, man. She's with me."

Now the young man was at her side, taking the bag from both of them. "S'OK. I got it. Thanks anyway, partner. We'll just be going now."

Her pulse still pounding, she breathed a sigh of relief when the drunken man stumbled away mumbling to himself. The young man turned to her, smiling. Gleaming teeth above the deep chin cleft. Hat brim cocked, just so.

"Bus stations. Don't you have a ride or something?"

She almost smiled back. "You were on the bus?"

"Way in the back. Where you headed?"

She stammered, looked around. "Well, I missed that early bus, and now I'm not sure…"

"I could walk you if I knew where you were going."

"The Mayfair Boarding House for Single Women," she said.

He laughed. "They don't call it that anymore. It's an old place, been around for years. But now they just call it the Mayfair Hotel. Not too far from here. Come on, I'll show you."

She reached for her suitcase. "Thank you, very much, but I'll be OK."

He stopped and looked at her, the fear still lighting her eyes. "OK, look. Let's do this. I'll start walking toward the Mayfair, and you let me get a good distance in front of you, then you just follow me. That way, you won't be walking with some strange man, you'll just be following one. I'll get you where you need to go. And if anybody tries to bother you, yell and I'll hear you. OK?"

She thought a moment. Reasonable. What could a man do to her if he was in front of her? And how else would she get there? She nodded. Olivia watched him walk away, straight-shouldered and head held high against the Kansas City night sky, a satchel strap across his shoulder, swinging a case of worn leather. An unhurried stride, confident but not arrogant. She stayed a few steps behind him, matching the pace of his walk with the click of her high-heeled shoes.

The streets were silent and the pavement shimmered beneath a glaze of just-ended rain. So this was it, the big city. The buildings were tall, but their tops faded like unfinished drawings into a foggy sky. An occasional car passed, emitting the tinny sound of radio jazz. There was the faintest smell of roasted coffee in the air. And bus fumes. The man turned down a street and Olivia followed, her heart calmer, her shoulders relaxed. The street was lined with tall oaks and old stone two-story houses with grand gables, wide porches, and white columns, big as mansions. He walked up the sidewalk to one building lit with a porch lamp, and she followed, almost even with him now.

He rang the doorbell. "I'll just wait here, make sure you get in OK," he said.

He seemed all right. At least he hadn't tried to talk to her or ask her questions. They both silently stood in the light of the porch lamp for minutes before they saw a light coming on and heard the clicking of opening locks.

Mrs. Hettie Peale answered the door, dressed in a red silk robe with white flowers, her hair netted in pink cushion rollers. "Olivia Benton? My God, you made it," she said, and opened the door. "Praise Jesus. Big Mama and Clo T. have been calling since nine o'clock. What happened? Did you miss the bus? How come you didn't call? Come on in. Who is this young man? I'm sorry, we only let young women stay here."

She let them into a wide, high-ceilinged parlor of elegant mahogany furniture, cream-colored sheers veiling French windows, dark wood molding, and wallpaper of powder blue and rose stripes. A walnut grand piano stood in a corner. The young man placed her suitcase next to the piano while Olivia apologized, embarrassed. "I'm sorry. I did a stupid thing. Got off the bus in Joplin, and it went on without me. Had to wait three hours for another one. I hope you weren't too worried. I never thought to call."

"Oh, child, bless your heart. Well, come on in," the woman said, her eyes shifting quickly between Olivia and the young man.

"Oh, uh, I just escorted her from the bus depot," he said. "I'll be on my way now."

"How nice of you." A small frown disappeared from the woman's face and she smiled. "I'd invite you in for a Coca-Cola but it's so late."

"No, thanks. I've got to go anyway."

"Oh, all right. Well then, let's get your bag upstairs. Child, you walked all the way from the bus station in those shoes? Your feet must ache something awful! Thank you again for your trouble, Mr., uh..."

"Yes, thank you," Olivia turned to him with a self-conscious smile.

"Louis," he said. "Tillman. Most people call me L.J."

"Tillman. You any kin to the Tillmans over at Pleasant Green Baptist on the Kansas side? The ones that run the funeral home over on Tremont? Been knowing them for years."

"No ma'am. I've only been here a few years. I play saxophone over to the Landmark Lounge at the Union Station."

"Oh? A musician?" she said. "We've had some ladies from the various gospel groups stay here from time to time. Sometimes they even sang here, rehearsed, you know."

He nodded toward the piano. "You had that tuned lately? I can tune it for you. You should keep 'em tuned, you know, otherwise they won't hold a pitch. And I work cheap."

The woman looked toward the piano. "Oh, that. We've not had much use for it, lately; nobody uses it, except we keep it polished. But we'll keep you in mind." She turned to Olivia. "Olivia here, from what her folks tell me, was quite a singer herself."

"That right? You sing?"

His perfect mouth now shaped a smile so wide it lit his dark eyes like the lights on Christmas trees, a smile that made you smile back before you realized you were doing it. Olivia felt herself smiling and looked down to finger the wooden buttons on her coat. "Not really. I sang some when I was a kid."

He shrugged. "Well, you know, once a singer." He took a deep breath and straightened the brim of his hat. She could feel nerves jump on the surface of her skin.

The three of them stood silent for a minute. Finally, he said, "Well. I better be getting on. Nice to meet you both."

He was leaving now, and she had an unsettling feeling. It was a big city. What if she never saw him again? There was really nothing she could do but hope. Hettie Peale was walking him to the door—*Thank you so much again, yes, so nice to meet you too, be careful going home*—then to her—*We'd better call Big Mama before she has a fit, let's get your things upstairs, your room is all ready*—If the woman hadn't hurried her upstairs with such mother-hen deliberateness, Olivia would have at least looked to see him walk away. As it was, she listened to the two/four rhythm of his steps and remembered it like a song.

· SIX ·

T HE THURSDAY FOLLOWING HER SINGING TRIBUTE at New
Hope, when the cool evening air of autumn beckoned, Olivia
took her plate of baked chicken and lemon almond rice to the porch.
On Walker Street the pale violet sky darkened, and from down the
block came the hoarse whispers of dry leaves, branch rustle, and skirt-
ing breezes. She sat on the glider, plate balanced on her knees. Winter-
tinged wind whistled through wood seams, raising goosebumps on
her skin, and she shawled her shoulders with her hands.

Olivia Tillman loved the smell of lavender, the skeletons of tall oaks
in winter, the taste of deep-fried fish, and old jazz. And old houses
with shutters and dormer windows and porches like the one she and
L.J. had bought quicker than it took to buy a dress. One walk-through
and they both loved it. Built in '48, it had nestled them perfectly, like
a soft, sturdy shoe: wood-shuttered against the wind, thick-walled
against August's raging heat, steep-roofed to shed the most drenching
rains. Most of all she loved the wrapping porch with the green glider
that creaked now under her slow-rocking weight, where she and L.J.
would sit on evenings like this before he went to work. It was covered
with a film of dust now; she hadn't sat on it in more than a year.

She took a bite of chicken and remembered the boxes. Winona had
come by earlier in the week to help her pack some of his clothes for
the church missionary barrel. Could she part with his things? So soon?
Was it time? From the closet she pulled out a gray collared sweater
she'd given him years ago when they were still dating. Moth-eaten
now, and two sizes too small, but carefully folded on a shelf in his
corner of the closet. His neatness amazed her; her new clothes hung

askew on wire hangers while this old sweater sat there so neatly. He'd held on to it for more than twenty years.

She remembered exactly when she'd given it to him. Days after the bus station, he started coming by—*Just was thinking about that piano, decided to swing by and tune it, no charge, no, I just hate to see a good instrument get out of shape.* She didn't care what excuse he'd made up; she was ecstatic to see him.

He opened the lid and pulled tools from a threefold pouch of felt—a screwdriver, a wrench-looking thing, a tuning fork, some strips of velvet—and spread them like a surgeon's instruments on the bench.

"I didn't know you played piano," she said, arms behind her, looking on.

"I don't, really. I just tune them. Extra money."

She watched as he leaned over and with a screwdriver carefully wedged strips of velvet between the strings. "This separates them, so I can tune each string," he explained, and then reached for the hammer.

"Can you use any old wrench?"

"It's called a hammer." He looked up at her, half smiling. "And no, it's special."

"Looks kind of like a wrench."

"I know, but it's a hammer."

"I thought those were the hammers." She pointed a finger to wooden things inside the piano pressing against strings.

"They are...uh...they're both called hammers. I never thought about...it's hard to explain."

He appeared to want to say more, but turned his attention to the piano. He fit the "hammer" around a pin and turned. Long fingers moving with easy grace, tapping keys, listening, turning, tapping again, the *ping-g-g-g* of tones ringing under the parlor's high ceiling, then dying somewhere in the seams of walls. She listened as tones that wobbled and wavered slowly rang true (and his face went through a series of looks—a frown, a querying look, a satisfied nod), the piano an ancient relic coming to life under his hands. She took note. *Such patience, such care.*

"How do you know when it's in tune? I mean really?"

"I use a pitch fork. But mostly you just have to listen. Here, you try it." He gave her the hammer and pointed to a pin. She fit the hammer on it and tried as he tapped a C.

"Don't be afraid of it. Give it a good turn. Like this." The warmth of his skin, a large paw of a hand resting firmly on hers, making her breath short. Another *ping-g-g-g,* this one vibrating somewhere in her chest.

"There, now, hear?" he said. "The piano knows. When it's in tune, it's just more alive. You can feel it inside you when it's just right. You know what I mean?"

She did.

Two pairs of eyes in concert, hers the first to look away.

He was older than she remembered but even more handsome, and had that shy way she had not known, until now, that she loved. A week later, he brought her cookies of oatmeal and chocolate from Mattie's Bakery and a clump of cellophane-wrapped daisies from the floral cooler at Milgram's. Sat at the piano and picked out a song she liked by Nancy Wilson. In time, fondness emboldened her to offer to cut his hair, buy him Miles Davis's latest. To sit by the phone in the Mayfair dining room on Wednesday nights when he got off early and wait until it rang, to talk with a girlish giggle in her voice, twirling the phone cord and laughing at his corny jokes.

But the night of the party at the house of one of his musician friends, everything had gone wrong. To begin with, she was too young. All of his friends were in their late twenties, some even thirty, and she was all of eighteen. And that might not have bothered her, had she not worn a polka-dotted Sunday dress and black pumps while all the other guests wore dashikis, halter tops, Earth Shoes. They talked about Angela Davis and Coltrane, drank Mateus Rose, and sported round Afros, while she silently sipped a Coke, her hair pressed into a flip. Why hadn't she just stenciled herself a nice sign? *Underage Hick Just Off Bus From Small Country Town.*

He seemed to see her discomfort and tried to make up for it, showing her off, introducing her to everyone in sight, making matters worse—making her the center of unwanted attention. And then there were his friends, the women especially, eyes rimmed in thick mascara, full lips glossed, breasts aimed at him like high-powered rifles, talking directly into his eyes without ever shifting to hers, as if she weren't even there. Fawning over him, making the jealous bones in her body prick the surface of her skin. Oh, women liked him, she already knew that, and why wouldn't they? He was handsome and kind. But when that fact wasn't making her beam with pride, it infuriated her. It wasn't that he flirted with them—he didn't seem to know how—but did he have to be so charming all the time? Did he have to smile that smile that she believed should only be meant for her? Did he have to be so polite?

At the party he'd left her alone only once for three minutes, while the host pulled him and two others to a side room to show off his new Conn trumpet. She'd gone to find a bathroom and had gotten lost down a hallway. Finally when she emerged from a closet door she'd mistaken for one leading back to the kitchen, two couples, drinks in hand, smiled at her mistake. "Party's that way, sister," one of the Afro-wearing women said, pointing an index finger half-curled around a wine glass. "Don't get lost, now."

Coming home in the car, her silence was icy. After ten minutes, he took the bait.

"Olivia, I apologize."

"Apologize for what?"

"Well, I'm not sure, but I apologize anyway."

"Well, if you don't know what you're apologizing for," she snapped.

"It's a general apology, let's just let it cover whatever I did wrong tonight."

"Well, if you don't even know what you did, it's meaningless."

"Well, why don't you tell me and then I'll apologize."

"What's the point if you have to ask?"

"Olivia, this is ridiculous. I'm sorry. Whatever I did, once I figure it out, it won't happen again. Now, come on. I'll buy you an ice cream cone."

Her eyes got big and she turned to him, her arms folded. "Oh, so it's like that? Buy the little girl an ice cream cone?"

"What's that supposed to mean?"

"Forget it. You obviously don't care about how I feel."

What she was saying was confusing even her. He gave her a "Where did *that* come from?" look, then shook his head in frustration and drove in silence. From the corner of her eyes, she could see his puzzled mind working, as if trying to calculate the square root of the earth's circumference. When they finally pulled up to the Mayfair, he turned to her.

"OK look, Olivia, I'm sorry if some of those people made you uncomfortable. The deal is, I don't think you're too young. If other people do, that's their problem. I think you are beautiful and intelligent and wise."

He reached for her hand, but—*No, don't touch me*—she wanted to be out of the car and in her room before the tears fell. Once inside, she cried softly. Feeling stupid and just plain wrong. What had he done? Nothing but provide her with something that her heart would break to lose. The next Monday she took her food allowance for the week, rode the Twelfth Street bus to Singleton's Men's Wear, and bought him the gray sweater. She lived on carrot sticks with peanut butter for six days. The sweater was inexpensive, not at all like the nice things he wore, but eleven dollars was all she had. The sleeves were a half-inch too short. But he went on as if it were cashmere stitched with gold. Wore it often for her to see. Years later, when the thin fabric gave way in a small tear on the shoulder, he still wore it under his blue blazer, the collar of it neatly turned out. Twice over the years she'd tried to throw it out only to find it retrieved from the Goodwill box she'd set out, and neatly folded on the closet shelf. Now, when she thought of giving it away, tears burned the corners of her eyes.

It was growing late. The sky was darker when she finished her chicken. She stood up, watched the transfer of light, the dimming sun's surrender to the street lamps crowned in blurred gold, the halo ringing the moon and the gathering of stars barely visible in the dusky sky. She could not go in yet because the sooner sleep came, the sooner came the disturbing dreams.

They were so bad, she'd begun to eat simple bland dinners, or none at all, just a cup of chamomile and sleep-aid herbs from the health food store, hoping that would help. But nothing did. Still he night-crawled into her sleep. Well, tonight she would not give in to the fear of sleep, she told herself, as she took one of the little white pills from her plate and slipped it into her mouth. Let him steal his way in all he wanted, she would gently turn him away, politely, like a suitor calling on her at an inconvenient time. He belonged to memory now, to be tucked away and brought out only when she was able to think of him without the panicky feeling of unresolved regret.

When her sleep-thick eyelids sagged and blinked, she turned to go inside. Winona would call tomorrow, she'd said, and talk some more about New York. Her divorce from Rex was final, so they both had men to lay to rest, she'd said. A trip would do them both good. Olivia was a homebody like Big Mama, who couldn't be bothered with travel. But Country had come back from New York about a year before she died, raving about the good-looking waiters in the Italian restaurants, the way the bellmen at the hotels smiled at you and held doors, and how good music blared from the uptown bars and the aromas of quaint kitchens could take your breath away. Maybe it was what she needed.

She dressed for bed. On her nightstand lay an unopened letter, still there after all these months, postmarked "Handy, Arkansas," with a return address from Big Mama. She took the white envelope in her hands and turned it, looked at Big Mama's cursive scrawl spelling her name. Resentment overtook her curiosity; she put the letter down.

She could not think about Big Mama now. Ninety and living alone since the others had all passed on, she was still as strong as an ox and stubborn as a goat, her mind and wit razor-sharp. Someday it would be easier to forgive her for what she'd done. But now the hurt was too fresh, like the icy burn that shocks the skin after a slap. Nothing to speed the cooling but time. She could wait for it and so, she thought, could Big Mama.

She lay down against the cool sheets and pulled the covers up around her neck. She glanced at his side of the bed, smooth, undisturbed, and for the first time in a year, she moved to the center. The sheets were cold in the new spot, uncomfortable, but she drew the covers closer, tucked the other pillow beneath her head, and closed her eyes.

She had only been asleep an hour or so when it happened, and though she half-expected it (she had planned what she would do if it happened), she still woke up shaking.

She answered the phone, shrieking like an alarm, and sat up. "Hello?" she'd said. A dream, for sure, but she almost said, "L.J., is that you?"

"Olivia, it's me."

She never fully awakened, wandering in vaporous half-sleep. But this time it was so real that she wondered if she was half mad. There had been background noise, like a nightclub, like when he used to call her from Jimmy's. And then the tone, the texture of his voice, the inflection, the familiar interrogative lilt in *Olivia?* It was all his, all there. And yet she knew it was not really him, refused to be fooled again by the dream state that had seduced her so many times before. Calmly, without speaking, she had placed the receiver back in its hook.

Go back to sleep, she told herself. It was a dream. The air in the room felt close and hot. Her heart would race for a while, she expected that. It would take a few minutes to calm down, as usual. She took deep breaths, slow and long, the way they had taught her in yoga class last year at the community school. *One, two, three, four...*you were supposed to count, exhaling slowly. *One, two, three...*how could a dream be so real? The counting wasn't working. Her skin was moist and warm. She turned over against the pillow and found a cool spot inches away from where she had lain before. *One, two...*Think of something else. Big Mama. No. Something else, something pleasant. The church, the singing. No. Something else. Winona, the trip. Yes, New York.

Maybe Cora could run the shop for a few days. Twenty-six years old and the girl could do hair in her sleep. *Sleep, sleep, come on...*and New York would be good a change of pace and they could see shows on Broadway and eat strange new food in nice restaurants and the tall buildings where you had to lift your head against the sky and the music and all the people and the nightclubs and they had good food there and up in Harlem and the bellmen who held the door and smiled at you and… the music and… the food and… the tall buildings and… the sky…

She slept until she felt the spill of morning's blue-gray light entering through her window and opening her eyes. She yawned, stretched, blinked emphatically. Another one, another damned dream.

But after her first cup of tea, she went into the living room, where the boxes of his things sat beneath the piano. She stared at them for a moment. Then, one by one, she carried them back upstairs.

III

· SEVEN ·

NIGHTFALL WELCOMES A MAUVE MOON and the still air is crisp. Just above the doorway of the club, one continuous swirl of blue neon spells out the name—The Baby Grand—then flows nonstop into a looping likeness of a piano lid. Yellow and Checker Cabs pull up to the glass doors, and out step silk crepe de chine and polished Ferragamos, Armani wool and Persian lamb. Hair swept up, or down and swaying, skin smelling of musk and Lancôme: denizens of the Upper East Side dress to the nines to cap the evening with a shot of bourbon and a set or two of jazz.

Arriving on foot are the employees—the waiters, the kitchen help, the musicians.

"Hey, Percy." On entering, L.J. nods to the overmuscled hulk of doorman standing outside the club. Dressed in a thin pullover that denies the chill air, Percy is black, almost seven feet tall, thick-necked, with deltoids and biceps so prominent that his arms hang slightly akimbo.

"'Sup, man."

Almost a month now, and the frowning behemoth (obviously planted to daunt the unwashed, the improperly dressed, and the up-to-no-good) has never spoken more than these words. L.J. guesses the man was hired just after his own foray into the club a few weeks ago, the night he'd straggled in to beg for a job, unkempt clothes full of rainwater and eyes full of pleading. No bouncer around then, but the first night he'd shown up for work, old Percy was standing sentry with all the humor and conviviality of a cigar store Indian.

A big black man hired to keep away others like him. But so what? Hell, he's got the job now. And he's glimpsed the misty-eyed looks of the regulars at the bar during his "Lush Life" solo, or his super-slow, note-bending "In a Sentimental Mood." The nodding heads, the wistful smiles, the warm applause all said they liked him here. He even looked like a different man: hair trimmed, a just-cleaned-and-pressed blue suit from the mission thrift store with a like-new pinstriped Oxford shirt. He was in. Let some bouncer try to keep him away now.

He only has to walk in, feel the swirling, ventilated air, see the bright, polished brass bar and Art Deco chandeliers, hear the state-of-the-art stereo piping the classics—Duke, Basie, Monk—to feel like a million, to forget that despite the promise of paychecks, he's still living on the street.

Or to forget the more painful fact of Olivia hanging up that phone. Slamming it in his ear without so much as a word. She made her message clear, all right.

But just like always, tonight he'll bury his discordant past in a maze of blue notes and sweet minor chords. Tomorrow, he'll think about her. He puts his horn down near the bandstand and heads to the back room to wash his hands. Just for habit's sake, a ritual: something he's missed living on the street. He's always liked to play with clean hands.

The piped stereo grooves at low volume, Miles and company doing "If I Were a Bell." On the way back from the washroom, Mel Samples, tending bar, catches his eye. Mel is thirtyish, white, and gay, with a southern accent that sings like a breeze across Georgia high cotton.

"L.J., y'all have got to do 'God Bless the Child' tonight. My mother and her boyfriend are in town for her birthday, and I told her y'all would play it for her!"

L.J. gives a thumbs-up nod. "Have her sit up front. Point her out to me." He'll play "Happy Birthday," too, always a winner, putting the whole crowd in a good mood.

L.J. steps up to the bandstand and unpacks his horn. The bass player, Wash, has arrived—lean and long-armed. "A long tall drink of water," his old man Purvis would have dubbed him. He unzips the canvas cover from his instrument, and nods—"Hey, man,"—to L.J.

He likes the men, fine musicians all and easy to work with. All three are black, and two are around his age. As he warms up the cold brass of his horn, the other members of the quartet join him: Larry, the piano-playing, preppy-looking kid, skinny, brown-skinned, and shy, from Juilliard; and Crawfish, short, round-faced, and stocky with monstrous forearms, the best drummer he's heard since Tony Williams's prime.

The men play noodling warm-up runs on their instruments. The filler music on the sound system fades and L.J. speaks first.

"Mel wants us to play 'God Bless the Child.' His mom's birthday."

"Cool," Larry says. "B-flat OK?"

"B-flat's good."

Wash uses his bow to tune the bass, then thumps out a bluesy walking step in D. "We'll take it from *you*, man," he says, smiling, nodding. "Just let us know when."

"Solid," L.J. says, then turns to Larry.

"Hey, man, I like that new tune you wrote. Want to start with it?"

Larry says, "You mean the blues one?"

"No, the other," L.J. says. "The ballad."

"Oh, 'Lovescape.'" Larry says, and fingers a haunting melody framed in block-chord harmony.

"Yeah, yeah," L.J. says. The boy was young, but could write his tail off. One by one they join the melody, first L.J. in breathy low tones supporting the tune in thirds, then Wash's bass in a lazy four/four, and finally Crawfish laying back, swirling brushes on the head of his snare, accenting strong beats on ride cymbals.

L.J., leading, takes the tune's head, straightforward at first, then carves it up into half-phrases, with improvised runs in-between. Caresses it into a husky whisper. Turns it upside down, stretches it out, floats from one octave to another. Quotes "Stella by Starlight" in the middle, just for fun. Plays with the tune as if he wrote it himself.

"Yeah, that's it!" An old man from the bar sips whiskey and yells out.

Larry looks at L.J. Nods his head, a smile in his eyes.

He's grooving now. This is the way L.J. likes to start with this kind of crowd. Slow, soft, easy. *Treat 'em like you treat a woman you want*, Purvis always said. They've come from dinner, so the music needs to go down easy, like smooth sherry. Don't start loud and aggressive: too challenging, and bad for the digestion. They're talking easy-like, so don't intrude, take your cue from the mood of the room. Meet the folks where they are, and when the time is right, they'll follow you wherever you want to go.

They applaud lightly at the end, but L.J. knows they'll build up interest as the night progresses, and sure enough by the time they finish "God Bless the Child" they are right where he wants them, involved, listening, clapping like crazy.

He starts a blues version of "Happy Birthday" in B-flat and Mel's mom (Clarice is her name, she says when he asks her) is beaming. She's looking around the room as the spotlight lowers to show her shining gray curls, feeling special, blushing with pleasure.

The crowd eats it up, sings along rowdily in harmony. Then, cheers and laughter.

"And now," L.J. speaks into the mic, "since our boy Mel's our favorite bartender, here's something special to you, Clarice, from all of us."

He begins "You Are Too Beautiful," a Johnny Hartman arrangement of a tender love song, and Clarice, halfway through, wipes a tear from her eye. Her date, a man named Ralph with horn-rimmed spectacles hiding sparkling eyes, places his hand on hers.

From behind the bar Mel produces a small chocolate cake lit with seven candles and brings it down front to Clarice's table, and kisses her on the cheek.

Clarice's eyes light up as she blows out the candles. More cheers, more applause.

They round out the set with "Seven Steps to Heaven" in a lively tempo. L.J.'s solo is a run of thirty-second notes at break-neck speed, up and down the scale, stretching outside the box, pushing the time. The men back him up—Wash laying down the bottom on the bass, Crawfish's drumsticks on fire, Larry framing the whole thing in perfect changes—tight as family. When they finish, a light film of sweat glistens on L.J.'s forehead, and he dabs at it with a white handkerchief.

This time, the applause is louder and several people in the back stand up. Break time, now. *Rev them up and leave them wanting more.* L.J. introduces the men, then himself, to the crowd. Each one takes a bow. "Thank you, thank you," he says to the wolf whistles and cheers.

"We're going to take a little break right about now, so don't go away," he says. "See ya in twenty-five."

It had gone so well, he feels on top of the world. And it has been this way every night. He couldn't have asked for more: playing in a good New York club with good musicians, himself in charge, getting paid.

"Going pretty good tonight," he says to Wash. "Good crowd." He puts his horn down on the piano. A smile coming on that's hard to keep down.

"Yeah, well," Wash looks up from the bass he has laid sideways on the bandstand. "Too bad everything's gone change."

"What's that?"

"Just something a little bird told me. 'Bout this club. They might be selling it."

L.J. looks dumbfounded. "What? Selling it? This place? You kidding."

Seeing L.J.'s face he says, "Well, it might not mean anything. These clubs around here always changing hands. Might be nothing. Just something I heard. Anyway, you sounding good tonight, man. Really."

"Hey, thanks, you too, man," L.J. says, still dazed by Wash's words. Selling the club? He just got this gig and already it's looking shaky. No wonder Covington left when he did.

He walks over to the bar, takes a seat, and orders a light beer.

"This is on me," Mel said smiling broadly, pulling a beer mug down from a wooden rack. "Y'all were great. Miss Clarice was in hog heaven. I thought she was just gonna die when y'all played that other real pretty song. What's it called?"

"'You Are Too Beautiful.'" L.J. shrugs. "It's nothing man. My pleasure."

L.J. takes a sip of his beer. He won't finish it. He hasn't had a whole drink since he drove his car into the river. But a couple of swallows will take the edge off.

He leans over the bar toward Mel. "Look, man. Have you heard anything about this place changing hands?"

"This place? No way. I can't see Frank giving up his baby."

L.J. nods, relieved, takes another long swallow, and pushes the glass away. He looks toward the bandstand, then back at Mel. "So what about that deal I asked you about last week? You find out anything?"

"What? Oh, you mean the place. As a matter of fact, my sister told me today that that apartment in her building is still vacant. She thinks the landlord has got to come down on the rent if he wants to rent it. And hey, I finally found out what happened there."

"What?"

Mel leans over, his eyebrows raised and his voice slithering into a gossipy tone. "Somebody died in that place. Some old man who drank himself crazy, then shot himself. Nobody wants to rent it, after they know. So the rent's gonna be coming down. I'll keep you posted. By the way, love your shirt."

"Look man," L.J. says. "I gotta have someplace now. I uh…I gotta move from where I'm staying. Can you give me the guy's number?"

"My sister can give it to you. Here's hers." Mel writes a number down on a napkin and slides it to L.J.

"Thanks," L.J. says. He pockets the napkin. He's been anxious to find a place to live for days and never knew it would be so hard, even with the $700 or so he's saved up. Who could afford first and last month's rent in this town? The times when he's tried to get a job before—dishwashing, anything—taught him he was going to have to write down a fake address on his job application to get hired. He'd done that. Now he worries that somebody will find him out, learn that he left the club every night to sleep on benches, steps, and in doorways.

"I'll check it out tomorrow."

"She gets home from work around—"

Just then, both men turn when there's a commotion at the door.

"I wasn't botherin' none of them people!"

The voice is familiar to L.J., even though he doesn't know it. It's the voice of a hundred other men he's shared the streets with for the past year: unruly, slurred and thick with years of jug whiskey, crusted over with bad times and bad breaks.

"Oh, oh. There's that guy again," Mel says. "Homeless man. We don't get too many of them over here in this neighborhood. He used to come around here a couple of months ago, panhandling. Lorenzo ran him off. Looks like he's back."

L.J. gazes at the man through the glass window. Percy is so huge over him, the two look like grown-up man and little boy. Percy is leaning over, yelling at him, pointing down the street.

L.J. leaves the bar stool, walks to the door to get a closer look.

"What you mean proper attire? I got me a jacket on!"

The man is small, old, with shiny weathered skin closer to black than any other color. He wears an army jacket, a wool knit cap pulled down over his ears, and overalls beneath his jacket. A red plaid shirt is buttoned to his neck, and a garish green and blue paisley neck-tie, too wide to be stylish, hangs to just above his waist. Above his beard—thick, gray, and uncombed—are eyes that are red-glazed and wild.

"I got the price of a drink! Looka here! I got a right to come inside!"

Percy is saying something, but L.J. can't hear. L.J. opens the door, steps outside where the men are arguing.

"I got the price of a drink, and I'm coming in!" the old man says, and tries to walk around Percy. Percy grabs his arm and pulls him back. The old man loses his balance and stumbles.

L.J. reaches for the man's arm as he nearly falls on the ground. He looks up at Percy. "Hey, brother, look, the cat's not bothering anybody. Cut him a little slack."

"Man, I'm handling this. I ain't need no help doin' my job," Percy says. He grabs the old man's arm again and drags him away from the door.

"Hey!" L.J. says. "No need to hurt the man!"

Percy turns from the man and stands in L.J.'s face. "Man, go inside and do your job and I'll do mine. This dude ain't doing nothing but trying to hit folks up for money."

L.J. just looks up at Percy for a moment. L.J. is over six feet tall, but even standing to his full height, Percy still has several inches on him.

He shakes his head. *Why, brother?* The things we do. The things we end up doing to each other, just because they pay us to. Percy's frown seems permanent, another feature on his face, like a nose or an ear.

"Look, man," L.J. says. "Just let me... I know this dude. Let me handle him."

He takes the little stranger's arm and guides him down the street a few steps away from the club door. The old man looks up at him, pathetic pride and indignation in his eyes, then looks down at his shabby clothes and dusts them with the backs of his hands, as if trying to recover some dignity that was never there.

"Shoot," the old man says. "I'ont know what's wrong with that dude. Say, man, how's about sneaking me in around the back?"

L.J. sighs. The man is a mess. He smells of stale alcohol, old sweat, and the street. It's true, the customers would freak if he came inside. And what if he did bug them about money? He shakes his head slowly. "I...I'm sorry, I can't do it. They got a cover in there. Fifteen bucks. I just started working here myself so I can't really...I'll lose my job."

"Humph," the old man says. "Fifteen just to come in out the cold!"

L.J. has seen so many like this. Burned out on booze. Roaming the streets like lost dogs. On his worst day on the street, he felt better than this man looked. The man looked as if he hadn't had a proper meal in a decade. L.J. reaches in his pocket and pulls out a ten.

"Sorry, man," L.J. says. He pats the old man on the shoulder. "But here. Buy yourself something to eat."

The man takes the bill, lifts his sad eyes to L.J.

"Well, I gotta get back to my set. Take care of yourself," L.J. says, unable to look him in the eyes. And he turns and goes back into the club.

Two hours later, after the last set, the wind outside the club has stilled as L.J. leaves for the night. It's one-thirty and now he has to deal with the usual problem—where to sleep.

So many things on his mind, he can't even think about sleep, even though he's exhausted. Olivia. He needed to think about what to do about Olivia. Maybe try to call her again. Make her see where's he's coming from. Convince her…of what? Of something he's not sure of himself? And he still doesn't have a place to live. He'd had to walk toward the same subway station every night after work so it would look like he had someplace to go. And then there was that old man.

That really bugged him, that old dude. OK, so he didn't belong inside. But there was no reason to treat him like something a dog dragged in between his teeth. That Percy. One black man roughing up another black man to keep him out of a white man's place. Same old story. Did any of the three of them really fit in there? And what was the difference between him and the old man? Not much. L.J. was a little younger and could play the horn. But it had only been a few weeks since he'd come to the club looking just about as bad as the old man. Carrying a gun, even. Thinking, if only for a moment, about holding the place up. And now look at him. Leading the band.

He walks south. For a while now he's had good luck sleeping at Grand Central. There's scaffolding there and plastic sheets hanging where construction men work during the day, so it's easier to hide from the cops. He'll find a good bench and put his feet up for a few hours before tomorrow morning when he goes out to find—*must find*—a decent place to live.

L.J. has only been walking two blocks when he hears a mewing sound, like a kid's toy trumpet, or no, like a harmonica. Somebody was in one of these alleys playing a slow down-home blues, and for a minute L.J. is a boy again, swimming creeks in the wet Delta heat. With every metallic simper and moan he could see boggy swamps, hear the reedy ring of cicadas in high weeds, smell the green smell of the bayou and the way the air above it held the breath of blossoming magnolias.

He turns in the first alley he comes to, and there, curled up against a tower of fruit crates, is the old man.

"Hey, hey! I knew you'd be coming this way."

The old man staggers to his feet, wipes his hand on his pants and extends it.

"Honeymoon, man. Franklin 'Honeymoon' Johnson."

L.J. shakes his hand. "L.J. Tillman."

L.J. apologizes again for not being able to let Honeymoon in the club, and the old man shrugs.

"I used to panhandle some there. Yeah, they had to run me outta there a coupla times. But tonight, man, tonight, I just wanted to hear the music. Man, y'all was soundin' so good! Whooo weee! Y'all was hot. I ain't heard playin' like that in a coon's age! Naw, tonight I just wanted to come in and hear me some good music."

He lowers his spindly body back down near the crates, folds his knees up against his chest. "And I had me some money, too, ten bucks, enough for a drink."

L.J. doesn't know what to say. Just an old blues man wanting to hear some sounds. He takes a seat on one of the crates in the alley, with his horn case and satchel at his side.

"This where you stay?" he asks.

"Yeah, mostly round here. For now. I keep movin'. Got all my stuff right over there." He points to a shopping cart full of old clothes, aluminum cans, and magazines wedged behind a Dumpster.

"Mind if I join you? Tonight, I mean."

The old man looks at him sideways from the corner of his eye. "Hey man, I don't play that funny stuff."

L.J. laughs. "Naw, man. I mean, I'm out here too. On the street, no place to stay. I figured we could, you know, hang for a bit."

The man's eyebrows fly up. He stares at L.J., his trimmed shining hair, his clean suit, his pressed Oxford shirt. Then shakes his head.

"Well, I be damned."

L.J. unlatches his case, pulls out his horn and attaches the mouth-piece. He wants to tell the man that his story might be a little like his own, that out here one man's story is pretty much like another's. Everybody out here's got one. They just look a little different. Some have a little drama behind them, some just the same old boring tale of living gone wrong. But anyway you sliced it, bottom was bottom.

Instead, he licks his reed. "You know, my old man played blues. He used to like this one tune by Blind Lemon. Check it out."

He plays four bars and taps his foot in time on the concrete. Then the old man takes his harmonica and joins him—his tones a treble whine across a Delta swamp, L.J.'s sax a fog horn above the deep.

"Good tune," the old man says. "Better in D, though. Ever try it in D?"

L.J. licks his reed again, looking at the old man whose smiling eyes now spread crow's feet across his face.

"OK," he smiles. "D it is."

· EIGHT ·

THE NEXT MORNING A BRIGHT LATE AUTUMN SUN wakes L.J. early, but not early enough to see the old man head off to be first in line for the hot pancakes in the kitchen of Trinity Lutheran. L.J. had begged off—six a.m. was too early to eat, even if the meal was free. He'd catch a bite at French's later.

The night before, they'd ended up sitting amongst alley detritus—crates and Dumpsters and shards of broken glass and cans—playing blues and talking until the bread trucks rolled out from the bakery down the block. Honeymoon had been a Chicago blues man until his career collapsed under the onslaught of disco and funk. When his wife left him, Old Crow filled the space she'd left behind. L.J. told his story: a working jazz man in flight from a woman he'd so wronged he had to put miles of serious road between them to dull the pain. He told about the life he'd left; the good clothes, the two-story with an almost-paid mortgage, the green lawn with juniper bushes neatly trimmed.

Funny where life takes you, they both said. And when words ran out, they played.

When L.J. stands and stretches, the joints in his knees and elbows pop. He shakes his legs to get the kinks out. He's got a lot to do today; his suit jacket needs pressing again, and he wants to buy a few things for the old man. Then, find a place to live. In his pocket, he finds the scrap of paper with the number Mel gave him.

At a gas station pay phone a couple of blocks away, Mel's sister's cheery voice offers the address of the building with the vacant apartment. But after another half-hour of walking, no luck; the super's place in the basement of the eight-story brownstone is empty. On the door a yellow hand-printed sign reads "Back at three p.m."

Hours to kill means time to think. In the city, he's learned the compatibility of walking and thinking: one seemed made for the other. Somewhere he'd read about a great stone labyrinth at some cathedral near Paris built a thousand years ago, and that back then people walked the serpentine path in search of themselves, believing the big answers were locked inside of you and busy feet helped set them free. He believed it was true. The city is his labyrinth, from Coney Island to the Cloisters, from the East River to the Hudson, and walking always puts his mind in motion.

So after strolling past the giant, naked trees lining the eastern edge of the park, he stops for a light breakfast at French's before continuing on his walk. In Kansas City a man's tires wore thin before his shoes did, but in this city, and with no address, walking serves as proof of life. Those who squatted, hovered, huddled, or sprawled too long were a step away from trouble—if death didn't snatch them, the law surely would. And as long as he could fake it (check his watch now and then, step briskly across a busy street and hurry off to nowhere in particular) he could claim a stake in the living game. He never loafed, never loitered, never allowed his shadow to linger in doorways; to do so would be to forfeit a visible connection with the upstanding and well fed. So all day, every day, he picks a direction and walks.

Brownstones and fenced-in churchyards, bodegas and bakeries, delis, rows of trendy and not-so-trendy shops dot the blocks of his path. Lebanese vendors hawk fried falafel in pocket bread, and Cubans under bright umbrellas serve up sizzling *platanos* fried while you wait. A bakery brandishes a Star of David on its polished glass front and the smell of potato knishes and fresh bagels and coffee drifts from its ovens and gives him a heady lift. His long stride is quick today, hands punched deep inside his pockets, eyes straight ahead as if the answer to his puzzlement is posted at the very next block. His thoughts are loose and jumbled, questions rattle inside. Even if he found a place, could he afford it, even with the job? He needs money, and that kid—the thief—is heavy in his mind. No void feels more hollow than a poor man's pocket emptied at gunpoint, and ever since it happened,

L.J. can't shake the thought: that three hundred bucks he's missing stands between him and a better life.

Sometimes his feet drift into East Harlem, the section where he'd gotten mugged. He's not exactly looking for that kid, but since he's walking anyway, he may as well walk where the kid might show up. Three weeks now he's done this, days and days of looking and not looking. And once he actually thought he saw the kid.

But after walking for only an hour today, he does.

L.J. does a double-take, to be sure. It's him.

He fills the doorway of a bodega, lanky, full of angles, dark-skinned, long-armed like L.J., with that unmistakable gold-flecked grin. An upturned bottle of orange juice pressed to his wide lips. Head cocked back, he drinks long and slow.

When the bottle is empty, he heaves it toward a wire trash basket on the street, but it glances off the rim and lands near a gutter. Grinning, he yells something to someone still in the store, all cocky bravado and mannish swagger. L.J. watches the boy leave, oversized T-shirt hanging below an open black leather jacket, denims bagging around his hips.

The boy has a handsome face with youthful bones not yet man-set, and the haircut is a tribute to geometry, with razored lines like little lightning bolts slicing the trimmed mat. But his eyes hold a careless look. Even at half a block away, beneath the lightning bolts L.J. can make out a neatly stenciled autograph in the boy's haircut. Roy.

Standing beneath the torn green awning of a fish market, L.J. stares, memorizing features—height, skin color, hair. (What kind of thief is stupid enough to carve his name into the back of his haircut?) Slick-strutting, pimp-limping, the boy starts in L.J.'s direction, though L.J. is certain he can't see him yet. Arrogance rides in the looseness of his joints, the swing of arms and hands. He lives around here, surely. No way this kid would stray far from his own turf.

Suddenly, closer now, the careless eyes angle toward him. Recognition passes like a current between them and both faces tighten with gathering heat. The boy's wicked smile falls like a branch from a dead tree. He stops, backs up, and turns to run, and L.J. takes off after him.

The boy darts down a street of tall leafless trees. L.J.'s legs are slower, but no less determined, chasing him through the alley, behind the soft drink truck, around the fence behind a coffee shop, and into another alley. The older man pants like an overheated puppy, his legs stiffening. A small cramping seizes his thigh. Limping now, but still running. The boy, still in view but losing size, runs with high athletic kicks, arms flailing, leather flapping around his wiry frame.

Weaving around trash barrels, the boy runs into the open street and into traffic, dodging the grill of a cab that skids to a stop. A swarthy cab driver spits out a curse and shakes his fist as the boy darts around the car. L.J. reaches the end of the street. His breathing is rapid, his chest rising and falling like bellows. He stops and leans against a car with his palm, then lowers his body onto the gritty, moist asphalt. His leg is throbbing.

"Damn," he exhales in a hoarse whisper, shaking his head. By now the boy is out of sight. Big huffs of air push from burning lungs through open jaws. He removes a handkerchief from his pocket and wipes sweat from his forehead and neck. He leans over, rubs his thigh with the palms of both hands.

"I'll see you again, don't worry," L.J. says to the air and the noisy traffic. As sure as I'm standing here, I'll find you."

An hour later, still sweating, breathing hard, and minimally composed, L.J. is back at the brownstone super's door, ringing the bell.

"What you want?" The voice from behind the bolted door has an accent, Persian maybe.

"Uh, I'm here about the apartment?"

The opened door unleashes a perfume of garlic, onions, and a curious eastern spice. The super is short, thick-browed with curly black hair and olive skin. "Let me turn off stove. I show you," he says.

L.J. follows him up a narrow staircase to the fourth floor, where the man unlocks a door at the end of a hallway with a thick layer of gray paint and a magenta carpet.

The apartment is smaller than L.J. hoped, so small he wonders if more than one person could actually move around in it. A thin, worn carpet of faded beige stretches across a floor tilted slightly upward toward the far wall. A bank of large windows with mini-blinds faces a red brick tenement building that is easily jumping distance.

L.J. steps inside. A tiny wall kitchen with appliances circa 1960, a small refrigerator and stove, an iron day bed against another wall. A wooden gateleg table and two chairs, a bureau of five drawers, and a nubby brown sofa with sunken cushions complete the furnishings.

The place smells of Pine Sol and cigars. He looks for blood and, seeing none, wonders just where it was that the man shot himself.

"Five eighty-five," the super says. "First and last month rent, and $150 for deposit."

L.J. adds the amount in his head—$1,320. With the seven hundred or so he's saved up, he's still about six hundred short. It's a dive, but looks clean, and cheap as Manhattan rents go. He'd have more by next week, but by that time it'll be gone.

"Any chance of coming down a little?" L.J. says.

"Already come down plenty."

L.J. can't handle the thought of another week on the street, especially now that he's employed. "Look, man, I just don't have that kind of cash. Maybe I could sweep the floors, help you clean up or something."

"How much you got?" the man asks.

"Seven hundred."

The man frowns, strokes his stubbled chin. "OK, you give me more next week. I take seven hundred."

As light from the window fills the room, a small roach crosses the floor from the sofa to the kitchen.

"I'll take it," L.J. says.

Within seconds of taking the apartment he's in the small bathroom, running callused fingertips through the burst of high-pressure hot water gushing from the faucet of the claw-footed bathtub. He rubs his hands together. Hot, but not enough for a year's worth of grime. With a pot he finds in the kitchen he boils water, carries it to the tub, and pours it in. His cast-off clothes form a wrinkled pile on the hexagon-shaped tiles, and stepping naked into the tub, he eases down to meet the ice-hot burn. His body quivers with a joy that eclipses the searing pain. Leaning back against the porcelain, eyes closed and tears melting into steam-sweat, he settles in, coughing a last lungful of rank city air, thinking *never again*. Never again stripping to his skivvies in pre-dawn cold to bathe in courtyard fountains. Never again checking over his shoulder in alleys before relieving himself against the brick. Or twisting into sleep on hard benches only to wake up to the insult of bird scat and cold rain. *Never again.*

In the cleansing boil, a new sensation surrounds him—a feeling of having crossed over, of having navigated some great gauntlet and living to tell the tale. He was *inside*. Homeless, drifter, vagrant described a man his pride had never let him claim—words to a tune he'd pretended not to know. He, L.J. Tillman, had only been without a room for the night, then another and another, as one night became two, then three, then incredibly, three hundred. For a year he'd denied the truth, believing a swipe of deodorant and scissor-trimmed hair ranked him above the unwashed skulking through the shelters and soup lines, who slept in the same hovels and crawls he did. But no matter how clean you tried to be, street living marked you, added a crust to you, and now he could feel it breaking away.

A half-hour of soaking, and now, mind blissfully blank, he's adrift to the sounds of indoor life: the percussive clank of steam heat, footsteps above, the distant trumpet of taxi horns cup-muted by brick and glass. He crosses both hands over his chest and sinks further down into the water. Even when Olivia wasn't in his mind, she was everywhere else in him. She was the slump in his shoulders, the lag in his step, the weariness in his eyes as he walked the streets. Out there, he could neither think nor plan. But with the lapping sound of water comes a certain settling peace, and he can seriously *think* about Olivia.

He splashes his face, closes his hands over his eyes, bringing her to life. Small-boned, delicate mouth, and on that night, mink-brown eyes watery and wounded. He can smell the sugary smoke from the burned pie, feel the fire from her stare. He'd never seen her so furious. But then, he'd committed the worst lie, the silent one. Caught between the two women, he'd felt as if life was being squeezed out of him from opposite sides; the long-ago promise to the one battling the longer-ago promise to the other, him in the middle gasping for air.

The first and last time he'd seen Olivia nearly that angry, it was a week after he'd met her at the bus station. It was early June, and he'd called to invite her to a poolside pre-wedding jazz brunch he was play-ing. After the brunch he suggested an evening walk by the lake at the eastern edge of the park. Already he had decided that this one, Olivia Benton, was The One.

Did she know it too? He could tell in her face she had no idea of that which he was absolutely sure. That every circumstance in his life—being born where he was and when, living every place he'd ever lived, taking every bus or train on every road or track or highway—had led him to this Sunday afternoon stroll along a lake with a young woman who had his future written all over her face. And that he could no more reverse the course of things than convince the wind-rippled water to flow another way.

She was young. Only a few years divided them, but he was twenty-seven and was she even twenty? Eighteen, he believed. In ten years it wouldn't matter at all. But now he felt old with her, weathered and worn, his roughened life a casement of leather over his skin. But she seemed as young and freshly formed as dew on morning grass.

"What did you say?"

"I said it's a little chilly here, by the water."

"Want to go?" he asked her.

"No, it's OK. I like it here." She wore a thin blue cotton halter dress with yellow things on it (pinwheels?), sandals, and the bud of a rose he had picked from a bush and placed behind her ear. The spring breezes off Lake Jacomo swirled at their backs and she folded her arms tightly against her chest. He removed his jacket and helped her into it, then considered drawing her to him.

No, not now.

Timing was everything.

Instead, he reached to hold her hand as they walked along the juncture of water and grass, and felt a twinge of joy edged with relief when her fingers curved around his.

"So you were telling me yesterday about playing."

"Huh? Oh, yeah. Well, I guess I'm mostly self-taught. Started playing tenor when the thing was almost bigger than me. Didn't go to school after I was seventeen. It didn't matter, though. I never saw myself doing anything else but this."

She began to walk ahead of him, and he grabbed her hand again as she headed around the other side of a small pine sapling. "Walk on this side," he said. "Don't split the tree. Bad luck."

She looked at him quizzically, and he wondered what she was thinking.

"Well, I mean," he began, feeling country and foolish, "they *say* it's bad luck."

"Superstitious?" she said, her eyes bright and teasing.

"Well, maybe," he said. "But when it comes down to it, why take a chance? It's just as easy to walk on the same side of the tree, or not step on a sidewalk crack. That way, if there is such a thing as bad luck, you're covered. And if there isn't, you're not out anything."

"Big Mama used to say if you think long and work hard enough you can make your own luck."

"She's right," he said. "I've never been afraid of a little hard work. I've done it all my life." He realized he'd said it to impress her, but it was true. Born with next to nothing, he always worked for what he wanted. And if he had to work to find that open place in her life that allowed him to slip inside and share it, he was more than willing.

"What's the luckiest thing you can imagine happening to you?"

Loaded question. He admired her small neck, the way her eyes brightened when she smiled, the way she made his cheap tan windbreaker look like a million bucks. She was turned to face him now, walking backwards in front of him slowly, hands in the pockets of his jacket.

He gave her his second best answer. "Well, I guess if someday I could own my own club. Then I'd always have a place to play." He dug his hands in his pants pockets and shrugged. "Considering right now I don't have a pot or a window, or two dimes to rub together, I'd consider myself real lucky if that happened."

"So I guess you want to be famous someday. Bright lights and all that."

He grinned softly. "Famous? Nah, I'm not that ambitious, not that way. I mean not that I couldn't be. I'm pretty good, I have to say. But I just want to play, you know. Play some good music with some good players. And make a living at it."

He looked across the water as a cool wind swirled its surface. "It's the only thing I've ever wanted to do. One night when I was about thirteen and I'd been playing a couple of years, I went to a joint in this little town in Mississippi where we lived. I heard these cats playing and it blew my mind. I couldn't believe it. Piano, bass, drums, and sax. The sax player was *crazy* good. Chops like lightning, you know, like a demon. He played a solo that lasted ten minutes and seemed like he never even took a breath. People were yelling like crazy."

"I went home and cried. Thinking I'd never play like that. Never in a million years. I felt like giving up. I found out later that guy was Horace Payne," and seeing the blank look on her face, he added, "one of the best tenor players out of New York. He was from there, that little town. He was just home hanging with the locals that night."

"Anyway, I started woodshedding…I mean, practicing, like I'd lost my mind. Scales in all the keys, arpeggios, listening to records, Coltrane mostly, studying the solos. A few months later I went back down to the club. Payne wasn't there, but the trio invited me to sit in when they saw my horn. I started playing and it was like…I don't know…something happened to me. I knew I couldn't play like Payne but I didn't care. I just played *me,* the best *me* I could play. I guess I'd had some hard times in those days and it all just came out of my horn. All that…life stuff, you know. When I stopped, the people went crazy. I mean, they stood *up.* They hadn't stood up for him. Then somebody said, 'Let the boy play!' They sat down and got quiet. I didn't know what to do. I only had that one tune ready, but I could see them wanting more, I saw it in their faces."

"So what did you do?"

"I played the whole thing again! But it was even better this time. Different, but better. They stood up again. I was in my world. I knew it, then. That's what I wanted to do."

He looked at her, saw her face lit up and shining.

"That's such a good story."

"So, I remember you said you used to sing. You must know what I'm talking about."

"Not any more," she said. "Used to. Now I'm just into the hairdressing thing."

He nodded. "So…you like doing hair? I hear there's good money in it."

Clouds moved, wind stirred, and she looked at the water as a chilling breeze set it in motion again. "Well it's not like playing on a stage and having people cheer you, but it's fun. I like to make people look good."

"So you make 'em look good, then I'll make 'em feel good. A shampoo and set, then a jazz set. We could open our own place, make a fortune. Whatcha say?"

"I like it," she said. And laughed. It was a bubble of a laugh that made his head light and his knees soft; it was girlish, sweetly giddy. His life, as far back as he could remember, had held few shining moments. A rare night of one perfectly turned phrase after another on a bandstand, a perfect groove of drummer and bass waiting for his lick. Red sky and evening sun slipping golden into hills from a bus window. But nothing matched that laugh, that shine of dark hair, a lake wind rustling pinwheels on a cotton dress. There was something about the honesty of laughter falling from a face shaped like a heart that made him want to tell her everything he knew about his life, the truth of it, who he really was and why he was here.

But what good was a promise if not kept, if not meant to last the whole of a life? What good was a promise that caved in at pinwheels playing on a dress, wind rippling water, or a laugh?

She turned to him as if she had something important to say. "Speaking of music, I wanted to tell you how much I enjoyed your…"

Thunder broke her speech as the sky opened up and unleashed a sudden torrent. Within a few seconds the rain was so loud he had to yell. "I didn't think it was going to rain. Come on," he punched her shoulder playfully. "I'll race you to the car."

Over his shoulder he heard her say something about her shoes, but he was running fast and suddenly she was on his heels, giggling. The rain was coming harder.

He let her catch him and pass him. Shoot, this girl can run, he thought. He tore out after her, laughing, reaching for her. He caught her by the shoulder, but his foot caught the back of her sandal and down she went in a thick patch of minutes-old mud.

"Oh, oww! Oh, my God!" she yelled. She was on the ground, rain soaking her face and hair, and she was holding her ankle.

He bent down to look. What the hell had he done? Her beautiful face was wet, muddy, contorted. The halter top of her dress was coming loose.

"Owww, oh no! I think I broke something." Her face now a mask of pain.

"OK, uh, grab onto me, around my neck. I'll carry you."

"No! No! It hurts too much to move!"

He lifted her anyway stumbling a little, and a yelp that sounded foreign to him, based on the little he knew of her, flew from her mouth. She was not heavy, but he held her awkwardly. She's whimpering like a baby, he thought. Then from nowhere, a memory like a shudder.

The world around him cold, wet and angry. Don't drop her, whatever you do. He paused, shifted her in his grip and ran toward the car.

She burrowed her face into his wet shoulder, sniffling. He arrived at the spot where he parked, now flooded with an inches-high river of pounding, splattering rain.

Where was the damn car? He looked at the gravel lot. He parked here, he knew it.

Olivia looked up from his shoulder. "Where's the car?" she said.

"Uh, I parked…" Still holding her, he turned full circle, looking everywhere, puzzled, panicked, and squinting through the hard rain.

"Oh my God!" Olivia said. "How could you lose the car?"

"Wait," he said. "There it is."

He must have forgotten to set the brake because the blue Plymouth had rolled several feet down into a gully along the downward sloping gravel road. He stepped carefully down the ditch, opened the door, placed her on the seat, got in and started the car.

The tires spun in futile circles, making a sputtering sound. No, no, not this, he thought. He banged his head lightly against the wheel. "I think we're stuck," he said. Olivia looked at him, her hair limp, tangled and wet, and drooping in her eyes. Finger-size stripes of mud scored her forehead and cheek. The front of her dress was torn. "I don't believe this," she said slowly in a dark tone that frightened him.

He got out and pushed with Olivia stretched across the front seat, her bad foot elevated and her good one gunning the pedal, sending mud flying everywhere, covering him in brown muck.

"Can't you push harder?" She yelled, and floored the pedal.

He slipped and fell, face down, in the mud.

"Not so fast!" he yelled through the mud on his mouth and the sound of rain and motor roar. "Press it lightly!"

She touched the pedal lightly over and over, and they inched their way out. When he got back in the car, Olivia was still wincing in pain.

"I don't believe this, God, I don't believe this."

He felt like a fool. They were both covered in mud, sweating, soaking wet. The perky rose he'd placed behind her ear drooped its sad head across her eye. (He started to move it back behind her ear, but thought better of it.) He wondered if her ankle was broken, and more importantly, if she would never speak to him again. If he had to choose, he'd rather her ankle be broken, or better still, his. He drove slowly through the rain, back through the soaked, flooding streets to the Mayfair. By the time they arrived, the rain had stopped.

Her silence pained him; he wished she'd say something. Finally, she did.

"Don't bother," she snapped as he reached down to help her out of the car and up the steps. And so he watched her hop one-footed, purse slung angrily across her shoulder, hair a tangled mess, up the steps and inside.

The next day he waited for her to come home from styling class. He parked outside the Mayfair until he saw her walk in, and a minute later he followed her in, asking a surprised Hettie Peale to point him to her room.

"Oh, it's you." Hettie smiled an amused, knowing smile. "Upstairs, all the way to the back."

He found her sitting on a sun porch off her bedroom facing the backyard where a clothesline full of sheets flapped in the breeze. A thick gray Ace bandage covered her ankle.

She sat on a plastic chaise, her knees tucked to her chin and her arms wrapped around them.

"Oh. Hi," she said. And seeing his horror at her bandage, she said, "It's better. Only a pulled ligament. Feels fine now that it's wrapped."

He sat across from her on the edge of a plastic lawn chair, feeling sheepish, his elbows resting on his knees and his fingers laced. He looked at her and admired the change from yesterday: her hair clean and pulled back away from her face, her eyes shining, her long legs in red shorts, no trace of mud. God, she looks good, he thought. Suddenly she sneezed with a sound so petite it made him restrain a laugh. Jesus, had he given her pneumonia too? She sneezed again, another baby sneeze that made him smile with pleasure.

Man, was he a fool. Even her sneeze sounded like music to him.

She wiped her nose with a tissue. "Allergies," she said. "Springtime's the worst."

Then she looked up at him, shook her head and smiled, a weren't-we-pathetic gesture. "Well, so much for not splitting the tree to keep the bad luck away."

He shook his head too. "God, I'm sorry."

"I must have looked horrible," she said. "I've never been that dirty in my life."

"Not really," he said. "In fact I'd say that you were just about the finest-looking mud-dipped woman I have ever seen. And," he said looking at her bare shoulders and arms, "I think it's done wonders for your skin."

She laughed at this. "Well, I have to admit that you looked pretty cute yourself covered in all that mud. I'm no expert on these things but I'd have to say, based on short observation, that brown is definitely your color."

He nodded, smiling. "Good thing."

She changed her position in the chair, unfolding her long legs to tuck her feet under her hips Indian-style. Young, he thought, but with a woman's grace. Then, she offhandedly stroked the length of her arm from her shoulder to her hand. At that minute, the late afternoon sun shone on her face, making her skin shine like gold, her wide smile even brighter.

She went on. "And you know, with that red tie you were wearing, you reminded me of a big chocolate bunny I got from Uncle Joon the Easter after I turned twelve."

He laughed. "That so?" Damn, he liked this woman. Really. *Liked* her.

"Look, Olivia," he said raising his palm to her, "Swear to God. I will definitely make this up to you."

She smiled again, and was that a wink he saw from the corner of her eye?

"When?" she said.

"Soon."

He got up to leave.

"Wait. I was going to tell you something, just before it rained. I was going to tell you that I really liked your playing."

"Huh?"

"At the brunch by the pool. I grew up listening to my Uncle Joon's records—he loves jazz—but I never heard anybody play saxophone live before. And it, well, it was just the best thing I've ever heard."

He walked to her, because he was speechless, because sometimes you just know when the time is right and because a team of thorough-breds couldn't have held him back. He felt pulled to her as if she were the earth and he were any small thing in gravity's range. He reached down for her hand and pulled her up from the chaise.

He drew her to him. Touched her hair with his fingers, kissed the small raised vein on her temple. The soap smell of her washed hair and the berry scent of her lipstick conspired to soften the muscles of his knees.

"Tomorrow?" she said.

"Come hell or high water," he said. "Well, come hell, anyway."

Years later when he remembered the bursting sky, the mud, the ditch, the car, he would also remember how *familiar* it felt, how the years melted in the curling of her body around his chest, his head shielding hers from the water as he carried her through the rain.

Pieces of memory like a patched-together quilt warm him when the water begins to chill. Things would be different now. He didn't know how, but they would be. He'd like to spend the whole night in the tub, but after forty-five minutes his fingertips are wrinkled as raisins. With the white washcloth from the rack he scrubs until his skin is red-raw and sore. He scrubs harder and harder still, his neck, his arms, his hair. Patches of soapy gray film float like dingy ice floes on the water. Layer by layer, the whole year falls away. And when he's done, he watches the black swirl of New York's streets spiral down the drain.

· NINE ·

THE NEXT MORNING, he remembers to take a bag of groceries—rolls, sardines, tuna, Spam, Hi-Hos, and orange juice—to Honeymoon, and tells him about the place he's found.

"OK," the old man says, looking down, munching on the crackers, curled up in a corner by the green Dumpster.

"Did you hear what I said? I found a place to live," L.J. says.

"I heard you." Honeymoon opens the box again, grabs three crackers, and stuffs them into his mouth.

L.J. is puzzled by the old man's reaction, and then he understands.

"Hey, look man, it's small. But there's plenty of room for a couple of dudes like us. There's a couch, and a bed, too!"

Honeymoon looks up at L.J. as if he's the stupidest man on earth.

"You thinking I'ma stay with you? Think again."

He takes another bite of his cracker. "You and me ain't the same, boy. Not at all."

The two men look at each other for a moment, L.J. confused, and the old man annoyed at his confusion. L.J. looks away, pondering what the old man is telling him. But he remembers a time when he was small and one of Purvis's Prince Hall lodge brothers invited Purvis and L.J. to stay at his house while he went home to Tennessee to bury his father. The friend's place had three bedrooms, a big kitchen, bathtubs in two bathrooms: a palace compared to the rented room where they lived.

But Purvis had said no, had made it clear that it served no purpose to sit a minute in luxury's lap, to eat the crumbs from the banquet table only to go home hungry with the taste on your tongue.

L.J. wishes he hadn't told Honeymoon about his neat little house in Kansas City, his nice clothes and trimmed lawn. But the man had only seen what he himself couldn't; sooner or later, L.J. would be gone, and he would still be there.

"OK, man, I hear you," L.J. says to Honeymoon. He reaches over to unlatch his horn case. He pulls out his horn and straps it on. "Come on," he says. "Let's play some tunes."

Days later at the club, L.J. is stunned by the news. Not only is the club being sold, but the whole band is being replaced—by a keyboard/synthesizer player.

"Can you believe it?'

Crawfish Malone is pacing back and forth under the street lamps in front of the building, while the men take a break after the first set.

"The place is packed every night," Crawfish protests. "But them jive-ass suits is always wanting mo' money. When they don't get rich quick enough, they bail."

"Man, wake up," says Wash, one hand holding a cigarette and the other, palm flattened, leaning against the brick of the building. "This place ain't been packed in months, since way before Cov left."

"That's right, man," Larry says. He has his hands in the pockets of his jacket, and the light from the blue neon of The Baby Grand sign gives his black hair a purpleish cast. "I hear they been losing money for a while."

L.J. is silent, thinking. If he'd not been blinded by his own success he'd have seen all the signs. It was just like Jimmy's. Little by little, the money folks had fallen away and mostly their audiences were filled with the hardcore jazz lovers—hearty and enthusiastic, but not spending enough money on drinks. Too busy listening. The drinkers were the ones who brought in the dough—the ones who threw money around and talked during the music.

"When's the last day?" L.J. says, meaning "when's the last check?" He's thinking about the six-month lease he'd signed, and the few hundred he still owed the super in his building.

"Friday," Crawfish says. "Listen. I say we make a pact. Tomorrow let's all get on the phones, see what we can find for the quartet. If that don't work, then we take whatever we can get, but everybody try to find some work for the rest of us, too."

And so they agreed.

For a week solid they worked the phones, and when they got nothing but answering machines and voice mails, they took to the streets. They checked the bulletin board at the union office, then trekked the pavement on the West Side and down in the Village. L.J. and Crawfish inquired at Sugar's and The Second Line, but they both had bands booked for the next six months. Wash and Larry checked out The Sweet Surrender, Newberry's, and Jezebel's, and all came up short.

After a few more days they got desperate. As much as they wanted to keep the band together, they came up with nothing for the whole group. L.J. thought he had a gig in an off-Broadway pit orchestra of *West Side Story,* but the tenor player recovered from flu and came back to work. They ended up playing freelance one-nighters: a bar mitzvah in Queens, a wedding reception on Long Island, the opening of a new health spa in Newark.

And every few nights, L.J. sneaked back to his old corner, playing on the street for tossed quarters and wadded-up dollar bills.

He was not only desperate but a little scared. He thought of what Purvis said. Was having his own place turning out to be just a tease, an unreasonable dream? Would his fourth-floor walk-up be something hanging in his mind when he's back curled up in doorways and sleeping on benches?

No way, damn it, no way. He opened his case wider and played his heart out to passing strangers.

On a Wednesday morning L.J. shows up at the super's door.

"Here's the money I owe," he says. "Well, most of it."

The super wears a sleeveless undershirt and shaving cream hangs from his chin. He takes the money from L.J.

"Only $475 here. You owe me six hundred. I already give you two weeks."

"I know, man, but see, I lost my job."

"I got bills to pay."

"I know man, but…I'll have the rest in a week. Swear it."

"One week?" the super says. "I give you. But no more."

"OK, man, thanks."

L.J. returns to his room and counts all his money, in his wallet, his pockets, the mayonnaise jar of bills he hides in the freezer. He has $14.17. He grabs his horn and leaves for his old corner. After two hours of playing he comes home tired, pockets noisy with coins and a little folding cash. But it only adds up to $18.50.

Finally, on a Sunday morning while L.J. lay staring at his precious ceiling and beloved walls, the phone rings.

"Hello?"

"Hey, man."

It's Crawfish. "What's up?"

"I got it, man. I got us a gig."

L.J. sits bolt upright on the bed. "Talk to me."

It's a road gig. L.J.'s heart sinks when he finds out it involves long bus rides through corn country, and in the middle of the winter at that. But he brightens up when he learns that a week of rehearsals in town will pay $785.

"Larry's going back to Juilliard, but Wash and me are in."

"Tell me more," L.J. says.

Rehearsals would begin in four days at the Ansonia Hotel. A big band to tour the Midwest during the holiday season, from Thanksgiving to Christmas, playing black fraternity dances, convention parties, and holiday gatherings at major hotels and ballrooms. The job lasts for five weeks.

"Where to?" L.J. asks.

"Nashville, Chicago, Cincinnati, and St. Louis, confirmed, and more coming," Crawfish says. But the only city L.J. hears is St. Louis.

Two hundred and fifty miles from Kansas City. A four-hour drive home.

"OK, I'm in," he says.

"Good deal," Crawfish says. And L.J. hangs up the phone, lays back on his bed, heaves a long hard breath, and grins until the muscles in his face begin to ache.

"So you going on the road," Honeymoon says, mouth full of food, mittened hands holding the thick pastrami on rye L.J. has brought him. A faded, fray-edged quilt of blue and orange is flung across his lap.

L.J. leans back against the brick. "Leaving today," he says. "At noon."

"How long?" Honeymoon says.

"Five weeks. We been rehearsing a ton of music. Nice charts, good tunes. I haven't done big band in a while. It's a whole lotta fun."

Honeymoon pulls his wool cap down around his ears and pulls the quilt up to his chest. "Don't they need a harmonica player?"

L.J. smiles. "I wish, man. I wish."

"Didn't you say your woman was in St. Louie?"

"Kansas City. Couple hundred miles away."

"Still…I know you gonna go see her."

L.J. puts his half-eaten sandwich down, rubs the back of his head with his hand. "She hung up on me when I called her."

"Shoot, man," Honeymoon says. "You need to get your ass back there and stay there. What'd you do, get you a little action on the side? That ain't nothin'. Ain't much between a man and a woman cain't be fixed, if they s'posed to be together."

L.J. shakes his head at Honeymoon's words, leans his forehead to his bent knees, and massages his temples. A little action on the side? He wishes it were that simple. He wants to tell the story but it's too complicated, nothing like what the old man thinks.

In his mind he can see the woman who'd complicated their lives. Vaughn, the thread that bound them, and then snapped them apart. He was young but not too young to appreciate her beauty, her mystery. She had only to look at him, and the woman's eyes pleaded, scolded, or demanded, depending on a certain arch of brow above them or angle or color of light shooting through. On one August afternoon, when the angled sun scattered remnants of light through her small living room, they teased. "Bring me a glass of water," she had said. And for no reason, threw her head back and laughed. The sound of it speckled the air like the fluttering of doves' wings.

He had laughed, too, though he didn't understand. He just stared at her.

Her laughter settled into a cajoling smile. "What you waiting for? Go ahead. Bring Miss Vaughn another glass of water."

He filled her glass with water from the faucet in her kitchen, found ice cubes, and brought the drink to her. The August afternoon heat burnished her skin to glistening and the shine of her shoulders nearly dazzled him blind.

"My shoes? Those satin slippers."

If she had said, "Bring me the moon," he would have gone looking for it. He found her shoes under the bed.

She wore a gown that settled onto the arc of her shoulder just below the curve, and beneath the diaphanous layer of the teasing silk shone her earth-hued arms. She took his hand and held it to her cheek. Her midnight eyes danced.

"Tell me again. Whose man are you?"

He blushed like a bride. Young as he was, his love was grave-deep. He wondered if, after it had swallowed him whole, there would be air left to breathe.

Olivia might have forgiven him for most of it, for knowing (and even loving) the mother she would never know, for never telling her. For that she might have forgiven him, eventually. But the other? For the other part of it, the part that fanned the anger flaming in her heart, he wondered if he could even forgive himself.

L.J. lifts his head from his knees, shakes off the daydream. He rises from the gritty alley floor and dusts off the back of his pants. "Gotta go. Where you gonna be when I get back?"

"Oh. Here, probably. 'Lessen it's real cold or snows. Then I'll be up at that men's shelter on 136th. They got decent beds, and nobody usually starts no trouble. Daytime, I like the central library. Newspaper section."

"I'll find you. Be cool, man." And he grabs his horn case and satchel and walks toward the bright daylight and noisy traffic of the street.

"Tillman?" Honeymoon says.

L.J. stops and turns. In the short distance, the old man's features are muted by the absence of light. But even across the few feet between them L.J. can see the eternity of sadness in his worn eyes.

"Lemme tell you somethin'," Honeymoon says. "Life don't love nobody, not really. Life ain't nobody's real friend. I ain't never seen not one person get all the way through it without one time or another feeling a boot up his behind."

L.J. frowns, a little puzzled to find the point.

"You got somebody tight alongside you, that boot don't hurt so bad." He waved a mittened hand across the alley. "This…is being old and lonely. Don't let it happen to ya. See your lady."

L.J. nods slowly. And without another backward glance, walks toward the light and on toward the waiting bus.

IV

· TEN ·

HER GREEN COTTON WINDBREAKER zipped to her chin, Olivia trod with city-girl awkwardness down the uneven sloping path to the river. Moss-covered stones and twigs, shards of old tires, a spill of big white rocks wobbled her step, but she kept on, arms outstretched for balance and lips pinched in.

Near that oak tree, umbrellaed out over the water in a big Y, that's where they said it happened. She found the tree and stopped, catching her breath. She looked around. The sky was a sharp gray, bright in the distance where the downtown buildings loomed like a mirage, darker where the sooty chimneys of the Fairfax factories exhaled black plumes beyond the distant bank.

She sat on a saddle-shaped rock, knees to her chest, her shoulders hunched and bare hands punched into pockets. She'd forgotten gloves, a scarf. The wind whipped her curls as if they were fine lace.

She looked out over the water, pale, rolling, mute as a ghost. There was nothing here, no sign. The water wasn't giving up a single secret about that night, whether it had spun him down or spat him out. But what had she expected? It had been a whole year.

She didn't know what she had expected. But after last night when he'd prowled her sleep (dressed in white, horn at his side) she had bounded out of bed, gotten dressed, downed a pair of scrambled eggs and black coffee, and motored the Jetta toward the river.

That bald-headed therapist on TV might as well have been talking directly to her. "Confront your fears," he said. "You can't put the past behind you until you've faced it." She found herself nodding like a bobble-headed dashboard dog right along with the TV audience. So here she was, ready to confront it, to relive the whole night. It wouldn't be hard to do. Time hadn't dimmed the details; it had made them brighter, like candle flame the longer it burns. A pot of greens at low boil over tiny kernels of flame. A peach pie on the range's bottom shelf sweetened with brown sugar and honey, the way he liked it. The dewy heat of the kitchen, the October air outdoors sing-songing through the window seams. With her eyes closed, it was as vivid as if it just happened.

She had come home from work in a girlish, giddy mood, so well had the day gone. The Battle sisters' mother had called to cancel their appointment, sparing her two nerve-vexing hours, and to add to her luck, she'd found a lost twenty wadded in the pocket of her smock.

And at the end of the day, she'd seen Doakes, and made herself a plan.

Home early, a perfect menu in mind, she bustled about the kitchen like a bride cooking her first feast: basil chicken from the K.C. Junior League cookbook, garlic-parsley potatoes by Paul Prudhomme, collard greens with smoked turkey, dill, and red pepper flakes, and the golden peach pie.

He'd bounded down the steps like the boy she'd married, smiling, whistling riffs of jazz. Wearing that nice navy jacket, smelling of Old Spice, looking good.

She couldn't wait to tell him her news.

As she reached to open the oven door to check on her pie, he grabbed her low around the waist.

"Damn, you smell good," he said. "What you wearing?"

"You like it? It's called 'Eau de Collards.'"

"Really? Well, I always said you were good enough to eat." He bent to peck her on the cheek.

"Hey," she laughed, playfully pushing him away. "Sit yourself down. Dinner's ready."

He sat at the table and drummed his knuckles. "OK, 'cause I wouldn't want to get in the way of a woman cooking up a feast for her main man."

She licked pie syrup from her finger and pushed the glass plate back in the oven.

"That's right," she said, and winked. "And he should be here any minute."

He laughed. "Ouch! Who is it this time? The mailman?"

She shook her head. "Him? God, no. Too short."

"Rucker, from church?"

She giggled at the image of the paunchy, myopic church janitor who spoke with a lisp, and shook her head again.

"Nope. Blind as a bat."

"Old man Fine?"

She let out a whoop at the thought of the septuagenarian yard man with six teeth missing in critical places, and ill-fitting plates he wore on special occasions. She stirred the greens, turned to him, and winked again. "You've found me out. It's those sexy brown dentures. I can't resist them."

He laughed again. "Yeah, they go good with that green church suit."

Now she laughed. She brought two steaming plates to the table, sat leaning forward with her arms crossed, and watched him taste the greens.

He leaned back and stomped his foot. "Oh. Lady, you have outdone yourself tonight."

"You like it? Good."

"So either I did something special to deserve this, or you got something special to tell me."

"The latter," she said, forcing back a wide smile. "I'm celebrating. I've got a plan to find my parents."

A beat passed, a discomfiting pause. "Yeah?" he finally said, swallowing a forkful of potatoes, and frowning. "How's that?"

Why did he do this? Every time she mentioned finding her parents, the same dark clouds hovered in his eyes, the same crease of concern in his brow.

But she told him anyway, about the tall ex-cop from Chicago who had walked into the shop today, a private investigator who had rented an office on the next block.

"I told him I'd keep his card in case any of my customers was looking for somebody. I was just talking, you know, because who uses a private investigator? Nobody I know. I mean, I know these guys are out there but…" She shrugged.

"But then I thought about my mother, my real parents. And I thought, why not? Isn't that the kind of thing they do? So anyway, I called him up, and he said he'd give it a try."

"Give what a try?"

"L.J., come on. What have I been talking about? Finding my parents. I guess I've been thinking about it a lot more lately, especially after Uncle Joon died, and Big Mama now the only one left. She's all the family I've got now. And, well, she's wonderful of course, they all were, but what if my real mother or father is out there somewhere? For years now, I've really wanted to know who they were. Anyway, I hired him."

"You hired him?"

"Well, going to. I haven't given him any money yet. I told him I wanted to tell you first. I've got the contract. There're no guarantees, of course, but…"

"Olivia." He placed the fork down near his plate, shook his head. "You don't even have birth records. I mean, you don't even know your birthday. What does he have to go on? Sweetheart, you were a doorstep baby. Those kind of parents don't want to be found. I'm sorry, but I just don't think—"

"I don't remember asking what you thought." *Doorstep baby*? She was angry now. They so rarely argued, they were inept at it, their clumsy words edging awkwardly toward each other.

She softened, drew back the claws that had sharpened her tone. "I didn't mean…look. This is something I want to do. I just need you to back me on this."

"This might cost a fortune, Liv. What about the club?"

The club. She hadn't even thought about how they'd agreed not to touch their savings until they had enough put away to look at properties for the club they both dreamed of owning, a small jazz place where he could play, and if and when she decided to sell the shop, she could manage the books. A place where she could even sing, if she ever got up the nerve.

But this was important. He didn't understand. Ever since the third miscarriage and their agreement not to try anymore, she'd felt the family she kept reaching out for were straws blowing in the wind, always eluding her grasp. Everybody couldn't be like him. Growing up with a great uncle and never curious about his mother or father. She was different. She needed the connection, needed to know.

"Look." She sighed. "I'll use my own money. If I need any from the joint account, which I doubt, I'll put it back. L.J., I'm *doing* this. I wanted you to be with me on it, but I'm *doing* it. I could have done it without telling you but I didn't want to go behind your back. I never want to keep secrets from you, just like I wouldn't want you to keep anything important like this from me. No secrets. Remember? Ever."

It was as if she had pushed some crucial button with the word "secrets." She watched his countenance change as the words ruffled his face like an unexpected gust of wind.

He had walked to the counter, where a stock pot sat soaking in the sink, and looked out the window. He had leaned his hands against the yellow countertop, his head down. She watched this, watched his back change, the muscles tighten, the tension gather in his neck. He turned to face her, and a stranger stood in his place.

"There's something I need to tell you," he said.

A rise of wind sent leaves scuttling across the river. *Enough. No more.*

As Olivia sat hunched on the rock she could still see the look of hurt shadowing his face after she told him to leave. He'd parted his lips to speak, but thinking better of it, closed them, and he was gone.

The wind from the water calmed and she could feel the sun's shimmer behind a sheer cloud, could begin to sense its heat. She looked at her watch. If she left now, she could have a few moments of quiet in the shop before Cora came in, full of gossipy tales and with her boom box set to the R&B station. Not that she minded so much; Cora was fun, perky, and clever. Smart. If Olivia loved owning her own place,

Cora loved hair, spent her time perusing *Black Hair* and *Ebony Mane*, and constantly altered her own style from long, flowing weaves to intricately wound braids, or if the mood struck her, a short cut with marcel waves pressed against her nicely shaped skull. Round-framed and thick-middled, Cora had large brown eyes set in a cherubic face that seemed to look at the world with a perpetual expectation of wonder and delight. And in the last year Cora's sprightly spirit and unburdened youth had been just what Olivia needed.

Lately, Cora had been the rainmaker, bringing in customers willing to trade a week's pay for a new look—weaves, extensions, braids, the trendy preoccupations of the young. In the last year, while Olivia was still tending the emotional bruises of sudden widowhood, Cora had saved her. "That's all right, Miz T., don't come in today. Stay home and get some rest. I'll cover for you," she had said so often, when Olivia, nearly two weeks after the accident, had still not been able to get herself out of bed. She was only twenty-six, but Cora had been more than an operator in her shop; she'd been a friend.

Olivia pulled her sleeve up to uncover her watch. Nine-thirty now. At ten, red-headed Janice would be in. Time to go.

She zipped up her jacket as the wind snapped, ballooning it around her. She was walking toward the car when she saw it, and wondered how she had missed it before.

She stared at the tree, then touched the boot-shaped patch of raw wood, browned with weather and age, fingered the gash that could only have been made by something large and forceful, like an out-of-control car. Of course, it really could have been anything, a speeding motorcycle, a bolt of lightning. Anything. But somehow she knew the tree had been gashed about a year ago on an October night, when the river was high and swift.

She released her fingers from the tree and covered her mouth with her hand.

"God, I miss you," she said half-aloud.

As she walked back up the steep bank to where the white Jetta was parked, she could hear in the distance the sound of an oncoming Union Pacific gathering speed. She watched its approach, its roar overtaking all sounds around it, and then watched it as it passed from sight. She looked again at the water, whose calm waves were now tipped with flecks of light.

Whatever happened to you, I can live with it, she said under her breath. *Dead or alive, I can live with it.*

But I just need to know.

Madam C.'s stood between K.C.'s Sundries and Boedecker's Dry Cleaners in a row of small businesses on the east side's Brooklyn Avenue, in the shadow of downtown's highrises. After two years at Idabelle Washington's and then seven scorching her hands in other women's sinks, Olivia opened her own shop. Sixteen years later, it still pleased her to open the door. When she accepted the fact that producing a child was not an option, it was the shop that became the fruit of long labor and birthing pains. They'd never discussed her owning her own place, but heading home from her doctor's visit one Thursday, he drove the wrong direction away from Walker Street and ended up on Brooklyn Avenue. It was as if he'd read her mind.

"What's this? What are we doing here?"

He got out of the car and opened her door. "Take a look," he said.

The old Palmer's Liquors, vacant for months with a "For Sale or Lease" sign hanging askew above the door, squatted in the center of the short block of red brick storefronts. Its windows were dust-covered and a hinged security gate stretched accordion-like across its front.

She got out and peeked inside the window at the light-filled space crowded with stacked boxes and debris.

"Very nice," she said. "So what am I looking at and why?"

L.J. started, "Well, I was thinking about how much you said you hated working for other women in their shops. And then Charles Palmer came into the club one night and said his daddy was retiring and selling this place."

Olivia let out an incredulous laugh. "Are you kidding? L.J., we can't afford this."

He pulled a white envelope from his pocket and gave it to her. It was a check for $8,700, his earnings from tours (one where he'd subbed for a player suffering from a herniated disc in Count Basie's band), run-out road gigs, and moonlighting at weddings, frat parties, hotel lounge dates, and anything else he could find in town.

"It's all yours," he said. Hands in his pockets, he shrugged. "I mean, you know, if it's something you want to do."

Olivia looked at him, at the check, and at the building. Tears came to her eyes. How long had he been saving for his dream nightclub? Longer than the years she had known him. Like a miser, shoveling away a stockpile for the day when he could blow in his own space and on his own stage. At first she was speechless.

"I—I can't take this," she finally said.

"Yes, you can."

The tears ran now. She knew why he was doing this. Three miscarriages, and the last one was the worst. Grief had tiptoed into their lives on baby's feet and sat between them like a giant. Dazed looks over breakfast, wide-eyed staring nights. It grieved L.J. less to think about the baby than to watch Olivia think about the baby. Now she wanted to call back every tear she'd shed in his presence over each of their not-quite-born children.

Her voice breaking, she said, "I'll pay it back to you."

He lifted her chin with one finger, brushed her cheek with his knuckles. "What's this? Tears, still? I just spent eighty-seven hundred dollars to see a smile. I'm about ready to demand my money back."

She couldn't help but smile, then laugh, then fling her arms around his neck.

"That's better," he said, squeezing her shoulders. "OK. Keep the money."

With the balance of the down payment borrowed from Big Mama, Olivia threw herself headlong into turning the dingy space into the good-looking beauty salon it was now.

It would be, she had decided immediately, not at all like Big Mama and Clo T.'s place. Olivia had returned to Handy for vacations away from cosmetology classes, and to her enlightened eyes The Beauty Palace, which once had seemed like wonderland to baby Olivia, and later seemed glamorous to little Olivia, now gleamed with backwater tackiness. The hot pinks with gold lamé borders and accents and the smoke-mirrored tiles marbled with bronze looked like a stab at city class that missed by a country mile. The homespun signs stenciled in glue-backed glitter (Pro-Line Products 50% off, While Supply Lasts), the chairs and stools covered in cheap gold-colored plastic, reeked of pretense to the nineteen-year-old who'd been to the city and returned as if from a mountaintop. She loved Big Mama and Clo T. dearly, but The Beauty Palace, she now believed, was but a country attempt at sophistication. Her place would be the real thing.

Sconces of fake pewter lined the walls and there were touches of forest green and black. Along one wall sat a row of dryers and along another were three deep stainless steel sinks trimmed in fake malachite. In the middle sat a double mirror flanked by long faux-marble counters and chairs on each side. At the back a circa 1930s barber chair (L.J. had found it at an estate sale in Mission Hills and had it reupholstered in deep red Naugahyde) sat beneath the framed likeness of Madam C. J. Walker, the guru of modern black cosmetology. Olivia had cut the photograph from a black history book she found at a garage sale, had it enlarged, sepia-tinted, and framed in ornate wood to look like period art. It was one of her favorite possessions because the woman with the round, delicate features and soft yet strong eyes reminded her so much of Big Mama.

This morning Madam Walker's queenly countenance, Olivia noticed, was washed in fluorescent light. Surely she hadn't left the lights on from the night before, she thought. Then she saw the reddish glow under the coffee pot in Cora's corner and heard the bathroom door open.

Cora was in. "Hey, Miz T.," she said, her Medusa-like extensions flopping in her eyes. "Didn't scare you, did I? I got in a little early on account of this woman, you know Odalee Martin, said she just had to have a touch up at nine, and then as soon as I got here, she called and canceled. Can you believe it? So I'm just waiting til my ten-thirty. Want some coffee?"

Olivia smiled. "Sounds great," she said, and sat in one of the swivel chairs at the counter. Cora filled a cup and brought it to her. Olivia thanked her, sipped slowly, and picked up pieces of mail that lay on the counter and began sifting through them.

The phone rang and Cora grabbed it. "Hello? Oh, hey, what's up," she smiled, sat sideways in a wash chair, and put her feet up on the chair next to her. "Oh, wait a minute, that reminds me," she said, and turned to Olivia with her hand over the receiver. "You got a couple of calls this morning already, Miz T. Somebody named Mr. Doakes called you and said he'd call back later, and then Winona said she wanted to pin you down on the dates for your New York trip."

"Oh, OK," Olivia said, taking a slow, thoughtful sip from the cup, trying to remember who Doakes was. She sat her cup down on the counter next to the stack of mail and rubbed the back of her neck. She felt tired already though she hadn't done much, but getting up two hours early, driving to the river, and remembering L.J.'s last night had left her feeling spent.

And she'd all but forgotten about Winona's trip.

"Winona said you could reach her at work until four-thirty," Cora said as an afterthought, and went back to her phone conversation.

"All right. Thanks." She'd call her at the cleaners later. And say what? There was no way she could ask Cora to take over for a week, as spotty as her attendance had been in the shop this past year, as many times as she'd sent apologies in her place after a sleepless night. It was a wonder some of her clients didn't switch over to Cora. This just wasn't the time for a trip. Later in the year, maybe.

She needed to work. Work was a perfect burial place for demons; as long as she was busy, they could not rear their heads. And if work wasn't enough, she could join a choir, the Sunrise Singers possibly, now that she'd at least sung in public once. She could not see herself a soloist, but could imagine her voice couched nicely in a cluster of others, edging above the surface just enough to satisfy her long desire to hear its sound. And there was her membership in the East Side Chamber of Commerce, where she'd been corresponding secretary the year before the accident. And she could do volunteer work, adult literacy, something like that. She could crowd her mind with so much as to leave no space for misery or regret.

Or dreams.

Cora got off the phone. "That was my mama," she said. "She was saying they got pork chops at Hy's Market for ninety-nine cents a pound right now. I'm going to run over there just for a minute, and I should get back before my ten-thirty. You want anything?"

"No. Take your time. If you're not back, I'll start her for you."

"Cool." Said Cora. "But Juanita Jones is always late. I'll be back by then." She headed toward the door, then stopped and turned around. "Oh, and I almost forgot, you got a couple more calls from church members, wanting to tell you how good you sang the other day in church. Why didn't you tell me you were singing in church?"

"I was afraid you might come."

Cora laughed and waved her hand. "I'll be right back."

A minute after Cora left, the door swung open again, letting in streams of angling sun and two middle-aged women, Janice Waverly and Davida Warfield. They were a study in opposites: Janice, stout and waistless, Davida, almost six feet tall and thin-boned. Both wore warm-up suits of colorful satin and baseball caps with spiky tufts of hair edging out beneath them.

"Morning, 'Livia," Janice said, placing a shopping bag full of knitting on the floor and letting her full weight fall into an armchair near a dryer. She removed her cap and raked her fingers through short stalks of dry, reddened hair. "Whew, mercy! Think you can do anything with this mess today?" she chuckled.

"I tell her all the time she oughta stop adding all that color between touch-ups," said Davida, who slipped into the chair next to Janice and pulled a Danielle Steel paperback from her purse.

"Morning ladies," Olivia said. "Let's see, Janice." She fingered the woman's hair. "Well, are you getting a perm today?"

"No, though I probably should. Today is parents day at Michael's school, and I don't have time. Just give me a wash and condition and set today, Olivia."

"All right, let's get started." She patted the back of one of the sink chairs, and the woman made her way across the room and sat down.

"Maybe just a trim, too, if you think I need it," she added.

"Right."

Davida reached for the remote control for the television perched high on a wrought-iron shelf above the row of dryers, and tuned it to *The Price Is Right*. Bob Barker was being wildly embraced by an enormous woman who had just won a Chevy Suburban. Davida clicked to a cable talk show hosted by a young black woman. "Leave it there, girl. I wanna see this," said Janice, as Olivia took a big-toothed comb and gingerly pulled it through the tangles in Janice's hair, then turned on the hot water faucet to full strength. When Olivia finished washing her hair, she reached for a big blue towel and began to rub Janice's head dry.

Janice cleared her throat, then spoke in a soft voice. "You know, Olivia," she began, "that sure was a nice thing you did, singing at the church like that. My sister, Doris Jean, she goes over to New Hope, she told me about it."

"Yes, well—" Olivia could think of nothing to say.

"I know it must be hard for you." Janice leaned her head back against the chair.

"It's getting better," Olivia said. "I'm OK."

"Child, I know it's rough. But the Lord works in mysterious ways, his wonders to perform."

"Yes, I know," Olivia said.

"Like the song says," Janice raised her hand for emphasis. "'His eye is on the sparrow, and I know'…however the rest of it goes."

"'He watches me,'" Olivia said, dousing Janice's hair with conditioner.

"Uh-huh, that's right girl. You just remember that. And anything I can do for you, you just let me know."

Olivia patted her on the shoulder, smiling uneasily. "Really, it's… thank you, it's all right," she said, and was thrilled when the phone rang.

"Hello?" She balanced the receiver on her shoulder as she combed Janice's wet hair.

It was Doakes calling again. Now she remembered the name. The man in the office above the drugstore, the private investigator from St. Louis. Or was it Chicago?

"Ms. Olivia Tillman? I don't know if you remember me. We met in your shop about a year ago."

He had a pleasant voice, deep and with a slight southern drawl. "Oh, hello, Mr. Doakes. Yes, I remember you. How are you?"

"Please. Call me Harlan. Oh, I reckon I'm doing fine. I was just wondering if you're busy this evening. I'd like to get together and discuss something with you. A business thing."

Olivia looked at her watch. "Well, I have customers until four. Is four-thirty OK?"

"Great. I hope you don't mind coming here. I'm just down the street from you…"

"…Above where the drugstore used to be."

"That's it. Third floor of the Davis-Reynolds Building. Just ring the bell and I'll buzz you up. And oh, pardon the mess. The guy who owns the building is painting the steps."

She really hadn't given the man a thought since that night she'd last seen L.J. Not a thought at all until this morning at the river. And she played the whole scene again in her mind. Odd that he would call today of all days. It was that conversation, about this man Doakes and his searching for her parents, that had begun the chain of events; the argument, L.J.'s confession, his leaving and disappearing.

Olivia worked quickly through the rest of the day, first finishing up the two women and then beginning Juanita Jones. Sidney Rae Jefferson's hair had grown so much it took forever to apply the perm and dry it on jumbo rollers. The tender-headed Murphy twins, two twelve-year-olds who wore bottle-thick glasses and had enough hair for four girls between them, arrived with their mother after school and wailed and fidgeted their way through a wash and hot combing. Busy hands helped her to slip into a mindless routine, and she was determined that nothing else—no well-meaning customers' advice or thoughts about her husband—would unnerve her.

Harlan Doakes was fortysomething, tall and athletic-looking, dressed in tan and black; a shallow beard speckled in gray and a receding hairline added years to his boyish face.

"Come on in, have a seat there," he told her, pointing to a low swivel chair in front of his glass desk. "Excuse me, I sometimes have to eat dinner at work." He leaned over a Crock Pot, fishing out a hot dog with a long-handled fork.

"Go right ahead," Olivia said. "I eat at work all the time."

She'd imagined something more like Jack Nicholson in *Chinatown*—a white-vested suit, a wide-brimmed Panama hat, and a brooding look. Feet propped up rakishly on a desk, electric fan swirling the humid late afternoon air. She looked around at the walls of dingy beige while Doakes slathered mustard onto a hot dog bun, loaded it with meat, and took a bite.

He wiped his hands on a napkin. "Sorry," he said. "I was starving. Now. Let me tell you about what I mentioned on the phone."

Business was slow since he'd moved down from Chicago a year ago, he told her, and he had wanted to give a networking party for East Side entrepreneurs to meet each other, exchange cards, maybe send a little business each other's way. Beauty shop owners, he figured, knew everybody, and he wondered if Olivia could provide him with a list of names and numbers of likely people to invite.

"My wife's idea, really. Parties are her answer to everything. Nothing big, you understand. Drinks and chips after work, kind of a happy-hour type thing. What do you think?"

She'd be happy to help out, she told him. "Call me Monday," she said. "I've got a list of East Side Chamber of Commerce members, with phone numbers, and a few others."

"Great," he said, leaning back and taking another bite. He clapped crumbs against the napkin on his desk blotter. "By the way, how did it go with your search? I guess you found somebody else last year to help you find your parents?"

Olivia reached up to grab a curl of hair, twirled it in her fingers. "Oh. I guess you didn't know. Shortly after I talked to you about that, my husband had an accident. His car sank in a river. The police think he drowned."

Doakes sat back, frowned. "Oh. I'm so sorry. I'd have never called you if I'd known."

"It's all right. You didn't know."

"No, really, I…." He paused. "What do *you* think? Are you sure he drowned?"

She told him what the police had told her, the swollen river's strong current, the wind that night, the likelihood that L.J. had made his way out of the car, only to be carried off to his death.

"Cops don't always do a thorough investigation," he said. "Believe me, I know. I was a cop for twenty years."

She thought about this, as she had thought about it before. The hasty investigation had still left her full of uncertainty.

"I'm not going to tell you what to do, but if I were you, I'd get someone to check it out, find out if he made it out of the car. If he's still alive."

"But I think I'd have heard from him by now."

"Not necessarily. People often wander off after accidents, dazed, suffering memory loss. Stranger things have happened. Like I said, I'm not telling you what to do…"

She thought about the way her morning began. *I just need to know,* she had told the secretive river.

"It's awful hard, not knowing for sure. I've seen what it can do to people. Maybe I can find something out that would at least give you a little peace of mind."

She wondered how much it would cost, but then wondered how much peace of mind *should* cost. She decided it was worth whatever she had, maybe more. She looked past Doakes through the window behind him, looked toward the street of her shop, past it to the skyline of downtown and further west to where the river began.

She sat up straight in the chair, then leaned forward. She reached in her purse and pulled out her checkbook. "How much do you need?" she said.

ELEVEN

THE MEETING WITH THE INVESTIGATOR, followed by a stop at the grocery store, got her home later than usual. She drove the Jetta through a thick soup of rush-hour traffic. But climbing the steps to the green-shuttered house on Walker, the sky above it deepening from violet to black, Olivia knew she hadn't felt this good in more than a year.

Since the night of L.J.' s disappearance, after the initial well-meaning rush of good will, Olivia had been a walking target of pity. Friends met her eyes with watery, consoling looks. She couldn't have normal conversations with anybody. Words directed at her were feather-soft, and usually accompanied by a casserole or a potted plant. The endless gestures of kindness only fed her misery.

But it wasn't as if she had done anything to discourage the torrent lavished on her by neighbors, friends, and church members. It was clear she had fallen on the most pitiable times. Even if she were as "pretty as a picture," as Big Mama and Uncle Joon had always told her, she was certainly less so in the months after L.J.'s disappearance. The Cherokee-sharp cheekbones had flattened, the tautness of her waistline and dancer's thighs had doughed out to a fleshy fullness, and her shining hair had dulled like roses after a three-month drought. Worry, sadness, and despair exacted this toll. Mirrors didn't lie to her, and neither did Cora, who could stand it no longer and took her aside one crisp March morning in the shop. The twenty years separating them made the younger girl sift through her vocabulary for respectful words, but there was no other way to say, "You're losing it, Ms. T. You just looking...bad."

Cora permed, patted, trimmed, and teased the desert-dry hair, rounded, buffed and painted the bitten-to-the-quick nails. She took her shopping and, with narrow-eyed scrutiny, supervised the purchase of two silk de la Renta blouses and a black crepe skirt of flattering, thigh-high length. When three-way mirrors finally threw back images of a woman on the mend, and heads turned her way as they once had, Olivia began to resemble the woman she'd been a year ago.

The external woman came back to life. She got her weight down, rolled her hair in pink foam every night, dyed away the creeping gray above her ears. She went to church regularly, served on committees, and even turned out six fine apple pies for the Pastor's Appreciation dinner.

But inside, she was still at sea.

Today was the first day in months she'd begun to feel like her old self. The breezy air and the sound of the river had cooled her to a peaceful state. She'd put in a good day of work and she'd hired an investigator. She was taking charge, had even written a check for a retainer. He'd check the police records, revisit the scene, conduct a real investigation. If her husband had died in the river that night, or if he was alive somewhere else—if the truth of it was knowable—he would find it out, he'd assured her.

Olivia entered her house, put her bag of groceries on the kitchen table, and laid down the smoke-alarm batteries she'd picked up from the store, along with a four-pack of Sylvania bulbs and a pound of Ghirardelli coffee, on the butcher block island. She'd take them into the shop in the morning. She arranged the ingredients for her dinner, turned on the little Sony to a jazz station, and hummed along to a big band playing "L'il Darlin'" while dousing the two chicken breasts in egg wash, seasoning the flour with basil, garlic, thyme, onion powder, and oregano. She coated the breasts with the flour mixture, sprayed them with canned cooking oil, and placed them on the hot oven rack. She was in the middle of tossing a store-bought Caesar salad in a wooden bowl when the phone on the wall by the window rang.

"Hey, girl." It was Winona.

"Hey, yourself," Olivia said. "You'll never guess what I did today."

She told her about the peaceful morning visit to the river, the gashed tree, the recollections of that night. The overwhelming feeling of needing to know.

"I hired an investigator."

"You hired an investigator? Who?"

"A man who came into my shop, about a year ago. Former policeman from Chicago."

Winona paused. "You still think he's alive."

"I don't *know* that he died that night, do I? There's no proof. Even this investigator, this man Doakes, agreed there was a chance he could have gotten out. And the police didn't say that there was no chance at all."

"I know, baby. I just don't want you to get your hopes up. You know as well as I do what more than likely happened that night."

Olivia paused. "Winona, we argued, worse than ever. I told him to leave. So it's not like he was planning to come back to the house that night, you know what I mean? He could have gone, I don't know, anywhere."

"I know. Of course it's possible. Anything's possible."

There was coolness in Winona's voice, but Olivia went on.

"At least there's somebody else thinking about all this, working on it, worrying about it so I won't have to, do you understand? I feel... unburdened. Somebody else is dealing with it now. And when it's done, when the investigation is over, if I'm lucky, I'll learn something that will help me better deal with all of this."

"I think there's more going on than what you're saying."

"What do you mean?'

"I think you're feeling guilty. I think you're so unsettled about this because of the way things went down before he left the house that night."

Olivia took a deep breath that she exhaled audibly. She'd never told Winona what she and L.J. had argued about. And now wasn't the time. But it was true; she'd as much as sent him off to the bottom of that river, or so she felt. Guilt and grief had rumbled inside her like irascible twins, each one powerful and so alike they were often indistinguishable.

For a year, Olivia told Winona, she'd felt as if she'd been pushed from an airplane into a freefall, spinning in the open air, and the seconds of time before her parachute opened up had expanded into months. Now, with Doakes's help, she felt the billowing tug of support, easing her gently to earth.

"Now I feel like somebody else is with me, taking on some of the weight. Tonight when I came home, I felt good. For the first time in a long time."

"Listen, girl. I know it's hard enough when somebody…leaves you. Worse when you end things mad at each other. So, if an investigation'll help you, I'm all for it. I hope something good comes out of this. Anyway I gotta go soon, so let me get to why I called you. The trip. New York. What do you think?"

She'd completely forgotten about New York. "Sorry, I would love to go, believe me. But I can't. Too much work right now. I can't leave Cora in the lurch again, after all the times I've missed going in this year."

"Oh, come on. She loves it when you're gone. Then she gets to act like it's her shop. I think she's got a sign that says 'Cora's Place' that she puts up when you're not there."

Olivia laughed. "You're probably right. She loves that place more than I do."

"What she loves is doing hair."

"Yeah. The way I used to. It's not that much fun anymore. Braids, blond extensions, purple hair, green hair, hair as straight as the Japanese. The youth thing is taking over. After twenty years, it's harder to fit in."

"I know what you mean. But a break will do you good. Listen, I'm not going to call my travel agent for a couple of days, in case you change your mind."

"You just don't give up, do you?"

"Why should I? You're weakening, I can feel it. You want to go to

New York with me. You just need a little wearing down. And I've got plenty of time."

Olivia had been asleep an hour when the phone shrieked, jerking her out of sleep to sit upright and wide-eyed in bed. Her heart pumped in rapid beats, and she felt breathless. The digits on the clock glared like neon: 1:17 a.m.

Ringing late at night could only mean bad news. A doorbell heralding uniformed cops ("We're so sorry to inform you that your husband…"), or a phone call bursting in a dream so real it made you crazy for days after ("Olivia, it's me"). So by now, she jumped at the sound of it, even if she was up late reading or watching TV.

Three rings now. At least it couldn't be bad news about her husband; he was gone already. Big Mama. Something was wrong with Big Mama. She gathered herself, rubbed her eyes to wakefulness, a hand to steady her pounding chest.

"Hello?"

It was Cora. "Miss T. You gotta come down to the shop. Something's happened. Come now."

"What? Cora? What's going on?" But Cora was gone.

What could have happened in the shop at one a.m.? And what was Cora doing there at this time of the night?

Olivia got dressed quickly, and by the time she rounded the last corner and turned onto Brooklyn Avenue where the shop was, it was clear what was going on.

A fire truck, no, two of them. Two police cars. A policeman in short sleeves waved his hands as she tried to pull into her parking spot. He was telling her to park further away.

"I'm the owner," she shouted to him, but he had already turned to go back to the building.

The building, Olivia could see even from the car, was billowing waves of smoke. It had blackened the windows. Long hoses trailed from the corner hydrant and snaked inside the opened door. Water was everywhere.

Olivia's heart sank. The shop had caught fire. How? Was there anything left? Men were going in and out of the shop, and some were bringing out furniture. A sofa that Olivia kept in a back room was being brought out by two firemen. It was charred and smoking, the paisley print no longer recognizable.

A straggle of onlookers stood in front of their parked cars. Huddled in the doorway of the office supply store across the street were Cora, a brown blanket draped around her and her braids covering her face, and a young man in his twenties dressed in an oversized orange T-shirt and baggy jeans.

Cora saw her and waved. "Over here! They won't let you inside."

When Olivia crossed the street, she could see that Cora was crying. The young man had his arm around her, consoling her. "Oh, Miz T. I'm so sorry, it was all my fault."

Olivia could smell their clothes, the pungent odor of smoke. "Cora, what happened? What were you doing here? Are you OK?"

Cora was sobbing so hard she could barely speak. "Well...we, I mean, me and Raymond... Excuse me, Miss T. This is my boyfriend Raymond Shayles."

Raymond's face was a grim mask as he nodded to Olivia while kneading Cora's blanketed shoulder. "Hi," he said.

"Anyway," Cora continued. "My cousin and her baby, they're from Texas, they've been staying with me for a month while her husband's been overseas in the service, so me and Raymond came over here, just to have some privacy, you know."

"We...were just playing some CDs and we had some wine and we were on the couch, just...uh, just messing around. Anyway, we fell asleep. And when we woke up..."

She cried and lay her head on Raymond's shoulder.

"It's OK, Cora. Tell me what happened," Olivia said.

"I don't know. We woke up and we both smelled smoke coming from the front of the shop. I don't know what happened. We had to crawl on our hands and knees to get out of there, there was so much smoke."

Just then the fireman who had waved Olivia from her parking spot approached them. "This your place? You the owner?" He asked Olivia.

"Yes," Olivia said. "What happened?"

"Well," he said turning to look at the building. "It looks a lot worse than it is. Mostly water and smoke damage. The fire didn't get very far. Probably faulty wiring, you know how these old buildings are. You got insurance, you should be OK." He turned to Cora. "You all right, young lady?"

Cora nodded.

"You're lucky you had the good sense to crawl out. We can get a care unit to run you over to Methodist Memorial if you feel like you need to go."

"No. We're fine. We're OK," she said, looking up at Raymond, who nodded.

"OK." He turned to Olivia. "You might want to stick around. The police'll want to fill out a report. And you'll want to call your insurance company ASAP. The sooner they get on top of these things, the better." As an afterthought he added, "Sorry, Miss," and he went back across the street.

Cora began to cry again. "Miss T., I'm so sorry. I just don't know what happened. We shouldn'tna been down here without you knowing about it."

Olivia put a hand on Cora's shoulder, and could feel a shaking beneath it. "Cora, it's OK. It's insured. It'll be fine. These things happen. I'm just glad you weren't hurt."

"But if we weren't down here, it wouldn'tna happened."

"How do you know? Maybe it would have happened anyway. Maybe your being here saved the building from being burned completely."

She could tell Cora wasn't listening. "Listen, Cora," she said, grabbing her shoulder now. "Last year, I lost my husband in an accident. This…" She gestured toward the shop, "this…is nothing. It's just a building. You're safe. You're OK. That's all that matters."

Cora looked up at her with red-rimmed eyes.

"Now why don't you go home and get some sleep? I'll take care of this. I'll call you after I've talked to the insurance company. Go on now."

They walked to Raymond's car, Cora still wrapped in the blanket and leaning on his shoulder. Olivia stood looking at the smoked remains of the building across the street.

She meant what she'd told Cora. It was only a building, after all. And a well-insured one at that, thanks to L.J. He'd always been uneasy about the building's age. A month before the accident, he'd finally succeeded in getting her to increase her coverage when he decided she was underinsured. "Thank you," she whispered to herself.

Only a building. Not a life.

As she looked across the street at the charred, broken-out windows of Madam C's, the men worked quickly, efficiently, drowning what was left of the shop in blasts of water.

Strangely, after the initial excitement had calmed, Olivia did not feel the least bit upset or angry. She was mostly concerned about Cora, distraught as she was. The poor girl prided herself on being so responsible. True, she shouldn't have been there, but what if they hadn't awakened? She might have gotten hurt, or worse.

She thought of the smoke alarm batteries, still on the butcher block in her kitchen.

Olivia reached up to run her hand across her hair, and realized there were rollers in it. Then she looked down to see that she was wearing her fuzzy bear slippers, and a white cotton Snoopy nightshirt under her brown trenchcoat, which gaped open. She chuckled to herself. She pulled the rollers out one by one and put them in her pocket, pulled her coat together, and walked across the street to the policeman standing in front of his car, beckoning to her.

"Honey, I'm so sorry that happened. How bad is it?"

Olivia parted the curtains to let a wider shaft of sunlight into the kitchen. The winter sun blazed like summer, and there was a coolness as if just after a rain. She balanced the phone receiver on her shoulder, poured hazelnut coffee into a giant clay mug, and punched down the toaster's lever a second time.

"Hard to tell," she told Winona, sipping coffee. "So much is soaked in water, or black with smoke. They did manage to save my barbershop chair, though it'll need reupholstering again. And that big framed picture of Madam C. J. Walker on the back wall. I'm so glad that didn't go. That couch I kept in the back room is gone, though, ruined with smoke and water, and the countertops and chairs and shelves and part of the walls are charred."

"And the dryers?"

"Gone. They think that's what caused the fire. They found something weird about one of the dryer outlets closest to the front door."

"So it just happened? It wasn't anything that Cora and that boy did while they were there?"

"No. Apparently just a freak thing. As I see it, it would have happened anyway, sooner or later. The fact that they happened to be there at the time was just a weird coincidence."

Winona sighed. "Well, girl. I guess you've been through it this year."

"You know what? For some reason, none of this even fazes me. This is nothing like what happened this time last year. I told Cora that to try to make her feel better."

"Well, so what are you going to do now?"

"The insurance people are coming by this afternoon. It'll take a few days before I know anything. Then I can start getting remodeling estimates."

"So it looks like you won't be doing any hair for a few days."

"Weeks, probably."

"Well?" She stretched the word with a long lilt.

The toaster ejected a golden waffle. Olivia put it on a plate and spread margarine on it. "Well, what? Oh. So you think now I can just run off to New York, just like that."

"Why the hell not? Deal with those insurance people, and then start packing."

Olivia chuckled, taking a bite out of the hot waffle she held in her hand. "Actually, I'd already decided. This morning at about five when I couldn't sleep. Let's go."

"Really? Great. We leave next Friday. I've already booked for two on United at six p.m., flight 119. Five days, four nights."

"No, you didn't. A little presumptuous, aren't you?"

"That, or psychic. I knew you'd give in. But, Lord, I sure didn't think it would happen this way."

An hour later, Olivia still sat at her oak kitchen table, shuffling the papers of the State Farm policy between sips of herb tea. The coverage was good, much more than adequate. There was nothing to worry about.

She sat back in her chair and looked out her window at the walnut tree in the yard, the sun a newly minted gold coin in the Kansas City sky. In one year, a business burned, a husband drowned. Fire and water taking everything that mattered. Why not go to New York? *You know I'm not into travel. Besides, you know how hard it is for me to get away…go without me, I won't mind…take your horn and have a good time…*

How many times? A dozen. Maybe more. And her answer to him was always the same. What had Uncle Joon said about hanging onto regrets? Like worrying about yesterday's weather.

But she remembered something else he'd said, as she recalled the ghost-quiet river that had kept secret the one thing she wanted to know: *Every shut eye ain't sleep, Baby Doll,* he'd told her, *and every good-bye ain't gone.*

V

· TWELVE ·

THROUGH THE WIDE, SMOKED WINDOWS of the Trailways, the plains states race by in cut-time—Ohio, Indiana, Nebraska, Illinois, each with its own patchwork plaid of farmland and untended stretches of green and beige, fenced-in Holsteins and Jerseys and baled hay, barns and silos and limitless cover of sky. And small in the distance, a passenger train, the Union Pacific or the Burlington Northern/Santa Fe, forging east.

Outside the bound-up grid of Manhattan, the seventeen men of the Excelsiors take fatter, deeper breaths, there being more air to breathe. L.J. takes a last swig from his Coke and tosses the can in the empty seat next to him. Long ago he'd learned to love the road; all that good air cleared his mind for thinking.

Torn between past, present, and uncertain future, he chooses the past for thinking on—and not the past with her. Rather, something that will not make his heart skip, his blood race. He remembers instead his first road gig with a big band—Wes Seldon and his Royal Keynotes. Young and green, the smell of the country still in his clothes, he set out for Indianapolis, Cincinnati, and Des Moines on a rickety bus bouncing over two-lane roads that stretched from one glittering ballroom to another, playing proms and frat dances fueled by Cold Duck and Thunderbird. No air-conditioning, so they fanned themselves with lead sheets, and pulled iced Buds and Nehi pops from the red cooler in the aisle. And when the ride got to be a bore, they pulled out their horns—L.J. playing a homemade tune, Cecil Pulliam the drummer slapping his palm to his thigh in "hambone" rhythms, and Sylvester Shaw blowing mean trumpet with the mute jammed in. Hot times. And then the gig itself. Playing their hearts out, one eye on the music and the other on the women: *this one in blue, that one over there in pink.* And at the end, their chops dragging, playing "Ebb Tide" behind the drowsy foot shuffle on the dance floor, the last couples' skin glistening under blue bulbs, arms draping shoulders in a slow-dance hug while half-notes swirled in the half-light of the rising dawn.

But now the men are older—most are in their fifties—and the air is filled with deep snores, the popping of middle-aged joints, heady aftershave, and cigar smoke. L.J. shifts into one of the few positions he can fix his body in semi-comfortably to keep the blood flowing through his long limbs and ease the pressure on his bladder. Twelve miles to East St. Louis, Illinois. He can hold on til then.

The bus engine groans as the driver wheels into the lot of a brand new Howard Johnson's, and outside the crisp wind belies the country-summer sky, a reminder that it's the beginning of December. The men pile out of the bus and into the motel, lugging suitcases and instruments across the lobby's carpeted floor. L.J. checks in at the desk, finds his room, and after visiting the small bathroom, checking himself in the mirror, and testing the bounce in the springs on his double bed, takes his horn and heads down the hall to the rehearsal.

The musicians enter the executive meeting room/ballroom and look up and around as if they've never seen one with two bright new chandeliers—one at each end—and brand-new gold-flecked carpet beneath their feet. Many of them haven't. At least not recently, or not often. Veteran road warriors all, they are so glad to be back in a band and playing together that they let their joy spill in belly-laughs as they help themselves to the free coffee the motel management had set out for them on a curtained table. L.J. finds Wash and Crawfish and Dizzy, the band's only white player—a short, bespectacled baritone sax man—near the tall coffee urn, shooting the breeze and filling their white Styrofoam cups.

"Hope this stuff is turbocharged," Crawfish says, sipping. "All those country fields made me sleepy."

"You mean made you sleep," says Wash. "I thought one of them Holstein cows along the road had got into the back of the bus."

"I don't snore, man."

"Like hell you don't."

"That wasn't me. That noise was behind me."

"You must be a damn ventriloquist, then."

The men laugh. Wash takes a sip of coffee, then slaps a friendly hand on L.J.'s back. "This beats Cincinnati, don't it?"

"Yep. Sure does," L.J. nods.

He's talking about a run-down hotel where the fire alarm kept going off by mistake, and the men had to dress and stand outside at four a.m. two nights in a row.

"And what about that place in Michigan?"

They all laugh and nod, remembering hotel food so bad that Mike, the trombone player and Baptist-turned-Buddhist, convinced them that fasting was the way to go. Not to mention the bug situation.

"Wasn't that something?" Crawfish pours cream into his coffee.

"The roach motels in that place had no vacancies," Wash says.

They laugh again.

Wash looks up at the chandeliers. "Ain't this nice? And this is just for the rehearsal. The hotel downtown is new, too, somebody said. The St. Louis Regal. Right next to the river, the ol' Mississip'. The place we're playing in, the Riverboat Room, got a big window on the water. You can see the Arch from it, they say."

Crawfish refills his cup and asks, "How come we having this rehearsal, anyway? We changing the program?"

Dizzy, the bespectacled man, speaks up. "We got some new charts, new arrangements. The presenters requested their favorites. Hap just finished 'em."

Across the room a clapping of hands calls them to their seats. L.J. sets his coffee next to his chair and thumbs through his folder as Hap Winters, bandleader/arranger and lead trumpeter, steps up on the carpeted podium.

He looks over a clipboard through half-glasses, then up at the men. "All right! Everybody OK? Everybody find their room?'

A nodding of heads, a soft rumble of affirmative grunts.

"OK. Here we go. First a few announcements."

He tells them about the schedule changes for the next few days. The choices of dinner restaurants, the motel shuttle.

"Tomorrow's a whole day off. After this rehearsal, go anywhere you want. Just be back here by Thursday morning. Ten o'clock bus. Sound check at the Regal will have to be in the morning, even though the show's not til eight."

The men groan in unison.

"I know. I know. But there'll be tour buses at the Regal that'll bring you back here or take you anywhere you want to go in between. Now there are a few new charts we gotta go through. Won't take long. Look in your books for charts fifteen through eighteen. A few solos, so lead players, check 'em out. And these'll be standup solos."

L.J., seated on lead tenor, thumbs through his folder, finds the music.

"L.J.," Hap calls, "Big solo for you on number seventeen. Letter A. Little free-form cadenza, then back into tempo, but slower. You'll see how it goes."

L.J. finds chart seventeen in his folder, stares at the title of the song written in bold black print across the top, and feels blood and heat surge to the surface of his skin.

"Number seventeen?" He looks up at Hap. Just to make sure. Then back at the music.

"Yeah," Hap calls back. "That OK with you?"

"Huh? Aw, yeah. Yeah," says L.J. and his eyes glaze over, staring at the title.

Of all the pieces to have to play, and to solo on, no less. Why this one? Why not one of the upbeat new tunes, or any tune he doesn't have some personal thing with, why the one he's not had the coolness of heart to play since the two of them were together? And no way would he have played it lately, alone and on the street, given what went down between them. No way.

L.J. sits back in his chair, sets his sax on the metal stand next to him. He crosses his legs and breathes a long stream of nervous air. At least they're not starting with it. The first tune, a Horace Silver piece, features piano, bass, lead alto, trumpet, and trombone.

Twenty some-odd years ago. Twenty-five, maybe. It was in the spring. It was the first time in years he'd heard the song sung like that. The way it was supposed to be sung.

Talk about somebody who could sing. Jesus. How long had they been together before he'd heard that voice? He'd just stumbled upon it one day, and lingered outside the closed bathroom door of his downtown Kansas City apartment just to admire it, his jaw hanging in awe. Why hadn't she told him? A voice like that, hidden like a jewel.

"I'm…I'm not that good," she'd stammered. She was standing at the mirror inside the open door combing her short curls with his fist-handled Afro pick. Embarrassed, she looked down at the comb, pulled two strands of hair from it, and absently wound them around her fingers.

His scoff came out in a choked half-laugh and his eyes bugged. "You kidding me?" He was amazed that a woman he thought he knew could surprise him so, could fill a room with a sound he'd spent his whole life searching for in a coil of brass and a slice of beveled reed. She turned to the mirror again and raked at her hair in quick strokes, then patted it with cupped palms.

"Well, I told you I used to sing. Long time ago."

"Yeah," he said. "But I didn't know you meant…like that."

"You really think I sound good?"

"Better than that. Way better."

She stopped combing her hair and smiled. "Well, I used to do it when I was a kid, for fun. I had a lot more nerve then."

"I'm not kidding, maybe you oughta think about—"

She cut him off, hooked her wrist around his neck, and reached up to peck him on the cheek. "Thought you said we were going to eat? I'm starved."

She skipped down the steps, leaving him dazed, that amazing sound still silvery and cool in his head. When he mentioned it again days later, she became downright shy, almost defensive. He resorted to coaxing, prodding, teasing her for a phrase, a piece of a song, anything. Even got out his horn once and begged her. "Sing with me, Olivia. One time." But she always demurred.

Not until he saw Big Mama's scrapbooks—Olivia in saddle ox-
fords and pinafores at the Y.W.C.A.'s tea, the Sunday school pageant,
and standing on the Formica counter (hot comb poised like a mic) in
the Beauty Palace—did he know the story. He believed she wanted to
sing—he could see it in her eyes when an Ella tune came on the radio,
or when she tried, once, a little bit of "Lover Man." What was she so
scared of? He wanted to know.

Finally one day as they lay sprawled across his secondhand sofa,
his head in her lap while a Sunday afternoon rain drummed gently on
the roof of his radiator-heated apartment near the Folgers plant, he
tried persuading her to sing a song he'd played for her, "More Than You
Know." And why did he choose that particular song? When he realized
it, it was too late to change.

"*Now?*"

"Right now. Come on. There's nobody here but us."

Silence.

He sat up, reached in his pocket, and pulled out a penny. He took her
hand and closed her fingers around it. She looked at him, puzzled.

"For your thoughts," he said.

She closed the penny in her fist and held out her other hand. "Infla-
tion," she said, with a small sly smile.

He reached in his pocket again. "Damn, lady, you drive a hard
bargain. Here."

He put a quarter in her hand, said, "I just want to know why."

She looked down at the quarter, turning it in her fingers, then up
at him, her eyes changed with a far-away look. "I used to love to sing.
I was such a little ham. Big Mama and Clo would let me run all over
their shop. I loved an audience. I'd sing along with the radio and prance
around like some little princess." She laughed. "I was shameless."

"Nice they let you do that. Let a little kid run wild while they
worked."

"Oh, they encouraged me. They said it took their customers' minds
off how long they had to wait. As long as they were entertained, they
wouldn't complain about sitting with a head full of wet hair. Especially on Saturday mornings—that's when it was really busy—I'd sing

along with a show called 'Buddy Jackson's Morning Jazz' on the Little Rock station. Dinah, Ella, all of them. I knew all the words.

"I was like a little show. There was even this one lady—forget her name—from the church. She came one Saturday morning, and when she saw I wasn't there because I was in bed with a cold, she cancelled and said she'd come back on Wednesday."

L.J. laughed.

"And when I wasn't singing in the shop, I'd sing in my room. I'd curl up and dream I was on a stage somewhere. You know how when you're little, your problems seem so big? I always felt I was a little different from everybody else, and I guess it bothered me—I mean, I had all these *parents*. It seemed normal for a while, but then later, I knew it was kind of strange. Anyway, singing made me not care about it, about being different. It was the one thing I could do that made me OK."

"But you stopped," L.J. said quietly, not wanting to press.

"Yeah, well," she said. "There was a rumor, about my real mother." She sighed. "Or at least, the person who some people thought was my real mother. They said she had been a singer, and—"

L.J. said nothing for a moment. "And?"

She looked at L.J. "And a few other things no kid would want her mother to be."

They both were silent. L.J. lowered his gaze to his lap. Then he said, "Too bad. All that talent. A waste."

She turned to him with a shy smile. "How do you know? You've never really heard me sing. Not really."

"Yeah, which is why I want to hear you now. Look, I'll sing and you join in." He started the song in a gravelly, yodeled bass.

She held her stomach, laughing. "I think you should stick to the tenor."

He yodeled again, an octave higher.

"I mean the tenor *saxophone*!"

"Why don't you just show me how it's done?"

She sighed. "Well..."

Whether you are here or yonder, whether you are false or true...

While she sang he felt warm movement in his chest. And he

thought of colors, of sun-yellows and marigold-oranges, and when she reached the peak of her range, he thought of the elusive, indescribable colors between colors, the fine silver of sea-sky at first light, and the pearl-colored innocence of early evening stars. And through it all he heard the pathos of childhood summer mornings redolent with hope, and the slightest hint of sadness. And he felt he knew more of her than she could ever say with words.

When she finished the song, he nodded his head slowly. With his index finger he reached to trace the line of her chin.

"Hey," he said. "Marry me."

The words spilled as involuntarily as a cough, a sneeze. Unplanned. Nerves twisted his stomach, but then he relaxed, because the idea seemed right. Better than right.

It was her turn to be nonplussed, to stare blankly. After a moment, a smile. "Is that a request, or a command?"

"It's whatever will work. You want me to kneel?"

"Do people still do that?"

"If they want. You're evading the subject."

"You're serious, aren't you?"

There was disbelief in her face, and he leaned over to kiss her.

"I'm serious. I want you in my life, I mean, you know, to stay."

Suddenly a blush rose in her skin. "I can't believe you're asking me this. But I—"

"What?"

"I'll marry you on one condition," she said.

She wanted to know more about him. That's all. Who he was and who his people were and what they did, where he'd come from, what his life was like when he was a kid. Simple, basic information. He had stared at her for a moment blinking, trying to decide just how much to tell her, whether or not to tell her the whole deal. If he had, how different things would have been.

L.J. sits up when Hap, trumpet in hand replacing his clipboard, announces number seventeen. "This'll be in a slow four/four," he says. "Real mellow. It's a old tune. Y'all know it."

L.J. licks his reed and takes a breath to begin Vincent Youmans's 1920s ballad. An intro chorus of thick chords, the brass deep and dark and the breathy reeds swelling to a full *forte* on the melody. When he reaches the solo part at letter A, he stands up. He empties his mind. Or tries to. He begins at the bottom of the horn's range, stretches the note languorously, then glides up to the top.

She had wanted to know him, his whole story, and it had been his chance. But he decided then and there that some of it was plenty and all of it was too much. All of it might mean trouble he was loath to risk. And how could she ever find out?

It's the middle of April, the Kansas City apartment is warm and humid from the pots on the stove, and he is stirring canned spaghetti sauce in a broken-handled enamel pot over a low flame. Curtains of spring rain are lifting up under narrow shafts of late afternoon sun. She is shaking ice in the jelly jar of Coca-Cola he has placed in front of her, and dangling her crossed leg under the small wooden table he'd trucked up from Mississippi.

It wasn't easy, he tells her, following the dirt-poor path of a blues man in the backwater South.

She takes a sip of her drink. "I wish I could have met him, your uncle. What was he like?"

He thinks a moment. "Well, I'd call him a character. Drank a lot. Gambled. Played a hell of a blues piano. Liked women, young ones, even when he got to be so old he could hardly see them. Flirted with anything in a skirt. He would have loved you. Show Purvis a beautiful woman who could sing, and that old buzzard liked to died and gone to heaven."

He places a Melmac plate of steaming spaghetti and red sauce before her on the table. He gets another chair and straddles it backwards, next to her. "He wasn't what you'd call stable, but he took me in when I was a baby. I guess I was his only kin. He raised me. He was already old, you know, but he took me in and *raised* me." His tone the same as if he'd said the man had carved a mountain with a spoon.

He talks, she eats. And listens. He sips from a Coke bottle and watches her face, the lighting up and lifting of it, the little quick smile or giggle, the understanding nods as she hears the stories of him and the old man with sharp shoulders and a shiny bald pate, who had more music and liquor in his blood than one body should be able to hold.

He was a skinny, sly, riddle of a man: part lightning-flash genius, part floundering fool. He could make a piano stride like a king, shout like a preacher, or rant like a woman scorned. Wiry and frail-looking with thin arms that held bulging veins, he was strong as a young bull, and played every song on his lopsided Baldwin like a man possessed of the devil, the Holy Ghost, a long-legged woman, or all three. Money slid through his fingers as easily as cheap wine down his throat. But with L.J.'s own mama Nadine taking her last breath only minutes after he'd taken his first (premature, he'd struggled bloody and breathless out of her womb), and a long-departed daddy not even *she* could have pointed out, it was just the two of them: L.J. and Nadine's trifling uncle, Purvis.

Showing up at Nadine's funeral wearing dirty brogans, a greasy yellow fedora, and a wreath of Wild Turkey fumes while the townsfolk and church women wondered just what rock had unearthed him, Purvis claimed himself the girl's only living relative. Sadly, he was right. The church women gave the baby boy up without a fight, but warned, "Raleigh Purvis Starks, clean yourself up and give that child a decent home."

He tried, in his fashion. But past seventy and set in his awful ways, Purvis was barely fit for the task. Railroad worker, janitor, fix-it man, and drunk, he showed serious expertise only in the latter. But when he finally decided to pursue his life-dream (to become a blues-playing piano man), he and his little charge made their home and whatever living he could muster in every honky-tonk town from Baton Rouge to Tulsa and beyond.

Late at night, when he and L.J. came in from a night of Purvis's piano playing and L.J.'s wandering from table to table and one cotton- or silk-skirted lap to another, the old man would sit up with the chipped plastic radio tuned to the Memphis station and play along on the upright, laying down chords beneath his favorite women—Billie, Dinah, Sarah—his eyes closed, the Wild Turkey gliding his mind off toward the most blissful world it could conjure.

One hot July night in Tulsa when L.J. was nine, Purvis came home from a set at Midnight Jack's tonk up past the railroad tracks north of town, eyes hot with anger and fuzzy with drink. He had tried to collect a gambling debt but came home instead swinging a beat-up brown case trimmed in beige. He stood gap-legged in the doorway, reeling as if on a moving train, a tweed hunter's cap raked over one eye and his mouth fixed in a scowl. He sent the case sailing against a paint-peeled wall; it bounced and slid back across the slanting floor to L.J.'s feet. Purvis belched loudly, cursed, and disappeared behind a slammed bedroom door.

"Go to bed, boy," he yelled through the wall. "We eat somethin' tomorrow."

More curious than hungry, L.J. opened the latches and looked inside the case that smelled like dust and old shoes. Even at nine, he'd seen enough saxophones to know this one was a mess. Keys missing, brass plate peeling. But he screwed on the mouthpiece and put it to his lips. The sound came out in squeaks and squeals that made his whole body quiver, quelling the growls in the bottom of his belly.

It was not long after that L.J. forswore his budding career of petty crime for the horn. On summer Saturday mornings, he would roam streets and country roads with his accomplices, Dumb Willie and Fat Boy. When the sun was low enough they stole hubcaps from prayer-meeters' cars outside Mt. Zion A.M.E. (banged them like cymbals, then forced the dented discs back onto the wrong cars), copped watermelons from market-bound trucks (to crash them on the sidewalk from rooftops in the path of nervous old women), and, in the alley behind Fourth Street Drugs, dropped their drawers, filled empty Nehi bottles with fart gas, and struck matches, igniting a popping blue flame.

But when L.J. began to practice his horn for hours, Dumb Willie and Fat Boy waited outside his door listening to the groans and squeaks, then went away in disgust.

In less than a year, the sounds from the bell grew to something like music, then music so sweet it wouldn't let him go. The music was so sustaining it helped to warm his blood on frigid nights while it eased the aches of an empty belly and an impoverished youth.

A stubborn man, Purvis sidestepped death until he was ninety-two; he had the decency to wait until L.J. was eighteen, as if holding out for the boy to come of manhood age. The week after the old man died, L.J. was gathering up what little he owned in the tiny two-room place in Winslow, Mississippi, just outside of Memphis. He'd been to Kansas City, found himself a gas-pumping job, and had come back to clean out the old man's belongings and move on.

Packing up to leave (underwear, pants, and shirts in a brown grocery sack, sheet music in a plastic pouch), he heard a knock at the door. A fat, dark-skinned man with no neck and short arms stood squinting, his cream-colored, sweat-rimmed hat brim dipping down over his eyes. His blue-black skin glistened in the hard noon sun. The man asked for Purvis, and L.J. gave him the bad news. The man removed his hat, his eyes clouding.

"Aw, Purvis," the man said, "Aw, naw."

L.J. invited Mr. A.D. Baxter in to sit a spell, but he declined. Purvis owed him money and had told him to come by this week and he'd make good on the debt. "But now he's gone," said A.D. "I'll miss that old bastard. Sure had some good times with him. But naw, I'll just go on."

"How much?" said L.J. "How much did he owe you?"

"Two hunnert'n' fifty."

Purvis had left L.J. only a stack of bills and overdue rent notices, plus a quarter bottle of Wild Turkey. He told Baxter to look around, and if there was anything he saw that he wanted to go ahead and take it.

Baxter scanned the ramshackle space of uneven walls and floor, the two flimsy cots, a writing table with unmatched wooden legs, a green ladderback chair tucked under a small desk covered in chipped white paint. The upright slouched against the corner had eighteen missing keys. Baxter wiped his forehead again, put his hat back on, squared it against his head.

"Naw," the man said. "I'll just go on."

On the way out the door he told L.J. he was a blues man too, and that he and Purvis had met one night at Sam Lilly's Greenwood Bar and Grill in Tulsa at a nickel-and-dime game in the back. They'd been gambling buddies ever since, running into each other here and there on the road. They often settled up in trade, and once he'd been so broke he gave Purvis an old beaten up saxophone as payment. "But it was a fine horn, used to be. I made him promise me I could have it back one day, but I imagine it's long gone. Nah, I'll just be going on."

L.J. said nothing for a minute, then asked the man where he lived. Told him he was leaving town soon and heading north, but if he could scare up some money, he'd come by.

When Baxter was gone, L.J. sat on the cot, reached down and pulled out the brown case. If Purvis didn't do much right in life, he kept a promise. "My promise is better'n some folks' money," he'd said. And Purvis never told L.J. the horn was his to keep. Sensing the old man's presence in the room, hearing the echo of stride piano beneath the whiskey cough, he wondered how he would get around honoring Purvis' word. At the funeral organized by Purvis's fellow Prince Hall masons, he'd cried like an infant. Purvis fed him, though not that often, and clothed him, though not particularly well. But to young L.J., the threadbare castoffs from the children's closets of the white men Purvis cleaned floors for, and the brown sacks of someone's chicken lunch left on the trains he swept, and even that tattered case brought in and flung against a wall, looked for all the world like love. Surely, there must be some way he could keep the best thing the old man had ever given him and then still leave town with his mind at peace.

The next day he packed up his things in the pickup truck, the horn on the seat. He found Baxter squatting in his garden, pulling up dandelions and mopping his brow with a handkerchief. The grass was high and wild, and L.J. wondered how he knew what to pull and what to leave, and why he cared. Half a bicycle sat rusting against a chain-link fence, and a stack of bald tires stood piled in the shade of a pecan tree.

"I'm on my way to Kansas City," L.J. said. "But I could work for you for a few days, pay it off."

Baxter stood to his full height, which was still half a head shorter than L.J. "Can you weed gardens?"

He knew dandelions, but not much more. "No sir."

"Fix a backed-up sink?"

"No, not really."

He looked up at the roof of his clapboard house. "Got a roof needs patching."

"Well," L.J. said, "I could try."

"Naw. Don't reckon I like the sound of that," he said. "Forget it, boy. It ain't nothing."

L.J. stood frowning against the hot sun, then turned to get the horn. But from the corner of his eye, he glimpsed the truck. He could hardly suppress the smile.

"Say," he said, pointing to a gray rusting heap of a pickup behind the house. "That thing run?"

"Not in months," said A.D. "Engine's shot to hell."

L.J. smiled wide.

He had kept Purvis's truck humming since he was fourteen years old, he told Baxter. The old man had taught him that a good running engine was just like music. "You gotta tune 'em like a horn, boy, make 'em sing." And so the old Chevy had crooned like Billy Eckstein long past the point when it should have seized up and died.

He spent the next four days sleeping on an unrolled cot on Baxter's linoleum kitchen floor and mining every salvage yard in town for parts, hands black with grease and aching, but determined to bring the heap to life. By Sunday, Baxter's dead truck was resurrected. He was ready for the drive north.

"Leaving now, are you?" Baxter stood at the door, chewing on a straw, a solemn look on his face.

"Yep. Guess I'll be going."

Clearly, Baxter's good mood had changed. The evening before, they'd celebrated the engine's new hum with a six-pack and home-made beef jerky. Now the man looked as if he had an ax to grind.

Baxter cut a glance at L.J.'s truck. "Saw the horn. Saw it lying on your seat. Now I can pay you for the work. But that was my daddy's horn. You oughta give it back."

L.J. felt a grind his chest that he believed could be the shredding of his heart. Give up his horn. The man might as well have been asking him for a finger. An instinct to jump in the truck and drive sailed through his mind, but that hadn't been Purvis's way, and it wouldn't be his. He tapped his foot and a swirl of dust puffed up from the dirt yard. He heaved a deep sigh, then went to the truck and came back with the horn.

Baxter opened the case, ran his fingers along the smooth, cool brass. He whistled low and smiled. "Yup, this is it. Y'done fixed it up good, too."

Then he did something L.J. didn't expect.

"Play something," he said, holding the horn out to L.J.

L.J. took the horn, thought for a moment, then began a languorous "Body and Soul," sending phrases feathering skyward, one by one, to glide on the warm morning breeze. Realizing there was no limit to how long he could play, he took his time. He wondered how much gas pumped in Kansas City, how many floors swept, how many stacks of dirty dishes washed it would take to put another horn in his hands. He played a long while, holding notes to play against the silence, unfurling them like fragrant ribbons let loose in the wind. He played the song as if it would be the last one for a while, because he believed it was true.

He knew instantly that something had changed in his playing, in him. A confident swagger—almost brash, certainly bold. A cocky, careless freedom. It was as if in dying Purvis had left behind a part of himself that L.J. had caught beneath his keys. Whatever it was, it drove away the worry and told him that anything meant to happen would find its own way.

He closed his eyes and thought of Purvis, then thought of the man before him. He might have to give up the horn, but if he had to choose between the fortune of owning it or the talent to pull such sounds from it, there wasn't any question. Horn or none, he had the music in him—he was the lucky one.

He finished the last phrase with closed eyes, then stopped and stroked the smooth lacquered bell. Still looking down, he handed the horn to Baxter.

"Here you go, sir," he said. "Sorry." But when he looked up he saw eyes shiny with tears. Baxter wiped at his cheek with the end of his sleeve.

"Daddy woulda give his eye to play that way," he said. "Anybody who can play like that..."

He put the horn back in the case and handed it to L.J.

"It's all waiting for you, boy," he whispered. "Just get to it." And went back into the house, leaving L.J. standing in his yard, horn in his hands.

Early Monday morning, L.J. motored north along miles of red clay flanked by grassy shoulders, happy as a fool. The man had said he'd do fine, that something was waiting for him. So he opened his throat against the clattering engine noise and sang at the top of his lungs. Hot jazz and city girls waited, and the days of his future were strung like carnival lights in his head. The truck sang along, bound for the place where McShann had once ruled, the Blue Devils had worked magic, and Charlie Parker first cut wisdom teeth, then cut every player in town. Leaving behind outhouse squalor and the uncertainty of boyhood with a broken-down blues man.

Once in the city cradled in the elbow of the Missouri, L.J. grabbed onto his dream with both hands. When he wasn't pumping ethyl or selling Marlboros and Cokes at Towson's Standard station, he took gigs on the road. He rented a skimpy room below two old Italian brothers who played Mario Lanza records at three a.m. while the sweet odors of chianti and fried garlic seeped down to spice his dreams. He played his horn in clubs where the smoke burned his eyes to tears but the women smiled like red neon and smelled like country summer dawns.

With his first check he bought four new button-down cotton shirts, his first pair of black wingtips that he wore, the first night, to bed. He got a city boy haircut at a place where men waited their turn for the chair while joking and jiving over flat beers and a game of eight-ball or craps or five-card stud.

He worked hard, played his horn, and waited for his life to start.

"Then I met you." Finishing his story, he takes Olivia's empty plate to the sink, not telling how he had suddenly found himself all mixed up with her like she was some mysterious music, some Monk tune with complex changes he was on fire to play. Not saying how her mink-soft eyes had cold-cocked him, and her smile had turned his hands to cotton, and how, within days, she'd become busy in his mind, rearranging life-things. Women took time, prompted planning, and he hadn't planned on this. But in his small kitchen overlooking the east-west traffic across the river, warmed by steam and after-rain light, he clears away dishes, puts on hot water for coffee, scrapes plates and runs dishwater, whistles, and waits. A full hour has passed since the question stumbled from him and hung stranded in the air between them.

"OK," she said. And smiled, and nodded. "Yes."

L.J. puts down his horn and looks up at the glistening chandeliers, prisms refracting perfect diamond patterns of light across the otherwise unadorned room. Throughout the band there is a loud shuffle and stomping of feet for his solo, the highest possible praise. His face is hot, his pulse racing; he's still glaring at the sheet music. He stacks the loose sheets, puts them back into his folder, and finds the next tune.

At the end of the rehearsal, as L.J. and the men are filing out of the ballroom into the lobby of the motel, Hap calls across the room to L.J.

"Why don't you meet me in the bar for a minute? I'll buy you a beer. Got a proposition for you."

L.J. looks puzzled, but tells Wash and Crawfish he'll meet them in the parking lot to go to dinner in a few minutes.

The scent of beer hangs in the smoky air of the Rumpus Room, the motel's sports bar. Across from a nearby pool table where two college-age boys are finishing a game of eight-ball, Hap sits at an oak-trimmed booth. He's smoking a Salem while a mute television plays basketball highlights over the bar.

Hap is a round, compact, brown-skinned man of about forty with beaver teeth and large eyes that bulge when he smiles. His lips still show the purpleish imprint of a trumpet mouthpiece.

L.J. sits forward and folds his hands. "What's up?"

"Let me buy you a drink."

"I'll just have a Coke or something. Fish and them are meeting me in a minute. We're going for dinner."

"OK, I'll get to it. I like what you did with that ballad. Actually, I loved it. That cadenza you came up with? Wow. You got a awesome sound, man, and you know these old standards like the back of your hand."

L.J. looks down at his fingers. "Thanks."

A waiter brings over a Michelob, and Hap orders a Coke for L.J. When the waiter leaves, Hap leans back and slaps a hand on the table. "Here's the deal. Gotta little project I'm working on, could lead to something. I'm doing arrangements of old standards, my new stuff too, and making demos to send around to a few independent film-makers in the city. I've always had a thing about film music, half the stuff they write is crap. Anyways, these producers and folks are always looking for new material. The standards are hot right now. Ever hear of this young girl, Dana Kurl?"

He nods. Sure. She's everywhere. A young, smoky-voiced white singer raised by sixties-generation parents who weaned her on thirties and forties jazz. She's making a killing in record stores. And starting a big tour.

"Anyway, I know her manager; I'll send it to him, too. I'm working on the stuff now. I'd like to feature you on some of the cuts. I can just hear you and her on that tune. I can't pay much for the demo, but it'll put a little change in your pocket. Then later, if it sells, who knows?"

"Hey, great." L.J. takes a long swig of the soft drink the waiter has brought over.

"Glad you like the idea. We need to work fast. I want something down on tape the week after we get back to New York. We'll start with the ballad we did today."

"What?"

"The ballad. The one you just did."

L.J. freezes a moment. He shakes his head, and looks down at the table.

"Does it have to be that one? That tune?"

"The way you played today? That's the song. That's the one that'll sell the whole idea. Anyway, it's the only arrangement I got ready. You play the hell out of it, like you wrote it yourself."

What can he say that would make sense to anybody? He's not sure he understands himself why a tremble went up his back at the thought of recording that song with a woman other than Olivia. He is not usually given to sentimentality; it wasn't *their* song. But he believes in the wisdom of his gut. And when he played the song with the band, his gut moved on him as if he'd stolen something dear, as if he'd flaunted money with a big debt unpaid. He thought of them, the mother, the daughter, and what he owed them both. Until he's settled things, he can't play that song, or even hear it, without a stomach twisting with fire.

L.J. shakes his head again slowly. He turns up the glass of Coke until ice falls into his mouth, and swallows. He wipes his mouth with the paper napkin on the table. "Look, I'm sorry, I just don't care for the song. I mean I'll play it at the show. But it's just not the song for me. There're a bunch of other tunes out there."

Hap eyes him incredulously. "You don't like the song? I can't believe that. Not the way you played it."

L.J. runs a finger through a water spot on the table, then folds his arms.

"Charlton Shepherd. He's your man. He's good. As good as me. Get him to play it."

Hap shakes his head. "He's not as good as you, and he's young and green."

L.J. sighs. "Sorry, man. There's reasons...personal stuff. I can't explain. I appreciate your asking, though."

L.J. gets up to leave.

"Wait, L.J., sit down a minute."

"Well, the guys are waiting for me."

"Please." He gestures to the chair, and douses the cigarette in a water glass. He blows a final ring of smoke toward the ceiling, then talks with a low voice. "Look, man, I'm just trying to help out."

"Help out?"

He looks over his shoulder at the door, then leans across the table at L.J. and whispers. "I saw you, man. Couple months ago. I was on the way to my dentist in midtown. I was running late so I got off the bus and hopped into a cab, and heard this music coming from Columbus Circle, the east side. I saw you, man, and I said damn, what's a player like *that* doing on the street? When you showed up at rehearsal the first day looking all clean and whatnot I just about dropped my teeth. So, you know, I thought I'd drop a little work your way after this tour is over. Help out."

Their eyes meet briefly, but L.J. shifts in his seat and shrugs his shoulders. He turns his eyes away. "Man, you don't have to do me any favors."

"Didn't mean to offend you, I just thought—"

Jaws tight, L.J. rubs the back of his neck and stands again. "You didn't, you didn't. But I'm doing fine. I got the group, the quartet, other stuff, I'm OK."

Hap lights another cigarette and takes a slow drag. He nods. "Yeah, OK. I shoulda known. You played that piece like there was some, I don't know…history. Like you been through something. I don't know what but I could hear it. It's all in you, man. It's all in the way you play."

He sends a ring of smoke toward the lights. "We all got our little stuff, don't we? Baggage. All right, I still want you in. I'll see if I can find some time to write something else."

"Like I said, man, I'm sorry. It just doesn't set right with me."

Hap shrugs. "Whatever you say. And listen. I haven't told nobody."

L.J. nods, eyes to the floor.

"No hard feelings, right? We cool?"

He coughs into his fist, looks away. "Right. Cool, man."

A knot throbs against his temple as he leaves the bar. Feeling like an impostor. He wonders how many others in the band had seen him on the street, looking like something a river spewed up, hustling nickels and dimes.

Bass man Wash slaps a heavy hand on L.J.'s back as he and Crawfish walk toward the lobby door. Outside, the sky is darkening except for a corner in the west where a shelf of light just above the horizon shows long fingers of lavender and rose.

"Awesome solo, man."

L.J. nods without looking at him. "Thanks, man."

Wash looks to the west at the flame of sun above the horizon. "Man, you don't see these sunsets in the city, do ya? Where y'all going for dinner?"

L.J. says, "Oh, I don't know. It doesn't matter."

"Let's decide something. It's freezing out here." Wash hunches his shoulders.

Crawfish pats his stomach. "I'ma head right on over here. That place next to the Walgreen's across from the gas station."

"Where?" L.J. says.

"See where it says 'All you can eat Chinese buffet, $6.95'?"

"Cool," says Wash.

L.J. shrugs. "I'm not that hungry, but I'll go along. Maybe I can find some fish or something on the menu."

"Got a tip for tonight," Crawfish says, talking loudly over the roaring traffic as they cross the road. "The Dirty Dozen Brass Band's playing downtown at the Colony Hotel."

"No kidding?"

"Yep. We could get that bus driver to take us there, then get a cab back."

L.J. coughs, rubs the back of his head with his hand. "Well, I got something to do tomorrow, and I need to get up pretty early."

"Oh, yeah? What's up?"

"Got to go to Kansas City. Got some business to take care of."

Crawfish raises his eyebrows and forms his mouth in the shape of an O.

"Mmmm, *hmmm*," he says. He sniffs the air. "What's that I smell?"

L.J. shrugs. "What do you mean?"

He sniffs again, smiles and nods, taps L.J. on the chest. "I got it now," he says. "The scent of a woman."

· THIRTEEN ·

WITH A MORNING SKY OVERCAST and clouds fissured like mother-of-pearl, he wheels the rented green Toyota toward Kansas City's silver skyline. It was only noon. Eager to go, he'd gotten up early and arrived much too soon to see Olivia unless he planned to show up at her shop (scare her half to death—he hadn't planned this well) and that was out of the question. So he drives and drives, killing time.

He rolls up the tinted windows. It wouldn't do to be recognized. After all, he'd been a local star when he lived here; fans stood in lines to get his autograph, even when he played at funerals. So he crouches low in his seat as he wheels the car past the Hy's Market where she shopped on double coupon day, Frank's on Prospect that served her favorite catfish special, and the Uptown Theater, where he took her to see *Love Story*. He drives and looks and wonders what the night will bring. He would see her. They would talk. Or *he* would talk, and she would listen. He hoped.

Two times around the Plaza, once around the golf course at Swope Park. A cruise through Westport, downtown toward the river, and back. Two hours later, he's in front of the pale yellow, green-shuttered two-story house on a modest slope in the middle of Walker Street, where the chain-link fences hem in the neatly groomed yard of trimmed St. Augustine and junipers.

Someone is taking good care of the yard, and the house looks better than he remembers. The juniper bushes are neatly boxed, the green shutters glow with new paint, the porch is swept clean. Everybody on this block has a day job, at the post office, the gas company or the steel mill, thank God, nobody retired, no rocking-chair widows on porch patrol. He could sit here for hours, maybe, and nobody would notice.

Two more hours. On a Tuesday, she ought to be getting home by now. Wait. Does she still even live here? What if she's moved? She could even be seeing somebody. He's never even thought of that. Might have a man, somebody who cuts the grass and trims the juniper bushes, and paints her shutters and…Wait. Stop. He'll go crazy for sure, thinking like that. He'll just wait. That's all. Just wait and see.

On the other hand, people will be coming home from work soon. He starts the car and drives around through the alley to the back of the house. From here he'll be able to see her walking up the steps before she can see him.

Six-thirty now, still no Olivia. The sky is dark. He drums his knuckles on the console, plays with the blinker. He gets out of the car and walks around the row of junipers toward the back yard. The back door opens easily with the key they kept hidden beneath a broken step ever since he locked himself out four years ago.

The kitchen is dark, the living room darker. The piano still consumes the corner of the living room, and on its lid rests a cluster of photographs framed in fake silver, Big Mama and Uncle Joon sitting on a quilt on the church lawn, Country in a wide-brimmed straw hat posing on a street with the Empire State Building in the background. An old picture of Clo T. taken when she was young leaning against a new Edsel, and Glodean in a studio shot, a three-quarter pose with bouffant hair, pearls at her neck. And he and Olivia smiling, him in a black tuxedo and Olivia in white silk at the Alpha's annual dance. He inhales and swears he can smell the faintest trace of lavender.

He's home.

Palms moist and throat swollen with backed-up words, he sinks into his blue Naugahyde recliner. Olivia…Olivia, what? Olivia, I'm sorry. Let's start all over, let's forget what happened and just go on from here.

He'll have to do better than that.

He glances at the picture of Glodean and recalls the night he faced all five of them for the first time, feeling like a prime suspect before a jury bereft of his peers. He and Olivia had driven the nine hours to Handy after they had agreed to marry, but on the way, they'd had a flat. L.J. cursed quietly while he wrestled with tire irons and lug nuts and tried to avoid grease-staining his wing tips and good white shirt, while Olivia sat in the car checking her Timex and twirling hair in her fingers. They were an hour late and expected chagrined faces, but were met at the door with smiles and welcoming arms.

Uncle Joon was a big, round-bellied, round-faced man with smallish eyes that almost closed when he laughed. At the beauty shop door he grabbed L.J.'s hand and pumped it, hugged Olivia hard enough to lift her off her feet. "Baby Doll! Y'all made it! Come on in! Let's go back this way, everybody's already upstairs."

Talking, he led them across the squares of black and white linoleum past dryers, sinks, swivel chairs, and counter tops with wig stands to the rear of the shop, then up the stairs to the apartment. "Flat tire? Aw, man. That's too bad. Y'all made good time, though." Upstairs, throw rugs in deep reds and golds lined pinewood floors shined to a fare-thee-well, and brass-trimmed glass tables flanked each end of a long, flower-print sofa covered in plastic. A maple rolltop desk sat in a corner. Brass floor lamps threw warm light against cream-colored walls broken by arched doorways. A breakfront held what looked to be real china and crystal. The whole room exuded care. L.J. thought of the rooms he'd grown up in. For a moment he couldn't speak.

"Is that Baby Doll?" From the kitchen, women's voices floated out with the mixed scents of turnip greens and Lemon Pledge. Then came the outstretched arms of four women squealing their delight, talking at once and laughing and hugging Olivia. She looked toward L.J. between embraces with an embarrassed smile.

The women wore flowing skirts of soft, subdued colors, their hair in perfectly coifed, upswept hairdos glistening with pressing oil. They fussed over the young couple, clucking and cackling and fluttering around them, then gathered them both into silk-covered bosoms ripe with L'air du temps and Chanel no. 5.

Olivia had been right. Glodean was indeed short and box-shaped, with hair dyed the color of sweet potato skins, and her sister Country, with her worldly airs and glowing skin that belied her years, did look as though she'd stepped off the cover of some black version of the magazine for which she was nicknamed, *Town and Country*. Clo T., whose deep brown complexion contrasted sharply with her shock of silky white hair, did have false teeth that gave her a pronounced underbite. And Big Mama, with thick glasses and silver curls framing her cherubic face, sure enough carried herself as if she alone could run the entire town of Handy.

After the dinner of clove-studded ham, turnip greens, and black-eyed peas seasoned with Uncle Joon's smoked sausages and bell peppers, they moved to the living room, where Uncle Joon offered L.J. the wingback chair near the brick-mantled fireplace.

"So, y'all getting hitched." Uncle Joon's small eyes sparkled.

He liked this man. Affable, uncomplicated, low-key friendly. But the ladies were foreign to his experience; he'd only known another kind, and he couldn't imagine any of these ladies hanging around bars and clubs, swinging their hips to jazz and cursing the men they drank with. He'd heard about the talcum-breasted, upstanding church women who hand-scrubbed their floors, warbled high soprano in church choirs, and never approached a funeral without a casserole. These were women who loved fiercely and took care of their own.

He cleared his throat. "In the fall, we think." He folded his hands in his lap and scanned the women, and felt as if he were asking four queens for their crown jewels. Olivia had told him that all five of them were her "parents," all with equal privilege. L.J. searched the five pairs of eyes for ones that looked in charge. That failing, he concentrated on quickly shifting his focus equally around the room.

"Olivia tells us that you are a musician." Clo T.'s L'air du temps wafted past his nose as she leaned over him to present a tray of walnut cookies for his sampling. "Do they pay you for that?"

"Aw now, Clo, don't be asking questions like that." Uncle Joon fidgeted in his seat and stretched a leg across the floor. "He a grown man. He been taking care of hisself all this time."

"Oh, it's OK. No problem," L.J. said waving a hand. He took a cookie. He told them how much money he'd made in the month of

March when he subbed on lead tenor with Ray Charles's band, and they smiled and nodded and looked to each other with raised brows. He didn't tell them that that included per diem for a three-week tour, and that he didn't work at all in February.

"Only one cookie? Don't you like them?" Clo T. asked.

Olivia shot him an affirmative look. He took another one.

"Thank you, they're very good."

Clo T. beamed. "I'll fix you a sack for your drive back. I make them with just a dash of molasses. Molasses is so good for the elimination, don't you know."

Country sat forward in her chair, her hands pressed together. "We had a cousin who once played in an accordion ensemble at the state fair of Oklahoma," she said, then sat back.

"You mean Geneva's daughter? It was the Kansas state fair," Clo T. said.

Country frowned. "No, it wasn't. It was Oklahoma."

"It was Kansas. I remember like it was yesterday," said Clo T.

L.J. sat up. "They're both very good, from what I hear."

Big Mama looked at L.J. with an approving smile, then leaned back in her high-back rocking chair and began to rock slowly.

"And what church do you attend, Louis?"

He wasn't ready for that one. He looked over at Olivia who was twirling hair in her fingers. "Well…ah, I don't exactly belong to a church." He didn't know if he should tell her that he sometimes played for weddings and funerals that took place in churches.

"Coffee?" Glodean was leaning over him, powdered bosom close to his face and sweet-potato hair shining, offering a tray holding a china cup of hot coffee.

"Yes, thank you." He took the cup and saucer and sipped slowly. Big Mama had stopped rocking.

"Well, I'm surprised Olivia hasn't invited you to attend service with her at New Hope and Redemption," Big Mama seemed to say to Olivia more than to L.J. "We're a church-going people, you know."

Olivia sat up straight and uncrossed her leg. "L.J. works on weekends and usually has to work until real late on Saturdays."

"Church don't start til eleven." Clo T. frowned and punctuated her remark with a bite of her cookie.

L.J. cleared his throat. He looked to Olivia for more support, but she was now preoccupied with straightening the hem of her skirt.

"Me and Clo T.'s great uncle was the first pastor of New Hope," Big Mama said pointedly. "He built that church from nothing."

"That's right," Clo T. said, patting her white curls.

"From nothing," added Glodean.

"And our daddy was a preacher, too," Big Mama said. "Started Sweet Rock Revival right here in Handy."

"The next time you two visit, you'll have to come to church with us," said Country, who sat forward again. "We have a splendid choir. And we'd like you to have dinner at *our* house." She nodded toward her sister. "Glodean and I live across the street, and that's Olivia's home, too."

L.J. smiled. "I know. Olivia told me. She grew up in three different houses."

"That's right," Clo T. said. "My little place is next door. I got Baby Doll's old room all fixed up for you to stay in tonight, L.J. The mattress is kinda worn from Baby Doll's jumping up and down on it when she was little, but I put a big old piece of plywood up underneath it so it'll be nice and firm. I know how you men like your mattresses firm."

"I'm sure that'll be fine," L.J. said, not hesitating. Olivia had told him about the sleeping arrangements: him in a room in the house next door, a good walk from hers behind the shop. It had taken him a year, countless hours of old-fashioned courting, and a firm wedding date to convince her to spend nights with him. So he knew better than to even suggest a room with her. He took another sip of coffee.

Big Mama turned to face him again. "I just think it's so nice that you are a musician. Now, what do you do for a living?"

L.J. looked puzzled. "Uh, what do you mean?"

"I mean, for money. Your regular job?"

"Well, music is my regular job."

"She means," Clo T. said, "What do you do in the daytime? Like selling insurance, or plumbing."

"Well, I practice in the daytime. Rehearse, sometimes."

He could see four pairs of eyes frosting in front of him. Uncle Joon seemed less interested, preoccupied with pouring tobacco into the well of his pipe.

Glodean sat forward. "We are just concerned," she said, "that it will be hard for two to live on a musician's…ah, salary." The other women nodded.

"Well, I…" L.J. started, before Big Mama cut him off, changing the subject.

"Did Olivia ever tell you how she came to us? How she got to be our daughter?"

"Well, yes. I believe she mentioned…"

Big Mama ignored him, stretching her hands wide in a gesture of pronouncement. "It was a miracle. Biggest storm of the year," she said. The other three women bowed their heads and sat back and folded wrinkled hands across their laps as if the sermon Big Mama was launching into required a prayerful pose.

"Outside, the thunder rolled, dontcha know," Big Mama intoned.

"Ummm-hmm, yes, Lord," said the other women.

"And here was this tiny little baby wrapped in a little old scrawny quilt, and some little ol' boy, wasn't much bigger than a toothpick hisself, carrying her. The boy ran away and ain't seen hide nor hair of him since. Baby didn't have so much as a cold. Didn't even cry. A miracle. We used to tell her that she just dropped out of heaven, into our laps."

L.J. nodded solemnly and looked down at his coffee. "Yes, ma'am. Olivia told me that story."

Big Mama seemed annoyed at the interruption and shot him a cautionary look, then went on. "It was the Lord's work. We know it's kinda unusual that all of us call her daughter, but we believe a child can't have too much love, or too many parents. Ain't that right, sister?"

Clo T. nodded. "Sure you right, sister."

The others nodded too. "So you see, we want the best for our Baby Doll. She's our treasure. She's all we got."

"And we ain't about to give her up to just *anybody*," said Clo T.

L.J. looked at Big Mama with serious eyes. "I know," he said quietly. "Olivia's lucky to have all of you."

Feet shifted and shuffled in the silence that followed. Then Uncle Joon said, "Well, shoot." He stretched an arm to stroke the base of a gooseneck lamp on the rolltop desk. "The boy ain't sweatin' enough. Why don't y'all just turn up the heat and shine this here lamp in his face."

"Hush, Joon," Clo T. said. "We just making sure Mr. Louis know where we all stand. Don't you have any questions for him?"

"As a matter of fact, I do." Uncle Joon raised both eyebrows, leaned toward L.J. with an arm on his chair.

"You ever shot anybody, son?"

"No, sir."

"Good."

Olivia sat up abruptly. "Well. We had a long drive. I'm getting kind of tired. I think I'll turn in."

Uncle Joon exhaled a puff of cigar smoke. "'Sposed to be chilly tonight. Get you one of them new blankets out the chest. And if y'all ladies is through beatin' up on this poor man, I got something I want to show him."

He got up. "You ever hear of a tenor player name of Spider Walston? From down around south Louisiana?"

L.J. stood, too, smiling. "My uncle played with him once. He's a legend where I come from."

"I got the onliest record he ever made. 'Blue Moon Blues.' Found it at a garage sale in Pine Bluff. Collector's item." He put a hand on L.J.'s shoulder. "Come on back here, boy. You ain't never heard nothing like this in your life."

After two rounds of Spider Walston and three of Southern Comfort, L.J. couldn't sleep. He tiptoed around the back of the Beauty Palace, and found the back bedroom where Olivia was lying wide awake. He tapped on the window. She opened it as far as she could and he crawled in, leaving a tear in his T-shirt and a bruise from the window on the small of his back.

She sat curled up on the bed, knees to chin. He sat on the edge of her bed, looking down at his wrists a minute without speaking. He looked up again at the pale lavender walls, the shelf of ancient stuffed dolls above the bed, the framed picture of Olivia at about sixteen in a deep green formal dress, her hair piled high in swirls, a young man in a powder-blue tuxedo at her side.

"Prom night, huh? What's his name?"

Olivia smiled. "Darwin Maxwell. And that's all I can remember about him."

He looked around again, nodded. "So this is your room."

"One of them. There were three."

"How'd you manage that? Going from house to house like that?"

"It was great. I never got bored. Had different books and dolls everywhere."

He nodded, lowered his head again, and was silent a moment. "I don't guess they like me much. The ladies."

She smiled and took his fingers into hers. "Don't worry. I do."

He looked at her with a crooked half-smile. On the wall a trail of yellow daisies caught the moon's glow.

"You have to understand. I'm all they've got. I'm...everything. Their world."

"I don't know what to say, how to be. With them."

"Yourself."

"They're...hard. I mean, is there something about you I should know? Is your blood blue? Do you pee liquid gold or something?"

She narrowed her eyes and frowned. "How long have you known about that?"

She laughed. He did too, and shook his head.

"They'll be OK. They really like you. I can tell. They were like this with every boy who came within a mile of me when I was in high school."

"What do they think I'm going to do to you?"

"Take me away from them."

"Yeah. Well."

"Hurt me. Break my heart."

He looked at her. "I'd die first."

There was a seriousness in his tone that made her breath short. Their gazes locked, and she scooted back, lifted the spread away from the bed, opening it up toward him. He crawled in beside her, spooning her back.

His face pressed against her neck, he could feel her breath.

"Liv."

"What?"

"I want kids."

"Me too," she said.

"Six. Three horns and a rhythm section."

"Hush," she said, and slapped his shoulder. The smile gave her voice a lilt.

Later, she said, "What do you think we'll be like later on? When we're old, I mean."

He thought a moment. "I don't know. Bent over. Forgetful. Slow. I can see myself waiting for you to get dressed with your purse in my lap."

"Mmm," she said. "And I'll probably have to cut your meat for you."

"I'll tell you now. I like my meat cut in cubes, not strips."

"You'll have to remind me," she said. "Remember, I'm old and forgetful."

He smiled and squeezed her shoulder. After a silent moment, he said, "Liv. I can't sleep. Sing something."

"What? Go to sleep."

"No really, sing that song."

She turned herself and positioned her mouth close to his ear, and hummed the one she knew he meant, her hand resting on the tender place in the small of his back.

"That's the one," he said.

The touch of her voice against his skin became another touch and then another and another still until the song overtook them both and they rocked and swayed and danced, cradling each other like newborns. There was no other sound but the sweet throb of heart rhythms and the pulse of the near-silent jazz. They danced a tangled tango. And the unsung song lifted them and carried them beyond the dark of the small room and into the sun of each other's dreams.

L.J. remembers every minute of that night. Of Olivia and him together in her small bed. Of Joon and the four women, and how hard he worked to win their affections, and how he felt when he finally did, when they called him "baby" and "sugar" and fussed over him as if he were theirs. He missed them as much as Olivia did. Lucky, lucky woman. Five parents, five people looking out for her for most of her life. Five who loved her so much that even though they must have known his secret, never told her.

With the familiar mounds and valleys of his old favorite chair softening the tightness in his back, he drifts off to sleep. When he wakes, he fist-rubs his eyes, checks his watch. One-thirty, and no Olivia.

Thirsty, he checks the fridge: no orange juice. Olivia was never without orange juice. He scans the walnut-stained cabinets over the sink. No bread. She was never without bread either. Her appointment calendar, secured to the fridge with plastic strawberries, shows no customers at all this week. Five days blocked out with red Xs, and above them are the words, "New York."

New York. *Damn.* Her in New York, and him here.

What in the world made her go to New York *now,* of all times, after he was gone? And who did she go with? Country was gone, and she was the only one of the five who liked to travel. Big Mama, who sucked her teeth at every passing plane, swore her first, last, and only flight would be as an angel swooping up to the pearly gates. And with her bad joints, the trip by train would be too long for her. So who did she go with?

Winona. Of course. She loved to travel. How many times had he tried to get her to go? Well, no sense in her sitting around worrying over him. He'd been gone over a year. Foolish to think that she would just stop living.

When it has sunk in that she isn't coming home, that he'd driven all that way rehearsing contrite speeches for nothing, he sighs, exhausted.

May as well go. If he was ever going to get back with Olivia, it would have to happen some other way. He turns to leave, then stops, and goes upstairs to the bedroom.

He really shouldn't take anything. The least little thing like a shirt, or some underwear, or even his shaving stuff might be missed. But this one thing she'd never know was gone, because she didn't even know he had it.

Before he finds it, something on Olivia's nightstand catches his eye. It's a letter. Unopened. The return address reads Eunice Benton, Handy, Arkansas. It's dated months ago. Why would Olivia keep a letter from Big Mama and not open it for so long?

He ponders this as he looks for it. He'd always kept it in his nightstand drawer. Since he was a boy he believed in little good luck charms. Purvis, when he was in one of his sober moods, once told him, "If you think something brings you luck, then it as good as does."

Where was it? In his top drawer, left-hand corner. Maybe if he'd had it with him that night, he'd have had better luck. Maybe he wouldn't be here now, sneaking around like a thief in his own house. Mismatched socks, an old watchband, old copies of *Downbeat* and *Musician*—there it is. Still. He takes it out and puts it in his pocket, walks downstairs and out the back door.

In his car, he looks at it again, spreads the wrinkles. It is so old now, even the cellophane tape he'd used to reinforce the corners of it is cracked and yellowed. Thomas Jefferson's visage is pale and worn to near transparency. Funny that a president everybody thought was so great showed up on a measly deuce note, and then only every so often when the Federal Reserve had a mind to issue it.

He folds the bill in his fist and closes his eyes. There is music in his mind's ear: Vaughn in a blue dress under a soft blue bulb on a wooden plank stage singing that song. The one song he swore for years only she knew how to sing.

He is nine years old.

Later, deep in the summer, Vaughn's ruby-tipped fingers place the two-dollar bill in his pocket and gently tap his back. Hard, heavy rain, thunder resounding in the pit of his stomach. Vaughn standing beneath an awning, egging him on. And her eyes. Nearly thirty years of living and so much pain coming to light in a single look. Could he do what she asked?

The baby's head is small—small as his hand—with bright eyes, and she has tiny feet thumping his chest. Wrapped like a present in a blue-green quilt. He has never held so much as a ten-pound potato sack without spilling, much less a newborn baby. He is after all, only a kid himself. But he'll do it. He must.

He tucks the bill in his wallet. *The turns your life can take.* He looks up at the sky, marveling at the conjunction of fate and human will that led him to that bus station in Joplin years ago, the next time he saw that baby, fully grown into a stunning copy of her mother. So recognizable it made his heart leap.

Orion's belt blinks, three winter stars pulsing against the velvet night. In the shadowy craters of the three-quarter moon, he believes he can see a smiling face. He starts the car, then looks at his watch. Two-thirty.

Four hours back to St. Louis. If he hurries, he can still catch a couple of hours of early-morning sleep before the bus.

VI

· FOURTEEN ·

T HEY FELL INTO THE RHYTHM OF NEW YORK as if the city were a dance partner waiting to swing them in its arms.

They walked, ate, shopped, looked, and walked some more. Museums, restaurants, stores, and Broadway's lights. The city was too much—its sheer abundance of things, its variety. Think of it and it was before them, somewhere. (One day it rained, and from thin air, umbrella vendors appeared.) They found a restaurant on the East Side near the museum that served sixteen flavors of pasta and a waiter who sang *Vesti la giubba* from *Pagliacci* while he was dishing it onto your plate. There was a smiling Chinese woman on the street in the Village who would stitch you a silk blouse while you waited, and a blind street preacher in front of the Bank of America who proclaimed that Jesus had come back to earth in the form of a black woman who worked in produce at Food World. They were so impressed with this story that they dropped eight new quarters in the preacher's empty Chef Boyardee can.

They stumbled giddily along Fifth Avenue like drunken sailors on leave, do-si-doing in and out of shiny, revolving doors, laughing and pointing at store windows and punching each other as they walked down the street. They stopped at street markets and shopped like pros, bargaining for the best prices. Their feet were crying out to them, so they stopped and bought knock-off Nike cross trainers from an Ethiopian street vendor and put them on, carrying their heels in shopping bags. Every afternoon they bought thick, heavy bread full of scallions and nuts at Zabar's and took it back to their room, where they uncorked champagne and celebrated themselves.

Their room was a clean if spartan little affair in an old hotel on

Eighty-sixth near the Natural History Museum that Winona found in a book called *New York's Best-Kept Secrets.* At first glance they wished the secret had been better kept, but then decided it was quaint: two full-sized beds that consumed the room, a black floor lamp with a wrinkled shade, a small desk, a cracked leather chair, a thin carpet that showed patches of its print like faded tapestry. In Kansas City it would have been a dive. In New York it cost $165 per night.

"I'm exhausted," said Winona, flopped across the sheets on their fourth evening in town, "but I'm starving, too."

"We could order room service," Olivia croaked from her bed, where she lay with her face dug into the pillow.

"I got a cousin once ordered room service in a New York hotel," Winona said. "I think she ended up having to mortgage her house."

Olivia dragged herself to an upright position. "OK, where shall we go?"

"Not far," said Winona. "My feet don't exist anymore. They're two giant stumps at the end of my legs. And they're telling me to go to hell."

They put on their fake Nikes and found another Italian place three blocks down from the hotel, and ate pasta, again, with artichokes and mussels. They drank so much cappuccino that their energy was fully restored, so they took the D train to the Village to look for gelato and jazz.

The night wind was calm, the stars like flecks of glitter flung up between the buildings. People strolled in and out of bistros and bars. The women breathed in air that held a multitude of wafting flavors: vanilla coffee, wine, roasting chestnuts, frying garlic. And Olivia was not even thinking about L.J. From the time they arrived on the jumbo jet and dived headlong into the whirl of the city, she'd only thought about him twice. So she was not even thinking about him when it happened.

They'd settled into a booth at a brightly decorated Cuban restaurant called Havana Harry's, while four young black men dressed head-to-toe in leather hovered over a microphone singing "I Only Have Eyes for You" in tight, doo-wop harmony. Winona went searching for a restroom while Olivia sat sipping a mango margarita and thinking about tomorrow. Check-out at noon. A matinee on Broadway at two, after a light breakfast and a MOMA tour at ten. And maybe, before the plane left at seven, they would have time to go back to the Venetian Shop and get that little crystal turtle that seemed like something Cora would love.

She was leaning on the cupped palm of her hand and looking out the window at the people passing when she saw him. Her heart jumped and her throat tightened.

He had his back to her at first, and even then she knew it was him. When he turned to walk away, she could see the outline of the bones in his face, and she almost yelled his name through the window. She got up and rushed to the door, almost knocking over a woman as she was entering.

He'd disappeared around the corner. She returned to the table, paid the bill and sat, knuckles drumming on the table top while she waited. Winona returned from the restroom, laughing, shaking her head and waving her hand. "Child, you won't believe what just happened to me back there," she said, sitting down. "Girl, I got tripped up by one of those cutesy restroom door signs. Why can't they just put 'women' or 'men' on a door anymore? This place has got symbolic fruit on the toilet doors and you've got to guess which one is which. Well, I got to the first door and it had a pair of melons on it, so I'm thinking, hmmmm, melons. Balls. Men's room, right? Well, was I wrong. Without looking at the other sign, which, turns out, had a cucumber on it, I just opened up the door and marched in, and child, four men, lined up against the wall looking red-faced, zipped up those cucumbers faster than you can say Jack Rob—Olivia, what's wrong? You looking pale as a sheet."

"Come on, we have to go," she said. "I've already paid the bill."

Winona ran a step behind Olivia trying to keep up with her quick stride.

"What's the matter? Where are we going?"

"He's here. I just saw him."

"Who?"

"L.J."

Winona stopped, her mouth set to protest, but Olivia ran on ahead, leaving her to catch up, running. "Girl, slow down, wait a minute."

When they reached the next corner, Olivia looked both ways. Winona was huffing and puffing. "Olivia, come on. Just because you saw somebody who looked like him doesn't mean it was him," she said to Olivia's back as she tried to match her pace.

"There," Olivia pointed ahead at a man a half-block ahead in a blue jacket and black pants. He was going into a bodega next to a florist's shop.

They reached the door of the shop, and Olivia, short of breath and sweating, pushed it open. They didn't see him at first, then Olivia spotted him in one of the aisles, his arms crossed as he considered various flavors of Pepperidge Farm cookies, his back to them.

"L.J.," she said quietly, still breathing hard.

The man turned around. "Excuse me?"

Olivia blushed in embarrassment. He'd looked so much like him from a distance. Now she could see that he was shorter, about ten years older, his hair gray and thinning in front, and his face rounder.

"Oh, I'm so sorry," Olivia said. "I thought you were someone I knew."

The man smiled pleasantly. "Not at all." His West Indian accent was thick. "People tell me that all the time. I just have one of those faces, you know."

Olivia smiled, apologized again, and walked back to the entrance of the shop, where Winona was waiting for her.

"OK. Don't say it," Olivia said.

"I wasn't going to say anything," said Winona.

"Good."

They walked slower now, and in silence, back toward the subway station. "OK," Winona finally said. "If I was going to say anything, I'd say this."

"OK. Go ahead," Olivia said.

"I think when you get back home, maybe you ought to see someone."

"Someone like who?"

"Somebody professional. Like a therapist. I don't think you're dealing with all this so well."

"Winona, you saw the man. Didn't you think he looked like L.J.? I mean I don't think I'm losing my mind here."

"OK, yeah, he looked like L.J., a little. From the back."

"A lot. You think I wanted so badly for it to be him that I thought the man looked more like L.J. than he really did?"

"Maybe."

"All right. I admit, of course I wanted it to be him. But it's more than that. I've just had this feeling, this belief that he's still alive. I thought about it this morning. I woke up before you. I heard a sound coming from our window. I walked to the window and looked out. I saw another window open across the courtyard, and from it I could hear the sound of somebody playing a jazz tune on a saxophone. Of course I thought about L.J. Then this feeling came over me: he's somewhere playing his horn."

"So you took that as some kind of omen."

Olivia sighed. "Silly, huh?"

Winona shook her head, and smiled sadly. "You poor baby," she said.

She took Olivia's arm in hers as they walked. "OK, look. You remember when my first husband died in that car accident years ago?"

"Of course. How could I forget that? It was right after you and I met."

"Really?"

"You don't remember? You came in one day when I was working over on Prospect in Mrs. Knox's shop. I hadn't been working long and I was totally green. I gave you a perm and it took your hair out."

"Oh, my God. That's right. You felt so terrible, you told me you'd take care of my hair for the next year for free."

"And then, the thing happened with your husband. Then I really felt bad."

"That's right, I was a bald-headed, wig-wearing widow." She laughed.

"That was such a long time ago. Well, anyway, even though Quentin was a two-timing, no-good ass, for the longest time I just didn't believe that he was gone. I didn't want to. I kept thinking one day I'd wake up and he'd be there, that it was all a dream. That he'd walk in the front door and I'd say, 'Guess what I dreamed last night,' and our lives would go on as usual. It took me a while, but eventually I just had to accept the fact that it wasn't going to happen."

"Yes," said Olivia. "But that was different. You had real proof. It was just a matter of time of when you could accept it. I don't have that proof." She looked at Winona. "And maybe I never will."

"I don't mean to be cruel," she added, "because I know it wasn't easy for you. But I believe it was easier than this."

Winona said nothing, but squeezed Olivia's arm as they walked down the steps to the subway.

The next evening, as the United 747 took off from La Guardia and roared into the dark skies above Manhattan, Olivia sipped cabernet from a plastic cup. The cabin lights were off and they could see the lights of the city below from the window, like clusters of colored jewels flung about a black sea.

Olivia looked down. "You know, I can't shake this feeling," she said. "I've got a strong feeling the guy I hired, the investigator, is going to find something."

"Have you heard anything from him?"

"Not yet."

Winona put down her airline magazine and loosened her seatbelt. "Well. We'll see, won't we? Meanwhile, do me a favor."

"What's that?"

"When this man, Doakes, when he's done with his investigation and doesn't find anything that proves that L.J. is still around, promise me you'll try hard to accept the fact that he's gone, and get on with your life."

Olivia sighed and looked back at the blackness through the small airplane window. Though most of the sky was completely dark, in the far west she could see a glimmer of color, the faint memory of sunset reflected in a cloud.

She looked at Winona and nodded.

To herself she said, *And what have I been doing all this time?*

Olivia returned to find Madam C's in a state of deconstruction that brought a flutter to her chest and a twinge to her stomach. Charred walls were dismantled, furnishings removed, burned countertops gone, and water-damaged tiles and carpeting ripped up from the floors. But Cora had taken charge in her absence, and for that Olivia was grateful.

The report from the fire department determined that a faulty outlet for one of the dryers had caused the fire. The damage was more extensive than originally believed, but Olivia's coverage was substantial and the insurance company settled on a generous compensation. And in phone calls daily from Kansas City to New York, Cora assured Olivia that things were progressing at a reasonable pace. Cora still felt terrible about sneaking down to the shop late at night and being there when the fire broke out, even though she and Raymond had nothing to do with it. But she went out of her way to take control, supervising workmen, asking questions and answering them, making sure Olivia's wishes were met, following her instructions to the letter.

The morning after Olivia arrived from New York she spent most of the time on the phone, talking to the insurance company, contractors, paint stores, and clerks at Home Galaxy. She decided to keep the same colors for the shop, and except for a few changes—deeper sinks and modern sink fixtures, adding one more dryer, and an extended counter at the front of the store—it would be much the same. The next afternoon, she walked through the construction in awe. It looked as though the whole shop was being rebuilt from scratch.

"How much longer?" she asked the young workman in charge as he sat eating a ham sandwich out of a Star Wars lunchbox.

"Coupla weeks. Three, maybe."

But even before the three weeks turned into four, and then more, Cora had decided to take some customers in the kitchen of her apartment, while Olivia referred hers to Cleora Davis's House of Hair, where she'd worked when she was just out of school. And in New York, not once had she thought about doing hair.

In that city she'd felt strangely energized. It was like New York had shot oxygen straight to her brain; the air there seemed charged with a heat that made her muscles loose and her joints unhinge. She understood why L.J. had wanted so badly to go there, wanted them both to go, if only for a visit. It never happened. She fought back the tiniest twinge of regret when she thought of what might have been, the two of them, arm in arm, in that city.

But she was back now faced with the scene in her shop. Would her life ever be normal again? So much confusion. She sat at the oak table in her kitchen and sifted through the pile of unopened mail. Halfway through, she found an invitation to an opening of a new bookstore this Friday from five to seven. Good. Something to do. It was only a few blocks from her shop, and she remembered Winona mentioning it before they'd left for New York. The owners, she'd said, were friends of hers. There'd be other people she knew there. Something to do. Something to distract her from her life, which seemed somewhere between hopelessly boring and out of control.

Culturally Yours, at the heart of a district known in the seventies for incense, tie-dyed T-shirts, peace-sign jewelry, and marijuana paraphernalia, was long and narrow, with light oak bookcases that reached to the ceiling on opposite walls. Moveable bookshelves and racks of greeting cards, calendars, and African figurines stood in the center of the room. On a circular rack hung vests and dashikis in kente and mudcloth patterns.

By the time Olivia and Winona arrived, guests stood elbow to elbow between book displays, talking and drinking chablis and margaritas from plastic cups while balancing paper plates of peanuts and party mix. A Sweet Honey in the Rock folk song floated from suspended speakers, and the blended voices of the a capella women's ensemble droned beneath the din of conversation, which had reached a noisy pitch. While the two women surveyed the room from the checkout counter near the entrance, a tall, graceful bald man with a small hoop earring in one ear and dressed in a green and brown dashiki approached them.

"Winona, hey, glad you could make it," he said, and kissed her on the cheek. He stretched out his hand to Olivia, his deep brown eyes shining and a smile lighting his face. "Glad you came. I'm W.D. Johns. My wife Amaka and I own this place."

"I'm sorry," Winona said. "Let me introduce you. W.D., this is my friend, Olivia Tillman."

"Happy to meet you," Olivia said. "You have a beautiful bookstore."

Johns looked around in acknowledgement. "Yeah, thanks, we finally got it together. We just opened up two months ago. We're pretty excited about the response. People like the place. We plan to have author readings every month, if we can. Oh, and don't forget, Winona, we've got a poetry slam coming up next month. That's when we oughta really pack them in. We'll have a jazz group playing. Wine and cheese, too."

Just then, a woman garbed in African dress, her head wrapped in a colorful gele, slipped her hand inside the crook of his elbow and looked up at him.

"This is my wife, Amaka," he said. "You remember Winona, and this is Olivia. Can I get you ladies some wine?" They nodded and turned to Amaka, who had high cheekbones, deep brown skin, and a broad smile that showed perfect teeth. "Pleased you both could come," she said in a lilting accent that Olivia decided was Nigerian. "I was so sorry to hear about your shop. The fire. It was your place, wasn't it?" she directed to Olivia.

Olivia nodded. "One of those freak things. It happens with these old buildings. But we should be up and running again in a couple of weeks, they tell me." She smiled.

"Good," said Amaka. She looked at her husband, who'd returned with two full glasses of wine. "W.D. and I are so glad you could stop by. We are so surprised at this turnout! I never thought we'd get this many people."

"I'm happy you're off to such a good start," Olivia said.

As the door opened the circle of four widened to include a friend of Winona's, an elderly man who'd come out of retirement to help with his son's trucking firm, then widened again when two young men who'd opened a new barbecue restaurant arrived. From another huddle nearby, laughter erupted, punctuating the punchline of someone's joke. The music grew louder—vintage Miles Davis replacing Sweet Honey—and the voices of conversation raised in competition.

Later, Olivia was wedging her way through the crowd, in search of the restroom, when a man in a tan blazer and purple shirt caught her eye. She recognized him immediately, even though in the year that had passed he'd put on weight and grown a patchy, whitish beard. And the look on his face told her that he was as embarrassed to see her as she was to see him. Jimmy Bell, L.J.'s friend and employer, and the last to see him the night of the accident, was making his way across the room toward Olivia. His eyes were full of unease, his head angled down.

She'd always liked Jimmy. He'd been born in the south, like L.J., and the two of them had known each other since they were both young boys new in town, roving the music scene with high hopes. Jimmy, a piano man just up from Newborn, Georgia, had inherited the piece of property he turned into a club. For a while, with L.J. playing at Jimmy's, both seemed to have reached their dreams. But on the night Jimmy's club went under, so did L.J., and the dream ended for both.

This might be awkward, she thought as he made his way to her. She never blamed Jimmy, but he may have felt responsible in some way for what happened to L.J. that night, since it was Jimmy who'd not only fired him, but had watched him lope out of the club and into the night with a fifth of Jack Daniel's under his arm. She was thinking that she never heard from Jimmy after that, but then remembered the phone messages he'd left for her that she never acknowledged, and the small card and chrysanthemums that sat and wilted by her kitchen door.

"Olivia," he nodded his head in greeting.

"Jimmy," Olivia said, "it's good to see you. How have you been?"

He smiled faintly. "I guess I should be asking you that question."

She told him she was fine, even though her shop was undergoing restoration after a fire, but that she had taken advantage of the time to go to New York. She tried to put him at ease with small talk, telling him what a good time she had in the city, the restaurants, museums, the music, and that now she realized why L.J. always talked about going there. She hadn't meant to make him feel uncomfortable by mentioning L.J. so quickly, it had just come out. But at the mention of L.J., Jimmy's eyebrows lifted, as if he'd been waiting for her to break the ice.

"Olivia, I tried to call you a couple of times…after. I wanted to talk to you about a couple of things."

She held up her hand. "Jimmy, you don't have to say anything."

"Wait a minute, now, OK? I just want to say this." He took off the wire rimmed glasses he wore and rubbed the bridge of his nose.

"First of all, you know how sorry I was about what happened to L.J."

"I know, I got your card and the flowers. I'm sorry I didn't return your calls. I just couldn't…didn't feel up to…"

"No, no, Olivia, it's OK, really. The night of L.J.'s accident, that was the night I fired the band. The club was going under. Hell, it was gone. I couldn't keep the lights on."

"I know that, Jimmy. I heard."

"Man, I felt terrible. All the guys were down about it. But L.J., he was the worst. He looked like a man at the end of his rope, you know what I mean? I didn't know what was going on inside his head. He just looked dazed for a while. Then he said a funny thing. Said, I'll take my salary in one of those bottles. He grabbed the Jack Daniel's off the shelf and left. Swear I never seen him drink that stuff in his life."

He paused and looked down at his feet, then up at Olivia again. "You know how it is, when you think back on something that happened? When you look back on it, you realize all the signs were there. You just missed them. I shoulda never let him walk out of there like that. I shoulda gone after him. I'll always think about that."

Olivia folded her arms and looked across the room at the other guests laughing, talking. Someone had spilled a drink on the hardwood floor and there was a small commotion, then laughter as someone spread paper towels over the spot to clean it.

"Well, we've both got our regrets," Olivia said, looking at Jimmy. She lowered her voice. "I know what was on his mind that night.

Before he left for the club, L.J. and I argued. Bitterly. In fact, I told him not to come back. And…" She lifted her hand and made a gesture, letting the unspoken words hang in the silence.

He looked her in the eyes, then nodded slowly. "Yeah. Well. I guess we can either think about that for the rest of our lives, or we can just get on with our lives."

"I guess it's our choice, isn't it?"

"Yeah. Yeah, it is." He paused. "You know Liv, I been thinking on this awhile. You ever think maybe L.J. made it out of that car? That maybe he's still around somewhere? I think about that all the time."

She told him she had not only thought about it, but had hired someone to try to find him. "Yeah? Well, if I can help in any way, let me know. Boy, wouldn't that be something if he turned up somewhere? I sure miss that boy. Things just ain't been the same without him. But there's something else I want to talk to you about."

Jimmy told her about a plan he had to reopen the jazz club. To completely remodel it, expand it, and make it into a top-notch night club that would draw people from all over the city. Feature local talent, and occasionally bring in name jazz artists from out of town. There was city money available for low interest loans to entrepreneurs with an interest in the area just east of downtown, which had been slated for major restoration with the passage of the bond. His old place sat right in the middle of the area, and he planned to take advantage of the opportunity.

"There's every reason to believe it'll work this time," he told her. "There's money behind it now. The city, the mayor, everybody's real hot to bring back the jazz history of the town. It makes good tourism.

"So anyway," he continued, after taking a deep breath, "would you be interested in coming in with me on it?"

Olivia was so surprised she almost laughed. "Me?"

"Sure. But I don't just want you for a partner. I want you to sing." She was floored. "Jimmy, I…"

"Now before you go saying 'no' right off the bat, let me tell you. I've heard about your little debut at New Hope the other week. *Everybody* who was there is talking about it. And then L.J. He was always talking about your voice, how you used to be kinda famous in that little town you grew up in. So I know you can sing, now. I know you can do it."

She smiled at him, flattered. Then she thought, wasn't that her dream? To one day recapture that old love, to sing like she'd done as a child? The club idea had been a dream she'd had, but it had been a dream she'd shared with L.J. If she was ever going to sing again, she always believed it would be with him right there with her, encouraging her. The thought of doing it without him raised a cloud of doubt.

"I don't know, Jimmy. I…"

Just then a short rotund man in a wine-colored suit grabbed Jimmy's hand. "Hey, man, I thought that was you! I ain't seen you in a year! Oh, excuse me," he said, looking at Olivia. Jimmy introduced the man to Olivia as an old friend whose plumbing business Jimmy used when the club was open.

Olivia smiled. "I'll let you two talk," she said, excusing herself.

Jimmy said, "Please consider what I said, Liv."

"I will," said Olivia, knowing she wouldn't. And then disappeared behind the restroom door.

· FIFTEEN ·

THERE WAS SO MUCH TO THINK ABOUT when Olivia returned home. The shop. Seeing Jimmy. And, as always, L.J. But when she entered her house, all she could think about was the piano.

A Baldwin baby grand stood—an ebony centerpiece—in the living room. Lacquered black, polished every month, and tuned once a year. His pride and joy. They'd both saved for it, but she'd made the final payment and had it delivered as a surprise for his fortieth birthday. Close by, blue-gray light from the pale December sky shone through the window. Through it, she could see cottony clouds thick with the promise of snow. She walked to the piano, ran a finger along the lid. She looked at her finger. Dust. It made her cringe. How could she have forgotten to dust it?

She found a soft cloth beneath her kitchen sink, and swathed it across the top of the piano. She dusted the white keys, then the black. The noise of random keys being struck sounded bell-like, breaking the quiet in the room. It had been a year since she'd heard these notes. It was time for another tuning. With her index finger, she struck one key, then another. She pulled out the bench and sat down.

She hummed a tune she knew well and found the notes with two fingers. She stumbled through once, then played it again. She opened her voice and began to sing; she liked the sound of her voice in this room, against the quiet. After a while, she closed the lid, turned out the brass floor lamp by the piano, and went upstairs.

She thought of Jimmy. Nice of him to ask her to sing, but what was that about? Guilt? A sympathy gesture on behalf of L.J.? Maybe. Or maybe he really wanted her to. At first she had dismissed the thought.

But then the possibility of it intrigued her, offering itself to her like an interesting book spread wide open. *He'd* always wanted her to sing, always encouraged her to. Coaxed her, teased her, never giving up. But now that he was gone...

She was still too wide awake for bed. But she went upstairs anyway, lay across the bed, clothes on, and stared up at the ceiling.

She thought again of Doakes. Before she'd hired him, he'd asked her to tell him everything that had happened the last night she'd seen L.J. She had balked. How often would she have to relive the awful memory of those last few moments? It might help, my knowing what went on, he'd said. There might be a clue in something he said. OK, a good point, she said. She told him most of it, as much as she could. But there was more.

And the more that she didn't tell him was what she remembered now.

She could tell by the look on his face, a look she'd never seen before, that something between them was about to change.

"I want to tell you about something that happened to me when I was very young, a little boy." He stood facing her with both hands resting on the sink counter behind him. Then he scratched his head.

"I told you when I was growing up that I lived a lot of places, but I never told you about one place. The year I was nine, I lived in Handy, Arkansas."

Olivia looked at him and blinked. "You're kidding. You lived there? How come you never told me?"

He raised his hand in a gesture that quieted her.

"Like I told you, we were always on the road, going from town to town, never stayed in one place longer than a year or so. Purvis'd get a job, then he'd blow it, we'd have to move on. So I spent a year or so down in Handy. Purvis had gotten fired from the railroad in Little Rock, so we moved to Handy, and he got a job playing blues piano at a little juke joint out in the country. A place where they played what he liked to call 'down home' blues. But I hung out at a club on Lawson

Avenue where they played jazz. Purvis had brought home a saxophone one night and I tried to teach myself how to play it. I messed around with it some and then I started going to this jazz club."

"Was it the Night Owl?"

"Yeah. The Night Owl. You came in a side door off the alley, through the pool hall. The walls, I remember, were covered with posters of singers from the thirties—Ma Rainey, Bessie Smith, even Billie Holiday—to cover broken paint. None of them had ever been there, of course, but it gave the place a look. It was just a shack of a place, a few wooden tables and some mismatched kitchen chairs. There was a little piano and a small wooden bandstand, and a yellow bulb for a spotlight. People came there to get drunk on cheap gin, or just pass the time. There was always a lot of laughing, joking, people having a good time. Sometimes a fight would break out, but nothing serious. Nobody cared that I was there, a kid in the way. It was exciting to me, and the music there was something else.

"I wasn't anything but a little kid, and Purvis let me run wild. So I was there every chance I got, listening to the music, trying to pick up tips on how to play from the guys who were part of the regular band. The musicians treated me nice. Anyway, there was a woman singing there."

He reached for a glass sitting in the sink and filled it with water. He drank in long, slow swallows, and blotted his lips with the back of his hand.

He let out a long sigh. "Anyway. This woman, she was a singer, about thirty, I guess. She was tall, and beautiful, and had a voice like...well, I can't describe it. It seemed to come from someplace way deep inside her. Amazing. She knew all the tunes, jazz, blues, whatever.

"One night when she wasn't working, one of the cats who hung out there, man named Earl Ridley, told me to take something to her; she had a little place she was living in on the north side up past the lumber mill, and he gave me a quarter for my trouble. It was a letter. She looked at it, opened it, read it and smiled. Then she wrote something on it and gave it back to me. Told me to take it back to the man I'd gotten it from.

"Then she gave me a quarter. Sent me on my way. Anyway. It got to be regular. I was like a go-between for the woman and the man."

He hunched his shoulders. "I didn't think much of it. I was just happy running back and forth between them because this woman…"

He took a sip of water.

"Let me stop calling her 'this woman.' Her name was Vaughn."

He cleared his throat, and scratched his chest. "Anyway, Vaughn… she was…very special. A beautiful, beautiful woman. She could be wild sometimes. She drank and cursed at the guys in the band when they messed up her tunes, got in the way of her rhythm. But when she sang, she was different. She had this expression, like some kind of angel or something, her eyes would shine, her skin… Sometimes when she sang the slow songs, the ballads—I can't explain it. Her voice was like a finger pressing against your heart—a soft touch, but you couldn't move while it was there. When she finished, you could look around and see old men brush their eyes with the backs of their hands. There was something very different in her voice—I didn't know what to call it at the time. But now I'd call it pain. Pain in her voice. Sadness. I mean, like when she sang, her voice took over the room. There wasn't a thing anybody could do but listen.

"We got to be friends. She and I did. She'd look after me. I mean everybody in the club, all the guys kinda looked after me, I was like a little mascot. But she really took care of me. She called me her 'little man.' Taught me how to comb my hair. She'd feed me sometimes when she could tell I was hungry 'cause Purvis had drank up all the money we had. She even let me play with her on a set once, let me have a little eight-bar solo. I was awful. I was honking and squeaking like a rusty door. But when I finished, she acted like I was John Coltrane or somebody, making the audience cheer, telling them I was gonna be a star someday. It was that night that I really knew I wanted to be a musician. I'd have done anything for her. Anything she asked."

He stroked the back of his head with his palm. "So, anyway, one night I went to Vaughn's place. I wasn't sent there that time, no note or anything. I just went there because…I guess because it was a place where I felt like I belonged. Vaughn was always happy to see me, or at least she acted that way.

"But this night it was different. Vaughn came to the door and I could tell right away something was wrong. She didn't even let me in. And she looked terrible, her eyes all swollen and dark. She sent me away, said she didn't feel well. I went home. When I went back to the club the next night, she wasn't there. And I didn't see her for months.

"When I did see her again, a long time after, she still wasn't herself. But she was nicer to me. I went by her house for no reason except that I wanted to see her. She told me she wanted me to do something for her, said it was very, very important. She reached in her purse and pulled out a two-dollar bill."

He rubbed his hands together. He looked at her straight on and spoke deliberately. "What I'm trying to say to you is, the night of that big rain, the night you were carried over to Big Mama and them's. The little boy who carried you over there..."

Olivia couldn't make sense of the words. What was he telling her?

"The boy...*was you?*"

He nodded.

Olivia forced a swallow, felt the cutting pain of it. When she finally spoke, words spilled, cracking like ice, from her throat.

"So you...you knew my mother. This woman...Vaughn. You waited until now to tell me this?"

He rushed the words out. "I promised her I would never tell you. That was her wish. The man, Big Earl, he was married. She never wanted you to know who she was, what kind of woman... She was in trouble, that's why she gave you up. Big Earl had a temper. He beat her, I found out. More than once. And she had to..."

"So the man, this Big Earl. He was my father?"

A furrow appeared in the space between L.J.'s brows. A bulging vein danced on his temple. "Yes. Well...I'm pretty certain he was."

He stopped and looked down at the floor, then up again at her.

"I swear, Olivia, I'd have never kept something like this from you if she hadn't made me swear to."

"So why are you telling me now?"

"Cause I had to. I don't know which is worse, betraying her or lying to you. But watching you, hearing you talk about looking for your mother—I just couldn't do it anymore. I felt like a liar every time you mentioned anything about your family. Now you're saying you want to hire somebody, and I figured if you were ever going to find out the truth, it should be from me."

Olivia nodded slowly, a look of immense sadness weighing her features. "Twenty-four years," she said. "You knew my mother and my father, and you said nothing. Twenty-four years."

She got up and walked to the window, staring out with her back to him. Then she turned sharply to face him. "Tell me something, L.J."

"What's that?"

"You were in love with her, weren't you?"

He smiled warily, shook his head. "What? Come on Olivia, I was nine years old."

"But you loved her?"

"Well, I guess so. Yes."

"And she, my mother, she loved you?"

"Well, yeah. I think she cared about me."

Her eyes widened and her voice got louder. "So is that why you wanted me? Was that the reason? Just because I reminded you of her? That day we met in Joplin?"

"Now hold on Olivia, you think I planned that one day I was going to meet and marry Vaughn's daughter? You think I planned for that to happen? I admit when I saw you that day at the bus station, you looked so much like her, a dead ringer for her, really, so of course I was drawn to you. I mean, the resemblance was…uncanny. But I never, it wasn't because of her that I—"

"Why don't you just say it. It…this….twenty-four years. It was never about me, was it? It was all about her."

"What?"

"Tell me if it's not true. You never loved me. Never loved me…for *me*. It was only because I looked like her, was *her* daughter. *Tell me if it's not true.*"

197

Silence. He blinked twice, hesitated. Looked away, then back at her. "I…uh. Of course…it's not true."

Too late. He'd hesitated. A split-second silence wide as an abyss. Not long, but long enough. Long enough for a heart to split wide open. Long enough to believe more in the silence than in the sound that finally broke it.

"Olivia, did you hear me? I said of course, it's not true."

She shook her head slowly, tears streaming down flushed cheeks. "No, no. Please get your things and leave."

"Wait, now, Olivia, Big Mama said you'd…"

"What? She knows about this?"

"Well…"

Her tears burned hot. "And who else knows? Clo T.? And Glodean? Did they know? And Uncle Joon and Country? Everybody but me? All these years?"

He sighed deeply. "Olivia…"

But she could no longer hear him above the deafening ringing inside her head, the choking feeling of something knotting inside.

"Just go…get out. *Get out and don't ever come back.*"

Each time she remembered the events of that night, her emotions were different: anger, sadness, confusion. Tonight she felt tremendous regret at the lost opportunity. He had betrayed her, withheld the truth from her, and as much as admitted he never loved her for herself. As much as admitted that it was Vaughn who had led him into her life, Vaughn's memory that kept him there. But in the aftermath of that storm, she realized she'd let her anger and grief cloud her judgment. At least she could have found out from him what happened to her mother before he was gone. Was she still alive? And what about her father? Did her father even know about her? L.J. had those answers. She'd let him slip out the door, taking the only key with him.

She felt unsettled. She wanted to call Big Mama right then and talk to her, but for a year now she had harbored anger for her part in the deception, hadn't returned her calls nor answered her letter. When she was little, she'd always felt a special closeness to Big Mama, and even more after the others were gone. Uncle Joon went from a heart attack when he was well past ninety; Clo T. and Glodean, almost as old, went quietly in their sleep. And Country, well, no one ever said how old she was, keeping to her wish, but from what the others said, she was the oldest of all. But of all of them, it was Big Mama who seemed most like family. Big Mama, the small woman with the big shoulders and hands and the endless heart, who had time for everyone in town who brought her their troubles and still managed to make Olivia feel as if she were the only one who mattered. They were all so good to her, but it was Big Mama who was the most affectionate, the most giving, the most like true kin. Which was why her part in the deception hurt as much as it did.

But maybe it was time now to stop blaming Big Mama. After all, it was L.J.'s secret, L.J.'s promise to Vaughn. Her gaze fell on the night-stand by her bed. The old woman's squiggly writing on the envelope was hidden in shadow. She picked it up and raised it to the light.

She sighed out a long breath. Then she scooted up on the bed with her head against the headboard, opened the letter, and slowly read.

VII

· SIXTEEN ·

FUNNY, HE THINKS, how certain days in your life can stick in your mind and others are gone forever.

They'd been married just six months. He recalled the shush-shush of her house shoes on the steps and her soft soprano hum as she came upstairs to find him still asleep at noon on a Saturday.

"L.J., breakfast is ready," she said cheerily, bouncing down on his side of the bed. "Wake up, honey. I want you to see something."

Usually she left him alone until he awakened. But she was an early riser and sometimes couldn't bear the peaceful, blanketed lump of his body sleeping late. He'd had a late night at work and even the smell of fried bacon didn't faze him.

She held a *Ladies' Home Journal* in her hand opened to an article titled, "Test Your Marriage," a questionnaire, she told him, compiled by two psychologists at a northeastern women's university. "Come on, L.J., let's take this test, you and me." She began the questions. "You are realistic about each other's faults...A, very strongly agree, B, strongly agree, C—"

He pulled covers over his head. "Please let me sleep."

"C, agree—"

"Please, babe."

She put the magazine down in exasperation.

"You're not even listening."

"Of course I'm not listening. I'm sleeping."

"You're not sleeping. You're wide awake."

"Not by choice—" he said, turning his whole body away from her. "The gig let out at four this morning. You know that. Please let me sleep."

"But this is important. Oh, listen to this—" She went on to read another question, while he ignored her. Finally he felt her weight lifting from the bed. Later, he'd come downstairs to find cold bacon sitting in grease, toast turned to rubber, thick, cold coffee staining the inside of the pot. Olivia had been sulking for hours on the green porch glider, slow-rocking, hair twirled in her fingers.

She'd been young when he married her, barely twenty. Not as mature as other women he knew. She exasperated him at times. But he reminded himself that she had some growing up to do, so he waited patiently for the woman to come. It would take more than a little immature sulking to convince him he'd made the wrong choice.

He reminded himself again when the tulips he'd cut for her from the garden and offered in apology sat unwatered and dried up.

"Spoiled," Uncle Joon told him the next time they visited Arkansas. "Got to have her way. These women fussing over her her whole life. No wonder." But Country saw things differently. "Orphans always need a little more," she'd say. "Takes all five of us to try and do what one woman didn't." And he understood that. She often tested him in little ways; love was something she needed to see, to touch. Her outstretched hands a cup that never quite got filled no matter how much you poured.

L.J. sits in Crawfish Malone's hot, tiny Upper-West-Side kitchen on a sunny afternoon, lost in thought as the men in the band talk around him. She doubted him, he realized, probably even before that night. He thought about the split second of silence he'd give his right arm to call back. *You never loved me for me. Tell me if it's not true.* He'd stumbled, let a whole beat pass, enough time to pale the light beneath her ginger skin, to make her shoulders go limp. He'd looked in her eyes then and saw something crumble. She doubted him, and not because she was spoiled or insecure. He'd given her reason. Her doubt of him was no deeper than his own.

"Hand me that aluminum bowl over there by the sink," Crawfish, busy at the counter, says over his shoulder to no one in particular. Wash is sitting closest to him and hands him the bowl. "Now," Crawfish says. "I'll show y'all how to make a shrimp creole that'll make you cry."

Afternoon window light curls sharply across Crawfish's bald spot. He grabs a handful of shelled shrimp and dumps them into the bowl. He turns to the stove and stirs flour and butter in a skillet, then dices green pepper and garlic and sprinkles them in the mix.

Tate, the new piano player who replaced Larry in the quartet after the tour, leans back from the old oak table and taps his cigar ash into an empty Coke can. "I hope you planning on deveining them shrimp, man. I don't eat nobody's shrimp unless that vein is *out*."

Crawfish looks up. "I takes 'em out. But I ain't never heard of nobody dying from eating shrimp with the vein still in. You eat chitlins. You eatin' worse than a shrimp gut."

Tate lifts his bushy eyebrows, frowns, and waves his hand. "I never touch them nasty things. I don't eat nothing I can't stand to smell. Besides, chitlins is slave food. The part of the hog don't nobody white or in his right mind want. Trash from the master's garbage."

"White folks eat chitlins, too." Crawfish turns the fire down under the sizzling roux.

"Now that's a lie," Tate says. "I ain't never seen anybody white eat chitlins."

"That's cause they don't want you to see 'em," Crawfish says. "You think they sell 'em in the stores just for us? They send they help out to get 'em and bring 'em back. They don't want anybody to know they be eating that stuff."

Wash strokes his chin, then clasps his hands across the back of his head. "Shoot. Get you some chow chow and some cornbread, and you got some good eatin'. I grew up on 'em. They don't smell that bad, you clean 'em right."

"The hell you say. My mama had me cleaning those filthy things one time when I was little. She put fire up under 'em, and I'm telling you…I had to burn the clothes I was wearing."

"Was you wearing one of them cheap leisure suits?" Crawfish asks. "Probably needed burning anyway."

Crawfish adjusts the flame again under his roux and turns to the men seated around his table. "I thought we said we was gonna discuss this boy's record deal after we rehearsed. This here is a meeting. I didn't invite y'all here just to eat up my shrimp creole and then go home."

"CD." Tate says. "Not record deal. Nobody makes records no more."

"Well CD deal then. What we gonna do about this boy's offer?"

Wash takes a toothpick from a tiny plastic dispenser on the table and begins to pick his teeth. "Fill me in again. What did he actually say?"

"Said he was looking for a new band to record with." Tate frowns against the sunlight, and his gaunt face and gray beard make him look older than his fifty-five years. "Said his drummer went into a rehab program. His keyboard man left to play with some hot new funk group outta Texas. Then his sax player cut his own solo deal with some European label."

"What about his bass man?"

"Don't know about his bass man."

Wash leans over, elbows on his knees, and shakes his head. "I don't know. This cat is twenty-five years old and already got two Grammies. He's the hottest young trumpet player around here. Why he want to hook up with a bunch of old heads?"

Crawfish chuckles and wipes his hands on the dishtowel tucked into the belt stretched across his barreling stomach. "'Cause we good, and he knows it. We been playing since before that boy ever sat on his Grammy's knee."

"You mean 'cause some old heads like us won't run out on him, that's why," Tate says. He rubs his sparse gray hair with his palm. "It ain't like one of us is gonna join up with a funk band, or like we got European labels busting down our doors."

"Anyway, this is what he told me," Tate continues. "Said he realized a lot of young cats are getting all the work and a lot of us, folks that made it all happen back in the day, well, we getting pushed aside. And these young cats ain't playing no better than us. Some not as good."

"He said he wanted to do one album, a tribute to the old school, with a group of…what's that word he used?"

"Veterans," Crawfish says.

"Yeah. Veterans," says Tate. "That's what he said. Like we been in a war or something."

Wash raises his eyebrows and shrugs his narrow shoulders. "We have. The battle of the young bloods and the old school. The battle of trying to keep some food on the table all these years."

Tate says, "Yeah. Well, anyway. He said his daddy told him his trouble was he didn't have no stability in his group. Get you some mature players in that group and you won't have to worry about these young bucks jumping up and leaving. That's what his daddy told him."

Crawfish takes the last shrimp and separates the spine with a knife. He pours canned tomatoes into the sizzling skillet. "If that's the deal, what's to talk about? Tell him we're in."

Tate douses his cigar on the lid of the Coke can and pulls a small calendar from his pocket. "Well it ain't all that simple. The dates he got lined up for rehearsal and studio time come in May. First week."

"That's when that street festival in Harlem is. We already committed to that," Wash says.

"That's right," adds Tate. "And we'd have to cancel some other things, too. And that jazz cruise I booked us for leaves the next week. We gotta find some time to rehearse for that. We got to weigh all our options 'fore we jump into this thing."

Crawfish says, "Well, I been wanting to play with Ronnie Penner since I heard him play on that TV Christmas show with Natalie Cole a couple a years ago. I said then, this kid is for real. I'm in."

"Wait a minute. We decided we all gonna do it or none of us is. We said we wasn't gonna let nobody bust up the quartet."

Well, I say we do it," says Crawfish.

Tate looks at L.J. "We ain't heard from this man here yet. And he's the main one Penner's interested in."

"How you know that?" Crawfish says.

"Remember he rushed up to us after L.J. played that 'Lush Life' solo at that party at the Plaza right after we got back from the tour?"

"Yeah, L.J. was kicking some serious ass that night. Well, L.J.? What you say? Put that little old two-dollar bill you keep playing with away. We talking about making some real money."

L.J. sits up straight in his chair and blinks himself back from a haze of memories. "What's that?"

He has dreaded this moment. The men are looking at him and he has been trying to decide how to tell them.

"We want to know what you think about this deal with Penner," Tate says.

L.J. clears his throat and frowns. He puts the two-dollar bill in his pocket. "Well," he says. "I don't know how much longer I'm going to be in New York. I'm thinking about going back home. To Kansas City."

The men look at him, say nothing. The silence growing around him becomes uncomfortably thick and hot.

Crawfish turns the burner flame down to quiet the cackling roux, and turns to face L.J. "I had a feeling. Had a feeling you weren't here to stay, man."

L.J. shifts uncomfortably in his chair. "My wife…back home. We had some problems. That's why I'm up here in the first place. But now…now I'm thinking about going back."

"Same old story," Tate says. "Everybody come up here from Kansas City or Cleveland or St. Louis, before you know it, they done turned tail and ran back home."

"Man, I didn't know you had a wife," Wash says.

"Yeah. Well, I did when I left. It's a long story."

"You talk to her? She know you coming?"

"Well, not exactly," L.J. says.

"Oh, so you just kinda hopin' she'll let you come back? Man, come on. I know you want to get back to your lady and all, but we need you on this deal. Just hang with us til we get this CD done."

Crawfish nods. "Yeah. We need you, brother. Tell your old lady you got a chance to play with Ronnie Penner."

"Not just play," Tate says. "Record with Ronnie Penner."

A sidelong smile edges across L.J.'s lips and he lets out a sigh. He looks down at the table. "Well, I don't have enough money saved yet anyway. It's not like I'm ready to go tomorrow."

"Your lady. Is her name Vaughn?" Crawfish asks.

L.J. looks at him and blinks. He can feel blood rush to his face. "Huh? No…no."

"Just wondering," Crawfish says, seeing a wrinkle of puzzlement etching L.J.'s brow. "That time we went to Clef's Steakhouse after the Plaza gig. Remember that waitress had 'Vaughn Marie' on her name tag? Cute little blond white girl around thirty. We was all joking around with her and talking about what a unusual name it was for a woman. You didn't say nothing, just sat looking like you seen a ghost. I thought maybe that was your lady's name."

L.J. remembers the waitress. He had been taken aback. He'd never known another woman named Vaughn.

"Olivia. Olivia is her name."

"Now don't be all up in this man's business," Wash chortles. "Maybe he got two ladies."

"Yeah. You know what they say about them sax players. They always get all the women," Crawfish laughs.

"Who, L.J?" Tate says. "Naw, L.J. ain't the type. He as straight as they come."

L.J. is uneasy, and he tries to re-compose himself. He feigns amusement with a half-smile and shakes his head.

Crawfish puts white plates on the table in front of the men. "Rice is done. Are y'all ready for a culinary feast? Dish up your own plates from the pots on the stove. Who wants a Bud?"

Tate raises a finger. "I'll take one."

"Me, too," says Wash.

L.J. rises from his seat and looks at his watch. "Uh, I just remembered. I gotta go see somebody about some money they owe me."

"You gotta go right now? Stay and have some of this shrimp creole," Crawfish says.

"Naw, man, sorry. I'm late already. Smells good, though. Real good."

He hopes Crawfish doesn't take offense, his leaving before dinner. The growl in his stomach makes more noise than his footsteps down the hardwood stairs. There's gotta be a creole restaurant somewhere in Manhattan. Gotta be.

· SEVENTEEN ·

Two ladies. The words hung in his mind like a ring of hot, thick smoke.

He pushes open the thick glass door of the building and steps outside to meet sharp, bracing air and warming flashes of winter sun. On the street, dead leaves rustle on concrete like the sound of wire brushes swirling a snare drum head. An old woman dressed in layers of gray wool pushes a rickety grocery cart full of empty wine bottles, and a kid on a bike whizzes past L.J. so close he can feel the breeze. He checks his watch again, knowing there's way too much time. But killing time on the street is nothing new.

He's hungry and the food smelled so good. But good food or not, the weight of those words floating in the room, "Vaughn" and "Olivia," dulled his desire for it. He just couldn't stay in the room. Not with all eyes aimed at his life, and with his suddenly shaky loyalty to the men looming like a cumulus cloud. They liked his playing and that was good. But he had been back home to Kansas City, sat in his chair, walked through his house, and touched Olivia's things, and hadn't been the same since.

When L.J. had gotten back from K.C., his spirits had sunk so low he slept for hours during the day, surfacing from his room only to go to work, a rehearsal, or whatever gig Tate had lined up for the group. Two weeks in the lounge at the Riverview. A birthday bash for a judge's wife at the Four Seasons. Sunday brunches at a new restaurant in Brooklyn Heights. He's working enough to pay the rent, buy food. But being home had paled New York's luster, and now Kansas City loomed distant and bejeweled in that region of his mind where New York had been. The midtown traffic that had crooned in harmony now honked in strident discord. The buildings that had stood like majestic sentinels now just crowded out the precious blue that he and Olivia had watched grow to starry purple from that paint-chipped glider on the porch. He wants to go home. Work things out with Olivia. Or at least try.

But he needs money to go back. The little bit left over after rent and food couldn't buy him a one-way ticket to Chattanooga. He needs money to buy something decent to wear. He needs money to rent a car (or buy something cheap) for the drive back, money to live there until he finds some kind of steady work. He walks a little faster than usual, his stride quick and deliberate. Today is the day, he decides. He feels lucky. Today is the day that he'll call in the debt.

And in his pocket, he can feel the soft wrinkles and the frayed edges of the two-dollar bill.

It was the only thing he still had of Vaughn's. Most of what she'd given him, hot breakfasts of sausage and scrambled eggs, a warm bath, his own dirty shirt washed and pressed and returned to his clean arms and back, he had to rely on his memory to keep in his possession. But the two-dollar bill he could feel now as he had felt it then. It had been brand new in 1955, with edges sharp enough to cut, its crisp, clean surface rough to the touch. When she gave it to him that night, he'd felt like a fortune had been laid at his door.

Might as well have been a fortune, and unlike the saxophone, tossed angrily against the wall and landing fortuitously at his feet, this gift was ennobled by the splendor of its bearer. *She* had given it to him. He found an old wallet of brown plastic in the trash bin in the alley behind the Night Owl, discarded the grocery receipts and laundry tickets, and carefully placed the new bill between the folds. When he was older and could afford it, he'd bought leather. But long after he'd left Handy, he'd kept it unspent and unseen. It brought him more than luck. Those times when he wondered if she'd really existed, if she was not just the creation of his young, romantic imagination, he'd pull it out and rub Thomas Jefferson's face.

It had not been difficult keeping it out of Olivia's sight, and he had been amazed that you could keep secrets so easily and so long from someone who slept right next to you, knew your habits like her own. But she never looked in the nightstand drawer where his socks were rolled up and his handkerchiefs neatly folded. A good thing, for if she had seen it, she would have asked him, and he would have had to tell her the truth.

It had only been a year ago, the argument. How many ways had he wronged her? Keeping the story of Vaughn from her was enough, but his own uncertainty rose like a viper from some hidden place and stung them both. Was the thing between him and Olivia just the offspring of a deeper, long-treasured love? Was it Olivia he wanted, or just a real-life memento of Vaughn? Did he love Olivia for herself, or for the essence of the mother distilled in the child?

He could not deny how it had begun. It was all Vaughn. The grave-deep love of his youth delivered to him by Greyhound. Even with befuddlement contorting her elfin face when she learned it was Joplin, not Kansas City, there was that unmistakable contour of jaw and cheekbone, toast-colored skin, curl of lip, and the same almond eyes. He stared, dumb-struck, his throat as dry as dust. That trickster, time, had worked magic on his mind; the woman he'd missed for most of his life had reappeared, had not aged, in fact had grown younger. It could have been no one else. Vaughn's daughter, now a woman and the spitting image of her mother.

Through a bus-fume haze, he had tasted soft-as-clouds biscuits, heard kitchen linoleum creaking underfoot. Smelled cinnamon and sausage gravy. Felt the watery coolness of an ivory slip, and warm water in a holy-white bathtub that made him feel newly baptized. The woman who stopped his breath had taken him all the way home, and not the place where his twin-size cot and too-thin pillow were (a two-room box past the railroad tracks where the icebox never had ice, where the old man's phlegmy snore invaded his sleep), but the home her mother made him feel was his.

He'd backpedaled through time. In the seconds it took for his brain to complete the smallest synaptic connection (How old would she be? Eighteen?), he felt bright infant eyes gazing up at him, and small arms and legs beating his pounding chest in a pouring rain.

This grown-up baby—this woman—disarmed him, and every word from him sounded like garble. She was uninterested, clearly. But that did not stem his desire, which for a split second was animal-hot, then cooled by her liquid walk, the long, sobering line of her swan's neck. She was not interested. But that didn't stop him from wanting to proceed with making a fool of himself before her.

There was something in her that shamed the drab gray and dirt-rubbed green walls of that bus station—a manner, a gentle sleekness of style that made her look as out of place as a jeweled chandelier. A cleaning woman dressed in denim looked up from her broom at her, at him, then down at her sweeping, and smiled, knowing. Yes, there was something between them, all right, even if Olivia didn't have a clue. A molecular heat, a chemical tie. A bond.

But maybe Olivia had been right. Maybe it was only because of Vaughn.

On a day so hot that the sun-baked Arkansas dirt seemed to radiate shimmers of light, and stray dogs loped miserably on the grassless yards, he'd walked to Vaughn's tiny house in the black quarter of Handy just beyond the river. White clapboard, a small, uneven porch, crawl space between the cinder blocks on which it squatted. A warped and rusted screen door that wouldn't close after a good rain. Two rooms, a little kitchenette, and a bath. It was the bath he would never forget. The white-white porcelain of the sink, the graceful curves of the slant-back tub that stood on what looked to him like lion's feet. The way the sheer curtains above it billowed like a woman's skirt with the late-summer breeze.

He had had to knock three times on her screen door.

From inside he could hear the soft moan of an electric fan and music, a woman's voice. Dinah Shore was singing *"See the U.S.A. in your Chevrolet…America is asking you to come…"*

A huge, heavy fly buzzed around his head as he stood on her porch. The hunger in his small belly made him jittery, and he shifted his weight from foot to foot as he waited for her. The late morning sun burned his skin. The rotting wood of the floorboards creaked and whined beneath his feet. She came to her door, looked out over him, and then down.

"Oh," she said. "All right. Come in."

The rooms smelled of cinnamon, fry-grease, and mildew. Even with the fan going it seemed warmer inside than out, and the air in the small room was as moist as human breath. The television mumbled from a corner.

Her eyes slanted up at their outer corners below eyebrows arched in an expression of mild surprise. The smile that began in her eyes ended just before the full, peach-colored lips.

"You got something for me? Well, come on in. Don't just stand there all big-eyed with your mouth hung open. You lettin' flies in. What you looking at? Ain't you never seen a woman in a slip before? Wait. Wipe your feet."

No, he hadn't, he did not say, and for the briefest moment his eyes rested on the soft whiteness of the slip and the silhouette of the body that moved like water beneath it. Inside, he scraped his blue Keds against the naps of a fringed rectangle of brown carpet at the door. He handed her the envelope and she opened it. "Well, don't just stand there looking silly. Go on, sit down over there," she instructed him. She unfolded the letter and smiled at the twenty tucked inside, then put the money in her bosom. She stood in front of the fan, swaying from side to side, letting the whipping air undo the cling in her slip and holding its tail while she read. The smile spread wide across her mouth. Then she stopped swaying and ran her hand up the back of her neck to lift her hair. She let out a laugh, and shook her head.

When she smiled, so did he, so pleased was he to be the bearer of joy. He had noticed that the letters often made her smile and sometimes laugh out loud like that. He'd wondered why, since Big Earl was not particularly funny. Not to him anyway. He wasn't even all that nice; he hardly even looked at L.J. when he gave him notes to take to her, or even when he dug in his trousers to pull out a quarter. His hair was slicked back and he wore boots that came to a dull point. He only smiled when he watched Vaughn sing, sitting gap-kneed with a hand stroking his jaw stubble, another resting against his crotch. The rest of the time, he scowled. What could a scowling man have said in a letter to make her so happy?

While he sat and waited, he clasped his hands together and stared at the television. Something else he had never seen before, though he had heard about them. One of the boys at school had bragged about his daddy bringing one home in his truck. He watched, fascinated, as the images moved and danced inside the box. Somebody in a commercial was singing, *"Ohh, I love Bosco, It's extra good for me…"*

She must have noticed how he was gawking because she said, "Bet you ain't never seen one of them before, have you?"

"No, ma'am," he said.

"Birthday present. It's used, and it don't get all three channels, just two, but it works. I coulda had me a telephone, but I told him, this friend of mines, I rather get me a TV because they got all these music shows from New York and all. Like Ed Sullivan. You ever hear of him?"

"No ma'am."

"You ever hear of New York?"

"No ma'am."

She laughed. "You ain't never heard of New York, the best city on earth? Where all the folks go that can sing and play? You don't know much, do you?"

"No ma'am."

She laughed again. "Well, if you ever come see me, and I ain't here, that's where I'll be. New York."

His stomach growled in a long, slow moan and he could feel the hollowness. He grabbed his stomach, then cleared his throat and coughed in case there was another growl coming.

"My!" She looked up from the letter. "You ain't got nothing in that stomach of yours, do you, baby?"

"Uh no, ma'am, I guess not." he said, and she smiled.

"Well, it's some biscuits and pork sausage and rice back in the kitchen. You lucky, today I felt like cooking. Just let me get done reading this. Then I'll write something for you to take back."

She sat down next to him on the lime-green sofa and a sweet, soapy smell wafted toward him. She rolled her eyes up toward the ceiling, then smiled and scribbled something on the back of the note. She leaned toward him.

"There. Now remember, you not supposed to read this, 'cause it's kinda personal. I'ma feed you something, then you can run on back with that note, all right?" She placed the note in his pocket and patted it.

Then she sat back, her spine straight as she frowned and put her hands on her knees. "You smell like something the cat done dragged in. When's the last time you saw the inside of a bathtub?"

"Uh, I don't 'member," he said, knowing he couldn't tell her the truth; that he'd never sat in a bathtub of hot water. The rooming houses where he and Purvis lived never had full tubs, only a sink against the wall in the room or a common, tubless toilet down the hall.

"Well, if you can't remember, it's been too long. You ain't eating with me smelling like that. Come on back here."

He looked down at his jeans, once blue, now a faded blue-brown. He rubbed his hand against the torn seam of his red cotton shirt.

"Come on."

She couldn't mean this. But when she rose, he followed her to the little room, for what else could he do? The room had pale green walls, black and white tiles lining the floor, a window with canary curtains above the tub. He watched her as she leaned over to turn the faucet knobs. He stared down at the huge expanse of shining white porcelain. Sun streamed in from the window and outside he could hear a chorus of morning birds.

"Well, take off your clothes and get in. And don't be looking all shamefaced. You ain't got nothing I ain't seen before. Seen all that and more. You ain't nothing but a little boy, no how. A dirty one at that, needing a bath. So get in."

He was horrified. He stood looking at her, then looked at the tub, the steaming gush of water from the faucets.

"Go on, now, get those clothes off." She knelt beside the tub and ran red-tipped fingers through the rising water. "Shame that old man ain't taught you better. Leaving the house like that, not even washing yourself. And looka that head of yours. Bet it ain't seen a comb in a montha Sundays. Put them clothes over here. I'ma wash that shirt while you soakin'. Go on. Get in."

He did as he was told, sank his thin body down into the steaming water, his nakedness raw and horrid, his humiliation complete. He slapped water on his eyes to hide the tears, and he drew up his legs and pressed his knees to his chest. Nothing could be worse than having your beloved declare you unclean and unfit for her table. Unless it was her ordering you to strip to your skin to fully expose the crime. Salt stirred in his wounded heart.

But when the water stopped running, he could hear the humming of her voice blending with noises from the open window, and he loosened the muscles in his shoulders. The hot water felt good. The gush of water was replaced with a gentle sloshing, a lapping of hand-stirred waves that accompanied the sound from the window above, the singing of summer's birds. The sheer curtains billowed with the breeze, and Vaughn's singing glided over his head like ribbons of silk. *What a difference a day makes, twenty-four little hours...*

He listened. *There was sunshine and flowers, where there used to be rain...* The singing was sweet, the breeze soft, the water cooled now to skin-warm, and he felt encased in something he wanted never to leave. He rested his hands to his side as she stroked the washrag against his back, down his arms, and along his stomach. He lowered his legs and let her wash between them. He leaned back and closed his eyes and listened to the singing and felt the breeze cooling his skin.

He felt dizzy, pleasantly. "Give me your hands," she said, and washed his palms, and the backs of them, and each one of his small fingers.

"I like a man with clean hands. You can always tell a decent man by his hands." She rubbed the rag again against the bar of Ivory soap, then scrubbed his hair vigorously, wiggling his head. Soapy water ran down his neck, between his shoulder blades. He laughed, and splashed water against the tub walls.

Water splashed in her eyes and she blinked and laughed. "Watch that, stop it, now." She splashed him back, and they both giggled.

She picked up his hands in hers and looked at him. "You a nice-looking little boy with your face clean. Got nice skin. Pretty eyes. Now, don't that feel good? Ain't nothing like a warm bath on a hot summer day."

In her sunny kitchen, he sat barebacked at the yellow Formica table while his shirt flapped on the clothesline in the yard beyond the kitchen window. He felt cool and clean. He piled rice and sausages high on his plate. He took the knife and sliced off a quarter inch of butter, and stirred it into the rice. He spooned mounds of sugar on top of it, and stirred it well. Then he shoveled spoonfuls into his mouth.

"My goodness, boy. Wait a minute. What's your hurry? Wait. Don't just shovel that food into your mouth like that. Sit back. Take your time. Don't ever eat like you hungry. Folks get the wrong idea. Look at me, now. Do like this."

She took the paper napkin folded by the plate, shook it with a dramatic snap of her wrist, then placed it neatly across her lap. She placed one hand in her lap, and with the other she spooned a small portion of rice and daintily placed it in her mouth. She chewed slowly before forking a small bite of sausage.

He did as she said, took his time, shook the napkin and draped it across his lap, placed a hand against his knee, even as saliva was rising in his mouth like creek water during a heavy rain.

"That's so much better. Now you look civilized." She smiled her approval. Her eyes glistened like agates and her white teeth shone.

His young eyes swallowed the smile that was as rich as cream. If he had known he would never see her smile that way again, he would have burned it in his brain.

He ate as slowly as he could, imitating her graceful moves. Then, his stomach roared in loud complaint, a twisting squeal so long and slow it sounded like musical chords.

She laughed, and he smiled sheepishly. "Bless your heart. We can work on your manners next time, baby. Just go ahead and eat."

In the eighteen years that passed from the last night he saw Vaughn to the first day he saw the grown-up Olivia, he'd felt himself a wandering man. Rootless, finding make-do home in a rented walk-up, on a rolling bus, or deep inside the brass of his horn. Now and then, there was pleasure in the arms of women whose perfumed scents lingered longer than they did. But not until that day in the bus station did he feel as if he'd found his home.

But except for the duplicated features, the smile and the gestures that traveled the blood route from mother to child, no two women could have been more unalike. Olivia sipped wine slowly, savoring it like nectar pressed from gold. He'd once seen Vaughn throw back a double Scotch and chase it with a beer. Olivia's eyes were twin oceans in which a man could lose his bearing, while Vaughn's could consume him in bright pools of flame. Olivia was refined, sweet-natured, and leaning towards shy; Vaughn was forward and bold, a column of brass tempered by a steel-edged beauty. And then there was the singing voice, Vaughn's river-deep and dark as a cave, Olivia's high and light as mountain air.

But there were similarities, too, and how badly through the years he'd wanted to tell her. Whenever she grabbed a piece of her hair and twirled it in her fingers the way Vaughn did, the way she held a glass to her lips, or blinked her eyes slowly. And that first night on the doorstep of the boarding home, just before he'd turned to leave, there had been that smile, the one he'd waited eighteen years to see, come to life again on the face of a stranger.

As the years passed with Olivia, he sometimes joked perversely to himself at how things had turned out, how he'd gotten just what he wanted: Vaughn in his life. Of course, it wasn't really that way. It was only a private joke. He loved Olivia, he told himself. In time Vaughn subsided in memory, overtaken by his life with Olivia.

But there had been that dream.

He'd often dreamed about Olivia when he had to leave her overnight to take a gig on the road. They were newly married, and he missed her fiercely. The dreams left him comforted, smiling—him and Olivia sharing intimacies, him delighting in the smell of her hair, her skin, the golden map of her body open to his own. He awakened one night in a hotel in Wichita after such a dream. He could see

Olivia's face clearly, her mink-brown eyes, her cheekbones, the sickle-shaped birthmark on the left side of her neck.

But Olivia did not have a birthmark there. Vaughn did.

He'd sat up, shaking. His heart pounding. What had happened, what had he done? He felt heavy with shame. He wanted to call Olivia and say...what? Nothing. He could say nothing, ever. Instead, he would have to live with the fact of it, let it run free in his mind until he could tame it, make sense of it. In the meantime, he could not let it come between them.

But it lingered in his sleepless, late-night stares at the wood-beamed ceiling of their bedroom, in moments at dinner when she shared the details of her day, looking at him with love and trust. In moments when he could not keep Vaughn from his mind. It hovered like a circling bird, ready to swoop down and spread its wings between them, pushing them apart. It had stayed aloft until that split second of silence—*tell me if it's not true*—and then descended, tearing at every thing that had been precious between them.

The dream had occurred twenty-three years ago. Only once. In all the years of his marriage, he'd never been unfaithful to her. Had never betrayed her with another woman, except once, in the deepest enclave of his heart.

The half-hour he has spent walking in the city has made his feet ache, but now he is where he wants to be. The building before him is gray, eight stories high, torn curtains and ragged blinds visible through open, dirty windows. He takes a position across the street. Not too close, trying to look inconspicuous, he leans against a dented and rusted old Chevy and turns pages of the magazine.

It isn't like he's stalking someone; after all, the kid ripped him off for every dime he had. Couldn't be stalking if you're just trying to get what's owed to you, could it? He had leverage over the kid; he had his address, his gun. He could threaten to give him up to the police, and he would, too, if the boy didn't pay up. He'd even give him a day.

He looks up from his magazine to the building across the street.

No one has entered or left for fifteen minutes. But that's OK. Patience is the key here, and he has nothing but time.

Two hours pass. He has had to shift his position several times, right leg, then left, then a full lean against the wreck of a car when his back began to hurt. Still no one has entered or left. But this has to be the building. This was the street he'd chased the kid to that day. Of the three tenements on the block, this was the only building that looked likely, with hungry, hard-looking kids going in and out and the front stoop littered with trash. The other buildings were neatly kept, retired fixed-income types trudging through the thick glass doors. No, this was the place. He tucks the magazine under his arm and walks across the street.

The tiny foyer of the building is painted in a dingy beige with dirt smudges, handprints, and graffiti scribbled on the walls. A wooden staircase banister with chipped varnish leads to the upper floors. From somewhere above there is the smell of frying fish.

"What's hap'nin, pops?" A man in his forties wearing a porkpie hat and red-striped knit shirt passes him on the way out the door as L.J. stops at the row of twelve mailboxes.

"Hey," L.J. says casually, then turns around to the man. "Uh, say, my man. Did Roy and 'em move? I just came down from the fourth floor, and somebody else is living in four-twelve now."

"Roy Price?" the man says, looking quizzical. "Roy ain't never lived in four-twelve."

L.J. scratches his head. "Coulda swore Roy said he was staying in four-twelve."

The man eyes him curiously. "What, you a cop or something?"

"A cop?" L.J. laughs. "That's a good one. No, I ain't no cop. Far from it."

The man hesitates, then he walks toward the door, and calls over his shoulder, "Go knock on four-sixteen. Top of the stairs."

The ruse worked. From behind the door of four-sixteen L.J. can hear a television game show in progress. He knocks slowly and loudly.

"Who is it?" A woman's rough voice from behind the door bellows throughout the hallway.

L.J. clears his throat. "Excuse me. I'm looking for a young man. Roy Price is his name."

Silence for a moment, then, "What you want? You a cop?"

"No, no, ma'am. I'm a musician. I just want to see Roy for a minute."

He hears metal bolts rattling from the inside, then the door opens a few inches, as far as the chain latch will permit. A pair of red-rimmed eyes meet his through the opening.

"He ain't here. Ain't seen him today."

"Do you know when he'll be back?"

The door slams in his face.

L.J. lets out a sigh, gathers himself, then knocks again. "Miss, I'm sorry to bother you. But could you tell me when Roy will be here?"

Silence.

He turns to walk down the steps when he hears the apartment door open again. He turns around and sees a small boy standing in the open door. He is round-faced and large-eyed, not more than eight or nine years old.

"Hi," L.J. says. "Are you Roy's…brother?"

"What you want with him?" the boy says.

"I just want to talk to him for a minute."

"He ain't here right now." The boy opens the door wider, stares up at L.J. through deep brown eyes.

"Is this where he lives, where he sleeps?"

"Yeah, sometimes."

L.J. rubs the back of his neck. "Yeah, well, I think I'll just sit out here and wait for him for a while."

L.J. notices that the boy is still staring at him, his young face registering recognition.

"I know who you are."

"Really? Who am I?"

"You're the man who plays that horn, on the street," the boy says. "I seen you a lot."

L.J. smiles. "You've seen me play? What's a little guy like you doing way over in that neighborhood?"

"I go anywhere I want to go," the boy says. "Roy ain't here, but I know where he is."

"You do? Can you take me to him?"

"What you want with him?"

L.J. shrugs and takes a small step toward the boy. "Well, he's got something that belongs to me. I just want to get it back from him. Will you take me where he is?"

The boy cocks his head to the side. "Where your horn at?"

"My horn? It's at my house."

"I'll take you to see my brother if you let me play on your horn."

L.J. smiles thoughtfully and nods. "So you want to learn how to play the saxophone?"

"I already know how to play it, I mean, I played it once before. Somebody showed me one time. It's easy."

L.J. squats down to the boy's height and rests his elbows on his knees. "Tell you what," he says. "Show me where your brother is, and I'll show you how to play."

"OK." The boy closes the door behind him as he steps into the hall.

"Wait," L.J. says. "Don't you want to tell your mother where you're going?"

The boy is halfway down the steps before L.J. can say another word. He follows the boy out the door of the building, and into the street.

Outside, night has fallen, and a full moon lights the dark street. The heavy bass of rap music and the garble of television wafts from open windows. The boy leads him to a red brick apartment house on the next block, where, in front, a man sits on the ground, blankets heaped around him, cradling a bottle of wine. Trash is scattered by the night breezes from the river. The boy takes him to the third floor and knocks loudly on the door.

When there is no answer, the boy turns to L.J. "He ain't here now, but he probably gonna be back here later on."

"OK, well, I guess I'll just come back another time."

"You still gonna let me play your horn?"

"What? Oh, yeah, sure. One day."

"Tomorrow," the boy says. "You come back tomorrow. Roy be here then."

"Yeah. OK, tomorrow, then." L.J. turns to walk away.

"Wait a minute," says the boy. "You got some money? Buy me a hot dog."

"What?"

"I said buy me a hot dog. And some French fries."

"Why should I do that?"

"'Cause I'm hungry," says the boy. "I'm starving. I ain't had nothing to eat since yesterday." He holds his stomach with both hands and fakes a pained expression.

Hands sliding into his pockets, L.J. looks pensively at the boy. He doesn't believe him—at least he doesn't want to.

"What's your name, little brother?"

"Marcus."

"How old are you?"

"Ten. I mean, umm, I will be next year."

He looks down the street toward the corner where street lights are coming on. The sky has turned to deep blue and against his face he can feel the feathery rub of a soft night wind. Up the street he can hear the sharp, high-pitched sounds of little kids playing in the street.

He looks down at the boy and remembers the red-rimmed eyes that met him at the door, and the door slamming in his face.

"OK. All right. I guess I'm a little hungry myself. I haven't eaten yet. Where can we get us a coupla hot dogs?"

The boy's wide, dark eyes light up. "Over this way," he says, and grabbing L.J.'s hand, leads him down the street.

VIII

· EIGHTEEN ·

Dear Baby Doll,

Well, I figured I'd set down and write you a letter. Doctor give me some new medicine for my arthritis. You know how my hands used to get with these cold, wet winters. So he done give me these little long, white pills. I told him, that ain't going to do no good, don't no medicine help. But he said try it, and I did. Now my hands feel like they did back when I used to do hair. So I said let me set down and write a letter to Baby Doll.

I figure even if you don't feel like talking to somebody sometime, a letter is different. A letter ain't about talking, it's about listening. You ain't got to say a word, just listen to what's on the page. And once you done heard what the letter got to say, then its your own business what you do with the news. But at least you done heard it. So Baby Doll, I'm going to tell you now just like when you was little, just set on down with your little cup of that funny tea you like, and listen to what I got to say.

I guess you not answering and not returning my calls cause of what L.J. done told you about your mama and how we all got together and decided not to tell you nothing about her. I know you mad cause that's how you would get when you was little, just get mad and don't say nothing to nobody for a while. You was always a stubborn little thing. After time pass, maybe you'll understand better and figure out we didn't mean no harm.

Lord knows, child, we thought we was doing the best thing for you, not telling you all this time.

When L.J. come to me that night in my kitchen, you and Joon and Clo T. was down to the Piggly Wiggly picking out a pot roast for Sunday dinner. (I remember cause the weather had just turnt cold and the leaves was turning red and orange and falling off these trees out here, except for the magnolia and the pines.) I said to myself, like I did the first time y'all came down here, I done seen them eyes before. That night we got you, I only seen him a couple of minutes. Rag-tailed little thing, scared to death carrying you all that way in his little skinny arms, covered with rain and jumping like a jackrabbit every time lightning flashed. Never would of thought he would grow up to be so tall and fine and handsome looking. But soon as I seen that boy standing there in my kitchen, them pretty, deep-set eyes shining, I said to myself, I done seen this child before.

That night during the storm, if I hadn't of been so taken with you, looking just like a little basket of flowers, grinning and not even thinking about crying, I would of made him come in that night and set hisself down and tell us the whole story. Asked him who you was, made him tell us what a little thing like him was doing carrying a little baby in his arms in the rain. But no sooner did I take you in my arms and start holding you and trying to keep you warm, that that little boy tore out of my shop like he stole something, instead of doing what he really did, which was bring us the best thing anybody ever give us. You.

Before he left though he told me what your mama, Vaughn, said to him that night. Said, don't tell nobody nothing. Said she was hell bent on you not ever finding out who she was. Well, that wasn't his exact words, him being just a little boy, but you know what I mean.

So when L.J. come to me that night in the kitchen twenty years later, I thought maybe he was just going to offer to help me roll out my dough for scratch rolls. Not that I would of let him, because he sure didn't look like much of a cooking man. And anyway you know how I can be about my cooking. I just don't like nobody in my kitchen when I'm serious about my cooking, sucking up all the air, getting in the way.

But he didn't want to help do nothing. He just come in my kitchen, stood in my doorway looking all serious, them pretty deep eyes fixed on me while I'm working, rolling out my dough. He started talking bout this and that, not saying much of nothing really. Got downright embarrassing cause I could tell he wasn't saying what he really wanted to say. Finally neither one of us said nothing for a long time. I was just fixing to open my mouth to say, "What's troubling you, boy," when he says, "Big Mama, something on my mind I got to tell you.'

He didn't say nothing at first, just reached into his pocket and pulled out something. I thought he was pulling out a letter or something, but when I looked, he done pulled out a two-dollar bill all folded up. He looked at me and said, "This mean anything to you?"

I looked at him and wondered, "What this boy talking about?" He held that bill up by his face and just looked at me. Then I thought for a minute, and it come to me. Well, you could of knock me over with a feather. I remembered the boy who brought you to us had a two-dollar bill sticking out of his shirt pocket.

I said to myself, Lord a mercy, life is strange.

Then it seem like the whole story done spilled from that man like river water over a levee that just can't hold it no more, all about the woman, Vaughn, and him. I could tell he was upset about it, look like he had some kinda big old weight hanging on his shoulders. So then he put it all on me. Big Mama what must I do? Tell her? Tell her about her mama? So I said, if you was going to tell her, why come you waited til now? Why didn't you tell her way back when you saw her in that bus station up in Joplin?

Then he look at me with them eyes, looking like the saddest man in the world. Big Mama I done promised her mama I wouldn't never tell her. I ain't told a soul about this til now, and I feel bad enough just telling you. Her mama wasn't real proud of the kind of woman she was and the kind of things she done, and Handy was such a small little town, she felt like that her reputation would hurt the child.

Then he said, "I know Olivia want to know who her mama is. I just don't know what to do." Then he sat down with his head between his hands. I could tell right then there must of been something special between him and your mama. Something real special and deep. Could tell by the look on his face.

Then he start telling me more, telling me about his old man and what a no-count he was. Said the old man didn't mean no harm, and he reckoned he did the best he could by him. But he told me, 'Big Mama, Olivia's mama give me something I ain't never had before.

231

The feeling like somebody really cared. She taught me how to hold a fork, how to say thank you and please.' He say he owe her for the kind of man he turnt out to be. Then he said, 'Big Mama, I just couldn't go back on my word to her.'

I put down my rolling pin and I sat down too, and there the two of us was. Nobody saying nothing.

Finally, he said, Big Mama, Olivia always talking about what a wise woman you are. That you always knowing what's best. That you always got the best answer. She told me how you be helping folks in town, this one and that one, with they problems. Giving advice and such. So he look at me and said, Big Mama, tell me what to do and I'll do it.

Now you know that was the last thing I wanted to hear. It's one thing to be telling somebody from church how to fix up they credit so they can buy them a house, or tell somebody how to get rid of they baby's whooping cough, but my own family, my own Baby Doll, that's something else.

Well, I told him I'd sleep on it. So I did. Child, I wrestled with that one. The boy made a promise and him being the sort of boy he was, he was set on keeping it. On the other hand, they's some things that everybody got a right to know, regardless of what somebody else want.

Well, I told Joon. Then I told Clo T. and Glodean and Country, thinking if we put our heads together we could figure out something and come up with some kind of answer. We even had a meeting on it like we used to do when you was little. We talked long into the night one night after supper. First we said, tell her. She got a right to know. Then we said don't. What she don't know won't hurt her. Back and forth, back and forth. We just couldn't figure out nothing.

So I told L.J., boy, I'm sorry. I wrestled and wrestled, but I don't have no answer for you. You the one made the promise and you right for wanting to keep it. But then you the one got to live with Baby Doll. You got to decide for yourself what to do. You got to do whatever's in your heart.

I could see the boy was troubled bad, caught up between two women special to him, you and your mama. But I couldn't bring myself to tell him what to do. I said whatever he decided, the rest of us, well we would go right along with it.

Well, I didn't hear nothing else about it. Finally, the night of the wedding, during the reception in the Y.W.C.A. parlor while you and Joon was cutting a rug and everybody was drinking punch and laughing and having such a good time, L.J. came over to me. Big Mama, he says, I decided I would not tell her. Then he look over at you, just dancing and smiling all happy. He said, Look at her. Sometimes it's better just to let things be. If I tell her, she be so upset, be asking me, why come you didn't tell me before? Why come you kept this from me all this time? But mostly, it was the promise to your mama. So I said yes, that probably is the best thing. This is the last we'll speak about it.

Sometimes the truth is a hurting thing. The older the truth, the bigger the pain, and this one was so old it was wearing whiskers. So L.J. and me figured it best you not ever know nothing about it.

I guess we shoulda knowed better, cause the way it turnt out, the boy had to tell you. You would of found out on your own, and if somebody just got to know the truth, it's better they find out from somebody that love them. And that boy, rest his soul, love you. I tell you, it breaks my heart that he done went off and did what he did, going off into that river. But I tell you what, I never did believe that he was gone. I just got a feeling he's cooling his heels somewhere, that someday he's going to come back to us.

I just got a feeling.

I got more to say but I'm going to end this letter now because my chicken's about to burn and because the rest I got to say I want to say when I can see you. It's been a good little while since you been down here, and the folks at Sweet Rock been asking after you. They always talking about when you was little, how you used to sing so pretty. I tell them you doing just fine. I just know you going to stop being so mad after while and come on back to visit, cause you ain't never stayed away too long. I'll be waiting, cause like I said, I got more to tell.

Love,
Big Mama

Olivia stared down at the handwriting on the onion-skinned paper, the pages now frayed and rippled with handling. She placed the pages in order, from first to last.

More to tell.

It was the eleventh time she had read the letter since the night she'd opened it more than two months ago. And each time she read it she hoped that somewhere, in a missed word or misunderstood phrase from the last reading, she could now better understand why Big Mama and L.J. had taken it upon themselves to withhold information that it was her right to know, and that might have changed her whole life. But reading the letter now hadn't much changed the way she felt about what they'd done. They had conspired against her, the two of them, and the others, not having a choice really, went along. They had kept her from knowing the identity of her own mother and father, and that had hurt her deeply. Unforgivably, it seemed at the time. But now, after so many readings, the letter did not make her angry. Finally, she could read it with reason (detachment, even), her questions clear and rational. What was it about her mother, what dark thing loomed in her past that would make her not want her own daughter to know about her very existence? And why, when it was so obvious that Olivia, a grown woman, should have been told the truth despite her mother's wishes of some forty years ago, the two of them still felt bound to hide the past from her?

The night L.J. and Olivia argued, the echo afterwards had filled the house with a hollowness befitting a forest after a felled tree. Olivia lay sprawled across her bed listening to it, the swelling noiselessness of L.J.'s departure, staring up at the ceiling with her hands tucked behind her head. She knew he would come back. Yes, it had been a terrible fight, their worst. Yes, her anger had scared even her, and she had sent him away and told him never to come back. But surely after playing his heart out at the club, losing himself in the music the way he always did, he would come back if only to get his things, and they could talk like two rational adults.

She'd gone to the kitchen. A glass already sitting out by the sink, enough bordeaux in the bottle on the door of the fridge to flatten her senses, to ease the waiting.

She'd gone back to the bedroom. Sat her glass down on the nightstand, and waited. Sipped a small swallow of wine. Leaned back again, waited. Maybe she should call the club. No, better just to wait for him. He'd have to come back eventually. But the longer she waited, the angrier she became. She picked up the phone and called Big Mama, tearful, her thoughts tangled and her mind in disarray. Why? she'd asked her. How could you? Both of you? "Oh, Baby Doll," Big Mama had said. "Come home. Come home now."

"No. I want to stay here. I need to talk to L.J."

"I can explain everything that happened. We had reasons why we did what we did."

"Tell me now."

Big Mama was silent. "I'll come up there."

Sure she would. Big Mama hadn't traveled outside of Handy since Johnson was president. Scared to death of anything that traveled above the ground and the pain in her joints too bad for anything that traveled over it.

"No." She collected herself. "I'll be all right. I've got to go now."

So she waited. In a million years, she would never have dreamed that he would not come back.

Big Mama had called back the next night, and Olivia spoke only long enough to tell her about L.J.'s accident. But she already knew, of course. Big Mama always had ways of finding out such things. Once again, Big Mama had asked her to come home, and again she'd said no. Because she wasn't up to a trip, not now, and besides, what if he hadn't drowned but managed to save himself, came back, and she wasn't there? "Slim to none" meant only that; it didn't mean no chance at all.

Big Mama's calls came, three in all in as many days, and thank God for a machine that let you listen to the caller's voice and decide whether you wanted to speak. She could not stand to hear any more reasons, excuses. And so the long letter, arriving a week later, sat on a corner of the night table, Big Mama's swirling hand staring at her as she closed her book at night and turned out the light for sleep.

It sat there, unopened, for months.

Now, sitting in her kitchen sipping tea and looking out at the chain-link fence that separated her house from the Fortman's next door, she watched a busy squirrel scamper up the walnut that threw dappled shade against her kitchen window. She folded the pages carefully and slipped them back into the envelope.

More to tell.

Olivia tried to imagine what she could mean by that. Did she know something about L.J.? Had he contacted her? When she first read it, she thought of calling Big Mama, then remembered—Big Mama wasn't giving up any more news over the telephone or in a letter, that was clear. No more news would come until they were face to face. Meanwhile weeks of reading and rereading the letter had softened Olivia's heart. For Christmas, she sent Big Mama gifts in abundance (a year's subscription to *Southern Living*, a soft flannel nightgown in powder blue, a ten-pound Smithfield ham, something for the table Big Mama always spread for Uncle Joon's two sisters, who made an annual Christmas pilgrimage to Handy from Lubbock, Texas), along with a note saying, "I'll be home as soon as the shop repairs are done."

Olivia poured loose tea grounds into the sink, ran warm water over the white Corning Ware cup and told herself a trip home would be good for her, what with all the stress of overseeing the renovation, choosing paint, tiles, carpeting and light fixtures. The repairs, which had dragged on longer than expected, were days away from completion, she'd been promised. Meanwhile, she could make plans to travel, with any luck, as early as next week.

She leaned against the sink counter, her chin in her cupped hands. She looked at her watch. This time of morning, Big Mama would be done with her breakfast and her wash, and ready to sit down to watch *The Young and the Restless*. It had been so long since she had seen her that it was difficult to shape a satisfactory image in her mind. It alarmed her for a moment that she couldn't rightly recollect her face, but what came to her mind most readily was Big Mama's hands: big-boned and strong-looking, veiny and weathered with brown spots on their backs. Over time, arthritis had knotted her joints and made her hands seem bigger than Uncle Joon's. When she was little they seemed like hands that could move hills from one county to another. Big, but quick; they could snap peas fast as lightning, whip batter into smooth-textured cakes that were a marvel of scratch-baked perfection. In the shop, they'd whipped up miraculous bouffants from two spoonfuls of hair and turned dull, yellowed gray to shiny ringlets of Autumn Sunset or Midnight Mink. Clo T. could do hair all right, Glodean and Country could stitch up a dream. But Olivia had seen Big Mama's hands massage away killing pain, swab moist foreheads until burning fevers cooled, and pull new, slippery life from women's bloody wombs.

And once, she'd even seen them raise the dead.

Olivia was about eight years old. It was Saturday, her day of the week to stay with Big Mama and Uncle Joon. The shop phone rang late in the evening while Uncle Joon was out on a plumbing call. Clo T. had gone home and Olivia sat in her usual corner drawing and singing, waiting for Big Mama.

Big Mama grabbed the phone in the middle of her work—washing sinks and sweeping up hair from the floor—and right away, Olivia could tell something was very wrong somewhere in Handy.

"Lord no," was what she could make out, as Big Mama's face turned down and her balled fist rested on her hip. "What?" she said. "Did you call Doc Robicheaux?" Then a long pause, and "I'll be right there."

Big Mama went upstairs to the kitchen and came back with five mason jars, which she stuffed into a potato sack. She moved about the shop with such a swiftness of purpose, turning out lights and locking doors, that Olivia knew they'd be going somewhere in a hurry, and there'd be no time for dilly-dallying. Without so much as a word from Big Mama (just the set of her jaw was instruction enough), Olivia began gathering up her Betsy Wetsy and her Romper Room blanket for the trip. Before Big Mama even said "Baby Doll, let's go," Olivia stood beneath her, clutching doll and blanket, ready to travel.

"We got to make haste," Big Mama said.

Uncle Joon had taken the truck, so Big Mama climbed behind the high steering wheel of the green Rambler wagon, craning her short neck and gripping the wheel to see above it. Off they went at the highest speed Big Mama could manage in the twenty-year-old heap, bounding along the red-dirt roads of the piney woods and around the creek bend as a light mist fell on the pine trees.

Old Lady Hathaway lived in the woods about three miles from the town, her small cottage tucked within a cluster of giant poplars and spruce just beyond the final loop of the river. The sun was just setting when they pulled up into the sand-covered yard, and four chickens clucked and scurried toward the crawl space beneath the house. The old woman's black housemaid, Ginny, ran out onto the wood-slatted porch, sobbing. A bright red checked bandana sat askew on her head, barely covering wayward tufts of nappy black hair. "It's too late," she said, wiping her eyes and rubbing her hands on the skirt of the loose-fitting yellow housedress. "I'm waiting for a call back from the funeral home."

Big Mama did not speak; she walked right past the girl into the house, with Olivia, her blanket gripped under one arm and Betsy Wetsy headlocked under the other, following close on her heels. At the bedroom door, they stopped. Lying on a small brass bed with faded red-and-blue cotton quilts pulled up to her neck, Old Lady Hathaway was the whitest white woman Olivia had ever seen; her skin was eggshell colored and translucent as wax paper. "Baby Doll, sit down there in the corner," Big Mama told Olivia, and pulled the five mason jars from her sack.

The wood-paneled room was dark except for a single lamp on a round table by the old woman's bed, and in the air hung the musky odor of damp wood, fried fish, and bay rum. Ginny stood at the doorway dabbing at her eyes with a handkerchief, while Big Mama placed two fingers against the old woman's forehead, then her neck.

She dispatched Ginny to the kitchen to boil a pan of water, and when she returned with it, Big Mama mixed the powders and weed-looking roots from the Mason jars into a greenish, acrid-smelling paste. She spread the paste onto a towel, then lifted the woman's night-gown and placed the towel across her bony, white chest.

Olivia watched in wonder as Big Mama worked, her large hands busy, her forehead etched with a frown of determination and purpose. The woman did not stir, her hands and arms limp as a rag doll's, Olivia recalled. Then Big Mama called for cool water, and when Ginny brought back the pan, Big Mama began blotting the woman's forehead gently with a water-soaked cloth.

After what seemed like hours, Old Lady Hathaway still lay motion-less. "It ain't no use," Ginny said, now composed and resigned. "Big Mama, you done all you could."

"Hush, child." Big Mama looked at Ginny crossly. Then she asked an odd question. "What time do the robins out back start to sing?"

Ginny shrugged. "'Bout six, I s'pose."

Big Mama went to the window above Old Lady Hathaway's bed and opened it wide. "Well," Big Mama said. "She might be all right by then, if she gonna make it at all. But we got to sit watch, though, in case she wake up in the night. Meantime, go get a glass of water and set it right by her bed. That'll be the first thing she'll want, come morning."

And so the three of them sat watch like sentries, Ginny in a straight-backed chair, Olivia on the floor in a corner, and Big Mama, some-times sitting on the side of the bed rearranging the towel and dabbing cool water on the woman's face, sometimes kneeling at the bed, her large hands folded steeple-like, her eyes closed. As the night wore on, Olivia drifted in and out of sleep using her doll's tummy as a pillow and her blanket pulled up around her shoulders.

Morning brought a yellow-orange glow of sunlight that pierced the pine branches visible through the window and glinted against the brass of Old Lady Hathaway's bed. Olivia yawned and stretched. Through the window floated a damp breeze carrying the scent of honeysuckle. Both Big Mama and Ginny were fast asleep, Big Mama in a wicker rocking chair she'd brought in from the porch, and Ginny on a cedar chest she'd moved near the bed, where she sat snoring softly, her head leaned back against the wall, her mouth agape.

Olivia looked at the old woman whose face caught the glow of the early morning sun, and though she still looked pasty, it seemed now as though blood moved beneath her skin.

Olivia felt the urge to pee and got up from the floor to search the house for a bathroom. She looked at Big Mama, whose head had dipped sideways against the rocking chair back, her glasses sitting lopsided on her nose. She looked at Ginny, head still leaned against the wall, a trail of spittle runneling down her chin from a corner of her mouth.

She would have to find the bathroom on her own. She moved to get up and go look, but then had a frightening thought. What if there was none? She'd heard of places in the woods like this that had outhouses still, and she would have to go scrabbling through tall weeds and thickets to relieve herself over some wooden hole surrounded by bees, mosquitoes, and ticks.

She hated this thought, but quietly put on her sneakers and laced them up. She was about to leave the room when she heard a sound that made her stop. There were birds chirping through the open window. They started quietly at first, then a full chorus of tweets and twitters overtook the breezy stir of tree rustle.

Just then, something happened that Olivia could hardly believe. The old woman, Mrs. Hathaway, opened her eyes. She leaned forward, raising herself up on her elbows in bed, then reached a purple-veined hand over to the nightstand and took the glass of water. She turned up the glass, swallowing long and slow. Olivia just stared at her, mouth open, and the woman gave her an angry look. "Who opened up that goddamned window?" she yelled hoarsely. "Y'all know I don't like to hear those damn birds disturbing my sleep!"

With that, Big Mama and Ginny both awakened. Ginny jumped up from the cedar chest and said, "Praise the Lord!"

Big Mama rushed to the bed. She attempted to feel the woman's forehead, but the woman swatted her hand away as if it were a gnat. "Leave me alone!" she said. Then she looked angrily around the room at all three, her eyes darting from one to the other.

"Well?" she said. "What y'all looking at? Git on out of here and let me be! Every one of ya!"

Sensing her work was done, Big Mama got her things together to leave. "Come on, Baby Doll," she said, and Olivia detected what she believed to be a smile buried just below the surface of Big Mama's cool expression.

"That's right, y'all git!" The woman was really yelling now, sitting completely upright in bed and waving her arm. "Lucy?" she said. "Lucy, get in here an' get these witches out of here! And bring me some food. I'm hungry as a goat!"

Big Mama whispered something to Ginny, who nodded, and then she grabbed Olivia's hand and said, "Let's go now." On the way back to the car, Olivia was puzzled. Who was Lucy? And she thought the old woman would have been a little more grateful to have been raised from the dead. Big Mama started the car, and as they backed out of the yard, chickens squawked and scattered, flapping their wings.

As they rounded the bend at Turtle River, the sun was peeking through the tops of pines as straight as broom straws. Olivia rubbed the sleep from her eyes, and wrapped her Betsy Wetsy in her blanket. She still puzzled why anybody, least of all Big Mama, would want to sit up all night long to help an ugly, mean old white woman. Big Mama must have been reading Olivia's mind, because she explained that Lucy was the old woman's daughter, who had died some thirty years ago. Big Mama said Mrs. Hathaway had kind of "lost her mind" years ago after her husband Joseph, Handy's only colored doctor, drove alone to Shreveport one Friday to pick up medical supplies and never returned. They found his brand new Studebaker in a ditch near the main road. Night riders, they said, got him. "She ain't been right in the head since then," said Big Mama. She told Olivia that everyone who knew her looked out for her, because they remembered the way she used to be.

A breeze stirred up red dust on the road, clouding the pine trees in brown haze. Big Mama shook her head, looking straight ahead leaning forward against the steering wheel, her mouth tightening. "Shame," she said. "Shame what they done to that man. Wouldn't never hurt a flea, but he married her, and well, we knowed it was just a matter of time before sumpin' bad happened."

Big Mama turned to Olivia, her face showing a hint of smile as they passed a stand of evergreens. "She old and mean now but she used to be as kind as can be," Big Mama said. "That girl, Ginny? Mrs. Hathaway took her in when she didn't have no place to go. Raised her like her own. I owe her myself," Big Mama went on. "Something that lady once did for me I'll never forget," she said, peering over the steering wheel at the narrow road unspooling itself through the dense woods. "Yes, Lord. I owe that woman plenty. Yes, indeed."

Olivia looked at Big Mama, her eyes fixed on the bending road as the yellow globe of sun lifted higher in the sky. She was hardly listening to what Big Mama was saying. Instead she remembered the dead white woman who'd raised herself up on her elbows, ranting with life. She looked at the wide palms and long fingers gripping the wheel. It was then she believed that no harm could come to her, as long as those hands were near.

Olivia touched her fingers to the rushing stream of water that filled the sink with suds, and began to wash the morning dishes. Big Mama's round face now arranged itself in her mind and filled it up. Now Big Mama could not resurrect her mother from the buried past, nor wrest her husband from the blue-black deep (if that was his fate), or from his wandering (if he had been lucky enough to live). Finally, Olivia thought, Big Mama had come across something not even she could fix.

· NINETEEN ·

Things were not going at all well.

When Olivia reached the shop, the workmen were there, along with Cora. "We got a problem," said the man dressed in paint-spackled blue coveralls, a tool belt dangling from his waist. He introduced himself as Stanley. He was short and squat, thirtyish and muscular with cornsilk hair tied in a ponytail and a cigarette drooping from his lips. "Come on back this way," he said, in a Texas drawl. And they stepped over swaddled sheets and paint cans and around ladders. When they reached the back by the bathroom and storage closet, Stanley pointed to a spot on the floor.

He bent down and ripped up a piece of the old carpeting from its stapling. As he stepped on the wood beneath the carpet, the floor gave off a creaking sound.

"Termites, ma'am," he said. "Big time. We can't lay new carpeting over this. We'll have to put some new flooring down."

"Oh, wow," said Cora.

"I know, ma'am," Stanley said, taking a slow drag from his cigarette. "If it ain't one thing, it's another. We run into this a lot though, in these here old places."

Olivia reached up to her head and twirled a piece of hair in her fingers.

"How bad is it?" Olivia said. "And how long will all this take?"

Stanley blew a thoughtful stream of smoke toward the ceiling, and shrugged. "Depends. Can't tell what we're dealing with until we get into it. I checked out your toilet, too. It's a wreck. The wood is rotten all around the bowl. We'll have to take it out, redo the floor, reset the whole thing."

Olivia frowned and shook her head. Already, it had been weeks, slow delivery due to a truckers' strike, the men had said. She wasn't so worried about finances, the nest egg in First Savings hadn't dwindled much, but since the fire not a dime had come in, and she'd already lost two customers to Cora, who'd turned her small kitchen into a temporary salon. Olivia could have taken customers in her house if she'd wanted to, but the relief at not having to go in every morning and face the sometimes impossible demands of women with dirty hair and illusions of unattainable beauty, well, that was something she couldn't deny. The tenderheaded Murphy twins vexed her nerves so with their flinching and squirming. And there was Mrs. Johnson, who never wanted those ragged split ends trimmed. But with L.J. gone, she'd needed to keep them coming, it was her job, and who would have thought it would have taken this long? She fully expected to be back in business by now.

"Will my insurance cover this?"

Stanley hooked his thumb into his belt loop, hollowed his cheeks and narrowed his eyes as he took another puff. "Should," he said. "This whole area was messed up from the fire. You oughta be OK on that score. If I was you, ma'am, I'd get them to replace all of this," he said waving his hand across the back room floor. "It'll take a while, with the strike and everything, but then you won't have no problems later."

Olivia sighed, and Cora spoke up. "It'll be OK, Ms. T. Just think how nice it'll all look when it's done. It'll be just like new. New floors and all."

Olivia nodded resignedly. "Yeah. All right," she said to Stanley, who was pulling up pieces of rotting, water-and smoke-damaged carpeting. "Sounds like I don't have much of a choice, do I?"

"Not if you want it done right."

"All right, then. Just do whatever you have to do."

"You got it, ma'am," Stanley said, nodding. "I'll get an exterminator in here. This looks like old damage, but you never know. Tomorrow I'll order some wood. We'll get you all fixed up. Be careful on your way out. It's a regular obstacle course out front."

Olivia and Cora left the back room and walked to the front of the shop, retracing their steps around the paint cans and between ladders. A younger, dark-haired workman in a New York Jets jersey stood high on one ladder wiring a light fixture, and another boy, who looked all of fifteen, was spackling Sheetrock tape on the back wall.

Olivia looked around the shop, remembering how much she had liked it before. She'd chosen new light fixtures of a modern brass design, and when she couldn't find the right shade of deep green, had decided to go with a lighter color, a pale mauve with magenta molding for the walls. It was a mess now, and the progress seemed to her unbelievably slow. Eventually, she knew, it would look beautiful again, better than before. But the work was taking so long now that she almost didn't care.

Cora had walked ahead of Olivia and turned to her at the entrance. She'd been unusually quiet today, Olivia noticed, and wondered what was on her mind.

"Ms. T." she said. "I got something to tell you."

Something in her tone caused Olivia's mind to brace.

"What's wrong, Cora?"

"Well," she looked down at her shoes, then down at her hands before turning to look back at Olivia. "It's about Johnice Crenshaw and Quintelle Tynes. They want me to do their hair."

"Well, I knew that you were taking care of them until we get opened up again."

"Well, not exactly. They want me to keep doing their hair. Even afterwards."

Olivia blinked. "Oh."

"I didn't know when to tell you. This might not've been the best time. It's just… they want braids now, both of them, and since you don't do that…"

"No. It's OK. Really."

"Really? You know I told them no at first. I didn't think it was right, taking customers away from you like that. I mean, it being your shop and everything…"

Olivia smiled. She could see how uncomfortable the girl was, and she couldn't believe that she was concerned about putting her at ease. But she found herself reaching a hand out to Cora's arm.

"Hey. Don't worry. Believe me, it's all right. I probably had more than I could handle anyway."

Cora smiled now, and spoke with a rush of relief. "You know that's what I kinda thought. I know this year's been kinda hard on you and so I figured, well, maybe she could use a lighter load."

"Cora, like I said, it's OK. Really."

The smile she wore felt pasted on her face, and she was beginning to lose her grip on it. She could hardly wait for Cora to leave so she could walk to her car, close the door, and let it go.

When Olivia did close the door of the Jetta and pulled roughly away from the curb and into the street at a speed that betrayed any sense of caution, she pinched in her eyes and lips.

Damn it.

At the first light on the Paseo, she stopped and reached for a strand of hair. She wasn't sure why she was so angry. The two women were her favorite customers, her friends, she thought, and had been with her forever. But it wasn't like the girl had stolen them from her. She'd actually told her customers, when they had called about the shop re-opening, that Cora was taking customers at home. She, on the other hand, was taking a long-desired break from the shop until it was up and going again. There was nothing underhanded about this. She'd taken a risk, and this was the way it had worked out.

But she hadn't expected the repairs to take so long, and this made four customers she had lost to Cora. Two others had gone to her after one appointment with Cleora Davis (her styling skills, they said, were old-ladyish); others were either doing their own hair or patronizing other places around town. She began to wonder if, when the shop was going again, she would have any customers at all.

Three o'clock in the afternoon and already she was exhausted. Talk of termites, trucker strikes, and deserting customers had made her neck muscles tight, and her head ached. She stopped by Hy's Market and bought three take-out cold pasta salads, red wine, and a box of

Pecan Sandies. She parked her car in the driveway and walked the steps to her house as if her ankles were trammeled in iron. Inside, she dumped the plastic containers of pasta salad onto the butcher block island in the kitchen, got a fork from the drawer, and opened each container.

She leaned her elbows against the island, flicked her shoes from her weary feet, and started with the bow-tie pasta, then moved to the fettuccini with parsley, and then on to the tortellini. She wondered if she should get a plate, a chair even, but decided not to bother. She found a corkscrew in the kitchen drawer, opened the beaujolais, and poured a brandy snifter half-full. Then she opened the cookies and took one bite, then went back to the bow-ties. If it was going to be a depressing evening for her, the least she could do was satisfy her every childish whim.

This was the time when she missed L.J. most of all. He knew her moods and how to handle them. When she complained about something at work, he knew to sit quietly and listen, nodding his head at intervals. When she was depressed, like now, he would put her feet up into his lap and knead her arches until she forgot her complaints and moaned with pleasure.

Later, looking down at the three half-empty plastic cartons and the half-full bottle of wine, she felt a little light-headed, and her neck and head muscles still ached. She drifted into her red-tiled bathroom and turned on the hot-water tap full strength. She ran her fingers through the water as the tub filled, removed her clothes, and got in. She leaned her head back and closed her eyes. In the darkness behind them, she saw L.J., seated on a wooden bench beneath the giant clock, leaning with his elbows on his knees, his head between his hands.

How long ago was that? Twenty-five years? It was in winter. She'd begun to wonder which she loved more, him or his music—the blue notes from his horn reaching inside her, pinging against her bones like a tuning fork finding its common tone. The music opened her up, and she followed it like rivers leading to places in her mind she had never been. She couldn't contain her admiration, so she didn't try, lavishing it on him, leading the applause after his solos, telling anyone who would listen, "The sax player, he's my friend. Well, I mean, we're going together." In no time, they were as inseparable as twins.

When he wasn't playing and she wasn't doing hair, they spent all their time together. They went to the Kansas state fair in Topeka, held hands along the midway, ate themselves silly with corn dogs and cotton candy. They went bowling and belly-laughed at each other's pathetic gutter balls. They made piles of leaves in Gillham Park and dove into them like preschoolers. They made love in his room on rainy Saturday mornings after she fixed pancakes and coffee, and then again during Cary Grant movies on late-night TV. They were inseparable, except for the weekend she decided to take the bus to Arkansas, and he, after first planning to go, stayed home to play the Kappa's winter dance.

"Can't turn it down, the pay's too good," he said, seeing disappointment shade her eyes. "And you know I've got to start putting some money away."

He'd meet her at the bus station Monday, he'd said. When she returned.

But by Sunday evening, the snow and ice buried the roads. The bus left Handy at dusk and was due in K.C. the next morning, but by eight Sunday night it had skidded off the icy road into the deep ravine off the highway shoulder outside Little Rock. She was not among the few passengers with minor bruises who were taken to the hospital, nor among those who (wisely, it turned out) waited three hours on the bus for the next one to come along. She'd gotten a ride to the train station in Little Rock with two policemen when she'd asked them how she could get to Kansas City sooner. But the trains were running even later. There was snow and ice on the tracks, delays, and more delays. She tried to call L.J. but he was gone. Finally, the train rolled into Union Station at ten minutes before midnight.

Later he would tell her how he spent that whole day, first waiting six hours at the bus depot (while two late buses pulled in, and then a third, each one without her), then how he'd heard about the accident, the bad roads, the injured passengers in the Little Rock hospital. How he'd called. No one had seen her, no one knew where she was. And hours and hours later, someone suggested the trains.

She'd gotten off the train, exhausted, frazzled. She saw the lone figure, sitting on a wooden bench under the big clock in the grand hall, rolling the brim of his gray hat beneath his fingers. His body, dwarfed by the high ceilings and cavernous empty space around him, was worn and slack, and worry defined the set of his back.

She'd called his name and almost ran to him. He met her at her fourth step, grabbed her and pulled her close enough for her to feel the tremble beneath his skin, then held her tightly enough to stop her breath.

Breathless, she'd sputtered out apologies, and even if he hadn't told her he was half-mad with worry, she would have known by the water that turned his dark eyes to glistening globes. "It's all right," he said, voice ragged and breaking. "I'm just so glad to see you." Then he cleared his throat and smiled. "Seems to me like you have a little trouble with buses."

She remembered Joplin, too, and laughed, taking his arm. Walking back to his car, she asked him how long he'd been waiting. "Let's see," he said, holding her door for her. "About sixteen hours, I guess."

When she realized he wasn't kidding, that he had actually sat on benches, checked schedules, called, paced, worried, and queried her whereabouts for a whole day, she became quiet; here was a measure of devotion that embarrassed her. How could she have been so stupid? And how could he have waited so long? He got behind the wheel and she turned to him. Before she could utter a word he spoke, looking straight ahead. "I just wanted you to know," he began deliberately, "that I'm gonna always be there. That you can always count on me."

She turned the hot tap on again. Lifted a wet sponge to her neck, squeezed warm water down her back, letting rivulets trail down her spine. She had never forgotten those words, or the way he'd held her that day beneath the big clock. Now she wondered if, buried in some bone-deep store of memory, there was a shard of recollection of the first time he had actually held her in that summer storm—her, an infant, him, all of nine years old—shuttling her from one life to another so different from what she might have known. Her rock-solid man, a little boy. *I'm always gonna be there,* he'd said. *You can always count on me.*

The irony of his words.

But Olivia's heart felt more wounded than cynical. He *had* been there. From the beginning, and every day, until the day when he wasn't.

The small digital clock on the porcelain vanity top projected 6:05 in even red digits. Olivia's skin felt shriveled. She stood up in the tub, dripping, her hair frizzed and beads of sweat studding her face and neck. She grabbed a towel from the rack, wrapped it around her and, still dripping, went to her bedroom.

Too early for bed, but her temples throbbed and weariness blanketed her. She sat on the gold chenille chaise in the corner by the bedroom's only window and, still wrapped in a towel, turned the small Zenith on the TV stand to the evening news. She flipped channels, half-hearing about the Dow Jones plunge and a cold front moving in from the north and the three percent drop in crime. Meanwhile, the alcohol, the hot bath, and thoughts of her husband tugged at her body like redoubled gravity.

She slumped into sleep, and in minutes she was on a stage in a big theater—her only audience Big Mama, Uncle Joon, Clo T., Glodean, and Country. But behind them, standing far in the back, were L.J. and a woman who looked like Olivia, only taller, darker, prettier. They waved to her, then turned and walked away, arm in arm.

When she awoke, hair still wet, towel twisted around her legs and torso, she sprang to her feet. It was morning now and the arm that she had tucked under her on the chaise was tingling numb. She looked at herself in the wood-trimmed dresser mirror—mistake; early morning nakedness was a crude and merciless thing. Eyes puffy, red-rimmed, and baggy stared at her from a mirror that rudely held nothing back. Her hair stood up like waves of black wheat. She grabbed the towel, rummaged on the dresser for a big-toothed comb, and tried to rake it through her tangled mess of half-dried hair.

That day, and for the rest of the week, Olivia had the idea that if she stayed in motion, kept her mind and body moving, she could outrun depression, leaving it collapsed and out of breath several laps behind her. On Tuesday morning she got into her car, having gotten it into her head to search the city for just the right shade of throw pillow for her avocado sofa. But after buying and returning three pillows in almost indistinctly different shades of red, she finally settled on a blood-dark crimson, which clashed horribly with the sofa and everything else in the room. It depressed her, so she returned the pillow for a bright yellow one (to improve her mood), and then focused her attention on just the right candlesticks for her dining table. They had to be wooden, hand-carved, with brass trim, Spanish-looking, like the one Erica had on *All My Children.* She spent five hours vainly driving from one shopping center to another, then settled for a gigantic lunch overlooking a fountain at Chez Marguerite's on the Plaza, and went home, depressed. The next day she continued her mission.

She could not find the right candlesticks, and decided that the world was a mean, uncooperative place (were carved wooden candlesticks so much to ask?) and felt perfectly justified when, sitting in the Jetta at the edge of the Hall's parking lot, she cried, loudly, luxuriously, for half an hour.

She went home. When it occurred to her that the days could possibly continue in a similar pattern for the rest of her natural life, she panicked. Nothing she was doing actually resembled living. Something big was needed, a shake up, a spark, something had to rattle the dice in her desperate, empty cage of a life.

The idea came as she was washing laundry in the tiny washroom off the kitchen and listening to the radio; a young woman with a five-note range and no style was singing a jazz standard. Olivia added an extra scoop of Tide to her whites and sang along, weaving florid notes around the tune. The child clearly could not sing—well, maybe she could sing a little, but she had no breath support, no real sense of pitch, and was singing through her nose. The placement was all wrong. Anyone with a real voice could do better. *She*, for example, could do better.

She sang long after clicking off the radio, and felt her shoulders spread and heart lift. She sang the song in a slightly higher key, and finding her true voice, sang it over while she handwashed her yellow silk blouse and gray sweater in the kitchen sink. Testing her upper range, she floated the song in a higher octave (ah, this is it, the right place) and sang louder while the white clothes clopped noisily in the dryer. When they were dry and put away, she danced a little cha-cha step over to the piano, and sat down, picking out notes and accompanying herself with one finger.

Before she knew anything, an hour had passed and she was still singing.

She reached down and found the phone number in L.J.'s old black leather-bound phone book right there in the piano bench. She felt her head spin at seeing his handwriting there, but moved past the feeling and dialed the number.

"Hello?"

"Jimmy, it's Olivia Tillman."

"Olivia!" he said.

It helped that he was glad to hear from her.

"Jimmy, I was thinking about what you said."

"Yeah?"

"At the bookstore, that time? About the club? Well, I was thinking I'd like to try it. I mean, I don't know if I can, but…well, it's been so long. But I do want to try it if you still want me. I want to sing."

Men everywhere. Olivia's house remembered the bass tones of men— walking heavy-footed across her floors, deep voices bouncing from wall to wall—and came alive. The guys were moving the piano out into the room, carrying drums and lugging cases of cymbals and horns and boxes of sheet music. Laughing and joking with each other, telling her how good she looked, how glad they were to see her.

It was early afternoon, cool outside, but sun streamed in from every window of the small living room, and scents of pine and patchouli aftershave mixed with husky laughter made Olivia feel that things had returned to what used to be. Whenever L.J. and the guys had needed to get together to rehearse some new tune, or had a special gig coming up that called for a little more polish than the usual casual outing, the men, L.J.'s oldest friends, would gather by the piano in their living room. They were like parties. Olivia would prepare enough food for an army—ham with tomato gravy, potatoes au gratin, black-eyed peas, and rice with okra—and then would sit close by listening, humming, her foot tapping on its own to the rhythms in the room.

Jimmy had been so excited about her singing at the new club that he'd immediately called up the members of the old house band. The renovation of the club was underway (Jimmy had started with his own money but was still looking for investors when Olivia called), and the new place would be opening in a few weeks. So the old trio—Walter, Cornelius, and Ace, and John Paul on alto sax—would back up Olivia, and Cornelius would teach her enough songs for a couple of sets. It would be the featured event at the grand, black-tie opening.

On her dining room table, Olivia laid out platters of garlic-creamed chicken, smoky baked beans, sweet-and-sour cole slaw, and pineapple upside-down cake she'd spent most of the previous day preparing, and watched them while they turned her living room into a jazz lounge. A drum set consumed half of the room, the piano the other, and a string bass and music stands fit in whatever space was left.

It was the first time the men had seen her since before the accident and they went out of their way to make her feel comfortable. This, after all, was not church music, and Olivia would need guidance through the complex maneuvers of jazz. Cornelius, a big shouldered, broad-framed man of sixty, put his black leather jacket and his fisherman's cap on the top of the piano, and rolled up the sleeves of his white shirt to his elbows. His wide fingers skipped up the keyboard in a flurry of broken chords, followed by a progression of block chords.

"Ah, still in tune," he said. He smiled at Olivia. "All right. Let's get to work."

Olivia sat leaning forward, her hands clasped, on the edge of a wing-backed chair they had pushed aside to make way for the drums, until Cornelius beckoned her to stand in the piano's curve.

Her face broke into a self-conscious smile, and she placed one hand on the piano while the other fumbled at her clothes, then dangled at her side.

"You got it, darlin', now you look like a singer," he said. "A star."

The first few tunes went well. The men praised her pitch and easy flow. "Sing that song, girl," John Paul called out when she glided through "Someone to Watch Over Me," wagging his head from side to side and smiling. Cornelius nodded from the piano, Walter swirled brushes against the drumheads, grinned, and grunted his approval. And "Autumn Leaves" clicked along in a steady groove. But "Send in the Clowns" faltered and stumbled a little. Olivia couldn't manage the changes, and kept forgetting the words to the second verse.

"I'm sorry," she said. "I'm not sure what it means, 'me here at last on the ground, you in mid-air.' Maybe it would help if I understood what the words mean."

Cornelius sat up straight. "You don't have to know what the words mean to sing them. It's just music. Just let the music lead you."

He played the beginning again. When they got to the second verse, Olivia stopped. "I'm sorry. I'll get it right. I promise."

Cornelius looked at her and smiled. "S'OK. Let's just go to another song for now."

They tried "You Don't Know What Love Is." Olivia liked the tune, but Ace frowned from behind his bass. "Uh-uh," he said. "That song ain't right for her. Her voice is too high to pull it off, plus it's in a minor key. Too sad for a club opening."

Cornelius didn't agree, but they put it aside. They got through "Embraceable You" in a slow, easy four/four with few problems. But when they tried "I Loves You, Porgy," Olivia had trouble with the pitches, and couldn't sustain the long phrases without taking a breath.

"You got to keep the line going there," Cornelius told her. "Don't break it up in the middle of the phrase."

"It's too slow. Speed it up a little," John Paul offered, and played the beginning of the tune on his alto a little faster.

"No, come on," Cornelius said. "That song can only be so fast. It doesn't work in a fast tempo."

Olivia tried again at the slower tempo, but by now she was exhausted. They took a break for twenty minutes, and while the men ate, Olivia looked through the pile of tunes Cornelius had set aside, some twenty in all, fast and slow, some with complicated changes. The task at hand suddenly seemed impossible. They started again, but Olivia felt she was singing worse. She was running out of breath, and she felt hoarseness coming on. She looked at her watch. They had been rehearsing two hours and forty-five minutes and had gotten through five songs. Of the five, only "Autumn Leaves," "Embraceable You," and "Someone to Watch Over Me" felt prepared enough to perform.

"We got plenty of time," Cornelius said, sensing Olivia's downcast mood at the way the rehearsal went. "Don't worry, we'll get you ready. You're gonna be great."

When the men had left, Olivia flopped into the wing-backed chair, leaned her head back, and closed her eyes. Who did she think she was kidding? The rehearsal was a disaster, and she was no jazz singer.

She thought of L.J. describing Vaughn's singing, the way it quieted a room. A spell-casting sound. What had he said? A sound like a finger on the heart. Olivia could not imagine having that effect on people; she couldn't even get through the songs. *She* had been the singer, and even though Olivia had never heard her voice, she believed she could never compete with it. Not now. She was no longer a girl of six or seven, spunky and cute, and she had long ago lost the fearlessness of ignorant youth. She tried to envision herself on a stage, microphone in hand, tables full of people expecting a show from her, and suddenly felt terrified. She was no singer, she could not do this. There was no way.

The doorbell rang. She thought one of the men might have left something, and sure enough, there was Cornelius's music case still under the piano. Good. There was no sense in delaying telling him. She went to the door.

Out of habit, she looked out the window onto the porch. What she saw made a small noise come involuntarily from her throat. There on her porch standing next to the paint-chipped green glider was that familiar worn-gray wool tweed coat with the black and white scarf tied loosely around her neck, the one she rarely left the house without. And that hat. Black, with a small brim, and a trim of red satin. How old was it by now?

Olivia stood at the door peeking out the window, dumbfounded. The old woman saw her and frowned with impatience.

"Well? It's colder than a witch's patootie out here," Big Mama said loud enough for Olivia to hear through the glass. "You gonna just stand there gawking, or you gonna let a tired old woman in?"

IX

· TWENTY ·

I N THE FULL SWING OF SPRING, uptown Broadway teems with shoppers, cyclists, joggers, dog-walkers, vendors, office workers, truant students, and camera-toting tourists. Today L.J., working musician, falls in step with the pedestrian parade. The expensive-looking thrift store jacket hugs his back snugly, and the hat—stylish, clean—is a nice touch. Deep gray, like the hat he was wearing the first time he met Olivia. The jacket was a steal. After a dozen trips to the Junior League Store, the first decent jacket he'd found in a forty-two long turned out to be a Harris tweed. Three hundred when it was new, he bet, maybe four. One tiny moth hole under the sleeve you could hardly see, and a tag that said $39.95 (there was a tear in the brown silk lining). So with a cool spring sun at his natty back, he celebrates his good fortune with an afternoon walk.

At the light at 110th, he waits for the green, the noon sun sweetening the feel of the herringbone weave. A middle-aged woman next to him, dyed blond and dressed in a navy business suit, fumbles in her Vuitton purse, and before the light changes drops a brass fountain pen on the pavement. L.J. picks it up. She smiles, gushes her thanks. "No problem," he says, touching a finger to the snapped brim of the smooth gray felt.

He smiles at her (and himself), remembering a woman months ago who'd given him a damning look and grabbed her purse at the sight of his rumpled form rising up from a park bench.

He crosses at the light and switches the alto horn case he's carrying from right hand to left. He has forgotten how much lighter the alto is than the tenor, he hasn't played one in so long. He'd practically tripped over it, lying in a box on the floor of the thrift store when he was headed to the checkout counter with the tweed jacket and hat. Good key action, and they weren't asking too much for it. If anything will make the boy break into a skip, this will.

He'd caught the boy skipping once, and it told him all he needed to know.

One childhood Christmas day, L.J. himself had skipped like a girl, happy as a clam. There'd been a knock at the rooming house door. Purvis' new lady friend, MayElla Rule, big-breasted, round-hipped, with a broad gap-toothed smile (and smelling faintly of roses and Vaseline), looked down at him with her wandering left eye, and adjusted her deep red wig. "Hi, baby," she said, rubbing his cheek with the back of her hand. L.J. looked over his shoulder to see who she was looking at, and then realized she was looking at him as best she could. She planted a rose-scented kiss square on his cheek and said, "Now, ain't you a handsome-looking young thing."

The box she placed in his hands was wrapped up in red and ribboned in green. The red fire truck was the same one he'd been eyeing in the Christmas window downtown at Jackson Brothers, but how did *she* know? Later that afternoon the aroma of fried chitlins and cornbread, potato casserole, and ham and pineapple rings mingled with the music—Purvis singing and pounding out a new tune he'd written, "Moonlight and Mistletoe"—as pots clanked in the kitchen and L.J. played with that truck. Outside, a gentle snow fell. After the biggest dinner of L.J.'s young life, Purvis pressed eight dimes to the boy's palm and scooted him out of the house with a plate of hot food to take down to MayElla's bedridden friend Easter Jenkins, while he and MayElla retreated to his bedroom. L J. skipped the whole six blocks, catching snowflakes on his tongue, spilling nothing.

A perfect Christmas.

So he knew the joy that sparked little-boy feet into that slide-shuffle-hop, had seen it that first day Marcus devoured that hot dog, then skipped and danced like a jumping jack, as if the sweet meat and hot mustard were just too good for plain walking.

At a fruit stand on Ninety-sixth, L.J. stops and buys a peach. One bite and the perfect, sweet juice runs down his chin. He grins, buys another one for the boy. It'll be a reward for a well-played C-scale.

That first day he pegged Marcus's life as a trial no young boy should suffer, given that a hot dog sparked rhythm in his feet. And he was right. The stench of poverty gagged L.J. even before the apartment door was wide open: dirty diapers, urine-soaked mattresses, stale beer, and week-old cigarette butts. One minute inside revealed more: the ratty, cheap coat (the boy grabbed it at L.J.'s order), the flimsy-soled sneakers, furniture more fit for sidewalks than living rooms, and clearly, nobody at home to call him back for a warmer wrap, or to question his leaving with a stranger.

The kid might as well go to a house where somebody would actually be there. There was no law that said a woman had to be at home evenings to be able to get those government checks, and that woman with the red-veined eyes sure wasn't. And no law saying she had to treat her deceased cousin's kids (both Marcus and Roy) as well as she treated her own. And forget about the daddy; there wasn't even a *picture* of a man around. No wonder the boys were turning out the way they were, the older one ripping off strangers and doing God knows what else, the younger one roaming the city like a stray puppy in a world overrun with wolves.

Today the younger one, the one worth saving, will meet him after school at his apartment for the surprise.

He turns the corner to stop in at Clyde's. The little bodega always had the best coffee, good and strong and hot, and good fresh bread. And he needs a few things since the kid is coming. He picks out a fresh salami, Muenster cheese, a jar of horseradish mustard, and Clyde's specialty, Jewish rye with scallions, before turning into the familiar alley behind the dry cleaners, the bakery, the shoe repair shop.

"So you telling me this kid is the brother of the dude that ripped you off?"

Honeymoon Johnson sits hunched over on an orange crate slathering mustard on rye bread, then fills the sandwich with slices of salami and Muenster cheese.

"Yeah. But Moon, the kid is different," L.J. says. "He's got some serious talent. Serious. And he's only nine."

Honeymoon smirks, then takes a bite of sandwich. "You forget where you are? This here's New York. You ain't seen nine-year-old kids like we got up here."

L.J. takes a long swallow from the bottle of orange juice he's brought. He hasn't seen the old man in a while, and he swears he looks years older, or maybe he's just forgotten how the street can scale your skin, crust your body like a hardened shell. Between the work that's pouring in now—recording jingles, punch-and-cookie fashion shows, Rotary Club receptions in Jersey, well-heeled weddings in Benson-hurst—and the boy, L.J.'s had little time to check in with his friend.

"This kid is different." L.J. rubs his hands together, pacing up and down the alley while the old man eats. "You ought to hear him. I gave him one lesson, and man, the kid…he's something else. The first day, he's playing scales. The second day, he's thinking about tone, playing in tune better than me when I was his age. Plus he loves it. He'd play all day if I let him. I even picked up this alto horn at Sam's. Can't wait to give it to him."

Honeymoon stares at L.J. between bites. "How you meet up with this kid? And sit down. I feel like I'm being picketed."

L.J. tells the story, how after three trips to an east-side tenement and no sight of Roy, L.J. figured he could kiss that three hundred good-bye. The thief wasn't stupid; he knew how to lay low. But the boy had a little brother, and he was a different story. A decent meal and his eyes lit up. He seemed in need all the time, and not just for food. So L.J. reached deep and found enough for a haircut, T-shirts, and a new pair of drawers (he couldn't bear the sight of the dingy beige creeping up above the boy's bagging blue jeans). One look at Marcus reminded him of days he'd wanted to forget.

When it came to food, though, L.J.'s childhood had held more prom-ise. Dirt poor, a missed meal here and there, but nobody starved in the country. In the tiny farming towns of L.J.'s early youth, a hungry boy could stumble on a watermelon patch to crawl into, a row of snap peas just lying in the sun. A pecan tree ready for shaking. Sugar cane, maybe, depending on where you were. And even in the winter, a kindly neighbor's back door. But hunger in the city was a different thing. So when a city kid says he's hungry, you feed him. Marcus didn't say thank you, but grabbed his hand, held it, walking down the street. L.J.'s eyes fluttered, his stomach twinged; a little boy's hot, tugging hand was an odd sensation, catching him off guard.

When he finishes, L.J. waits for the old man to speak. Honeymoon closes his eyes slowly and opens them again. He looks tired. And the bushy hair beneath his cap has gotten even whiter the last few months.

"I didn't mean to bend your ear like that, man. It's just—"

"I got you, man. Ain't much happens in a man's life like that to get your juices going. Something like what you talking about, or some good music, or maybe a woman somebody done left back home." He raises his eyebrows, cocks his head toward L.J.

L.J. looks away, sighs. "I'm working on it."

Honeymoon leans back against the wall and folds his hands in his lap. "Now, then," he says. "Where you say you from? Kansas City? They must grow 'em foolish down there. Cause only a fool in New York would go looking for somebody that held him up with a gun. You get took for your money, you say, OK, you win. And go on 'bout your bidness. You take your lumps. Hope it don't happen again. You go trying to make it right, you just asking for some hell to come knocking on your door."

"Now you got yourself mixed up with his brother." He shakes his head. "You better watch your back, boy."

L.J. leans over and looks at Honeymoon. "I'm through with that punk. It's the boy, the little kid. I just want to—"

"I know. You just want to help."

He says these words with a tone of sarcasm, as if L.J.'s breaking some kind of unwritten law, and any idiot should know better. What's wrong with helping the kid? He's offended. Try and do a good turn for somebody and this is what you get.

"Well, I gotta go," L.J. says. "The kid's coming over after school." His words are callused with resentment.

"Suit yourself."

He fills a plastic bag with slices of bread and a few slices of salami and cheese and sits them on the ground near the old man.

"Here's some dinner," L.J. says. "Knock yourself out."

"Thanks," Honeymoon says, and pulls out his harmonica. As L.J. walks away, he recognizes the song he's playing: "I Got a Right to Sing the Blues."

"Marcus, that you?"

"Yeah, it's me." His voice is as high pitched as a little girl's.

L.J. unlatches the door, and Marcus tumbles into the room, a tiny bundle of motion. He runs to the bed, sits on it, and begins to bounce up and down.

L.J. winces as the springs squeal. These kids today, jumping around all the time. The constant energy is baffling. L.J. figures he must be getting old, because sometimes it just gets on his nerves. "Marcus, hey, don't bounce on the bed like that. You'll ruin the springs."

He stops and looks sheepish. Then he hops off the bed and looks under it. He reaches under the bed and gropes around for L.J.'s horn.

"Wait, Marcus. Aren't you hungry? I thought we'd get something to eat, play later."

He figures the kid won't want to eat once he's seen his new horn.

The boy's moon eyes grew bigger. "Ooh, yeah. Can we go get a Mighty Burger?"

L.J. reaches in his closet and grabs a gray and white windbreaker, another thrift-store special. The salami can wait. It's too nice a day to stay inside. "Yeah. We could do that."

Marcus darts toward the door and L.J. pulls him back by the tail of his jacket. "Not so fast. Come on. Let me zip you up."

Marcus is short for his age. Standing to his full height, he only comes to L.J.'s belt buckle. He stands quietly looking up at the tall man while L.J. pulls the zipper up and pulls his collar up around his ears.

"This the only jacket you got? Kinda thin. It's nice outside, but not that warm."

"This all I got. This and that big coat I wore last time."

L.J. remembers the coat. A decent weight, but sleeves so short they were up past his wrists. "Well. All right. Let's go."

They've been on several excursions in the city since meeting. But the boy is so excited and rambunctious he's hard to control. When the Circle Line ship cruised the Statue of Liberty, Marcus climbed rails like a monkey and leaned so far over that L.J. had to hold on to his belt for the whole trip. In the planetarium he darted from room to room like a crazed mouse (once knocking over a blue-haired woman's walker), and at the zoo he almost lost an arm trying to feed popcorn to a lion through its cage. So L.J. considered the entire city, looking for a place with no rails, rooms, or cages.

Coney Island clings to Manhattan's skirt tail like a hem of antique lace, a cobwebbed relic dusted with a century's memory. As they ride in the clattering D-train car, Marcus presses face and hands against the window as New York whooshes by in quicksilver flashes—skyscrapers and tenements, bridges leaping across rivers, factory chimneys spewing curled scarves of gray smoke. And finally the flat sprawl and uncluttered sky of an island near its ancient shore.

By now the day is hot, the sky a sharp blue and the sun splendid overhead. L.J. walks and Marcus skips along the uncrowded streets, in and out of old shops along the boardwalk that hawk T-shirts, sunglasses, saltwater taffy. The arcades draw them in and they play games, tossing little basketballs toward too-small hoops, plastic rings at impossibly distant Coke bottles, dollar games that steal you blind, and then laugh at themselves losing.

When finally Marcus glimpses the ocean his skipping stops. He stares for a moment, eyes bugged, mouth slack, then tears out across the pale sand like an arrow shot toward a distant mark. L.J. watches the little boy, his own face stuck in an uncontrollable grin. Suddenly, he realizes he has never seen the ocean before himself. There was that one night in Biloxi when he was seven and Purvis had played a party at a seafood joint a block near the shore, but it was too dark to see. That night, while they slept in a five-dollar room at the YMCA downtown, Purvis told L.J. to listen—he could hear the ocean pounding a samba rhythm against the shore.

L.J. couldn't hear it then, but didn't think he'd missed much. But here he stands, a man of more than fifty seeing the ocean for the first time, listening to the riffs of the swelling surf and grinning like a fool as the spidery dot that is Marcus dances like a little dervish along the water's edge. Silhouetted by the sun's slant, he chases three skittering seagulls, teases waves that tease him back. L.J. only watches, hands deep in his jacket.

Ocean breeze swirling his shoulders, L.J. fixes on the spot where the two hues of blue bleed into each other, one like simmering steel, the other muted and fine as bone china. The air is quiet with few sounds, a gull's forlorn caw, the crush of water pounding sand. It's early in the year for the beach crowd, but a stout middle-aged couple strolls along the beach as a dirt-colored terrier scampers after them. A salt breeze gusts up and the woman grabs her enormous yellow sun bonnet, giggling.

Just beyond them, Marcus, sneakers in hand, dances toward the outgoing tide, then runs squealing as it chases him back. He turns to face L.J., laughing. His smile is a diamond in the sun.

Far out to sea, a giant wave of dull silver rises, crests, curls in upon itself, and surges toward land. At shore, L.J.'s eyes follow a foam-tipped tongue of ocean licking land, rolling in to erase itself, then rolling out, and in, erasing itself again. There's always another wave, he thinks. If only his mistakes were as easily swept away as the tideprint of lapping water on sand.

Or maybe they were.

Watching the sea, the boy, he feels almost happy. One thing is missing, and he wishes Olivia could see this big wide ocean, big enough to hold all the possibilities of a life. As another wave rises, crests, and crashes, he's suddenly overwhelmed with feeling for her. How long had it been since he'd seen Vaughn? Forty years. And yes, he'd missed her. But these last months away from Olivia were becoming unbearable.

He couldn't stand to think of Olivia gone from his life even a fraction as long as Vaughn had been. Of course he loved her for herself. Vaughn had been the bright light of his youth. Her affection had buoyed him above the murky and uncertain currents of his childhood for as long as he needed it, but in Olivia his heart had found its home. In the space behind his eyes, he could see Vaughn's arms outstretched, handing him her child. Maybe the friendship with Vaughn had been all about Olivia from the beginning. Her gift to him. If Vaughn had been his life raft, Olivia was his shore. He sucked in salt air, taking a deep breath. He needed to go home. Tell her the whole truth this time. All of it.

In the distance, a giant tanker is a speck beneath the sun before it disappears between the two blues. Walking along the shore, his collar upturned, he keeps the wild, dancing boy in the corner of his sights. Tonight, after practice, he'll fix dinner, give him a hot bath before sending him home, then write a long letter to Big Mama. Why hadn't he thought of this before? Tell her he's alive and well, wanting to make a new start. He'll plead his case and she'll understand, and help him get through to Olivia. Then, he'll make a plan.

It has grown cooler in an hour, the surf stronger now. L.J. remembers the thinness of Marcus's jacket, and though he hates to, calls him in from the shore. To his surprise, Marcus comes happily, giggling, without complaint. He's a mess, his rolled-up jeans salt-stained, his hands and feet covered in sand.

They find a water faucet near a stand of beach umbrellas. L.J. turns the faucet handle and Marcus washes his feet.

"Wipe your hands, then roll down your pants legs and dust them off." L.J. hands the boy a paper towel.

"Good. OK, pal. Put on your shoes. We'll come back another time."

Walking back, they see a castle rising from the sand, more than five feet wide. It is elaborately detailed with towers, moats, drawbridges. Nearby, a water stain like a giant shadow stretches toward it in the shape of a four-fingered hand.

"What's going to happen to it?" Marcus asks.

L.J. shrugs. He kneels down, and points to the water stain.

"The monster'll get it," he says.

"What monster?"

"The Coney Island Sea Monster. That's the hand of it, right there. At night the hand stretches across the sand and grabs all the castles and pulls them out to sea."

Marcus cocks his head and looks incredulously at L.J.

"Man, come on. That's some shit."

A little startled, L.J. shakes his head. So much for the innocent little boy he brought here.

"He also grabs little boys who curse."

"Sorry," Marcus says, and L.J. sees a look of real remorse. "No, but what really happens to it? Will it be here tomorrow?"

L.J. stands and claps sand from his hands. "Naw. The tide'll wash in. Drown it."

"It'll be gone?"

"Yeah. All gone."

"Oh." Marcus says.

"It's OK. The tide wipes everything away, makes it all clean and new. Gives everything a fresh start. So somebody can build another one even better."

"I wanna come back here and do it."

"Deal," L.J. says.

"Can we come back tomorrow?"

"Supposed to rain tomorrow. Maybe next week."

This pleases Marcus and he skips ahead of L.J. He doesn't stop skipping until he reaches the subway station.

Back in town, coming out of the Fifty-ninth Street station, they both squint at a sun that sends hard angles of afternoon light from beneath roaming clouds. The city air is cool but still soft, and a westerly breeze balloons Marcus's jacket. "I'm hungry," he says.

L.J. stops and looks at him. "It's not dinner time yet, and you just ate."

"That was a zillion hours ago," Marcus says, and frowns. "I'm hungry again."

It was an hour and a half ago. He just had two Mighty Burgers at the beach. How could anybody eat so much? L.J. sighs. He'd planned on fixing the boy a decent, healthful meal for dinner, but he fingers the bills and change left in his pocket. "OK. All right. We'll go down here and get some French fries and a drink. But then we gotta get back so you can practice and be in before dark. Before your...before Nita gets home."

"Aw, she won't care," Marcus says, and L.J. is sorry he mentioned the red-eyed woman's name.

They walk to a red-and-green-umbrellaed vendor's stand, and L.J. orders two cartons of curly fries and two lemonades. "That'll be four-eighty-five," says the tall, dark-skinned black man with a Jamaican accent.

L.J. reaches into his pocket, but before he can get out his money, Marcus has reached inside his own jacket.

He pulls out a crisp, new one hundred-dollar bill.

"I'm treating you." Marcus' round face stretches into a grin. "You paid for me. I'll pay for you this time."

L.J. is dumbfounded. "Marcus, what...where did you get that money?"

The vendor raises both his palms. "Whoa, buddy. I can't change that."

L.J. pays the man with a five, puts the change back in his pocket. Marcus walks away, eating, and L.J. follows him, circles him until he stops.

"Where'd you get the money, Marcus?"

He shrugs his shoulders. "I don't know. I don't remember. I already had it."

"Did somebody give it to you?"

Marcus takes a long slurp from his drink. He turns to walk away again. L.J. reaches for his arm.

"I'm talking to you, Marcus. All I'm asking you is where you got the money."

"Leggo of me," Marcus whines, and as he jerks his arm away, a dozen sea shells spill onto the ground, along with a small, plastic bag of white powder.

The boy quickly reaches for the spilled shells and the bag, but L.J. is quicker. He turns the bag in his hand and examines it.

"Gimme that back!" Marcus cries.

The boy grabs for it and L.J. swipes it from his reach. He is breathing hard now. "Marcus. Damn it. Roy gave you this, didn't he?"

The boy says nothing, slurps on his drink with his eyes cast toward his sneakers.

"Who'd he tell you to deliver this to?"

Still nothing.

L.J. exhales a huff of air in exasperation. He squats down to look at Marcus eye to eye. "Marcus, your brother sells this stuff, doesn't he?"

"I gotta take that someplace. You gonna get me in trouble."

L.J.'s heart is racing. He tries to keep his voice low, calm. "Marcus, you know what your brother is doing is wrong. And let me tell you something else about him. He stole money from me. A lot of it. Held a gun to me one night when I was walking in your neighborhood. Look at me, Marcus. That's right. Your brother's a thief. And this…" He looks at the bag again, turning it. "How long do you think he can keep doing this and not get caught? He's headed for prison. You can bet that money you got in your pocket on it."

Marcus finally looks up at L.J.

"I gotta pee."

"Marcus, have you heard a word I said?"

"I gotta pee, now."

"OK, OK." He gets up, and puts the bag in his pocket. He looks down the street. "Uh, all right. Down this way. I think I saw a McDonald's over this way somewhere."

They trek the short block to the McDonald's, and Marcus no longer skips. His hands are deep inside his pockets, and he walks looking down, his shoulders hunched. Once inside the McDonald's, Marcus races to the back of the restaurant toward the men's room.

"I'll be right up here," L.J. calls out to Marcus's back, and takes a seat in a booth up front.

Two young black women sitting across from him, both dressed in hospital uniforms, are drinking shakes and discussing the weather. He leans both elbows on the table, puts his head in his hands.

Damn that punk brother. How old was Marcus? Nine years old and delivering. Scoring. Using? He shudders at the thought. He'll have to think of some way to get through to Marcus. Probably idolizes that fool brother. Talking to him might not do much good. Maybe he can convince the boy to stay with him tonight. No, that's no good. Red Eyes might suddenly turn into a righteous parent and have him arrested or something. He could go to the police. But what would they do to Marcus? What would become of him? Naw, no police. He'll just have to see Marcus when he can and slowly drum it into his head that his brother's a criminal, and taking money from him and delivering that crap will land his butt in jail someday.

Or worse.

He looks at his watch. Five minutes since Marcus went back to the restroom. What's taking him so long? Sick maybe, from all the food. He gets up and goes to the back to check on him.

He slips inside the door and calls out. "Marcus, you OK?"

He doesn't hear a sound. He walks further in. The urinals are vacant. He looks in each stall. Marcus is gone.

L.J. runs out and sees two teenage girls, both with blond ponytails, seated in a booth near the door eating hamburgers. "Did you see a little boy run out of here a minute ago?"

They look at each other, then at him. "No, sir. Sorry."

L.J. sighs deeply. He rubs the back of his head with his palm, and walks out the door to the street.

Two buses roll by and the shriek and hiss of brakes ring in his ears. It's cooler now, and he pulls his jacket collar around him. The sun has dipped behind a slate-gray cloud. He arrives at his apartment a half-hour later, bone-tired, an ache pounding in his temples. He pauses to look around the spare room at the faded sofa, sagging bed, small wooden, gate-legged table, two-drawer desk. A four-burner stove with a coffee pot sitting on it. Through the open window a maze of sidewalks, streets, and boulevards fade in the dimming light. He sighs deeply, with an audible rush of air.

Somewhere out there is a nine-year-old child finding his way alone. Surely he'll be OK, L.J. thinks, pushing back the urge to worry. After all, he's come and gone as he pleased, traveled the subways and buses long before he met L.J. He goes to the bed, reaches under it and pulls out the little alto sax. *Damn.* If only he had gotten the chance to give it to the boy. Then maybe he could have convinced him that his life had other possibilities.

He'll be OK. Please, let him be OK.

He sits on his bed, and as he moves he finds an offbeat rhythm in the squeak of rusted springs. He attaches the mouthpiece to the instrument, then licks the cold reed, and blows a somber, bluesy scale.

· TWENTY-ONE ·

CLOUDS GATHER OUTSIDE L.J.'S WINDOW on a Thursday evening as he sits perched in the windowsill, eating from a Styrofoam carton. He sips from his coffee cup, places it in the sill, picks up his tenor horn, and runs through a high scale. A soft rumble of thunder plays in the distance, like the flapping of metal sheets. A storm coming, the evening news said, an hour or so away. Glancing at the alto sax case where he left it days ago, he wonders if he'll ever see Marcus again. He'd waited a day, then gone by the apartment, knocked on the door. No answer. The next day, the same thing.

He takes the cup to the sink, runs water over the dirty dishes, squeezes in a few drops of liquid Joy, and watches the rise of white foam in the sink. The water pressure is so loud, he can barely hear the knock at his door.

"Who is it?"

"Marcus."

Thank God. He opens the door. Marcus, moon eyes sparkling, wears a wide grin. Relief cools L.J.'s mind only briefly; the tall boy standing behind Marcus makes his heart jump.

"Roy," L.J. says.

A broad smile circles the prominent gold tooth. "Yeah. It's me," he says.

L.J. just stares at them both, inhales sharply. *You just asking for some hell to come knocking at your door.*

"This my brother," Marcus says, still smiling. "He say he gonna give you all your money back."

"Yeah, yeah," Roy says. "Like, uh, you know, I'm real sorry about what happened and everythang. You gonna let us in?"

L.J. watches Roy as he pimp-limps into the room, one shoulder dipping with every other step. He flops onto the sofa, sprawls long legs, while Marcus goes to the bed and gropes beneath it for the saxophone case. He finds the alto and pulls it out.

"What's this?" he says, his eyes wide.

"That's for you, Marcus, it's yours."

"Mine?" His eyes are like plates, and his mouth is wide open. "Oooooh, weee!"

This isn't the way he'd planned for the boy to see his new horn. "Marcus, put it down for now. We'll play it later, all right?"

Roy must have grown six inches since the time he mugged him on the street, L.J. realizes. He is lanky, long-limbed, mounds of muscles raising the thin black cotton of his T-shirt. He head is shaved, and black wire-rimmed shades hide his eyes.

"Put that thing down, Marcus," Roy says as Marcus begins to take out the horn. He crosses his long legs at the ankles. "Me and Mr. L.J. got a little bidness to take care of."

"Yeah, OK," Marcus says. "But after you give him the money, I got me a song I made up I want to play."

Roy sits forward and puts a hand in his pocket. "OK but first, little man, run on across to the store and get me something cold to drink."

L.J. eyes Roy warily. He stands at the window facing them, arms outstretched and palms flattened against the windowsill. "I've got Cokes here in the fridge."

"Coke? Never touch it." Roy lets out a laugh that shows the gold blinking like prisms in his mouth, and slaps himself on the chest. "Marcus, get me one of them large Orange Crushes, and a package of Juicy Fruit."

"OK, I'm going. But you gonna give him the money now? L.J., he got a lot of money with him and he say he gonna give you more than what he took from you."

"Little man, get on out of here before that rain hits, all right? Get you something to drink for yourself too."

"OK," Marcus says, taking a five that Roy had peeled off from a wad of bills, and he is out the door.

L.J. can feel a roiling uneasiness in his gut as Roy stands up, stretching his frame nearly to the height of the room. He removes his shades, and his eyes are two small, black agates.

"Aw 'ight, man. Where is it?"

"Where's what?"

"Hey, don't play me, man. You know what I'm talking about."

He is circling the room like a caged lion, eyes to L.J.

"Aw, you mean that bag of white stuff? Man, I thought it was sugar. I threw that stuff in the trash. Couple of days ago."

"You lyin'. You know how much that bag was worth? I know you ain't that stupid."

"I'm telling you, it ain't here. Sorry."

In a moment, the steel flashes before L.J.'s eyes. The gun is bigger this time. L.J.'s heart pounds with the rumble of the thunder.

"Move away from that window."

"All right, all right." L.J. raises his palms in the air. "I'm moving. But I'm not lying to you, man, it ain't here."

His gun cocked sideways and leveled at L.J.'s chest, Roy paces the room, snatching cushions from the sofa, rummaging through cabinets, opening and slamming doors. He picks up three books from the table and hurls them toward L.J. They bang against the wall and crash to the floor.

"Myas well tell me where it is, man, cause I'ma find it with you or without you."

"I told you."

The thunder claps.

Roy opens the alto case, lifts out the horn, and looks into its bell. He lifts it high above his head as if he plans to throw it across the room.

"No, no! Hey! That's Marcus's horn! Don't throw it."

Roy tosses the sax on the sofa where it lands with a thud. He strides toward L.J., his gun pointed at L.J.'s ear, his eyes aflame.

"Tell me where it is."

L.J. looks him dead in the eye. "It's not here."

Roy snorts, an evil laugh with gold-trimmed teeth. "You feel like dyin' today, Mister L.J.? I'ma smoke your punk ass right now. I can find it quicker with you out the way."

A heavy clap of thunder rocks the room. The lights blink, then go out, leaving the room in darkness.

A sharp pain shot up the side of his temple, and as he sank to the floor in floating slow motion, an airy lightness filled his head. His eyes closed to find a shining light, glowing like the sun. Then, behind his closed eyes, the bright light dulled to gray, and slowly faded to black.

When the light rose again, he was nine years old.

If I had to choose one moment,
To live within my heart,
Darling it would be,
When you smiled at me...
Recalling how we started..

The wind teased at the trees on Jefferson Street and made their branches rustle like a dancing woman's skirt. Beneath the faint rumble of distant thunder, as he was rounding the corner to her house, came the satin tenor of Nat King Cole.

New born whippoorwills
Were calling on the hills,
Summer was coming in, and fast...

The soft crooning between the pops and cracks of the worn vinyl quickened his steps along the cobblestone into a near-skip. She must be home. Home from wherever she had been these last months. Finally, after weeks of passing the house and seeing the warped screen door latched, the small porch darkened, the house veiled in ghostly quiet, finally, she would be there and he would see her.

The last time she hadn't looked well and hadn't been happy to see him. She had come to the screen door and even through its rusted darkness he could see the dark puffiness under her eyes, and the swollen corner of her bottom lip. It sent a ripple of fear up his spine.

"I can't see you today," she said in a raspy whisper, an unrecognizable voice that made him quiver inside. "Go on home now. I'm not feeling well." He left and came back the following week, and every week after that for months to find the house as dark and tightly locked as an empty church.

But now Nat King Cole sang the announcement sweet to his ears. As thunder growled from the far corner of a summer evening sky clay-colored with the threat of rain, the air smelled green and wet and raised the hairs on his arms. As he walked up the steps the wind shifted slightly and gusted. He was cold but he would be warm soon, the threat of storm eased by the promise of her living room, the sound of her humming voice, the smile, the hair that shook when she lifted back her head to laugh.

But she did not laugh, or smile, and Nat King Cole sang unaccompanied by her familiar hum.

"Oh," she said, looking down at him, the darkness of the rusted screen aging her face. Then, after pausing a while as if to ponder the weight of her next move, she let him inside.

Her eyes looked cool and empty, dazed, as if drained of whatever it was that had made them beautiful and warm before. "Sit down," she told him. He wanted to smile, he was so glad to see her, but something, he didn't know what, kept the smile from his face. The record reached a word that made it stutter, and the sticking needle—and her ignoring it as she silently gazed out the window—made him uneasy. He waited for some explanation of where she'd been, that she'd been visiting a sister or a mother somewhere, or for her to bring out the pretty new things she'd bought while away, singing maybe, in Little Rock or New York. He thought she might offer him refreshment like always, a cold cherry Kool-Aid, a plate of store-bought cream-filled cookies, but she sat across from him, staring past him with absent eyes, and twirled the ends of her hair in her fingers.

Finally, she got up to silence the stuttering Nat King Cole. Then she turned facing the door with a hand to her cheek, alarm coloring her face, as if some startling news had been delivered. "Oh Jesus," she said, apparently to no one. "He's coming back. I know it."

Her mood changed, her steps quickened. She hurried toward the bedroom. Her dark blue dress had bluer circles under the arms, and the thin strap drooped down her shoulder. The back of her hair stood away from her head in spikes. Her dress was torn in back. While she was gone he looked around the room. Everything was the same, except covered in dust, and there was a sharp, musty odor in the air. He considered the items on the square wooden coffee table: a teacup and saucer of unmatched blues, a yellow ashtray shaped like a piano with a Lucky Strike dangling on its keys, a red Big Chief tablet, a black-handled gun.

The gun held his stare, and he couldn't unloose his eyes from its grip. That was the odor, he suddenly knew, the same smell as when Purvis shot his rifle in the air across the field behind their house early one New Year's Day. It hung heavily in the room, sharpening the air like a prickly mist. He was transfixed by the object, until she reentered the room with something even more compelling.

It looked like it might be a girl, the baby she held in her arms, although he really couldn't say for sure. He'd not seen many newborns in his short life. She rocked it softly as it cooed, held it close, and said without looking his way, "I got something I need you to do for me. Something real important."

He wondered why she looked so sad, and now so nervous, what had brought the pale color to her eyes, and what had crusted the edges of her voice. And most of all, where in the world did she get that baby?

But he said nothing, just watched her and the baby in wonder. "Hold out your arms," she said, and she placed the baby's head in the crook of his elbow, and wrapped the little blue-and-green quilt around her. "Watch her head, put your hand back there, like this." He held her stiffly, the bundle of heat warming his chest, looking down at the wide-open eyes that seemed to look right through him.

She sat next to him, writing something on a sheet of tablet paper. When she was done she tore the sheet from the tablet, folded it, and placed it in his shirt pocket. "I'll tell you later what to do with it," she said. She picked up the baby and stood. "Now I want you to come with me."

A gun, a baby, a note? He had the feeling there was something she wasn't telling him. But he followed her out the door, and as they stepped onto the porch, they both glanced up at the sky.

"Better hurry. There's a storm coming."

She carried the baby close to her chest with her chin covering its head. The wind whipped stinging dust at their legs as they walked eastward on Sycamore, past the pool hall on Maple Street, past the Night Owl. Trees swayed in a frenzied dance. When they reached Third Avenue the sky had turned deep silver, and a flock of birds winged noisily southward. Lightning crackled in the distance from the west.

He had no idea what she was doing, where they were going, but he had the odd feeling that there was something final about their journey. She was silent, her steps purposeful, and he had to walk as fast as he could to keep up. When the first drops of rain fell, they both ducked their heads and walked faster.

They came to the yellow awning of the Piggly Wiggly and she stopped and looked down the street at the row of businesses ahead, the Easy Street Diner, the hardware and electrical repair shop, the Handy Dandy Five and Dime, the Beauty Palace.

She turned to him, rainwater glowing on her face. "This is as far as I can go with you," she said.

She pointed to the only building with its lights on, the Beauty Palace at the end of the block, and then handed him the infant. "Give her to the woman who answers the door," she said. "And give her the note I gave you. She'll know what to do."

When the baby was tucked into his cradling arms, she bent to cup his chin in her hand. "Look at me," she said. "This is my baby girl. Something happened, and I can't take care of her, but that woman over there, she can."

She busily rearranged the quilt around the baby's face, shielding it from the open air. She stared at the child a long while, then pressed her lips to her forehead.

"Such a good little baby," she said, brushing her fingers against its cheek. "I'm sorry it's gotta be this way. Someday you gonna understand."

She wiped the corner of her eye with her hand, and looked at him again. When she spoke, her voice broke. "I done something I shouldn't a done, and now I...now I gotta go away. But..." she paused to swallow and blink. "But I want my baby to be safe. Can you do this for me?"

He nodded.

"Good." She reached inside her blouse and pulled out a two-dollar bill. "This here is all I got. Buy yourself something you might like with it." She put the bill in his pocket along with the note.

"And one more thing," she said. "Don't tell nobody. Promise me, all right? Don't you ever tell anybody about this. Long as you live."

He nodded yes.

"Cause it'd be better if my baby grow up not ever knowing about me, about what I done. You been a good friend to me, Louis," she said. "I...I might not see you...for a while."

She reached over and planted a kiss on his cheek, and smiled. "Be careful with my baby," she said. With a soft hand to his back she sent him on his way. He took small steps forward, then looked back to see her gesturing him on with a quick nod and a flick of her hand. He turned and walked ahead.

By now the air was blue-gray; sheets of water were pouring down, and he squinted his eyes to see where he was walking. Puddles formed around his sneakers, and he tried to dodge them. Slowly, he walked on, head bowed over the baby's eyes, shoulders tightened, his whole body a balled fist against the rain, against whatever obstacle he and the little baby girl might meet. He could hear the baby's muffled whimpers beneath the quilt and he kept his face down as the rain thickened. For a second, he lost his balance on the water-slicked cobblestone of the sidewalk, but caught himself and walked on. What if he fell with this baby? he thought. He erased the thought from his mind. He would not fall, couldn't. He passed the electrical repair shop. Two more doors and he'd be there. His heart raced wildly. It never occurred to him to ask who the baby was, what its name was. He wondered. Maybe she didn't have one, maybe the lady would give her one when she took her in. One more door now, and he is there. He raised the palm of his hand and knocked flat-handed with all his might. But the thunder exploded in a rapid volley of crackles and claps. He knocked again, louder. Finally, the woman appeared in the window above, looked down, and let him in.

The deed done, he raced through the rain back to the spot where he had left Vaughn, but she was not there. So he hid under the sheltering leaves of the giant magnolia in the town square until the rain subsided to sprinkles, and the sky lightened to a pale gray. Walking home, he'd gotten lost, but didn't care. He was not at all ready to go back to the tiny rooming house on Jackson Lane.

He wanted to think about her, because he realized that it was likely he would not ever see her again. She was gone from him now, for good. So he wanted to remember her face, and not the way he had seen it tonight, or the last time. He went back to the hot August day she invited him in, the humiliating bath in her tub, the sound of her singing voice floating above him, and the smile that shot gold through the mink-brown eyes.

As he found his way home beneath the lightening sky, Nat King Cole sang from deep in his mind. Before long the rain ended, reduced to drips from awnings, gutters, and tree leaves. The sky in the distance had faded to grayish pink, and arched across the breadth of the sky L.J. could make out a double rainbow of yellow, blue, and pink. Two multicolored ribbons striped in the colors of bubble gum and ice cream, perfectly formed, bowled over the wide sky. He stopped to gaze at it. *Didn't somebody say a double rainbow brought good luck?* He closed his eyes. He thought of the one thing he wanted now more than anything. He crossed his fingers on both hands, and made a wish.

Eighteen years later, he would swear it had come true.

· TWENTY-TWO ·

B IG MAMA'S TIMING AND FORESIGHT, as always, were impeccable. Olivia needed her now, and so she appeared, unbidden, on her porch wearing the same drab gray coat she'd worn to Olivia's high school graduation and the same felt hat that warmed her head during the winters of the Nixon years. Her head tilted up, her stance purposeful, she wore a self-satisfied smile, pleased to have arrived right on time at the exact place in the world where she needed to be.

Olivia had to flare her eyelids to stare back the tears that wanted to flood them. She wanted at that moment to sweep the woman in her arms to tell her that she was sorry. That she hadn't answered the letters and ignored every call only because she was confused, bewildered, and hurt, and that she was trying to understand all that had happened. That she had planned to come visit her soon. How could she have ignored her for so long? Of course she knew Big Mama would never deliberately hurt her, and how could she have been so cruel to the woman who had received her with open arms one rainy night on the other side of a storm? Saved her from a life of god-knew-what at the hands of a mother who, for whatever reason, didn't want her?

She wanted to say all of this but instead opened the door wide and extended her arms. Their embrace was warm and swaying, and scented with waves of Big Mama's flowery talcum.

"Big Mama," Olivia said. "Thank God."

Big Mama had never set foot in the house before, or the city for that matter, since Olivia moved to town, but once inside she made herself at home, finding L.J.'s old blue recliner immediately. "Ima set on down right here," she said as the taxi driver, dressed in a Shaquille

O'Neal jersey, who couldn't have been more than eighteen, brought in her five bags and placed them in a semicircle where Big Mama sat. Olivia raised up the chair's footstool and Big Mama let out an appreciative sigh. After removing her shoes, she wriggled her bottom into the Naugahyde cushion and folded her arms across her ample chest.

"Nice," she said. "Real nice."

Olivia offered everything edible or drinkable in her kitchen: a tall cool glass of Minute Maid, a turkey breast sandwich, leftover chicken pot pie that she could microwave in seconds. Or maybe she'd like to freshen up in a long hot bath with lavender beads and green tea with honey? "Give me a minute Baby Doll, I just got here." Once settled and comfortable, she allowed Olivia to bring her a cup of hot tea, not that strange stuff that smelled funny, but some real tea, some Lipton's. Then Big Mama pulled a drooping silver curl back from her forehead and closed her eyes. "Seventeen hours on that bus, and I feel like I'm still rolling," she said. A minute later she opened her eyes and pointed to a big brown shopping bag at her side.

Olivia knew the bus ride from Handy was only about thirteen hours, but said nothing. She reached into the big bag and brought out one small brown sack after another. "Right there, that one." Big Mama said. She slurped a tiny sip of the too-hot tea, frowned, and pointed a stubby finger at one of the smaller ones. "No, you open it. Go 'head, it's for you."

Olivia opened it and found the pair of diamond-studded earrings Country used to wear every Christmas dinner. Olivia stared at them and felt a twinge in her heart. Country's first husband, Webster Gaither, had given them to her right before he went off to fight and die in the second world war. With their young marriage stopped short by German tank fire, he had remained in a state of remembered perfection no other husband afterward could touch. The earrings dangled in a swirl of teardrop-shaped gold. Olivia had always been fascinated with them; when she was two, she would reach for them on Country's ears. When she was seventeen, Country had let her wear them, under threat of death if they were lost, to the Booker T. Washington High School senior prom.

"I finally got around to cleaning out that house across the street after Country went," Big Mama said quietly. "She always said she wanted you to have them."

Olivia slowly put them on, speechless. Big Mama smiled and pointed to another box. This one was wrapped in layers of green tissue paper, and another layer followed of yellowed newspaper comics. Inside the white cardboard box, buried deep inside folds of cotton, was a single strand of pearls. "Clo T.," Big Mama said, "got them things when she was about sixteen from that Jewish lady she used to clean house for over in Magnolia Heights 'cross the highway. Miss Kavner, I believe, was her name. Told her they was real, but I doubt it. But Clo T. was just as proud as if the queen herself had snatched them off her crown and strung 'em up."

Olivia folded them in her hands, then pressed them to her lips. She believed she could smell the faintest scent of L'air du temps wafting up from them and the feeling it triggered again made her eyes brim.

Another box contained a covered candy dish of heart-shaped crystal that Olivia remembered Glodean keeping on her dresser. Glodean always kept them full of Olivia's favorite candy, broken pieces of Hershey's milk chocolate bars with almonds. Olivia turned the crystal box in her hands and pressed the cool glass against her cheek. She looked at Big Mama's eyes, which glistened above a satisfied smile. Here they all were, Olivia thought. A while ago she'd called them conspirators plotting against her happiness. Now she could feel the love of all five of them distilled in the presence of this one old woman.

"Ain't been through Joon's stuff yet." Big Mama slurped more tea and placed the cup in its saucer. "Ain't had the heart, after all of these years. His sisters from Texas come up and got some things, but I ain't been through them myself really. I know there's some things of his he want you to have."

Olivia got up from the wing-backed chair where she sat and asked Big Mama if she'd like a nap. "I just put clean sheets on the bed this morning," she said. "I know you must be really tired."

"No child. I'm tired, but a few more minutes in this chair, and I'll be good to go. I want to see around a little bit. Ain't been in this town since I was a girl myself. You got time?"

And so for the next few days Olivia and Big Mama tooled around town in the Jetta, seeing Kansas City while Big Mama gazed awestruck at the traffic, the buildings, the clusters of people. Cool breezes swayed the evergreens on The Paseo as they drove past the site of the old baseball stadium where Big Mama and Uncle Joon, when they were young, had once gone to see the black team, the Kansas City Monarchs, play. In its place was a park with a manicured lawn of bluegrass and a circle of walnut trees. They window-shopped and people-watched on the Plaza, traipsed in and out of Saks and Halls, where Olivia bought Big Mama the perfect wide-brimmed straw hat for church. They oohed and awed at the Spanish-tiled roofs and fountains, the big rambling estates in wealthy Mission Hills, had fancy coffee in the lobby of the Ritz-Carlton, and sat in the balcony of the Lyric to watch a touring company perform *Guys and Dolls.* On Wednesday they picked up Winona and her friend Juliet and went to the racetrack, where Big Mama won $50 on a horse named "Mama's Pride."

Big Mama was having a ball. It was days before either remembered there had been ill feelings between them, and before Olivia remembered that Big Mama had ended her last letter with, "I got more to tell." When she did remember, she was loath to bring it up, they were having so much fun. So she decided to wait until Big Mama was ready to tell her whatever it was that she'd hinted at in the letter.

Big Mama cooked every day, finding her way easily around Olivia's kitchen to turn out collard greens, pound cakes, and apple pies while they sat around dishing the latest gossip floating around the hoity-toity circles in Handy: who the mayor had married again, what judge had divorced his wife of fifty years, and what second soprano in the Sweet Rock choir had been caught doing what with whom. One afternoon while the sun streamed in through the kitchen's yellow curtains, Big Mama hummed "Jesus Is the Light" waiting for her pound cake to rise, sitting at Olivia's big oak kitchen table, poring over piles of unread mail she'd brought with her in a big plastic bag.

"My hands feel so good now, I been writing all these letters to folks I ain't heard from in years," Big Mama said gleefully. "Now I got all of these here letters to answer." She spread an assortment of pens before her on the table and chose one as if she were choosing the right sword for a duel. "Look. Here's a letter from Matilda Wright. You remember her. She played organ at the church for years, then she went to visit her daughter over in Germany and decided to stay." One by one, Big Mama pulled envelopes from the bag, read cards and notes aloud, and in her slow, painstaking hand, answered them.

When the oven timer went off, Olivia carefully pulled the pound cake from the stove. It was a perfect golden brown. Big Mama nodded, not even looking up from her letter writing. Olivia suggested that they let the pound cake cool on the rack for a while. In the meantime, she had a surprise for Big Mama.

The shop was finally ready. Olivia had been saving the beauty shop as the culmination of her "city tour," even though Big Mama said over and over that she wanted to see it and didn't care what state of repair it was in. But Olivia wanted to wait until the work was completed, and on Thursday morning Stanley Newman called.

Even as they pulled up to the front, Big Mama's eyes were huge and her jaw dropped an inch. Olivia wondered what Big Mama had already seen that was so special. The front of the building—neat rows of small red bricks, brass lamp lights, and smoked windows with "Madam C's" in cursive swirls—was nothing out of the ordinary. But compared to the Beauty Palace down in Handy, Olivia realized, it must have looked like a Fifth Avenue salon.

Inside, Big Mama was half dazed, half dazzled. The place, Olivia admitted, looked beautiful. The polyurethane-coated hardwood floors shone like glass. The silver light fixtures glowed cool against the walls, which showed mercury-colored orchids trailing up embossed paper. The new dryers and sinks were state of the art, and above the wallpaper, which came waist-high, mirrored glass stretched from front to back on both walls, making the place seem twice as large as before.

Olivia could hear someone—Stanley probably—banging away at something in the back. Big Mama walked from one end of the shop to the other, running her fingers delicately along fixtures, wig stands, counter tops, and chrome-trimmed chairs as if she were a child strolling in a museum gallery while the guard's back was turned. "Child,

child," she said. When she arrived at the back of the shop, she stood transfixed under the huge portrait of Madam C. J. Walker.

For a moment she stood gazing at the guru of modern black hairdressing with the reverence she usually reserved for portraits of Dr. Martin Luther King, Jr. Then she turned to Olivia with mist-filled eyes. "This is something, Baby Doll," she said. "It's just like in my dreams."

Olivia blushed through a smile, swiveling in one of the dryer chairs and dangling her legs like a schoolgirl who'd been praised by her favorite teacher. She'd done well in the big city, and now Big Mama had seen evidence of it. Never mind the fact that this spanking new shop was owed in part to an unfortunate fire; the place was hers and she was proud of it. But as she looked around the finished shop, she couldn't help but wonder why the feeling of elation she expected was eluding her.

Now she would have to go back to work, it was true. There would be a client base to recapture. The twins would be coming back, with their fidgeting bodies, screaming mouths, and tender heads. And ancient Mrs. Forester, whose sparse head of see-through silver presented a weekly challenge to Olivia's imagination.

"Well, there's plenty of work to do," Olivia said. "I've got to see how many clients I've got left." She told her about the women who'd left her for Cora. "Don't matter," Big Mama said. "You the best hairdresser I done seen, next to me. Mrs. Tallifero and her daughter still talking about how nice you fixed they hair for Wanda Jean's wedding when you came home Christmas before last. You gonna do fine. You wait."

But Olivia couldn't bring herself to tell Big Mama that she really didn't care that much. That making women look pretty wasn't as much fun as it used to be. That with L.J. gone, clean and shining hair—like so many other things in her life—had lost its spark. That she was finally, just now, beginning to understand her life without her best friend.

"Big Mama," Olivia said, looking down at her nails, her feet tapping against the chrome footrest of the dryer chair, "I haven't told you this, but I'm singing again."

Big Mama smiled. "I know, Baby Doll. I seen that big case of music underneath your piano. I didn't want to say nothing."

"Well, I'm just trying it. Somebody asked me to sing for the opening of a new club, and I said I would. Only the first rehearsal last week didn't go all that well. So, I don't know."

Big Mama turned in her chair and a loud metallic squeak went up from somewhere beneath the plastic. "These new chairs always squeak so bad, don't they?"

Just then, Stanley came out from the back. An unlit cigarette dangled from his thin lips and his sagging tool belt clung desperately to his undetectable waist. He grinned, pushing strands of wispy blond hair beneath his paint-stained baseball cap.

"Well, you like it?" He looked around, his thumbs hooked in his belt loops, the cigarette flopping as he spoke. "I had to get you a new toilet seat, by the way. I ruined the other one, spilled some paint thinner on it. But the new one is better anyhow."

Olivia stood up. "It looks good," she said, then turned to Big Mama. "By the way, this is Mrs. Benton—Big Mama," she said to Stanley. "The woman who raised me. She's just visiting me for a while, from Arkansas."

Big Mama nodded. "Ma'am," Stanley said and lifted his cap and smiled broadly, showing dark shadows where two molars should have been. "Pleased ta meet ya."

Stanley pulled out a lighter, then said, "Oops, I'm quitting. Almost forgot." He tucked the lighter in the pocket of his T-shirt. "Miz Tillman, you look around today, tomorrow. Take your time. Anything you see ain't right, why you just make a list. Call me in a couple of days. Don't want you to sign off on the work til everything's just the way you want it." When Stanley closed the door behind him, the shop was quiet and mostly dark except for the new skylight in the ceiling. A shaft of light angled down and bathed Big Mama where she sat beneath it.

"Big Mama," Olivia said, "I want to apologize, for not writing you, for not trusting you. I know you were doing what you thought was best for me. I know all of you…none of you would hurt me on purpose."

A cloud passed over the skylight, casting a shadow on Big Mama's face and shoulders, but when she shifted in her seat the light found her again. Olivia figured she should probably get up and turn on the lights to make sure they all worked. But she sat there in the increasing darkness waiting for Big Mama's response.

Big Mama took her time, leaned back against the chair, and let out a deep sigh. "Well, Baby Doll, that's right. I sure didn't mean to hurt you. None of us did."

There was a new weight to her words. "Remember I said I had something else to tell you," she said, shifting again as if she needed to arrange herself comfortably for a long sitting. "Long as we're setting here, I guess now's about as good a time as any."

Taking her cue, Olivia leaned back against the seat and nodded.

Big Mama folded her hands together in her lap. "First let me tell you," she began slowly, "about my daddy."

She took a deep breath, as if she were about to make a speech before a congregation. "Like you already know, my daddy was a preacher man, just like his daddy before him. Preaching was a long tradition in our family, ever since slavery ended. After the war my granddaddy Welcome Harshaw and his brother Nimrod sharecropped a while on little parcels of land in Arkansas down close to Louisiana, and then later on they both took up the church work. Nimrod moved up north to Kansas City and helped build New Hope with his own hands, and my granddaddy stayed in Arkansas and became the first pastor of Sweet Rock Revival down there in Handy.

"My daddy followed in his footsteps and became Sweet Rock's preacher after my granddaddy died. So, I grew up every inch a preacher's child, and every day of my life when I was a young'un, I knew that's what I was. I sang in the church choir, me and Clo T. did, served on the Junior Usher Board, the Morning Sunbeams Circle, the Young Missionaries, and taught the Wee Wisdom Sunday school class when I wasn't nothing but a girl myself. You name it, if it had to do with the church, I did it.

"We was a real prominent family in Handy, the Harshaws. Lived in a great big old stone and wood parsonage the church members built theyselves. My mama, Elizabeth, was a fine upstanding preacher's wife. She was a real pretty lady, always dressed nice and wore big, fine hats to church. Come Sunday morning, she'd dress me and Clo T. in our nicest clothes. The three of us, Mama, Clo T., and me, would sit right up on the front row during service, lined up like little ducks, while daddy preached his sermons.

"My daddy was a real fire-and-brimstone preacher, dontcha know. Used to get so riled up shaking his fist and jumping up and down that sweat would start pouring off him like he done got caught in the rain. He was a big man, too, and when he raised his voice to a shout and stomped his feet, talking 'bout sin and eternal damnation, I tell you, the floor in that little church would shake and the windows would rattle with the fear of God. The congregation loved it. They handclapped and amen'd so loud, it looked like a contest to see who could outdo the other, the preacher, or the preached-to.

"Now, I was the oldest child, Clo T. come up a few years behind me. So I had to be the one to set the example, or so my daddy said. 'Eunice, make sure you set a example for your baby sister,' Daddy would tell me. 'She be looking up to you.' Oh, it didn't make me no never mind, cause I wasn't never one to misbehave too much nohow. I was a good daughter, never caused neither my mama nor my daddy no trouble.

"That is, til one day. When I got to be a young lady old enough to take a interest in the young boys, this one young fella in particular started coming around. We would talk at school a lot, and then one day he ups and asks me out to the picture show. Now Handy didn't have no movie house at that time, so we had to go way over to Jennings to the Crystal Palace Theater, where they allowed colored to sit up in the balcony. Well, when I told my daddy I wanted to go out on a date with Maurice Pierce, he hit the roof.

"He knew all about the Pierce family, you see. Now Maurice was a nice enough young boy, but his people had sort of a reputation. They was poor, sure enough, and that alone was bad enough in my daddy's eyes, cause the poor folks in town seemed to him to be the ones closest to sin. But on top of that, the Pierce men was drinking, gambling men, and had been known to patronize a place out in the country called Jethro's. It was a juke joint, just a barn of a place, with four bedrooms upstairs, and I don't guess I have to tell you what went on up there.

"Well, my daddy forbidded me from going out with Maurice. 'Absolutely not!' he practically screamed at me. I said, 'Why, Daddy?' Then he said, 'Why? You asking me why after I done give you my answer?' The fact that I asked him why seemed to make him even madder. He sent me to my room without supper.

"Well, I went to my room, sat on my bed, and just looked at the yellow dandelions in my wallpaper, my blood boiling. It wasn't like I was some young little thing, I was eighteen, almost done with high school by then. Old enough to decide for myself who to go out with. So I decided what I was gonna do. I was gonna defy my daddy and go out with Maurice Pierce. I put on my best blue shirtwaist dress with the white collar, my Sunday shoes, raised up my bedroom window, climbed out, and I was gone.

"This went on for a time, me sneaking out my window at night 'bout onceta week, my mama and daddy thinking I was in my room asleep. It went along fine until one night, all hell broke loose.

"About four months after that first night when I snuck out, we was all sitting around the dining table on a Friday night. Now, my daddy had this tradition where me and Clo T. would have to tell what we done wrong during the week, kind of like confessing our sins, like the Catholics did, before supper. Then we would hold hands and Daddy would pray over the food, and the bigger the sins the longer the prayer. Lord, bless this food that we ain't worthy to eat, he'd say, then go on and on. One time Clo T. said she had cheated on a spelling test, and we was sitting there praying for a half-hour before we could eat a crumb. I ain't lying, a half-hour.

"But this particular Friday night, I could tell Daddy was steaming about something. He was a dark-skinned man, and it take a dark-skinned man a awful lot to get so upset his skin gets flushed. But my daddy, that night, Lord if his black skin didn't look plum red.

"We all sat down to the mashed potatoes and pot roast my mama had fixed for us and Daddy turned to me, fire ripping all up in his eyes, his dark skin shining with sweat, and said, 'Eunice, confess your sins before God and this family!' Well, I didn't know what he was talking about. I hadn't done nothing that week that I knew of, 'cept sneak out to see Maurice, and I wasn't about to confess that, no sir. I wasn't crazy. And he couldn't of knowed about it, 'cause I was so careful not to get caught. So I said, 'What you mean, Daddy?' Then he slammed his fist on the table so hard Mama's pot roast shimmied in the platter, splattering juice on the table, and the good dinner plates rattled. I looked over at Mama, and she wouldn't look at me, so I knew something was up. Then Daddy said, near 'bout screaming, 'Eunice Harshaw, you in the family way!'

"Child, you could of knock me over with a feather. I didn't know what he was talking about. Me, having a baby? True enough, I had done gained a little weight around my middle, but I didn't pay that no 'tention. I just thought I musta been eating too much of Mama's fried corn fritters. That's just how dumb I was. Nobody had done told me how such things happen. Shoot, I didn't know.

"So, what'd I do? I looked my daddy in the eye and said as how I didn't know what he was talkin' about. Well, what'd I do that for? Daddy stood up so fast he almost knocked the table over, reached over his long arm, and slapped me so hard I fell outta my chair.

"Mama yelled something and grabbed Daddy's arm so he wouldn't do it again. I looked at his face and I couldn't see nothing but fire, his eyes all red and lit up, veins jumpin' outta his neck. Then Daddy sat down, leaned over with his head on the table and cried. Mama told me I best go to my room.

"Clo T. and me had never seen Daddy cry before, and it scared us somethin awful. Daddy wasn't one a them cryin' preachers. Daddy was always proud, always had control of things. So I felt real bad. I swear, that was the worstest night of my life.

"Mama and Daddy musta talked that night after Daddy calmed down. The next day I was took over to the Hathaways in Cross County. Remember old lady Hathaway, that old white lady that was sick that one time we went over to help her? Doctor Hathaway and Mrs. Hathaway let me stay the night after he examined me. Sure enough, I was three months along. I liked to died, I felt so bad. Mrs. Hathaway said not to worry, nobody would know. Doc Hathaway was good about not talking about his patients to nobody. His wife was the same way. Far as I know, they never told nobody I was in the family way.

"So I was sent up to Kansas City for a few months to have my child. The Hathaways had friends in Kansas City. You remember Hettie Peale? Her mama used to run the Mayfair Boarding House long before you stayed there. Back then, it was a place where young colored girls went so's they could be took care of when they was in trouble.

"I had my baby there, cute little old baby girl. I wanted so bad to keep her. But when I got back to Handy, Mama and Daddy had done already found a family to take her, raise her as they own. The whole thing was hush-hush like. I cried and cried 'cause I wouldn't never see her again. Or at least, that's what I thought at that particular time.

"The years pass by. I married your Uncle Joon when I was about twenty. I done met him up in Kansas City when he was there learning the plumbing trade. He was a home boy, from Arkansas too, little town over near Pine Bluff. When he come back from the trade school to Arkansas, he start coming round to my house. We started seeing one another. My daddy liked him right off, and so we was married.

"Then more time pass on. Joon and me set up housekeeping above the Feed and Seed in downtown Handy, then later we bought the feed store so Clo T. and me could start doing folks' hair. Everything was just fine. My shop was going good after while, and so was Joon's plumbing. Joon was such a good, good man. A good husband. Except for one thing. He and I...we couldn't have no chil-ren. I figured that was God's way of punishing me for what I done. I figured it was what I deserved for bringing shame and disgracement on the family. But I didn't let it worry me, it was my lot. I'd done wrong and now I was paying for it. So I made up my mind that I would make it up to the Lord. Anybody needed help, why if they came to me, I'd help 'em. Folks needed money, I'd loan it to 'em. Need a place to stay, I'd give 'em one, or find a place for 'em. That's when everybody round town started to calling me Big Mama.

"One day I was alone in the shop, cleaning out sinks and sweeping hair up off the floor. It was a afternoon right around Easter time, and the sun was high and hot. A young woman showed up at the door. Pretty young girl somewhere along in her twenties or thirties. Pretty, but with a kinda reckless look to her. Clothes was too tight for her, too much makeup, specially 'round the eyes. I could tell she wasn't no angel. Now mind you, I wasn't no saint neither, I'd done made my mistakes, but I was ignorant. This child has a 'easy' look about her, she wasn't no ignorant young thing like I was. Anyway, she come to my door that day.

"'Can I help you?'" I ask her.

She just looked at me and kinda smiled a slow smile, like she knew something I didn't.

"'Are you Eunice Benton?' she said.

"'That's right,' I told her.

"'The one they call Big Mama?'

"'Yes, that's me.'"

Big Mama leaned forward, took off her glasses, wiped them on the tail of her dress and put them back on.

"She didn't say nothing for a minute. I kept waiting for her to say what she wanted, but then I figured it out before she said another word. I'd done seen it before. Every now and then a young girl would find her way to my door needing help after getting herself in trouble. Some had done been throwed out they parents' house and needed someplace to stay, some just needed somebody to sit down with 'em and tell 'em the world wasn't gone end just 'cause they got theyselves in a predicament. When this girl showed up, I looked at her face and saw that look I knew so well. The child had a lot of pain she was carrying around. I said to myself, 'This child's sure enough in trouble, just like I was, long years ago.'

"But what she said in her next breath nearly took mine's away. She looked at me with those round, brown eyes of hers and said, 'I'm your daughter. Vaughn.'"

Olivia felt a rush of heat to her face. Had she heard right? What was Big Mama telling her?

"What?" she said. "Vaughn…your daughter?"

Big Mama sighed and looked straight into Olivia's eyes. She nodded slowly. "That's right. That's what she told me. My daughter." She paused to let her words take their effect. Then she continued. "I said to her, 'Are you sure? How do you know you are my daughter?'

"Then she told me that her people told her when she got grown where she come from, how it was all arranged. I didn't ask her no more about it, 'cause I believed her. She was just the right age to be my daughter. And there was no way she could of even known I was with child if it wasn't true.

"I told her I was happy to see her. That I was so sorry I had to give her up, but I didn't have no choice. That I had thought about her every day since she was born, hoping to God that one day I would see her again. And there she was, standing right there in front of me.

"Well, she just looked at me, no expression on her face at all. Then she flat out told me, 'I'm here cause I need some money. I need four hundred dollars.'

"I thought, mmm-hmmm, just like I figured. She was in trouble. I told her, 'If you in some kinda trouble, come on and stay with me. You can stay right upstairs with me and my husband Joon. We give you everything you need.' You see, back in them days, when a young woman went to somebody's door asking for four hundred dollars, there wasn't but one thing she could need it for. And I wasn't about to give her money for that.

"Well, she didn't like that idea at all no sir. She said no, didn't need no help like that, just needed some money. And if I wasn't gonna give it to her, she'd just be on her way. I told her once again, child, if you in trouble, just get your things and come on back here and everything be just fine.' But that girl…" Big Mama shook her head. "She just turned and walked away, outta the shop. That was the last time I saw her.

Big Mama sighed deeply. "I guess it was no more than a few months after that when you showed up at our door. Soon's I saw you, I wondered. Could it be? But then when you started to grow up, you looked so much like the girl that come into my shop that day, there wasn't much doubt who you was. My grandbaby. Vaughn's little girl.

I thought, God done forgive me now. I had to give my own baby up, but he done give me her little one to raise.

"When you showed up, Lord, we was so happy. Four of us women, and no children between us. Not a one, til you. I figured that was my fault, too. That what I did had done set some kind of curse on the whole family. Then you came along one stormy night, showed up like sunshine in the middle of rain. Like that double rainbow that crossed the sky after L.J. brought you to us and you was safe inside our house.

"Yes, we was all happy. But nobody was as happy as me, once I figured out who you were. It was like…like I had my daughter back."

Evening shadows veiled the women. In the growing darkness, Olivia could no longer see Big Mama's eyes, only small patches of reflected light on her glasses like tiny, shining moons.

Big Mama leaned towards Olivia. "Child, I'm telling you all this so you'll understand how it was. Times was different back in them days. Certain things you just couldn't own up to, specially if you was a preacher's child. Folks was used to carrying secrets around with them, weighing on they hearts, forever. Everybody had something, big or small, but something. It was a time of secret-keeping, not like now. You had something in your past, well, you kept it to yourself and just lived with it. Sometimes you took it to your grave.

"Seem like it was better that way, nobody asking no questions, nobody trying to know what might notta been meant for them to know. You know how they say the truth will set you free? Well, I don't know. Seem like a secret kept could keep you safe from harm. From pain."

Big Mama leaned back and rested the palms of her hands on both thighs.

"So you see, it wasn't just Vaughn trying to keep you from finding out about her, or L.J. trying to keep a promise he made, but it was me, too, trying to protect my reputation, my family's name and standing."

"Did anyone else know?" Olivia asked.

"All that time I didn't tell nobody 'cept Joon, and of course, my sister Clo T. She knew."

"Not Glodean? Not Country?" Olivia asked.

"If they knew about it, it wasn't cause of me."

Olivia paused. "So you're my...my grandmother."

Big Mama paused, then nodded. "That's right, Baby Doll."

Olivia considered the old woman sitting across from her, the lines of age sprouting like tiny branches from the corners of her eyes, the webbed, loose flesh of her neck, the shoulders rounded by the special gravity of a secret too heavy, and too long held. Grandmother, she said to herself again. Her mother's mother. This old woman who sat unburdening herself before her was not just a charitable stranger who had stood with outstretched arms between a rain and its rainbow, but her own flesh and blood.

Big Mama sighed heavily, placing a hand on her chest. "So if you looking for your family, your blood kin, look right here." Her voice was low and quivered with emotion. "You ain't got to look no further than me."

Olivia got up and went to the dryer chair next to Big Mama's. The old woman now looked weary, as if the story had taken its toll on her strength. Her eyes glistened with tears, and she dabbed at them with the back of her hand. Olivia reached for Big Mama's hands and held them in both of hers, and noticed how small they now seemed; arthritis had narrowed the once-large bones to normal size with one or two knuckles slightly misshapen. Or maybe her grandmother's hands had never been quite as large as they seemed.

Olivia thought back to an hour ago when she'd introduced Big Mama to Stanley. When she was a child, she called each of the four women "Mama" in the presence of others. Only when she became grown had she used the phrase, "The woman who raised me." She'd never liked it, and thought how hopelessly distant and inadequate it sounded, how awkward it made her feel. She wondered now how Big Mama, her grandmother, must have felt each time she used that phrase.

Finally, Olivia spoke. "I don't know what to say. I never thought—"

At that moment, Olivia thought about L.J. and water stung her eyes. Secrets. Her truth-seeking had forced him to tell her about her mother. And here was the woman who could tell her more, sitting before her. Was Vaughn the woman of the childhood rumors, who had shot a man, maybe killed him? The woman who sang in dives and sold herself to the highest bidder? The whore of Handy? One thread of truth-telling had set the whole skein unraveling. And now there was even more to know. A truck rolled by and blared its horn at an intersection not far from the shop. It was rush hour now and the sound of traffic filled the spaces of silence. Still holding Big Mama's hand, Olivia asked, "Do you know anything more about her? My mother? Do you know what happened to her? Where she is?"

"No, child. Did, I'd of done told you. No, the onliest one who knows something like that is L.J."

"Knew."

Big Mama sat up now, shaking her head. "Baby Doll, I just have a feeling, like I done told you, that boy's somewhere alive right now."

"I thought so, too. That's why I hired an investigator to find him."

"And?"

"I haven't heard yet."

"Well, I think we ought to pay him a visit."

Olivia looked toward the window. "Lately I've been thinking. What if he's alive? Would it change anything? If he's alive, he obviously doesn't want to be with me, or he would have called or come back or something. Of course I'd like to know if he's alive. But either way, it's over."

"Maybe. But it's not just about L.J. If that boy is alive and he knows something about your mama, my daughter, I want to know it." Olivia rolled a strand of hair in her fingers. It hadn't occurred to her until now that Big Mama had a stake in this. Now that her past was laid out in the open, she would want to know what happened to her daughter, just as Olivia wanted to find her mother. Big Mama must have read her thoughts. "When L.J. told me all about him and Vaughn, I thought, well, maybe I should tell him about me, that she was the girl I gave up. Maybe it would help him. But I just couldn't bring myself to tell him. Then when he decided to keep the whole thing secret, I decided maybe it's better this way for me too. Just to let the whole thing go. After all, my daughter didn't want any part of me back then. Can't say as I blame her either. I shoulda done kept her. Run off by myself and raised her. The Lord woulda made a way for us, somehow. She mighta been better off. I couldn't tell much about her that day she showed up at the shop, but one thing I did know. She wasn't happy. She done had a hard life already, and wasn't even thirty yet. No. She didn't want to have nothing to do with me, except for whatever money I could give her."

Olivia smiled a wry smile and squeezed Big Mama's hand. *She didn't want anything to do with either of us,* she thought.

"But now, I guess because I done got old, time to make my peace. Now I want to know what become of my only daughter, my girl. Course I want to know if L.J.'s all right, if he's safe. But he's the onliest one who can tell us what happened to Vaughn."

Olivia looked at her watch. "Everything around here is closed now," she said. "But first thing tomorrow morning, we can go see Harlan Doakes."

Big Mama sighed, and rose forward to the edge of her chair. "All right, Baby Doll. This is been a long day anyway. I'm wore out."

"Let's stop on the way home, get some ice cream to go with the pound cake," Olivia said. "Let's celebrate."

"Celebrate what?"

"Us. You and me. Grandmother and granddaughter."

Big Mama smiled sadly, shook her head. "I shoulda raised her. Shoulda kept my child. Can't nobody raise a child like her mama."

"Oh. I don't know about that." Olivia said. She took Big Mama's arm in hers as they walked out of the shop. "Look at me," she smiled, turning back once again to look at the new and improved Madam C's. She squeezed Big Mama's shoulder. "I think I turned out OK."

· TWENTY-THREE ·

BIG MAMA NEEDED HELP walking up the steps of the Davis-Reynolds building, so Olivia put her arm around her to steady the old woman for the two flights. "These here old buildings is hell," Big Mama said. "Oughta have a elevator in this place."

They found Doakes's office closed with no lights on inside, and a cardboard clock sign on the door with the black paper hand saying he'd return at noon.

"We'll just wait, then," Big Mama said, looking at her watch. It was 11:30.

They sat on a wooden bench between two philodendrons in the hallway. At 12:05 Doakes showed up, carrying a white bag in one hand and a steaming coffee cup in the other.

"Ms. Tillman!" he said, surprised, then looked at Big Mama, and nodded. He held open the door. "You ladies come on in."

Olivia and Big Mama sat in the two wooden chairs in front of Doakes's big desk. "This is Ms. Eunice Benton, one of my guard—my grandmother." Olivia said, catching Big Mama's eye and smiling. "We're sorry to just show up like this…"

He waved a hand. "Not at all," he said. "In fact, I was almost ready to call you with my report. I needed another day or two to confirm a couple of things. Would either of you care for a doughnut?"

Olivia shook her head. "You've found something?" Her heart began to race.

"Well, it would be better if we waited a few days, but since you're here, I'll tell you what I have." He took a sip of coffee and pulled a brown folder from beneath a pile of papers on his desk. "I did a lot of work here in town, called the police, went back to the scene, talked to a few people who he'd seen the night of his accident, including your friend Jimmy—" He shuffled through papers.

"Bell," Olivia said.

"Yeah. That's right. Anyway, I found nothing."

"Oh."

He held up a hand. "But wait a minute." He told her he'd happened to go to New York a week ago for his nephew's wedding, and a friend, also an ex-cop, suggested he poke around New York for information. Lots of musicians, his friend said, come to New York to start their lives over. So he checked the membership of the musicians' union, not only in New York but also Chicago, Los Angeles, and San Francisco.

"Those towns probably hire more jazz musicians than others, at least that's what my buddy said. I came up with twenty-one L. or L.J. Tillmans, six of whom play the saxophone. It's not exactly an uncommon name. But your husband has only been missing since October of last year. I'm still waiting to hear about that, about new members who signed up around that time, work records, social security numbers, and so on. I should know something conclusive in a couple of days."

Big Mama looked at Olivia and smiled. "See, Baby Doll," she said. "There's still hope. Betcha he's out there."

Olivia looked down at her hands and rubbed them together in her lap.

Doakes sat back in his chair, his fingers drumming on the wooden arms. "Maybe. It's possible one of those musicians is our man. It's also possible he never left the river. But Ms. Tillman, I think I know what you're thinking, and I know I don't have to tell you that a lot of guys who disappear like this, if in fact your husband did, don't want to be found. I'm not trying to tell you what to do, but I'd suggest that if we do find him, you should weigh your next move very carefully. Most men who wander off and don't contact their wives have their own reasons. If you go after him, you might not like what you find." He paused, then added, "If you don't mind my asking, were you on good terms when he disappeared?"

Olivia blinked. "Not exactly. Well, no, not at all."

Big Mama reached over for Olivia's hand. "One thing at a time, Baby Doll. Let's just find out first. Then go from there." She looked back at Doakes. "Thank you for your help."

Big Mama and Olivia got up to leave, and Doakes rose from his seat. As he held the door he said, "I've had a few cases like this before. I'm afraid whatever I come up with won't be the happiest news, if you know what I mean."

"Yes," Olivia said. "I know. But if you could find out something certain, something definite, believe me, it would help."

"I understand," he said. "I'll do my best."

Big Mama took Olivia's arm, and looked up at Doakes. "Whatever your best brings us," she said, "we'll take it."

Shadows from the dimming sun darkened the front porch, and the long branches of the pine sapling Forest Fine, Olivia's gardener, had planted in the front yard curled against the slow breezes. He must have read Olivia's mind. While she was out, he'd come by to trim the juniper bushes, which had begun to look a little shabby, and water the grass, which was beginning to take on the pale green of the coming spring.

Big Mama and Olivia sat rocking on the glider, the only sound between them the gnaw of metal against rusted metal. Someday she might oil the springs, but for now, there was a quiet comfort in their soprano squeals. Big Mama had suggested they sit out tonight. After all, it was a beautiful evening, and after such a day it would do them good. "Folks don't do enough porch-sitting these days, with air conditioning and everything," she'd said. "That's part of what's wrong with the world today." She'd concocted an elaborate explanation of how sitting on porches could end most of the ills of the world, especially the crime infesting northern cities. "Down south, we don't just let these here porches sit and rot. You sit on your porch, you ease your troubles, you get to know your neighbors better," she'd said. "Know everybody's coming and going, the way it used to be down south. Thataway, somebody come sniffing around looking for trouble, you spot 'em right away."

Olivia sat next to Big Mama in a T-shirt and jeans, a *Good House-keeping* article on low-fat cooking open in her lap. Big Mama had a straw bag at her feet from which she drew more of the mail she'd brought with her. She sat contentedly, occasionally reading a line or two of a letter from some friend she'd re-established contact with.

Olivia found herself reading the same sentence three times, so distracted was she by thoughts of her meeting with Doakes. What would she do if L.J. were found? She thought about the last night she had seen him, his revelation of the promise to Vaughn that amounted to a betrayal beyond words, the heartbreaking sliver of silence that shook Olivia to the core. What would she do? Go after a man who wasn't sure, after twenty-five years, why he wanted her? If he did? A man who let her think he was dead for a whole year?

"Looka here!" Big Mama said, holding up a new envelope postmarked from Nebraska and interrupting Olivia's thoughts. "Remember Sedona Johnson? No, I don't guess you remember her. You was just a little thing when she used to come in the shop. Liked her hair tinted bright red. I hated it, but I always give my customers what they want. She moved to Lincoln, Nebraska years ago. Lord Jesus, she used to love it when you sang around the shop. You cain't remember, you was so small, but she used to give you a quarter when you sang "A Tisket A Tasket" just like Ella. Remember that?"

Olivia put her magazine down. "The song, yes, but the woman... What was her name again?"

"Sedona—oh, never mind. You couldn't of been more than three." A pickup truck rolled into a driveway across the street and Big Mama looked up. A man and woman—the man in coveralls and the woman in a green trenchcoat—got out and went into the house. "See, that's what I'm talking about. Bet you don't know nothing about them folks. They ain't even speaking. And where's the kids in this neighborhood?"

Olivia watched the couple—the Jensons, who had a daughter, Sharita, in high school. "There're a few," Olivia said, looking back down at her magazine. She didn't feel like getting into a discussion on why kids didn't play stickball in the streets anymore. She leaned back and for the fourth time began to read the article. There was so much for them to talk about, so many questions she wanted to ask the woman who had, as her grandmother, taken on a new aura. But Olivia decided to wait for Big Mama to broach the subject.

"By the way, Baby Doll," Big Mama licked a stamp and placed it in the upper corner of a beige envelope. "When's that club opening up you were talking about? You say you singing again. Ever since I been here, I ain't heard a note of music coming from you."

Olivia hadn't thought about that in a while, she'd been so busy entertaining Big Mama. She'd talked to Cornelius once since the first rehearsal, and they'd agreed to talk again to set another time after Big Mama had gotten settled in. In fact, she remembered, she was supposed to have called him today. She sat forward on the glider and rested her elbows on her knees. "I don't know if I want to do it now. I just don't know if I can sing anymore."

Big Mama put down a letter, looked at Olivia, and shook her head. "What a voice you had when you was little. I swear, you was good enough to be on TV, everybody said so. Seemed like one minute you was singing and then the next minute you wasn't. It wasn't just because of them girls teasing you, was it? Or your teeth getting broke?"

Olivia remembered the day May Frances and her friend taunted her on the way home from school. It really had little to do with that, or her broken teeth, she remembered. She was too embarrassed to sing. She'd heard about this woman, a tramp, some of her classmates' mothers called her. A singing tramp. Then came the whispers, the rumors, the fingers pointed at Olivia. Singing no longer held the joy it once did. The less Olivia did that would connect her with that woman, the better.

"Well," Olivia started. "I never told you, when I was little, there were rumors about a woman singing down at the club—Vaughn. And me. The illegitimate daughter of the town whore. I didn't believe what they were saying, but I didn't want to give anybody else reason to believe it either."

Big Mama said, "I didn't know nothing about Vaughn back then, not til she showed up at my door. L.J. told me she was a singer down at that place where nobody but them rowdy liquor-drinking folks in

Handy hung out, and I guess it's true, she done had her way with more than one woman's man."

Big Mama looked up at Olivia. "But baby, that was a long time ago. That ain't got nothing to do with now. I always felt you was born to sing. It's been a long time but it ain't been too long. You still got it, buried inside of you. It'll just take a little time. You always was a impatient child." She looked down again, pulled another envelope out of her sack, and looked at it frowning. "I wonder who this is from. I don't recall writing nobody in New York."

Olivia sat back and the glider let out a long squeal. She wanted to sing. But she was not the same girl who sang around that shop, not at all. In fact, she didn't even know who that child was. Singing was a habit when she was little, and then for reasons she didn't completely understand, suddenly it wasn't. Could she really blame the overshadowing image of Vaughn, still, for shattering her confidence? "I don't know, it just didn't feel right," she said. "I know I need more practice. Connie said I just needed to believe in myself more, that I shouldn't expect to sing like a pro overnight—"

Olivia sensed that Big Mama was not listening. She looked at her, and the old woman's complexion was pale. She stared, unblinking, at the letter before her. Bad news from someone, Olivia thought. "Big Mama, what is it? Is there something wrong?"

Big Mama said nothing. She handed Olivia the letter, staring straight ahead. Olivia took it, and before she read a word, the handwriting made her heart drum wildly. The fiercely slanting "Ts", the looping "Ss." The dots above the "Is" so far to the right that they seemed part of another word.

It could be no one but him.

Her face became hot as blood rushed to it. She could not speak, but a tiny sound unloosed from her throat, which had suddenly gone dry. She looked at Big Mama, whose face mirrored her own shock.

Finally, the words choked out in a coarse whisper.

"My God," she said. "He's alive."

XI

· TWENTY-FOUR ·

"**H**OW MUCH?"

The toll booth attendant, middle-aged and bespectacled, leans forward from the window as his wire-rims drip water. "Just what the sign says, mac," he says, pointing. L.J. fishes out enough bills and change, rolling down the car window just low enough to hand over the exact fare, trying to keep out the rain.

"Thanks," L.J. says, rolling up the window. He pulls off, moving headlong into the torrent. With the rain increasing, parts of the New Jersey Turnpike are like little rivers, shoetop-deep, with beads of water spiking up off the surface. He's pushing the old Delta 88 a little too fast for the weather, maybe, and the visibility isn't great. But come hell or high water, he's got to get as much road under the wheels as possible before pulling into a Motel 6 somewhere along the way, maybe around Columbus. That way he can arrive in early afternoon with enough day left to find her, talk to her, before laying his head down to sleep even one night in Kansas City.

It's only afternoon, but the day looks much older. The windshield wipers fan a triangle of visible road through the sheets of water, in rhythms that sounds like calypso. A soaked maple leaf unlooses from a wiper blade and snaps away. How many miles has he gone? No use thinking about that now. Too early in the trip and too many miles to go. He checks the odometer, then sets it at zero, something he meant to do earlier. He touches his right temple, which is still throbbing.

He still can't remember anything that happened right after that big bolt of lightning. He remembers the boy, tall and dark, his big feet pacing like a panther's, stalking lunch. Sweat covering his face, eyes like lit coals. Spasms of light erupting in the far sky, the rain coming down, like now, in thick curtains, the thunder rolling like a metal drum. The blinding glint of steel, waving and pointing. The boy in a madman's rage, looking for the package that wasn't there, throwing books, shoes across the room.

The thunder bolt, the big one. The closing dark.

He'd awakened, head throbbing, on a white-sheeted gurney in a corridor of emergency at Mercy. Staring up at white drop tiles and long tubes of light, thinking he'd been shot for sure. But the ER doctor, a bone-thin Asian woman, told him it had been a sharp blow to the side of his head—the butt end of the gun maybe?—leaving him with a concussion and a knot that looked like an orange protruding from his skull. He'd mumbled something that made no sense, even to him.

"You're probably OK," she said. "Your X rays show nothing serious. But we want to watch you so we'll keep you a day or so."

His semi-private room faced west, and through the setting sun blazing in the window he saw himself making his way in the same direction; it was time to go. He didn't need to be beaten over the head to know it was time to get out of this town. Or maybe that was just what he needed. It had seemed so long ago that sweet New York had slipped its song in his ear, had lured him in at train-speed, and wasn't the big town every jazz man's dream? Like every music man given half the chance, he'd flirted with the lady for a time. Let her distract him from what really held his heart. He could spend forever getting ready and making a plan, pooling together enough coin, shaking off the crusty shell of street hustler and shaping himself back into a man Olivia might want again. The truth was, he was scared. But he wanted her like he wanted to keep breathing, and there was no sense waiting longer. There was nothing holding him here.

Except Marcus.

The police had come, had said a young boy, about eight or nine, had called 911 but disappeared before they arrived. They asked him about the older boy, the one who'd clocked him. L.J. told them all he knew, guarding his words for Marcus's sake. He'd spent that whole night awake, thinking about the boy, worrying himself into a state. What if they found them both together? Roy, he was sure, had a rap sheet the length of the Turnpike. Marcus was just a baby, but nobody was seeing nine-year-old boys these days the way they used to. What kind of criminal things had Roy been getting Marcus to do for him? He'd always been too scared to ask. Could they hold a nine-year-old, send him to prison? He'd heard stories, awful ones. No. The ones his age probably got carted off to some juvenile home. Marcus probably had done plenty in his short life to qualify.

What would become of him? He couldn't bear the thought.

His second full day in Mercy, his ears still rang like sirens, his balance was still off when he tried to walk to the bathroom, and he was seeing double. But he was determined to go on his own, no matter how much the room spun. He opened the door, and on the floor under the sink lay the curled-up body of a nine-year-old boy.

He felt dizzy as he reached down to grab the sleeping boy. Marcus awoke with a startled yell, his eyes as big as cue balls. He was cold, shivering, and running at the nose. L.J. grabbed the boy and hugged him with all his might.

"Boy, what are you doing here? I been worried sick about you."

"Roy, they got Roy," Marcus said, crying now. "They took him away."

L.J. said nothing, just crouched on the floor and held the boy for as long as it took him to fall asleep again. When the boy finally awoke, it was night. L.J. got his clothes on, walked out of the hospital room with the sleepy-eyed boy's hand in his, and never looked back.

He'd taken him to his apartment, still a mess from Roy's ransacking. He put him to bed, then paced the floor, deciding what to do. So strong was the urge to leave, to get the hell out quickly, that he could hardly stand it. But the boy. What could he do about him?

He'd have to leave the boy here, he knew that. Take him back to the red-eyed woman in that filthy place. He was hers, her charge. He had no rights to Marcus, as much as it pained him to admit it. The boy was not his.

"Take me with you," Marcus said, rubbing his eyes as he sat mop-ing over the bowl of cornflakes and sliced apples L.J. had set in front of him.

"I can't. I can't just take you."

"Why not?"

L.J. sat on the bed and stroked his chin, rubbed the back of his head. Maybe there was something he could do. Go to social services, see if there was some way he could be placed in a foster home. Pre-sent a case that the boy wasn't well treated, or something. He didn't know.

"You're a kid. You can't just take a kid somewhere because you want to. They got laws."

Lame. He thought. How could the kid possibly understand what he didn't understand himself.

"But don't you like me?"

L.J. leaned his elbows on his knees, his head between his hands. *Like* him. The last time someone had dug into his heart this way, he was standing in a bus station in a small Missouri town with a stupid look on his face.

He got up and walked to the table, sat across from Marcus, and looked him directly in the eye. "Listen to me. You're my main man," he said. "Don't you ever forget that."

"Then why can't I go?"

"You know I want to take you with me. It's just…it's illegal. Your cousin takes care of you. She's in charge of you."

Marcus lowered his head practically inside the bowl and shoveled a spoonful of cornflakes into his mouth. "She ain't even there most of the time," he said, his mouth full.

The boy was right. It didn't make sense, and it wasn't fair, like so much that happened in life.

"Let me talk to her. She can change her ways. I'll tell her you're not happy there. That she's not doing a good job of taking care of you. Maybe convince her to get some counseling. Something."

"It'll work out," L.J. said in a tone that wasn't convincing, even to him.

The next day, Saturday, he took the boy back. The red-eyed woman was there. This time she opened the door wide, so wide the layered odors hit L.J. full in the face: urine, alcohol, and somewhere beneath, the pungent smell of marijuana. Nita couldn't have been more than thirty-five, gaunt-faced, with two side teeth missing. She wore an oversized red T-shirt under baggy denim overalls. Her deep-brown skin looked sallow, and thick braids half-covered her crimson eyes. He recognized the look, but it was one he'd usually seen in doorways and under bridges. She was high on something, L.J. thought. And it wasn't a good high.

"Where you been, you little monkey-faced fool?" Her speech was slow, her words gnarled. She wore a smirking expression on her face as she looked down at Marcus, who without looking at L.J. took off running to a bedroom.

"You more trouble than you worth," she yelled after him.

She shook her head and looked up at L.J. "You want that boy, mister, you can have him. That money I get for him ain't near enough."

"That's some way to talk about your family, your cousin."

She had turned from him, and now whirled back around.

"What you say?" she said, her red eyes large, her finger pointing at L.J. "Looka here. You trying to tell me how to raise these kids?"

A pig-tailed girl of five or six, dressed in a dingy T-shirt that reached her knees, emerged from a bedroom, carrying an infant awkwardly in her arms.

"She sick again," said the girl. "She still hot, and she puking all over the bed."

Nita looked down at the infant and sadness covered her face like a veil. "Put her back in the bed, Shaunice. I'll see about her."

Nita turned back to L.J., and he considered whether the red in her eyes was from drugs or tears.

"Look Mister. I done buried one baby already this year. Now this one's sick. You come in here high and mighty but you ain't got no idea…" She stopped when the piercing wail of a screaming baby filled the room.

"SHAUNICE!" she yelled over her shoulder. "I gotta go."

315

"Can I come in for a minute? Maybe I can help…"

The door slammed in his face.

Days later he walked the streets, his mind a welter of tangling thoughts. To go or stay. How to help the boy. After hours of walking, he needed distraction. He bought a bag of groceries—a small canned ham, orange juice, poppy-seeded crackers, a loaf of oat-nut bread—and went to find Honeymoon.

The minute he turned into the alley, his heart sank. The alley was clean. No debris. No crates. No Honeymoon.

He went inside the bakery on the corner. "Where's the old man who used to hang out back here in the alley?" he asked the clerks.

Two white boys in their teens looked at each other and shrugged. "Dunno," one said. "Mr. Katz might know, but he's out right now."

L.J. sat at a small wooden table holding the groceries and sipping a mug of coffee until the owner, a thick-browed bald man who spoke in a Yiddish accent, appeared.

"Oh, that old fella? Yeah, used to play some nice blues harmonica, he did. I give him coffee now and then, you know, day-old bagel. What it cost me? Nothing. I say live, let live. But somebody complain I guess. He drank a little. Cops come around one day, see the old fella passed out back there. Wasted. Woke up coughing, kinda sick. I says, 'Leave the old man alone, he don't bother nobody!' But they send him on his way. Sweep him away like trash, I tell ya."

Katz shook his head as he placed a new filter in the coffee urn. "Don't know where he went, but he don't look so good. Like maybe he not gonna make it, trust me, I know the look. Ten to one he's dead by now."

"Awww," L.J. said in a voice that came from his gut, as if he'd been dealt another blindside blow. He stood there a moment, groceries in hand, his face a blank mask. Then he walked out of the bakery into the afternoon light.

He checked the library, the men's shelter. No luck. He called hospital emergency rooms, even morgues, but still no luck. Then it occurred to him, he ought to use the name "John Doe."

He went from one morgue to another, viewing the shriveled bodies of seven John Does. The eighth one, on a shelf in the basement of Lutheran Memorial, was the withered, broken-down remains of Franklin "Honeymoon" Johnson.

L.J. sighed long and deep, and caught himself when he reeled, feeling dizzy. "Thank you," he told the young woman attendant, who put a hand on his shoulder to steady his walk out of the room. The man at the desk had told him that if no one claimed the body soon, they would have to dispose of it themselves.

"No, wait, you can't...don't do that."

"Did he have any relatives, next of kin?"

"I...I don't know," L.J. said as if his answer surprised him. Still dazed, his own voice seemed to come from somewhere else. "I'll see what I can find out."

On a long shot, he phoned the musician's local in Memphis. A man he'd known from his days playing there had once been president of the old black musician's union. The man said he thought Honeymoon Johnson had died years ago.

Maybe he did, L.J. thought. But he asked if he knew of any kin.

"He used to talk about a cousin he was tight with when they was kids," the man said. "Fellow name of Anderson Quartermaine. Talked about him all the time."

"You know where he lives?"

"Got no idea."

Anderson Quartermaine turned out to be The Reverend E. Anderson Quartermaine, a retired Baptist preacher now living in Charleston, South Carolina. L.J. found his number from a librarian who searched the files of an online telephone directory. On the phone, Reverend Quartermaine didn't seem surprised to hear the news. "My wife and I will take responsibility," he said soberly. "We'll see to it that Brother Franklin gets a proper homegoing. We'll be there as soon as we can."

In less than forty-eight hours the Reverend showed up, a robust man in a black suit a size too small for his portly frame, with a full head of jet-black hair that was obviously dyed. His wife was a tiny, demure woman with a fixed, sympathetic smile.

"We'll take Franklin back with us," he told L.J. in the hospital corridor. He filled out forms, made phone calls. Later, as they sat over weak coffee in a booth in the cafeteria, Quartermaine said, "Sixty-nine years old. Two older than me." Then shook his head and turned up his coffee cup.

L.J. only nodded, stirring his coffee slowly with a plastic spoon.

"We used to play together, as kids, you know," he said. "Haven't seen him since, what, maybe sixty-five? That's when I got the 'call'. He went one way and I went another. He and Liz headed off to Chicago, trying to make it big."

L.J. tried to imagine Honeymoon thirty years ago, head full of hair and eyes full with possibility. "I liked him," was all he could think of to say. "I liked him a lot."

Quartermaine's wife placed a hand on his arm. "They want us to check in by five," she said.

Her husband looked at his watch. "Time to get on over there."

As he stood up, he said, "Almost forgot. They found something on him. You were his last friend," he said. "I think he would want you to have this."

From his pocket he pulled out a small, metal harmonica, trimmed in wood.

L.J. reached for it, and turned it in the palm of his hand. He cleared his throat and coughed around the wedge in his throat. He nodded his head several times, unable to speak. "Thank you," he finally managed in a whisper, looking down, averting his wet eyes from the preacher's.

The preacher nodded, shook his hand finally, and the couple walked away to deal with the end of Honeymoon Johnson. L.J. stood in the corridor for minutes, staring at the mouth harp, turning it in his hands.

He thought of Honeymoon's words to him, sitting in the alley, before he left to go on tour. *This is being old and lonely.* For nights afterwards he slept fitfully. Sleep came, but in pebble-sized lumps and watery trickles, his head rolling from side to side. Thinking, *If only he had*…and a string of hindsight possibilities followed.

He thought of how even a great city could claim you, chew on you until there was nothing left to stand. Honeymoon was gone. It was time to go. But it was not as easy as that. He was torn; there was the child to consider, another soul the street was just waiting to claim. He couldn't just walk out on a boy who'd come to depend on him. Could he?

The next few days he made plans to leave, changed his mind, then changed it back again. Thinking first about Olivia, then Marcus. With Marcus, he'd felt helpless. What could he do? He'd tried to give him something—music, a peek at his talent, a glimpse at another kind of life. Maybe the boy would remember that or maybe he wouldn't.

He'd gone to the police to see what happened to Roy, and learned he'd been picked up on carjacking, assault, and suspicion of murder. Sixteen years old. There was no telling what all Marcus had been exposed to, no telling what those babyish moon-eyes had seen.

He went to a police station and told them about Marcus, about how he was living. That the state should do better by him. They said they would "look into it."

Day and night, when he wasn't thinking of Marcus, he thought of Olivia. He had to see her, and now that he'd written Big Mama that he was alive and well, he needed to do it soon. He owed Olivia. Even if she didn't want him, he owed her. An explanation, the most humble apology he could muster.

And he owed her the story of her mother. The truth about what really happened to Vaughn.

There was no decision to make. He was gone.

The rain has stopped now, the sky light gray with pieces of sun peeking from clouds, as if the day has gathered a second breath.

He pulls off the highway into an Exxon station to check the oil gauge. Not bad, not even a half-quart low. He'd bought the twelve-year-old Olds, sight unseen, from Crawfish's nephew in Queens, who'd just finished dental school and was looking to buy a new Mustang. A new fuel pump, gas filter, a tune-up, and some brake pads, and he was good to go. The guys took his leaving well, especially after he'd found a replacement for the gigs coming up, a tall, light-skinned kid from California with a Sonny Rollins tone and chops for days. He'd be back for the recording, he told the men, but the truth was he didn't know what the future held. He decided to take a page out of Purvis's book. *No need to see around the corner, 'cause when you reach that corner, there'll be another view.*

He fills the tank with high octane, locks the car, and pays for the gas. When he returns, he hears yawning noises from the back seat.

Marcus is waking up. L.J. looks back at him and smiles.

"Guess you're hungry now," he says.

Marcus rubs his eyes, stretching. "Can we get a Mighty Burger?"

L.J. reaches back and gives the boy's head a playful rub. The watery air smells fresh, and the sky is light. He starts the engine. Further down the strip of the off ramp, he sees a pair of golden arches.

"Not out here," he says. "Quarter-pounder'll have to do."

XII

· TWENTY-FIVE ·

"**W**HERE IS SHE NOW? What's she doing?"
Big Mama opened the front door wider and pointed a finger toward the ceiling. "Upstairs, probably in the bed. Goes to work, then comes straight home, goes upstairs, and stays there til morning."

Winona stepped inside the house and followed Big Mama into the kitchen, her arms clutching a brown grocery sack.

"She eating anything?"

"Won't eat hardly nothing. Just some toast this morning, and some microwave popcorn last night, sitting up watching *The Sound of Music* on cable til dawn. She always was a stubborn child. I tried to tell her, ain't you at least glad he's alive? What if the boy turned up down at the bottom of that river 'stead of in New York? Would you feel better then?'

"What'd she say to that?"

Big Mama pulled a chair out from the oak table, sat down, and crossed her ankles. "Something smart. Said, I don't wish death on nobody, but at least he'd of had a good reason for not calling or something, for letting me go through all that grief. I told her, well Baby Doll, you done told him to get out and don't come back. She said yeah, but considering the circumstances, she had a right to say something she didn't mean. But that wasn't no reason for him to let her think he was dead all this time."

Winona put her grocery bag on the table and pulled out several slender packages wrapped in glossy white paper. "Big Mama, I stopped and got some fresh catfish from Hy's Market. Thought we could have a little fish fry tonight. Maybe that'll cheer her up."

"Just put it on that bottom shelf in the icebox, baby," Big Mama said. "I don't know. Since she read that letter, it's like she found out he was dead, 'stead of finding out he was alive. Moping around all sad and pitiful, looking like death riding a Popsicle stick. *Then,* seem like she got angry at him, walking around here spittin' nails. Like he got his nerve, being alive!"

Winona opened the refrigerator door and placed the packages on the shelf. "So what did the letter actually say?"

Big Mama leaned forward across the table and folded her hands beneath her chin. "Seeing that letter liked to knock me off my feet. Like carrying around a ghost with you and not knowing it. Couldn't believe I had it with me all that time." She sighed. "It was short. Didn't say too much. Just that he was living in New York. Said he had a real hard time at first, but he's better now. But then he said a funny thing."

"What's that?"

"Said he could understand why Olivia hung the phone up on him when he called. He said he was coming back here soon as he could, and could I please talk to Olivia to help make her understand he didn't mean to hurt her so. That he didn't mean to cause her all that pain. He musta called the wrong number, or something."

Winona shook her head. "Dialed his own number wrong?"

"What else can you figure?"

Winona shrugged. "I don't know. I don't get it. But there's a lot of stuff happens I don't understand."

"By the way," she said. "Does L.J. know you're Olivia's grand-mother?"

Big Mama's voice quieted, and she shook her head slowly. "No. Before I told Olivia, I never told that to nobody but my sister and my husband."

Big Mama looked toward the open kitchen window as the evening light sifted in. A finch sat on a thin branch of the maple for a second, then took wing. "Days getting longer now," she said. "Spring already. Funny how time moves on, and things change just 'cause of that. A month ago, I never thought I'd be sitting here in this kitchen talking about Olivia being my granddaughter and waiting for L.J. to come back."

Winona said nothing for a moment, then reached back into the bag and pulled out two plastic cartons. "Now Big Mama, you know I don't cook. So I got this potato salad from the deli counter."

Big Mama frowned, got up, and took one of the cartons. "From Hy's? They can't make no potato salad. They too stingy. No eggs, and too much mayonnaise. Give it here. I'll doctor it up a little bit with some onion and some mustard and sweet pickle. Some celery and paprika too if Baby Doll got any. I guess you want me to do the fish, too?"

"Big Mama, from what I hear, nobody else should even try to fry catfish while you're in the house."

"Well, now, that's true." Big Mama smiled. "'Cept my husband. Joon could do a mean barbecued catfish on the grill. Olivia loved it when she was a little thing. I brought some sauce with me from home, but I don't see no grill around here."

"There's a grill," Winona said. "We used it last summer when we got those steaks from Mr. Fine's son, who works at that cold-storage place. Olivia'll know where."

Winona pulled a head of romaine lettuce, four tomatoes, a bunch of carrots, and some green onions from the bag, while Big Mama pulled down a large yellow plastic bowl from the cabinet.

"Well, at least Olivia's back working again," Winona said. "Maybe that'll take her mind off things."

"Working?" Big Mama said. "Barely. Got that pretty shop all fixed up, and act like she don't care nothing about it. Ain't hardly got no customers, and don't seem like she want none. Said—get this—said she's thinking about giving up doing hair, selling the shop."

"What? Selling it to who and then doing what?"

"You know that child that works for her? What's her name? Cora. Cora and her boyfriend Raymond is getting married. Olivia been making noises about quittin' the business, so Cora and Raymond jumped up, said they'd get a loan and buy the shop from her whenever she was looking to sell. Olivia said she was actually thinking about it.

She might take the money, take some time off, decide what to do with the rest of her life."

"The rest of her life? She's not but forty-five years old, a couple of years younger than me."

A noise from the doorway, the sound of a throat clearing, made them both turn.

"Forty-three. If you're going to talk about me, at least get your facts straight."

Olivia stood in the kitchen doorway, her hair tied in a flowered scarf, her worn yellow buttonless robe gaping wide open revealing a wrinkled gray nightgown.

"How long you been standing there?" Winona said.

"A while," Olivia said. "I heard your car pull up." She let out a small, dry laugh. "Then my ears started to itch."

Big Mama dumped potato salad into the yellow plastic bowl, and mixed it with a wooden spoon. "Well, I guess that old wives' tale is true cause we sure 'nough been talking about you. We worried about you, is all."

"What's this about you selling the shop?" Winona asked.

"Oh, I don't know what I'm going to do. Did Jimmy call?"

Big Mama dipped a finger in the potato salad, tasted it, and wiped her hands on a striped dishtowel. "Nobody called you today."

"I'm going back up to take a bath," said Olivia. "If Jimmy calls, Big Mama, tell him I can't do it. I already left him a message, but tell him again, I just can't sing for that opening."

Big Mama looked up from the potato salad.

"Now wait a minute, Baby Doll. You mean to tell me you just gonna leave that poor man hanging after you done told him you would sing?"

"I can't do it."

"Yes you can. And you will. Now listen. Ain't no use in you walking around here all sad and upset and not doing nothing else. Singing'll be the best thing for you right now. Believe me. The best thing."

"You seen the club yet?" Winona asks her. "Everybody's talking about how it's going to bring back the neighborhood to what it once was. And there's a new restaurant, lady from Harlem owns it, opening down the street. They even got a jazz museum and baseball museum planned less than a block away. I thought you'd be excited about it, Olivia, since you've got money in it."

Big Mama's eyebrows raised. "You got money in that club?"

"Oh, some. Jimmy was looking for people and it sounded like a pretty good investment. L.J. and I—we had been saving up for a while, you know, to start our own place. I figured it was the closest we…I'd ever get to having a club."

"Well, Jimmy Bell's my client now," Winona said. "He wants my cleaners to do laundry for the club—tablecloths, napkins, uniforms, towels. Anyway, I went down there to take a peek. Jimmy's down there every night unpacking boxes, getting stuff ready. Child, you won't believe it. Jimmy went all out. It's the best-looking club any black man ever opened up in this town."

Big Mama stirred yellow mustard, sweet pickle relish, and red onions into the potato salad. "Well, I think we ought to go down there ourselves after dinner and take a look-see. Maybe you'll change your mind when you see the place," she said, looking at Olivia. "You got any paprika? And where's your barbecue grill?"

"I'm not going," Olivia said.

"Nonsense." Big Mama said. She slammed the wooden spoon against the side of the bowl, and fixed a stern gaze on Olivia. "Child, I done had just about enough of your sackdraggin'. Now get upstairs and take your bath and put some decent clothes on. You one sorry sight. You been wearing that old ratty robe since baby Jesus was born." She whacked the spoon against the bowl again, sending a glop of mayonnaise flying. "And looka that hair. Don't look at me in that tone of voice; gone and get up there while I fix this dinner. Winona, baby, go bring in the mail. I don't want this child out there cause it's too many old people in this neighborhood with bad hearts."

Olivia ran her fingers through tangles in her hair, and pulled her used-to-be yellow housecoat around her waist.

Winona tried to hide a smile that itched to break into laughter.

Big Mama went back to stirring the potato salad with a vengeance.

"Now I'm a guest in your house, and I spects to be entertained hospitably. I say we going to that club, granddaughter. And you *gonna* have a good time." She tasted the potato salad again.

"Winona, put me two eggs on to boil," she said. "And where's that paprika?"

Jimmy met them by the new gray-stuccoed, smoke-glassed front of The Rhythm Room. As he unlocked the door and let them in, Big Mama's eyes grew large, and she sucked in her breath.

"Ummm, ummm," she said. "My, my."

"Like it?" Jimmy said. "We decided to spruce up the front a bit. Why not? Gives people an idea of what they'll see inside."

Inside, all three women were speechless. The black-topped circular bandstand stood under state-of-the art theatrical lighting, with a small, black-lacquered Yamaha grand off to one side. The walls were pale blue with black molding, and light fixtures above and on tables were designed to look like piano keys. In the middle of the room stood a U-shaped bar, oak veneer trimmed with brass rails, with twelve sleek, high-backed bar stools. Martini glasses and wine goblets hung upside-down from thin wooden racks above the bar, and along the walls the black and pewter geometric sconces added an Art Deco touch. There were framed impressionistic paintings of jazz greats: Billie Holiday, Lester Young, Duke Ellington, and the Kansas City-bred icons Charlie Parker, Count Basie, and Mary Lou Williams.

"Told y'all," Winona said as she stood by the bar, smiling, hands on both hips, rotating slowly to admire the view.

"What do you think?" Jimmy asked, directing his question to everyone but eyeing Olivia. He removed his baseball cap and the jacket of his warmup suit and placed them on the bar.

Olivia turned slowly, seeing the room from every angle. Her face held the expression of a child's first glance at a Christmas tree. Her gaze settled on the piano, the small bandstand, the lighting above it.

"A new piano?" she said. She ran her fingers across the lid's shining surface.

"Brand spanking new," Jimmy said, walking over to where Olivia stood.

"Well, barkeep, what's a lady got to do to get a drink in this place?" Winona said, hoisting herself up on a seat at the bar and crossing her legs. She slapped the palm of her hand against the counter. "I feel like making a toast."

"You got it, Miss Lady." Jimmy smiled, rubbing his hands together as he rushed to the bar, and Big Mama joined them, raising herself up on a bar stool with Winona's help. Jimmy reached beneath the bar and grabbed a bottle of Moët from a cooler.

"I've been serving this to folks, friends of mine that've been stopping by this week, like you all," He said. "Big Mama gets the first drink."

"Oh, my goodness," said Big Mama, her face lighting up. "I don't know as I ever had no champagne before."

"Well," he said. "It's high time." He uncorked the bottle with a loud pop that made Big Mama jump, then poured a fluted glass full. Bubbles danced around the rim.

Big Mama took a cautious sip. "Mmm, this is tasty." She took another long sip and licked her lips. "I could drink this all night. Better watch out. Y'all gonna have me sittin' up here drunk. And ain't nothing worse than a old drunk country woman."

"Tell you what, Big Mama," Jimmy said, pouring a second glass and setting it in front of Winona. His voice lowered, and he nodded toward the front of the room. "You talk Olivia into singing for the opening, you can have all the champagne you want."

Winona laughed and waved her hand dismissively. "If she can pull that off, it'd be worth a whole lot more than a little champagne."

"Well, I'll do my best," said Big Mama, "but that's one stubborn girl." She eased the glass up to her mouth again, then giggled. "Oooh, child, the bubbles do tickle, just like they say."

Jimmy poured another glass full and placed a rubber stopper in the bottle. He lifted his glass, leaning over the counter. "Well, ladies, what shall we toast? Hey, I know. This might be kinda sad, but I can't help it. We oughta toast my partner L.J., rest his soul. I swear to God, happy as I am about this place finally getting back on its feet, it just breaks my heart that L.J. isn't here to see it."

Big Mama and Winona eyed each other with a secretive look. Big Mama put down her glass, and lowered her voice. "Jimmy, honey. There's something we got to tell you. About L.J." She leaned toward Jimmy and spoke in a loud whisper. "He's alive."

"What?"

"I got a letter from him. He's been in New York all this time."

"Oh, my God."

"Don't say anything to Olivia for a while," Winona said. "It's a long story, but she's none too happy about him letting her think he was dead all this time."

"Oh, my God," Jimmy said again, putting a hand to his mouth, his features contorted in shock. "I just can't believe it. Is he OK? What's he been doing?"

"He's OK. The letter didn't say what he'd been doing." Big Mama turned up the rest of her glass. "We been, Winona and me, trying to get her to snap out of this mood she in. She been in a state ever since she found out. We thought her singing down here would be good for her."

"We gotta get her to sing," Winona said, looking at Big Mama.

"Well," Big Mama said, leaning back, "now I kinda think she might do it."

Winona looked incredulous. "How's that?"

"Don't everybody turn at once," she said, "but look over at Olivia now."

They did all turn at once to see Olivia standing on the bandstand, a black microphone in her hand. She was leaning into the curve of the piano, one hand resting on the lid, gazing out toward the room of tables and chairs. Then she closed her eyes, her head swaying. From the distance, they could not hear her. But she looked as if she were humming a tune.

She sensed the heat of silent stares and opened her eyes abruptly. "Well?" she said. "What are you all looking at?"

XIII

· TWENTY-SIX ·

A FTER THE GRAY SPRING RAINS of New Jersey, the Ohio Valley sported a crazy quilt of new spring blooms, sweet williams and blackeyed susans cocking their heads sunward along the grassy highway banks. Marcus, who had never been beyond New York's steel shoulders, leaned out of the car window wide-eyed at greening slopes awash with trees and the dome of blue overhead. The weather was perfect for travel, but even with the cooperating climate, the two-day trip L.J. had planned turned into four.

He would have cursed loudly the crawling, single-lane construction traffic in western Pennsylvania if the boy hadn't been with him, and had to temper his ire again in West Virginia when he was cited for speeding. "One-hundred fifty dollars," the beefy, narrow-eyed cop had told him, so he decided to pull into the sleepy mountain town and protest the ticket.

In the town he'd found the tiny traffic court building off the tree-lined town square and gotten the fine reduced to sixty by a tired, white-bearded judge with lunch and golf on his mind. Feeling like he'd won a bonus, he decided to relax, slow down, look around. Reconciliation with Olivia, after a year's time, would be no less easily won if he arrived a day later. Big Mama had sent him a note saying she was in Kansas City. "Try to get here by the fourteenth," she'd said, and didn't say why. He figured maybe they were going out of town or something. Anyway, it was only the eleventh; there was plenty of time.

He felt a hankering for a big, sit-down lunch, and he and Marcus found an old-fashioned diner that served real lemonade and smoky, thick-sliced Virginia-cured ham sandwiches with grilled red onions and sliced tomatoes. A young waitress with a button nose, her hair done up in a teased bouquet of blonde, recommended the hot Dutch apple pie with ice cream; Marcus consumed it entirely in four fork-fuls. L.J. had the peach cobbler, but only got two bites after he offered Marcus some.

Marcus was full of questions: How did the mountains get there? How come the roads were so twisty? How come there weren't any tall buildings, like in the city? Where'd the rivers come from? When L.J. got tired of saying, "I don't know," he made up stories. The mountains came when God stepped down from the sky and hills bulged around his footsteps. The roads used to be straight but then a big meteor crashed into the earth and shook it violently and scrambled the roads, and so on. Marcus believed him at first, but when the stories became more outrageous, he laughed. They both did. They laughed so hard they could hardly eat. After, L.J. fanned the AAA map across the stained Formica and showed Marcus how far they'd come and how far they had to go.

In Ohio they checked into a Motor Inn, then found a traveling carnival that had set up in the parking lot of a nearby Valu-Mart, roped with garlands of red, yellow, and green lights. They found burgers almost as good as the ones on Coney Island and tubs of warm popped corn dipped in caramel. L.J. held Marcus's hand as they climbed on the Rolla-Whirl, a huge Ferris wheel trimmed in sparkling lights of purple and gold. When they reached the top, while Marcus squealed at the lit-up night view of the whole town, L.J. sat back, his head raised to view the vast, starry night sky. For the first time in more than a year he felt warm, and cool, and easy, like a stream finally returned to its natural current after days of raging rain. He looked at Marcus and smiled. But then he asked himself just what the hell he thought he was doing, and how he planned to do it.

He wanted to keep this boy. Wanted to keep him for his own and raise him the way a boy ought to be raised. Music lessons and vac-cinations, braces and Little League. Father and son day at school. And maybe even, if he could work a miracle, a mother's loving care. But while he would not even allow himself to dream that far, he wondered what Olivia would think, him coming to her, begging his way back with a nine-year-old kid at his side. He must be out of his mind.

He'd felt bad about taking the boy away from school weeks before the end of term, and especially about taking the deal the red-eyed woman offered him: fifty dollars (to buy her baby some medicine, she'd claimed) in exchange for two weeks with Marcus. L.J. believed that for not much more than that she probably would have agreed to sell him the boy outright.

He'd felt bad until he'd seen the butterfly. As soon as he saw it, he knew the small voice guiding him in this unsettling direction was right. At a Days Inn outside Indianapolis, Marcus kept to his habit of hiding in the bathroom to undress. Shy kid, L.J. thought, and remembered himself one August afternoon in Vaughn's bathtub years ago. But this seemed different; after all, they were both men, weren't they? What could make a boy not want a grown man to see him with his shirt and pants off? L.J. wondered at this, and opened the bathroom door wide.

He looked at Marcus in horror. The butterfly he'd tried to hide had perfectly shaped wings, and stretched four inches across his stomach. A perfect arrangement of a connect-the-dots pattern, branded, he was certain, by a lit cigarette.

"What...who...did this?" L.J. stammered, inarticulate with rage. Marcus pulled away from him, said nothing the rest of the night. After that, L.J. only regretted not taking the boy away sooner.

The idea of raising Marcus as his son was a tiny flame warming the far edge of his mind. In that remote corner, it had dimension and light. Was it possible? The boy had a legal guardian, such as she was. But wasn't the best parent for a child sometimes simply the one who wanted to be, and could be?

It is dawn. The sun piercing the bluish clouds of the eastern sky of Missouri looks like an envelope spilling gold. The damp air smells of remembered rain, and as the sleep-quiet houses in the distance awake, lights blink on like morning stars. As the car cruises along, L.J. and Marcus play a game they have played since Indiana. L.J. got so tired of hearing Marcus practicing his scales in the backseat that he wanted to scream, so he taught the boy songs by dictation. First he sang the song in rhythm, and Marcus clapped it, then he called out note names four or five at a time, and had him play them back. F#-G-G#-A-G-E, for "Stardust," and so on. By the time they reached St. Louis, Marcus had learned "Stardust," "Billie's Bounce," "Joy Spring," and "C Jam Blues," in four different keys.

But as they enter the limits of Kansas City and pass the huge king's crown of the sports complex looming in royal blue over Interstate 70, Marcus puts down the horn, too excited to play and again full of questions.

"What do your house look like?" He is standing in the backseat leaning his elbows over the front and bouncing on his toes.

"What *does* my house look like."

"How I'm supposed to know? It's your house."

"Marcus...sit back a little. You're screaming in my ear."

"What do your wife look like?"

"What *does*...never mind. She's pretty. She's nice. You'll like her."

"How come you left, then?"

"It's a long story."

"She kick you out or something?"

"Marcus, didn't I ask you to sit back?"

Marcus sits back. After a moment he pops up again. "Are we gonna get some barbecue now, like you said?"

"Maybe later."

"When?"

"Later. You just ate twenty minutes ago."

"But I just saw a sign that said Gates's Barbecue..."

"Marcus—"

"OK. OK."

He doesn't want to admit it, but he is every bit as excited as Marcus. Sometimes the ache of loneliness, of missing her, is like the wounds on Marcus's back, sealed by time and numbing scars, but indelible. On the road ahead, between flickering trees and hills, he can see her soft smile. She'd talked about letting her hair grow long. Did she? He wonders about her face, if the pain he has caused her has left its traces in the mink-brown eyes, the sun-shot skin.

But whenever he thinks of Olivia, Vaughn is not far behind, and he can feel his whole body slacken. Vaughn. He will have to tell Olivia what happened. He realizes that in never telling her he'd known her mother, he had unburdened himself of telling what became of her, and now wonders which had driven him more; sparing Olivia the knowing, or himself the telling. Was that the reason he didn't tell her—cowardice? Or protectiveness? He'd been protective of her (and look where that had gotten him), but all the while he'd been protecting himself. It didn't matter now, because it was time to lay all the cards face up on the table and see how it all played out.

When they arrived it was early afternoon, and he drove directly to the house. His heart beat rapidly as he climbed the steps. Big Mama answered the door, and squealed her joy at seeing him. She took him in her arms and gave him a fierce, rocking hug. She looked down at the boy and without wanting or needing an explanation of his presence, hugged him too.

"Big Mama, is Olivia…?" L.J. said.

"She's at the club right now."

"The club?" he asked. And she explained. Olivia was singing at Jimmy's remodeled club, which he'd named "The Rhythm Room." The opening was tomorrow night.

Olivia singing. L.J.'s smile was uncontrollable and his eyes became wet. "Big Mama," he asked quietly. "I know you got my letter. Did she say anything, when you told her, did she say anything about me? About us?"

Big Mama first looked down at the boy, then up at L.J., both hands on her hips. "It's better," she said slowly and deliberately, "if Olivia speaks for herself."

L.J. gave a resigned nod. "Yeah, I guess so."

"If you go now, you can catch her alone. She went early before the rehearsal to go over the songs by herself." Big Mama looked down again at Marcus. "You can leave the boy here, with me."

He brushed a kiss on Big Mama's cheek. Then he leaned over toward Marcus, put a hand on his shoulder. "Remember all the things I told you about how to act in somebody's house. I'll be back for you later." He turned again to Big Mama. "You got any food?" he said. "This little guy eats like a horse."

Olivia stared at the mannequin. Curled her finger under her chin, cupped a palm under her elbow, walked around it, and viewed it from all angles.

"It's beautiful, isn't it?" The salesclerk at Walter Klein's on the Plaza was dressed in a black smock, her raven-colored hair pulled severely into a small bun at the nape of her neck.

"It is," Olivia said. "It might be just what I'm looking for."

The sleeveless black dress of matte silk sheathed the slender mannequin, its hem falling well above the knee. Its waist was cinched, the square neckline dropped, and three thin spaghetti straps crossed each shoulder.

"It's not on sale, unfortunately," said the clerk. "It's a new item, but the regular price isn't bad. It's a classic little black dress. It'll never go out of style."

Olivia had put off shopping for a dress. But when her debut night approached, she'd begun to envision herself on the stage. Every part of the image was clear—the people, the band, the club and its lights—except what she would wear. In her closet she found clothes that would take her almost anywhere—church, brunch at the Ritz-Carlton or Crown Center, even a night on the town with Big Mama and Winona. But everything suggested seeing a show, not *being* one. Even Big Mama told her, "Child, quit looking in that closet cause there ain't nothing there. I done looked myself. Get yourself something special, something that'll make you look like you belong under them bright lights."

"My name is Mindy," the clerk said, burgundy lips smiling. "Let me know if I can be of assistance." Olivia nodded and stepped away from the dress to get a better look. She could not recall the last time she was as excited as she had been just standing on that stage in the club, looking out at the U-shaped bar of brass and wood, the bar glasses hanging like Christmas bulbs, white-draped tables and chairs aimed at her. It was the feeling she missed when she looked at the new Madam C.'s. On that stage she felt like a girl again in Big Mama's Beauty Palace, where the women with rolled-up hair smiled and waited to praise whatever came out of her mouth. Where she made the whole shop come alive above the roar of hair dryers and the clicking of curling irons. *A tisket, a tasket, a green and yellow basket*...The small Motorola backing her, women snapping their fingers, their wet heads nodding.

"May I try this on?" Olivia asked.

"Of course. What size?"

"Six."

"Six. I'll get one off the rack and meet you in dressing room number two."

"Thank you."

Olivia hung the dress on a brass hook opposite the dressing-room mirror. She stepped out of her running shoes, took off her slacks, and hung them across the back of a wooden chair. She unbuttoned her blouse, took it off, and draped it over the slacks.

She slipped the dress on and looked at herself in the three-way mirror. For the first time in a while, the reflection thrown back at her was not a disappointment. In the warm light of the dressing room, she looked exactly like her best self, the woman she was used to seeing when she felt good about her life. Her eyes looked clear and bright. Her waist had slimmed down to its normal size. Her face was beginning to look, again, like the face of a woman with a peaceful life.

The dress's length, inches above her knees, made her feel a little self conscious about her thin thighs. She tried to imagine the look with black pantyhose. The waistline hugged hers perfectly, though. When she moved, the silky fabric of the lining chafed her skin with a soft hiss.

From the beginning of the second rehearsal she'd known, absolutely, that this was something she truly wanted to do. She'd been nervous at the beginning, but then Big Mama did something that immediately put her at ease. She reached into her purse and pulled out an object wrapped tightly in a brown paper sack. "Here, Baby Doll, use this."

Olivia opened the bag, looked at the object, and laughed. It was Big Mama's steel straightening comb, the same one Olivia had used as a make-believe microphone when she was singing for the ladies in Big Mama's shop. By now the wooden handle was worn and the teeth were curved and oiled black with years of use. "I carry it with me all the time for emergencies," Big Mama turned to tell Winona. She patted at her hair. "You just never know."

Olivia shook her head, still laughing, and put the comb on the piano lid. "I'm serious," Big Mama said. "Use it."

Big Mama had to be kidding, Olivia thought, but she believed she should humor the old woman. She lifted it to her mouth. Strangely, her hands around the familiar object gave her a sense of physical grace and confidence. Suddenly she remembered gestures she hadn't used in years; it was as if she had unlocked some door to a memory long forgotten. And the problem she'd had before, of what to do with those hands, how to use them to help phrase the music, was solved. Her "audience"—Big Mama, the musicians, Winona—loved it. The sight of an old greasy hot comb being handled like a cordless mike brought a smile to everyone's face and made Olivia relax even more.

The looser Olivia felt, the more her voice opened, her volume increased, her pitch became sure. Within and around the melody, she worked scales and rhythms that were her own. She took tasteful liberties with the tune—some notes up an octave and some down a third. Shaped notes at will, bent them into blue notes. Lingered languorously on some phrases, raced through others, as the mood struck. And with Big Mama and Winona sitting in front of her on the couch, both grinning, it seemed impossible to fail. They applauded every sweet turn of phrase, pleased with her and with themselves for convincing her to sing.

Cornelius was so startled at the improvement that he began bringing out new material, songs with complex key changes and changes in tempo. John Paul grinned and nodded when he wasn't playing, and Walter and Ace's pleasure showed in their play. Beads of sweat dotting his forehead, Walter held the upbeat tunes to a tight groove, his quick wrists working his sticks against the drumheads in intricate patterns, driving the pulse like a master. Ace stretched his arms around the bass's shoulders as if they belonged to a beautiful woman, his fingers dancing on high tones close to the bridge—his notes inspired by Olivia's.

In addition to the songs she already knew, Olivia had memorized "All of Me," "Embraceable You," "Love for Sale," "Autumn Leaves," "My Romance," "The Nearness of You," "Stormy Weather," and "It Never Entered My Mind." For the second set, Connie suggested keeping a few from the first and adding a few more ballads for the late, mellow crowd. Olivia lapped up each new song like a child eager for more dessert. By the end of the rehearsal, Olivia was not only ready, but giddy with anticipation. Tomorrow night she would sing in a room bereft of hair dryers and church pews, full of people who had come for only one purpose: to hear her sing. This was the beginning of something, she believed, as she turned to admire the dress in the three-way mirror. Her life was about to change.

It couldn't have come at a better time. She needed a distraction now, needed to think of something else besides L.J. Of course, she was glad he was alive. But when she'd pushed back the grief of his death, up sprang another kind, for something surely had died between them. *Tell me if it's not true.* He hadn't drowned in that river, he had merely stayed away. And while she had told him to go, his willing absence confirmed what she had thought; he was unable to separate mother from child. Whatever he felt for her was overwhelmed by his obsession with Vaughn, the one he really wanted. The real love of his life.

The letter had said he was "coming back to town" and asked Big Mama's help to "make Olivia understand" he needed to talk to her. And what was that about some phone call in the middle of the night?

Thank God for the singing, for the song lyrics crowding her mind, the complexity of tempos, key changes, and rhythms, because she didn't want to think about him. Didn't want to think about how much longer it would be, how many more hours before she would see him again. Didn't want to think about how she cried the night she learned he was alive as if the greatest prayer of her life had been answered. And when those tears were gone, how she cried again, bitterly, for all that he'd put her through.

Most of all she didn't want to think about seeing him, and what she would do, what she would say, how she would act. The thought brought a twinge of uneasiness to her stomach, so she put it aside and replaced it with "the autumn leaves fall from my window, the autumn leaves of red and gold," slow and easy, in E-flat minor.

She turned to see the back of the dress in the three-way mirrors. Then she turned around to see its front.

How would he look? She wondered. And how would she look to him?

"Everything OK in there?" Mindy's high-pitched voice cut through Olivia's thoughts from the hall outside the door of the dressing room. She looked at her watch. She hadn't planned to take this long. But if she left now she could still have some time at the piano to vocalize before the rehearsal.

"Fine," Olivia said. "I'll take it."

After L.J. left Marcus with Big Mama, he'd driven directly to the spot where the old club had been and was dazzled by the new front of the place, gray stucco, a bright red awning, block letters spelling out "The Rhythm Room" in neon tubes. Jimmy had gotten some money from somewhere. This club looked better than the places he'd played in New York. He drove up and down and around the block looking for where Olivia might have parked her car. Not seeing the Jetta he drove away, going nowhere in particular. Maybe she stopped somewhere along the way, he thought as his racing heart threatened to break out of his chest. He made a complete circle around the downtown area, and thirty minutes later returned to the club.

The white Jetta was there, and he sat in his car staring at it for ten minutes, trying uselessly to fashion some kind of speech. Nothing seemed right. He would just have to say whatever came to his mind when he saw her. He breathed a deep and long breath, got out of the car, walked to the door of the club, and opened it.

He stood at the back in the dark and listened for a moment. He could see a figure sitting at the piano bench toward the back of the club, and could hear the slow pinging of single piano notes, and a small voice softly singing straight tones above it. The figure's head tilted up toward the ceiling and the voice opened up. Now it was clear and full. But even with its volume it was poignant, nearly sad, moving, and made him feel heady and light. He'd never heard her voice sound so rich. It was the most amazing sound he'd ever heard.

He moved quietly toward the bar to get a better look. Her head was bowed slightly over the piano, a hand resting in her lap, the right hand on the keys. Light from above the stage struck her face and he could see her now.

He thought about the last time he had seen her. Purple flowers edging her skirt, her faced flushed red with anger and kitchen heat. In this muted light, she was incandescent. A shadow defined a worry crease between her brows he swore wasn't there before, and he realized he'd been the one to put it there. The sight and sound of her made his breathing short. The voice seemed a miracle to him, but he could barely focus on it; he was too busy taking in the mink skin, deep brown hair, subtle angles of shoulder and arm. The curve of her wrists as she fingered key after key with an awkward, though delicate grace. And as he looked, all of the trials of the last year dissolved into a feeling of ease. He thought of old-time travelers, weary, spent, seeing green landscapes they'd long ago left. He was one of them. Home, now. And what would be would be.

XIV

· TWENTY-SEVEN ·

N O NO, SHE THOUGHT. Not that way. Make the notes flow out, as if being pulled by a thread, the way Connie said. She tried it again. Easy, effortless, no forcing. Search your voice for the purest tone. She took a deep breath, and ascended the scale. There, that was better. She shuffled the music on the rack searching for a certain song, a ballad.

She found it, and played the first note of it, a C. It was a sweet, melancholy song with a haunting tune. The verse described a roaming man, a waiting woman. I don't want to sing that song, Olivia had told Connie when he suggested it. Too sad. He'd told her it suited her voice perfectly. He'd said the song was playing on a jukebox in a café bar in Pensacola, Florida, the night he met his wife. He was with a band touring the southeast, and on his night off he went to a place called Sid's with the guys, and she walked in. He bought her a beer and asked her to dance. They were married a year later. And even though she packed her bags and left him for her chiropractor one March night fourteen years ago, he still played that song, even recorded it once. "A no-good woman, but a damn good tune," he'd told Olivia, and they'd both laughed.

She was smiling at this when the noise, like the complaint of wood beneath feet, came from the front of the club near the door. She looked up, beyond the tables and chairs and the long U-shaped bar, and stopped singing. The band wasn't due for another hour, so it couldn't be them, but Jimmy had said he'd probably stop by and bring lunch after one-thirty. She looked at her watch. It wasn't even noon. He was early. He stood in a shadow near the entrance. She smiled in his direction. Jimmy often liked to stand quietly, listening while she practiced.

She shaded her eyes with her hand to block out the glare of the lights as she looked at him, still smiling. The man stepped out of the shadow and into the light.

He was tall, and his arms were long and hung loosely at his sides. His shoulders were broad, his head tilted up. It was not Jimmy, she could see now. And then she knew. Recognition did not illuminate her at once like light splashed on a darkened object, but slowly, like rising heat, it started inside, her knees, her chest, the tips of her fingers, and finally the surface of her skin, which became hot with the knowledge. L.J. was here. He was in the room standing before her.

It had been so long. What should a woman do or feel at this moment? Could feelings be more complicated than hers, now? She felt a weakness overtake her, a sudden softening of muscle and bone. Part of her wanted to run to him and hold him, another wanted to run to him and beat his chest with her fists. And another part wanted to, and did, hold back and stand as still as a stone.

He spoke first. He knew that it was his place to do so even though he could see, as that smile obviously meant for someone else disappeared slowly from her face, that she knew it was him.

"Olivia…" was all he could manage to say.

She stood up with one hand on the piano.

She was wearing a shapeless, sleeveless gray dress of thin fabric, silk, he thought. It was simple with clean lines, hanging below her knees, but somehow it made her look extraordinary. He waited for a thought to come into his head, a word or two that could impart his emotions—sadness, longing, regret, contrition, inexplicable joy. He was never good at this, at saying what he meant with words. These were things better expressed in a dozen or fewer notes blown freely through the bell of his horn. But his musician's hands were empty, and he felt that even volumes of words from his lips would seem useless and pale.

When no idea came to him, he just said her name again.

She waited for the slowing of her racing pulse, then touched her fingers to her lips. "L.J.," she said, her voice breaking. "How…why did you…"

"First let me say this. I know I hurt you. I'll spend the rest of my life wishing I could change that. I'm sorry."

A short fluttering laugh, nervous and sarcastic, spurted from her throat. She arched her brow. "Sorry?" she said. "L.J., I thought you were *dead*. For a year. How could you not even call me?"

"I did, once. Remember? You…you hung up on me. I didn't blame you for not wanting to talk to me."

She thought a moment, searching the months back and arriving on that night in the fall after so many nights of dreams. He *had* called. She had hung up.

"I thought I had dreamed it," she said. "I was so sure it wasn't you, I'd had so many dreams. Why did you wait so long?"

He walked closer to her, his hands absently touching the backs of chairs as he moved. "I was too…I was living on the street. I just couldn't tell you that." He looked straight into her eyes. "And I guess I didn't know what to say."

Standing in the new light so close to her, she could see him better. He looked almost unchanged, except for a few gray hairs that had crept along his temples, and the hang of the tweed jacket revealed the loss of a few pounds. But the skin still reminded her of darkened butter, and the cleft in his chin was pronounced.

She considered him homeless for a moment, trying to imagine his broad shoulders rounded and cowering in some doorway the way she had seen those people in New York.

"The night you left…" she started to say, and he lifted a hand to quiet her.

"Olivia, could you sit down for a minute?" He gestured toward a chair.

Watching him, she sat, and he sat opposite her, and crossed his hands over the table, lacing his fingers.

"I know you have a lot of questions. Let me just tell you first what happened. There's so much I want to tell you."

He told her about the night of the argument, and how devastated he'd felt when she told him to leave, and even worse after losing his job. The bottle he'd emptied in a few swallows. He told her about the accident, the car sinking and about fighting the river for his life, the train and the summoning music of whistle and bell that carried him out of the misery of that one night and into the misery of many others. He told her about arriving in New York with nothing but river-shrunk clothes and his tenor horn, about the mugging, the job, and the trip he'd made back with the band while she was away in the city he had just left.

The only sound in the room was the electric hum of lights, and of their breathing, hers slow and measured, his staggered and shortened by his nervousness. He talked on and on, unable to stop even when she indicated with a raised brow or parted lips that she would like to speak. When he finished telling her about himself, he wanted to tell her about Vaughn.

"So many times over the years I thought about telling you. It was unfair, I know. I made a decision. It was the wrong one. But let me tell you something," he said, and sat back in his chair, "about why I did it."

He went back to the last night he saw Vaughn. He told her about how she looked that day, haggard, worn, distraught. And how her face brightened when she came out of the bedroom with the baby in her arms.

"I remember holding you," he said, his face now forming a smile. "I remember how you felt to me, small, warm. I remember walking down the street in the rain, holding on to you. I was thinking, this baby trusts me. It scared me to death. It was the longest block I've ever walked. But it was the most important thing I ever did in my whole life."

She lowered her head when he said this, and he wondered what it meant, if it was an act of understanding or simply an acknowledgement that he had spoken.

He told her again what Vaughn had told him. "'Don't ever tell anybody as long as you live. I don't want this baby to ever find out I'm her mother.' Like I told you, I would have done anything for Vaughn. And so I promised her."

He paused, allowing her room to speak.

"Promised her?" Olivia felt heat in her eyes. "What about the promises you made to me? What about honesty? You lied to me. Every time I mentioned her and you were silent."

He bowed his head and nodded slowly. "Let me finish. In my whole life, I've never told anybody this story. And when I'm done, I'll tell you why."

He rubbed together his palms and placed them both flat on the table between them.

"That night, I waited a while," he said. "Then I went back to Vaughn's house."

A storm-swept sky of pale violet. The sharp sweetness of wet pine needles. The *tap-tap* of water dripping and the green-scented perfume of rain-sogged leaves and earth. After the punishing storm, Handy collects itself like a teary child after a mother's disciplining hand. Winds that howled now whisper and sigh, air-drying trees and sagging roofs, shrinking swollen eaves and floorboards. Two rainbows arc contrite banners across the sky, blackbirds surface from cover, and L.J. finds his way back to the small house on Jefferson Street.

She hadn't asked him to come back, but there had been warning clouds in her eyes. He was a boy with a man's protecting instincts, and could sense something wasn't right. From outside, the clapboard house stood dark except for a single light in the living room. No music, no satiny Nat King Cole, no deep hum of ballads. But a dark green Ford, the same one he had seen at the club, is parked at the fence. Seeing it sends an icy chill up his back.

But it's the scream—quick, desperate, hot—that springs his body forward before his mind knows where it's going. His legs bound up four steps in a single move, and he yanks open the warped screen door.

There is Vaughn, barefoot in royal blue, eyes wild, body pressed against a wall. Before her, with his back to L.J., a mountain in bib overalls, a shirtless arm raised high like a salute.

And before L.J. can blink, a fist flying like a brick hard across her face.

Another scream, and Vaughn slumps against the wall, her hand to her cheek.

L.J. yells something and Big Earl whips around—the bulk of his madness filling up the room, but with eyes unnaturally calm. From his wide-open mouth, a sickening whiff of liquor.

"Get on away from here, boy, go on home, this is grown folks' business."

Heart pumping wildly, fists balled, L.J. flips through his nine-year old life, searching for some plan to stop another flight of fist to face.

"L.J., get out. Get out now," cries a pain-thinned voice. But L.J. doesn't move. And Earl turns back to Vaughn.

Whiskey-oiled words roll out too loud, thick and slow. "Look, ain't nobody gonna get hurt if you just tell me where the baby is. What you gonna do with a baby? You got money? You got a husband? If I 'member correctly, you ain't got nothin'."

Vaughn's hand presses a cheek turned the shade of roses. Her voice low and brittle.

"Go to hell."

Whapppp. This time a wide, wound-up backhand across her mouth. A tiny red speck springs to her bottom lip. Big Earl shakes his head and sucks his teeth.

L.J. grabs Earl's arm and sets his small teeth in the skin, but Earl flicks him away like dust. The man pauses a moment, then looks down.

"Boy…you know something about all this?"

A giant hand locks L.J.'s arm with an awful burning pain. He tries to jerk free from the grip.

"Leave him alone!" More power in her voice now. L.J. and Earl turn to see her on her feet, shoulders arched high and eyes blazing, body rocking from side to side. Her hands stretched forward, the gun pointing at Earl's chest.

352

Big Earl reaches two hands up, backs away with palms flat against the air.

"Whoa now. Now you 'bout to mess up. That thing go off again, somebody like ta get hurt this time."

Two gun-holding hands shake and the words rapid-fire in one breath—"Move away from him L.J. get out of here and go home I don't want you to see none of this."

Earl puts his hands down and walks back toward her, head cocked to the side, muttering something under his breath. Grinning.

L.J. watches, frozen, his mouth open. With the gun still pointed at Earl, she turns back to L.J.

"Go!" A splitting, spitting scream with something desperate in it. Something that rips through him like fire, jerks his feet into motion, and sends him flying out the door, the screen door flapping behind him.

Outside, he runs half a block before he stops and looks back at the house. Takes a few more steps before hearing the popping noise—a crackle like a hot spark up his spine. It scares him to think of the scene inside, but a cooling relief sweeps his hot skin. She shot him, and now he can't hurt her.

Good.

At home, sickened by rain and shock, he's in bed for two days. The next day he goes to the club, then back to the house. Then the club again. Vaughn is nowhere to be found. But two weeks later, when L.J. passes the club, the dark green Ford is parked outside.

L.J. walks past her house, tearful, for days. Watching, waiting. Finally a sunny blue-sky afternoon brings two old, church-dressed women who go inside and come out with boxes, and padlock the door. A man with a straw hat and dark suit is with them. He boards up two windows that were broken by the storm.

L.J. shook his head slowly, staring down at the table. He folded his fingers and rested his chin on his knuckles. Minutes passed. Somewhere in the club an electric buzz starts up, like a generator. Outside, the dull roar of cars, tree branches in motion, a trash truck.

"I should have stayed. I should have done something." His voice somber, quiet.

Olivia took a short breath, parted her lips, then closed them again.

"You…you were a child," she finally said.

"I know," he whispered.

Another minute passed by in silence. L.J. pulled from his pocket a white handkerchief and blotted his whole face.

Olivia was about to speak again, when L.J. held up his hand.

"There's more."

He sighed long and deep. "The story was that when Vaughn got pregnant, Earl told her to, well, you know, 'get rid of it.'" He said the last words almost apologetically, and watched Olivia for a reaction, but when there was none, he continued. "He'd been giving her money—kept her, you could say—but wouldn't give her money for that. Then when she decided to give birth, he changed his mind. His wife couldn't have children and she wanted Earl's child, badly. That's when Vaughn gave her baby—you—to Big Mama, when she found out Big Earl's plans."

"You mean, to her mother," Olivia said.

L.J. hesitated, then nodded slowly. "Well, you know, I suspected that all along."

He continued. "Earl's wife knew he ran around, and didn't seem to care. He liked to slap them around when he was drunk, Vaughn included. But for all the women he abused, he never laid a hand on the wife. Jessie was her name. I found all this out years later, when I went back to Handy."

Back to Handy. Olivia sat back in her seat again, and folded her arms across her chest.

"When I was about eighteen, I was living in Winslow, Mississippi, a few miles outside of Memphis. The night after my great uncle died, I had a dream about Vaughn. She was telling me to find out about her baby, find out where she was and make sure she was all right."

"I didn't think much about it then, I blew it off. But years after that, after I'd moved to Kansas City, I went back to Arkansas—Little Rock—

on a gig with a band. The manager rented us a van. But I stayed over, decided to take a Greyhound back so I could stop through Handy."

Olivia sat forward in her chair.

"I hadn't been there in eighteen years. It looked different. I remembered it was real pretty, real green. Full of magnolias and smelling that sweet smell of pine. But the places where I used to run around, the fields and stuff, were all overgrown with weeds and bushes and trees. I tried to find the rooming house where me and Purvis lived, but it was gone. There was a Save-All supermarket where it used to be. The Night Owl was boarded up, broken down and leaning. The Beauty Palace was still there, though. Nobody was there. It was a Sunday. I guessed everybody was at church.

"It was September, but still hot and sunny. I just walked around, talked to folks—black folks, that is. I didn't even know before that almost the whole town was black. It wasn't hard to find out stuff. Everybody knew everybody and everybody trusted everybody. I'd find somebody bent over in the garden, weeding, or sweeping their porch, or hanging clothes, and I'd just say 'Beauty Palace, young girl, about eighteen?' and they'd smile and nod. I found out you were heading to Kansas City to go to school. That same week.

"I got a room near the bus station and just hung around it for a few days. Practiced my horn and ate at the little cafeteria next door—remember that place? Had lunch and dinner there every day. Checked the schedules. Bought me a ticket and just waited. There were two buses a day that went all the way to K.C., and I checked every day to see which one you'd show up for.

"But after a few days I gave up. I got bored hanging around town, I didn't know anybody there anymore—we'd only spent the one year there when I was nine. I figured you'd left early in the week and I missed you, or maybe I just didn't recognize you. After all, I didn't even have any idea what you looked like. Then I thought maybe you got a ride to Little Rock and took the train.

"I felt pretty silly, hanging around all that time for nothing. I finally got on the Greyhound on a Friday afternoon, the last K.C. bus out of

Handy for the week; I had to get back to work by then, to be at my part-time job pumping gas.

"So I sat in the back of the bus and fell asleep. I guess I didn't even see you get on. When the bus stopped in Joplin, I got off like everybody else to go to the bathroom, or whatever. That's when I saw you. I saw you, and it was like…a thunderbolt. Like I was seeing her again. I couldn't believe it when you stayed off the bus in Joplin. What's she doing? I wondered. But I just stayed off, like you did, and then just got back on the next bus, like you did."

He shrugged a little, as if perplexed by an unasked question. "It might have been because of that dream, I don't know. Or maybe I was just curious." He looked up at her. "But once I saw you, everything changed. Everything."

Olivia had been frowning so long, her brows furrowed with such an intensity of interest, that she wasn't even aware of the tightening in every muscle of her face. She had to rub the frown from her forehead, her temples.

He sat back in the chair, his feet spread apart, and closed his eyes, then opened them again. He patted the table lightly with his hand. "Maybe checking on you was the one thing I thought I could do for her, to make up for…" He stopped and stroked his chin. His voice was low and soft. "If I could have back one night of my life, it would be that one. For years, I felt responsible for what happened to Vaughn. I never told a soul, but I don't know if I ever really got over it. I'd have given anything to be bigger, stronger, older. Smarter. Just for that one night." He shook his head. "I had to live with that feeling for years, til I met you. Even after, a little." He taps a foot and rubs his thighs.

She finally spoke, her voice sounding deliberately calm and even. "And what about this man, Big Earl. My…father."

He raised his eyebrows. "I asked around. Tried to find out stuff. I hung around the pool hall next to Piggly Wiggly, met a little guy named Bunny, short dark fellow with a badly curved spine, like he had scoliosis or something. Anyway, this Bunny used to run his father's place—a little joint called Ray's. He remembered them, Vaughn and Big Earl. Vaughn sang there before she started at the Night Owl. He did know about the shooting—Earl told him—and he did know that Earl went to jail for a couple of months. Not long at all. But when he got out, he left town. And that was that."

L.J. leaned forward on his elbows. "OK, Olivia, look. I guess, I mean, I know I should have told you all this. Vaughn didn't want you to know—ever. She didn't want to burden you with her life, what kind of woman she was, her…reputation and stuff. All the trouble she had. Who your father was. She wanted you to have an easier life than she had. And I understood that. But I also understand that you had a right to know.

"After what happened to her, what went down, I just didn't have the heart to break my word to her, or the guts to tell you…any of it."

Olivia mulled over this in her mind, saying nothing, letting silence consume the space between them. Outside there was the sudden noise of a Pepsi truck making its delivery across the street, the squeal of its brakes and the loud *haaahhnnn* of its horn. Olivia seemed not to hear it. L.J. wondered if he should speak again, say something to ease the sadness that now rested on her face below her eyes. But he could think of nothing to say.

Olivia seemed completely lost in her thoughts, and now L.J. began to feel he was intruding on them. It was time to leave. He looked at his watch. He'd been gone from Marcus for almost two hours now. "I guess I should go," he said. He stood up. "I've got to pick up someone. There's a little boy traveling with me that I met in New York. He doesn't have much of a home. He's got lots of troubles, and I've been kind of looking after him. I actually left him with Big Mama." He smiled. "He's always hungry, and he's a little wild, sometimes. You know, like kids are. I've got to go pick him up while there's still some food left and the house is still standing."

She smiled faintly, relieved to hear about something else. "How old is he?"

"He's nine. Only nine and you should hear him play the alto sax. Olivia, he's so talented. And he loves it. He's a good kid too."

Olivia took note of the change in his eyes when he spoke of the boy. A sharpness of focus, a light.

L.J. turned to leave, then turned around again to face her. "Olivia," he said, "Let me say this. From the time I left, not a day went by that I didn't think about you, want to be with you. Not a day that I didn't wish things had been different. I came back here only to see you. And how long I stay depends on you. I know you've got the show tomorrow night. You already got a lot to think about. Me and the boy are staying over at the Holiday Inn near the viaduct. I hope we can talk after the show, when there's time, when you've had a chance to think about all this. There's more I want to say. There's more I think that needs to be said."

She nodded, still silent.

"By the way," he said. "I heard you singing. It was…remarkable. I knew someday you would do it. I mean, really, it was amazing. Good luck tomorrow night."

"What was hers like?" Olivia said suddenly. "Her voice."

L.J. thought a moment, turned from her to look at the window. "Her voice? Different. Deeper, darker. Not prettier than yours, though. No more special. You know, it's funny. Long time ago, before the first time I heard you sing, I thought that maybe you would sound like her. But you've got your own voice. Nothing at all like hers. Your voice is, well, it's you."

Olivia considered this, nodding. "And what was she like? I mean really like?"

He scratched his head. "Well, she was…she had a way about her, elegant, kind of like a queen. Sometimes that tough side would come through, but then she had a vulnerable side, too. Olivia, no matter what people said or thought about her, or what she thought about herself, I knew her to be a good and kind woman. A generous woman. A lady, in her way. I'll never forget her."

And I'll never know her, Olivia thought.

He was about to leave again when she spoke.

"The show, by the way, starts at nine."

He looked at her for a moment to be clear of her meaning. Then he smiled again, nodded, and left.

· TWENTY-EIGHT ·

OLIVIA FACED HERSELF in the bathroom mirror and rubbed her eyes. She tied the belt of her white terrycloth robe and turned on the faucet full-strength to let the water heat up. To her surprise, she had slept straight through the night. She had been dead tired after the hours-long rehearsal. She told the guys about L.J. coming to the club and their mouths fell open in unison. Was she OK, they asked her, did she still want to sing? Absolutely, she told them. She took over, driving the rehearsal with a fierceness that surprised them, detailing every nuance of phrase, adjusting tempos, cleaning up ragged intros and transitions in every song. Finally it was the men who threw up their hands well after midnight. "I'm beat," Connie surrendered hoarsely. "We got a good show. Let's go home." By the time she got home, Big Mama was asleep and the house was dark and quiet.

The reflection of the bathroom wall clock in the mirror read 7:05. She'd awakened thinking about Vaughn, then about L.J. About what future, if any, they had together. Now all the curiosity she'd been harboring about what would happen if they finally were together had ended. She had seen him. They had talked. And now she had to decide what she wanted.

She honestly didn't know. There was still so much unresolved between them. She had missed him terribly, grieved over his disappearance, wanted him alive. But beyond that, what she wanted was as vague to her as the steam-clouded image in the mirror.

She soaked a washcloth and covered her face with it, letting the wet heat soothe her eyes. There was too much to think about, too much to sort through, and there was a show coming up tonight. A small knot gathered in her stomach at the thought of the show, but as it relaxed she knew she had nothing to fear. Everything she wanted was happening. She took the cloth down and smiled at herself. Big Mama was here. L.J. was alive and well. And she was singing.

The door opened abruptly. "Uh, scuse me," a high voice said.

She turned to see a small boy waiting at the door, a T-shirt with a New York Knicks logo on it reaching below his knees.

She put a hand to her chest, startled.

"You scared me."

"I didn't know you were in here," he said. The boy rubbed his eyes sleepily.

Olivia, settled now, remembered about the boy. "What's your name?"

"Marcus," he said. "I was over here yesterday and Big Mama and me was playing dominoes and then we ordered a pizza and Big Mama said I could stay all night and she would rent *The Lion King* if it was OK with L.J. and L.J. said it was OK."

Olivia smiled. "Oh."

"Big Mama said this morning she was gonna let me help her make biscuits."

Olivia smiled again at this. Big Mama never let anybody help her do anything in the kitchen.

"Well, I think she's still asleep," Olivia said. "You're an early riser. It's only a little after seven."

"Oh. OK," Marcus said, and turned to leave.

"Wait a minute," she said. "I think we can find something for you to eat until she wakes up."

He smiled shyly. He was a cute little boy, she thought. Had beautiful eyes. She wondered what the troubles were that L.J. mentioned.

"Let's go downstairs. But first, I think you should wash your face."

She handed him a clean towel from the pantry. He turned on the water, rubbed his face once across and said, "OK, I'm ready."

She looked at him. "I don't think so. You didn't wash the corners of your eyes. Or your ears. Like this." She turned the faucet on, and when the water felt hot to her fingertips, she took the towel and rubbed it against his face as he squirmed beneath it.

"Now let me have your hands," she said.

He smelled of little-boy sweat and bubblegum. Probably could use a nice, hot bath, Olivia thought. After breakfast. A nice bath with Ivory liquid bubbles. She washed his palms and the backs of his hands.

"Now," she said. "You're ready."

In the kitchen she put raisin bread in the toaster, scrambled four eggs, and fried six patties of sausage.

Seeing all of that food in front of him, Marcus's eyes grew big. He took his fork and stabbed at a piece of sausage, plopped it on his plate, and then put the whole thing in his mouth.

Olivia said, "Marcus, wait. Why don't you put all your food on your plate at once? Then eat it."

Marcus looked sheepish. "Yes, ma'am."

"You don't have to call me ma'am. My name's Olivia."

"I know. But L.J. told me I had to call you ma'am."

She smiled, put a spoonful of eggs and toast on his plate. "What else did he tell you?"

Marcus took a bite of sausage, frowned, and looked toward the ceiling. "Oh, yeah. He told me I had to make sure I put the lid back down."

Olivia smiled again, this time with a small laugh.

He looked up at her curiously. "You the only one that live here?"

"Yes."

"Ummm," he said. "I ain't never been in a real house before. It's kinda big."

She paused at hearing this and studied him, putting more eggs on his plate. She watched his eyes, large and bright, shining with delight at every awkward mouthful of food. He was beautiful, she thought, especially with his face scrubbed clean. She didn't know what had happened in his life, but at the moment, at least, he looked like a happy child.

She watched him, thinking how pretty his eyelashes were, long, like a girl's. Making a face as if he'd forgotten something critical, he took the folded napkin by his plate and shook it once, then put it across his lap. It was the same gesture L.J. always made before eating. She almost laughed aloud.

She put another sausage on her plate. "So, I hear you're a musician?"

"I play saxophone. I can play 'Stardust' and 'Joy Spring.' I play two more songs but I can't remember the name of 'em."

"Well, maybe when Big Mama wakes up, you can play for us."

He grinned, his eyes wide. "OK. I'll play 'Joy Spring.' I can play that one good."

She watched as he tried to force another whole sausage patty in his mouth.

"Slow down, sweetheart. Eating fast is not good for you. Watch me. Take your fork and slice off a piece of sausage. Like this."

He imitated her moves, her graceful hand in her lap, her small bites.

"That's better, much better." She leaned forward, smiling at him, taking her napkin and wiping his cheek. "Now. I almost forgot. What would you like to drink?"

Olivia had arrived early to find the club in total chaos. At 7:00 the plastic champagne glasses and party favors hadn't been delivered and two of the waitresses hadn't shown up. The phone was ringing off the hook and a plumber was trying to unstop the toilet in the men's room. The piano tuner was driving everyone crazy banging on a D that he couldn't quite get in tune. Jimmy's rental tux had no cummerbund so he had to drive back to Sir Knight's, and several huge bags of Guy's Party Mix sat unopened on the floor behind the bar awaiting candy dishes no one could find.

But by 7:30 the waitresses Saundra and Denise had shown up, gushing apologies and babbling about freeway traffic, the piano was tuned, and the toilet was working. Tall wine glasses and cloth napkins sat on every table, and cashews and pretzels filled fake crystal bowls placed by every glass. The house lights were dimmed and the brass table lamps and sconces gave The Rhythm Room a warm golden glow.

Twenty minutes after eight, the doors swung open and within ten minutes every chair was filled, and the scents of perfume, aftershave, and champagne were mixing in the charged air. Jimmy stood near the curtain behind the stage with Olivia, watching the crowd grow.

The noise level rose, competing with the piped recording of the Oscar Peterson Trio playing "This Could Be the Start of Something Big."

Jimmy wore a gleeful grin. "We're already getting bookings for New Year's Eve," he said, and winked. "You busy?"

"I just want to get through tonight," Olivia said. She looked at the door and saw a group of people she recognized from New Hope—Ann Sloane and Martha Hedley, who had come to Olivia's the day after L.J. disappeared, and Peter and Cynthia Curry, who waved at her as they took their seats. Pauline Jacks was sitting next to her husband Marshall, and smiled widely beneath a small-brimmed, blue felt hat. Cora and Raymond beamed at her from the two bar seats where they sat (Cora held up a hand to flash her engagement ring), and Big Mama was just coming through the door in her favorite green suit on the arm of Forest Fine, who looked to be sporting a new partial plate and a brown pinstriped suit for the occasion.

Winona came backstage and gave Olivia a hug. "This is it, sweetie," she said. "Sing pretty." Then she looked toward the door.

"Is he here yet? Is he coming?" she said.

"I haven't seen him since yesterday. I don't know."

"Well, he'll be here. I can't believe he'd miss this."

Winona went back to a table occupied by her daughter and son-in-law, who waved to Olivia and smiled. Olivia's eyes scanned further for some sign of L.J. and saw none. She didn't know if she was disappointed or relieved, or both. Disappointed mostly, she decided. But she could understand why he wouldn't want to show up like this after being gone so long. Causing a scene with his presence. It had always been her dream that whenever she sang, he would be there. But this was an absence she could understand.

At ten after nine Jimmy took to the stage, his black tux jacket opened to reveal a too-tight red cummerbund, his hands folded together in front of him.

"Friends, I want to thank all of you all for coming out tonight and helping us open the brand-new Rhythm Room!"

"Hear, hear," someone yelled out, and applause filled the room.

Jimmy nodded in the direction of the yell. "That's right! It's been a long time coming. And I especially want to thank all of y'all who supported us in this, and a special thanks to our good friends at First Republic Bank!"

Laughter and applause bubbled up from each table. Jimmy raised his hands palms up. "Seriously, though, thanks to the good folks at City Hall and the mayor's office for getting behind us on this, and helping us try to get this part of town back to where it used to be when it was the hottest jazz district in the country!"

Applause and yelps echoed, and Jimmy nodded and clapped his hands. "And now, do we have a treat for you. Most of you all remember our house band from the old place. Walter Davis, Cornelius Beverly, and Ace Jones, and the new addition to the group, John Paul Stubblefield on alto sax."

Applause again. "And we've got a special treat for you tonight. Someone most of you know, and somebody I hope I can convince to be a permanent headliner down here at The Rhythm Room. In a minute you'll see why. Y'all give a big hand for Miz Olivia Tillman!"

Olivia stepped up onto the stage to a roar of applause and shouts. The band played a bouncy intro to "Love for Sale," and Olivia started in good voice after the eight bar opening. The crowd was with her, she felt. Smiles and rhythmic nods and patting feet fed her and there was an electric spark in the air that made her skin tingle. Behind her bass notes thumped in a jaunty step, cymbals sizzled, the piano pulsed in rocking chords. It was going to be a good night; she could feel it.

The first three tunes were upbeat, and the fourth, "More Than You Know," was a slow ballad that flowed lazily. As the piano chimed a block chord intro, John Paul left the stage; this song was meant for Olivia and the trio. The lights lowered, narrowing into a spot that glowed around Olivia's face as she began:

Whether you are here or yonder,
Whether you are false or true,
Whether you remain or wander,
I'm growing fonder of you...

After the free-form verse, the drums began with soup-stirring brushes, and the bass began its slow, steady beat.

More than you know, more than you know,
Man of my heart, I want you so,
Lately I find, you're on my mind,
More than you know…

And when her mouth opened for the next phrase, she drew a blank.

She couldn't remember the words, couldn't call them to her brain. As well as she knew this song, her mind was empty. She looked at Connie, vamping the chords. She waited for the next entrance. But nothing came to her. She was silent. Connie began the phrase again, giving her more time, but it was no help.

Her eyes felt liquid, her skin hot. This was what she feared most, and it was happening. She couldn't do it after all. She would fail in front of a room packed with people. Her friends. Her neighbors and church members. Accepting the failure staring her in the face, she only wanted one thing: to get off the stage.

Suddenly, as if someone had opened a window, the air in the room changed. From a corner of the stage a sound emerged. It was a hushed sound at first, like an ocean's whisper, but at its core was a backbone strong enough to lean on.

The gasps from the audience came in waves, first from the left side by the entrance where the light was better, then working their way around the room as his friends and fans recognized him. One man even pointed. A woman's voice floated the word "alive?" in a high, squealing pitch above the din. Cupped hands closed over parted lips and whispers rose like feathers above the vamping music, and from way in the back a Sunday-morning-witness "Praise the Lord!" cut through it all. In time, the shocked room calmed and cooled, and smiles appeared like bright bulbs of light at tables through the lamp-lit club.

He continued to play, walking toward her at the center of the stage. His own eyes seeking permission in hers, not imposing, but ready to help at her cue. Her gaze acquiesced while her voice poured wordless, a humming of the tune. He led her, first cushioning her an octave below, then following her in thirds. A sweet, breathy sound like the sea's low tide. It lifted her and carried her, buoyed her above the deep. She rode the wave, dancing with it, unloosing melodic syllables from her throat. Their two tones coiled, interlocking like fingers as higher and higher they climbed; she scatted, he riffed, in and out and around like weaving threads, up and down scales lacing together like ribbons. Then she took the arm of his melody as it guided her, and she found the words.

Connie smiled, and reading the moment, shifted the tempo to an upbeat groove. Something they hadn't rehearsed, but he was right on the money. This was the time.

They played on, the two of them, with the trio kicking a mean groove now. Solid, sure. Somewhere in the audience, hand-clapping in rhythm began, and the tapping of feet on the offbeat. It grew and grew. A few people in the back stood on their tapping, dancing feet, hands clapping and shoulders shaking, unable to resist the pull of the music, of the two souls dancing and taking their turns.

If she could have remembered a raining night before memory began, it might have seemed like the beginning of her life, when he had carried her through a thundering storm down a dark and cobbled street to an opened door.

· TWENTY-NINE ·

"MARCUS! Please!"

Olivia took the phone from her ear as Marcus raced by, his small frame a torpedo hurtling from one end of the house to the other. The midmorning light sifted through the green shutters in the house, and Olivia shifted the phone to another position on her shoulder.

"Wait a minute, Winona. Marcus?"

He was no longer within earshot. "Never mind," she said. "Go on."

"Well like I was saying," Winona said, "I couldn't believe it when I saw him leave before you did. After that crowd of people around him thinned out, seemed like he just vanished. I thought sure you two would have got together. I mean, the sparks were flying up on that stage, honey. And I swore I saw steam coming out of that man's horn!"

"Well, it wasn't really—" Olivia started, when Marcus tore past her again, this time making a noise like an airplane. "Marcus, honey, I'm trying to talk!"

"Sounds like you got a handful over there, Liv." Winona said. "But just answer me one question. Are you really gonna sell the shop? I spoke to Cora last night and she acted like it was a done deal."

"You heard right. I'll be working with Jimmy full time down at the club, keeping books and singing too. Jimmy said I can start whenever I want to."

"The way you lit up that room last night. I'm surprised he doesn't want to sign L.J. up right along with you."

"He does. But that's another story."

367

"Ummm-hmmmm. I'm not *even* going to open up that box."

Marcus raced past Olivia again, this time sending a brass floor lamp reeling on its round base.

"Gotta go," Olivia said, and ran to grab the wobbling lamp before it fell. She didn't make it in time. The lamp went crashing to the floor, shattering the bulb.

She grabbed Marcus' arm. "Marcus, you know not to run in a house like that. You could have been hurt!"

Remembering what Marcus had said earlier about not ever having been in a house before, she regretted her words immediately. But Marcus cowered into a ball, turning his tearful face away from her and hiding it with his hand. "Don't hit me!" he said. "Don't hit me!"

She stopped, stunned. She had barely raised her hand, and certainly not to hit him, but he was sobbing beyond control. She thought of what L.J. said about the "troubles" in his life.

She knelt beside him, grabbed his shoulders and pulled him to her, pressing his face to her chest. "I'm not going to hit you, sweetheart," she said. "Nobody's going to hit you."

Just then Big Mama descended the stairs humming something like "Autumn Leaves," but not quite. She was dressed in a blue-and-white striped bathrobe, but her hair still held the swirling uplifted curls of the night before.

"What's this?" she said, looking at the fallen lamp. "Lord Jesus, y'all little boys is hard on furniture." She raised the lamp and set it upright, got a broom, and swept up the broken glass. Then she said, "Come on, Mister. I feel like making some biscuits."

"That's a great idea," Olivia said, brushing the tears from Marcus's cheek with the back of her hand. "Let's *walk* to the kitchen."

Big Mama rolled out dough and let Marcus cut biscuits with an overturned water glass. Olivia sat at the table sipping a cup of chamomile tea.

"Child, I can still hear that music. I ain't had such a good time since your wedding," Big Mama said. "Speaking of which, is L.J. coming by today to pick up Marcus? You better call him up, 'cause I got some plans for tonight."

"You?" Olivia said. "What plans?"

Big Mama put a tray of biscuits in the oven, then poured a glass of milk for Marcus, who sat at the table on top of a fat phone book. "Me and Forest Fine. We going out to the Ponderosa over on the Kansas side for steaks."

Olivia stifled a laugh. "You're kidding. That man is at least seventeen years younger than you."

"That's right," Big Mama said, wiping flour from the counter top. "And just what is your point?"

Olivia smiled into her cup of tea. "I guess I don't have one," she said. "Who kept Marcus last night?"

"The Jensons' daughter over across the street. Sharita. She a cute little thing. Plays the cello, dontcha know. Smart, too. Her mama said she's going to K.U. in the fall."

"So you met Imogene?"

Before Big Mama could answer, the doorbell rang, and Marcus dashed off into the living room. When he came back, he was hanging on to L.J.'s hand.

"Well, well," Big Mama said, grinning. "If it ain't the man of the hour."

"Morning, Big Mama." L.J. said, smiling at her.

"Sit on down here, child. I'm just making breakfast."

"I'm sorry, I can't stay. I got to go soon." He turned to Olivia. "Liv, I got something to tell you. I'm headed back to New York. Today."

"Why?"

"After I left the club last night, I called New York. This job I heard about came through. I told you about the recording with Ronnie Penner next week? Well, another one, a four-day session for a low-budget movie soundtrack, starts Wednesday. It'll pay about four thousand, more with overtime. And I need the money. It's a long story, but I got a hospital bill to pay. If I leave now, I can make it."

"Well," Big Mama said to Marcus. "We better get your things together. Come on upstairs with me."

Marcus followed Big Mama, and L.J. turned to Olivia, his voice quiet.

"About last night, I hope I didn't, you know, intrude or anything. It was your show. It just seemed—"

"Come on," Olivia said with a half-smile. "You saved my life and you know it. I thank you for that."

"Well. You were sounding great. I was so proud of you, the last thing I wanted to do was steal your thunder." He looked up the staircase, and back at Olivia. "Come out on the porch with me for a minute."

Outside, the sunny May air was warm, the shaded breezes cool. He looked at the green glider, its worn and rusted seat. "You know, nobody sits out on porches in New York. I missed this place. And you."

Olivia wrapped her arms around her shoulders. "Like you said, there's a lot we need to talk about."

"Olivia, come with me."

"What?"

His eyes brightened like a boy's. "Get some stuff together real quick and come with us. I'll bring you back in a couple of weeks."

"I…I can't."

"Sure you can. Olivia, we'll see New York. Then we can take the long way back. It's spring up in the Blue Ridge Mountains. You ever drink water from a rock, or put your ear to one and hear the water running through it? And there's a diner in West Virginia that's got the best ham sandwiches in the world. And in Ohio there's a little carnival with a Ferris wheel where you can see lights on the boats riding the river. Come on, Liv."

She shook her head, felt a crowding sensation in her chest. She wished she could open herself up like church doors on Sunday, wide and welcoming. But she crossed her arms and considered a worn place on the toe of her shoe. "A year is a long time to be angry or hurt or confused or whatever I was." She looked up at him. "I can't just go, like nothing happened. I can't reverse what I've felt for a year in one day. I need time."

He dangled his gray hat on the ends of his fingers, searching her mink-brown eyes for an opening to a certain place inside her he used to know well. He saw fences, borders, bridges he couldn't cross. His mouth stiffened.

"Yeah. OK. Time? You got it."

Marcus burst out the door onto the porch, a green backpack over his shoulder. "OK, I'm ready." He held up a brown bag. "Big Mama gave us some biscuits for the trip."

Olivia looked down at him. "Don't I get a hug?"

He hugged her as she kissed his cheek. He blushed and ran to the car.

"That little boy has stolen my heart," she said, looking after him.

L.J. nodded, watching the boy climb into his car. "He's got nobody. He needs a home, badly." And turning to meet her eyes he said, "You know, I never told you, but I can see the future. Know what I see? You, me, and that boy. Us three—doing things families do. Going to the movies, to the park. Just regular stuff. Making a go of it.

"All it would take is a little bit of luck." He fiddled with his hat. "There's one thing for sure I learned from living on the street."

"What's that?"

"That everything else is easy."

He pulled his jacket collar around his chin as a sudden breeze swirled around the porch. "I guess I'll be leaving. But you haven't seen the last of me. I'll be back."

When he reached the end of the porch, he stopped and turned slowly. "Olivia," he said. "A year ago you asked me a question, and I...I guess I acted like I wasn't sure about my answer. I was a little confused back then. I'm not now."

He took a few steps toward her. "I could tell you that the way things started with us—that it was all about you from the beginning. I could say that but it wouldn't be true. You were right. It was her. When I met you, all I could see was her; she was in my head. Maybe I thought I owed her, that taking up with you was the last thing I could do for her. Maybe I was trying to make things right. And I guess part of me thought if I had you, I'd have a little piece of Vaughn again.

"But Olivia, that all changed for me. I'm not sure when. Probably the first time you smiled, or I heard you speak or heard you sing, or just got to know you and realized that you were you, and not really like her. You were your own woman, special.

"Anyway, I stayed away, because I wasn't clear about all that. I wasn't honest, and the truth scared me—about Vaughn and what happened to her, about how things started with us. I was wrong not to tell you everything from the beginning. It wasn't fair."

He sighed as he looked down to smooth the felt of his hat, then looked back up at her.

"But no matter how things started, at a certain point, I knew I loved *you*, not just Vaughn's daughter or even Vaughn's memory. Loved *you*, Olivia." He focused his gaze on her eyes, and felt his throat catch.

"I still do."

He held her eyes for a moment, then put his hat on his head, turned, and walked down the steps.

She watched him leave and remembered the first time years ago she'd listened to his steps, the rhythmic click of heels as he walked down the street from the Mayfair into a September night. His shoulders squared and high, his head tilted toward the trees.

"Well, what happened?" Big Mama had her hands on both hips when Olivia reentered the house.

"Oh, he's gone. He wanted me to go with him, but I said no." Olivia flopped backwards into the wing-backed chair.

"You what? You not going? Child, you ain't got the sense God gave a goose."

"What do you mean?"

"You and me both know there ain't but one thing stopping you from going off with that man."

"What's that?"

"Don't be asking me. Ask yourself."

Olivia shrugged, folded her arms, and looked toward the window.

Big Mama glared at her. "I know one thing. That green-eyed monster'll eat you alive, you ain't careful."

Olivia turned sharply to her, eyes narrowed, shaking her head. "I can't help it. All I can think about is her having me only because you wouldn't give her that four hundred dollars. Thank God for your good sense, or I'd have never been born. Then she gives me away but treats *him* like her child. I come along, looking just like her, so of course he wants me just so I can remind him of her. He as much as admitted it. Admitted that it was only because of her that he wanted me."

Olivia looked wistful. "You know what I do sometimes? I think about them, together. Her and him. Her fixing him breakfast, combing his hair. Singing to him. But when I think about her, it can only get so far, because I don't know what she *looks* like. Oh, I know she looks like me, but I don't really know, you know, the shape of her hands, the color of her eyes, the sound of her voice. But *he* does. Do you know what I would give for one day of knowing her the way *he* knew her? What I would give for *his* memories?"

She refolded her arms across her chest, arched her shoulders. She remembered what L.J. told her; at some point she'd have to tell Big Mama the whole story. "She had a choice," she said, almost whispering. "She could have found a way to keep me, if she'd wanted to. And L.J. He kept her to himself—the memories of her, everything—away from me all these years. How can I forget that?"

Big Mama let out a long, tired sigh and draped the dishcloth she was holding on the back of a chair.

"Baby Doll, I see you still got a lot to learn about life. All I been hearing from you is what you *ain't* got, about what *ain't* right. If you'd spend time thinking about what you got, maybe you wouldn't have no time left to be feeling sorry for yourself. Now, true, L.J. made a promise, and maybe it wasn't his to keep. And maybe you still thinking he favored your mama over you. But, Sweet Jesus, Baby Doll, that boy married you, and was a good husband to you all them years. He *loved* you. Gave you a good life, a happy home. You think he done all that 'cause of a woman he ain't seen since he was *nine*? You so jealous of him and her—would you trade your young life for his growin' up? Who you think had the best go?

"My daughter didn't just give you away; she gave you to *me*." Big Mama patted her chest with the spread fingers of her hand. "But no mama gives her child away without a price. I didn't know much about my daughter, but I knew she done had a hard life. Child wore her pain on her face like a big old scar, didn't take a minute to see that. All that pain and then here come a little baby. Little piece of life. Ain't hardly a baby born nowhere without some joy behind it. You probably the only real joy she had, quiet as it's kept. If she coulda kept you, she would of. Think what it cost her. Think what it musta cost to give you away."

Big Mama looked pensive, and suddenly sad. "Sometimes, Baby Doll, giving your baby away seem like the onliest choice you got," she said, shaking her head. "Believe me, I *know*. But I'll tell you something, when *your* mama gave *you* up, she did a darn sight better by you than..." She stopped, a tiny ripple in her voice.

"Than what?" Olivia said.

She whispered. "Than I did by her."

Just then, Olivia looked up to see regret shadowing Big Mama's face like a passing cloud. Olivia sat frozen for a moment, closed her eyes, letting the words settle in her mind. Big Mama was telling her something that she should have known, and how could she not have? She'd never thought about the pain. Big Mama and Vaughn had given their children away. One who might have raised a child, and one who surely couldn't. And instantly Olivia went back to her own losses: three babies born but not born, and the pain born in their place. She wondered what she would have done in her mother's circumstances. Looking at Big Mama now, she knew. She'd have given her child to the woman standing before her. And lived with that. And if, for the briefest time, L.J. received whatever love Vaughn had left to share, that had to be a good thing, too. God knows, he had needed her. And maybe just as much, she had needed him.

Olivia frowned, looking away, her head and heart now heavy with the weight of so much knowledge. She thought of L.J. trying to protect her from all of it, and wondered briefly how much better it might have been never to know all this. Her mother was an abused, broken woman. Her father, as mean and dark-spirited as a man can be. What good had knowing any of this done her?

Then a sudden realization washed over Olivia—she'd *needed* to know all of it, needed to know every painful thing. When had she started singing again? After she had squared herself with the truth. After her husband and her grandmother had given up the hiding and denying of it. After knowing and coming to accept her mother, failings and all, and in doing so accepting the gift she had given her. A gift she had taken for granted, even rejected, for so many years. But a gift Olivia treasured now, in spite of herself, in spite of everything.

"Big Ma—Grandmother, I'm sorry," Olivia started to say, but turned when she heard her squatting to pick up something that had fallen on the floor near the sofa.

"Oh, my Lord," Big Mama said. "Looka this."

In her palm was a two-dollar bill folded over twice, faded with age, its edges frayed and ragged.

"What's that?" Olivia asked.

Big Mama unfolded the bill and stretched it out. "It's L.J.'s. It's that two-dollar bill Vaughn give him years ago. His good-luck piece, he said. The one he's been carrying around with him for forty years."

Olivia looked at it curiously, thinking of Vaughn. "I'll put it in my room and I'll make sure he gets it when he comes back."

Big Mama shook her head and said, "No, Baby Doll. You got to get it to him now."

Olivia looked dazed, staring into space. "I'm not even sure where he is."

Big Mama reached into a console table drawer behind the sofa, pulled out an envelope and stuck the bill in it. "They staying over at the Holiday Inn near the viaduct. Ain't but one Holiday Inn over that way."

"I'll probably miss them. I'll mail it to him in New York. I'll get his address off that letter he wrote."

"Didn't he say he gave up the place he was staying in? Stop being lazy, Baby Doll, and take him this bill. I guess you don't know how important a good-luck piece is to some folks. He's been carrying this thing around with him almost since the day you was born. He needs it to bring him luck. Ain't nothing worse than realizing you done lost your good-luck piece. Why, one time when I was a girl I had me a little rabbit's foot—"

"All right, all right, I'll go," Olivia said, cutting her off. "Just give it to me."

Big Mama smiled. "Hurry up, or you'll miss them."

Olivia took the bill, grabbed her purse and headed out the door. "I'm gone. There's leftover baked chicken in the fridge for your lunch, if you want it. I'll see you in a bit."

And as Big Mama watched Olivia get in the car and drive down the street, she smiled again, satisfied.

She didn't see his car in the asphalt parking lot of the low-slung, off-ramp style motel, and for a moment her breath stopped. She'd missed him. Let her chance slip away. But she wheeled the Jetta around to the back of the lot and there was the gray Delta 88.

She'd driven like a madwoman, speeding down the highway, dogging semis on the overpasses, scraping a curb at the exit. When she pulled up to the motel, words were still gathering in her mind like pieces of a forgotten song. She drove up before the picture window framing the cheap gray curtain drawn across it and paused before knocking at the chipped blue door. Over and over the words rolled in her mind, a jumble of half-built sentences, tumbling, colliding, refusing to arrange themselves in some sensible order. She stopped trying to think. She would have to rely on whatever spilled from her when she faced him.

He took a minute coming to the door. He wore a sleeveless white undershirt, bright green boxer shorts revealing slightly bowed hairy legs, and a pea-size spot of white shaving cream on the underside of his chin. After twenty-five years, he still managed to miss that same spot. He'd shampooed his hair and it stood in small matted clumps from his head. She smiled at the sight of him like this, familiar as her own reflection.

He opened the door wider, revealing pairs of sneakers, socks, and T-shirts, and two jumbo potato-chip bags strewn across the two un-made beds. In the background, Marcus was squealing a song above the sound of water splashing violently in a bathtub.

He stood there looking at her with a smile that slowly grew to consume his whole face, which took on a delight she could only call goofy, and for the first time in all of these years she saw how he must have looked when he was nine years old. She would have laughed if she hadn't been so busy trying to figure out what in the world to say to him.

"May I come in? May I talk…"

Then there was no need to figure it out, because suddenly long arms were reaching around her shoulders and back, pulling her tightly into a shelter of chest and chin. Against her face she could feel the familiar coarseness of rough stubble on half-shaved skin hinting of evergreen soap and Old Spice, and in her ear was the soft bass murmur of something that sounded like her name.

After a time, she felt something gathering in her throat. Words. She wanted to call them up, but they stumbled and tripped over each other somewhere in the middle of her mind, and in doing so convinced her that they were needless. In a movie one of them would say something about forgiving but still remembering, or starting over new and not looking back. About beginning again together and taking whatever time it took to get it right. She could say how much she'd missed him, how desperately she'd wished him alive, how the love she felt for him now crowded out every other feeling she possessed. But words paled against the here-and-now rhythm of this man's speeding heart. So instead she leaned into the feel and smell of skin-heat and shelter-arms, and a heart beating wildly next to her own.

They stood together in the middle of the room for a long time while above the noise of truck traffic from the viaduct there was the wild splashing of water from the bathtub and more of Marcus's singing. At least Olivia *thought* it was singing. It was an unrecognizable squawking, laughing, gleeful song, full of nonsense. Anyone passing might have thought the boy had lost his mind. It was the kind of noise children make when they feel safe, Olivia thought, playing in backyards on hot summer afternoons with love and lemonade waiting for them inside.

Olivia listened to the boy's caterwauling as if it were instructive, as if the nonsense babble held some burning truth. She thought of Marcus flinching at her innocently raised hand and knew one thing for sure—here was a child who knew pain. Yet the air around him pulsed with joy. She decided it was the sound of a child for whom the discovery of such joy was still brand-new.

Holding on to her own pain had surely been her choice, just as it had been to resist the peace of knowing who she was. All right, now she knew it—now she could work with it. *All I hear about is what you ain't got,* Big Mama said. Olivia dug her cheek into the crook of her husband's neck, and listened to the beautiful, laughing, singing boy. This was what she had: a husband she loved alive and near as her own arms, and a child not far away, giggling and laughing with joy.

Marcus let out a whooping squeal now, and began singing an octave higher, even louder. He sounded even more playful and wildly jubilant, slapping the water with the flat of his hand. This new outburst was so startling to L.J. and Olivia that they pulled away from each other laughing. Olivia laughed so hard she felt a cleansing coolness rushing to her face.

She nodded toward the bathroom door. "Is he OK in there?" she said.

L.J. shrugged. "What can I say? The boy loves a good bath."

This made them both laugh again.

"Oh, thank you," Olivia said softly, "for bringing him here."

"Does this mean you'll go with us?"

She gave him a wry half-smile. "I don't have any clothes. I'd have to pack."

He smiled back. "I'll buy you anything you need. Let's just go."

Pick up and go, just like that. New York. She remembered the many times before when he'd asked her. She'd never done anything so spontaneous in her life. But she listened to the boy's gleeful noises again and nodded.

"But you know, I've always been a little afraid of driving through the mountains."

He nodded slowly and pulled stray hair back from her eyes. "Well, the mountain roads are sometimes a little rough, twists and turns, you know, but it's worth it for the view. It shouldn't be too bad. Not if we just take our time."

She liked the way he said that. As if there was all the time in the world. And for the first time in a long time she believed there was.

Remembering the two-dollar bill, Olivia reached for her purse and fumbled through it. "Oh, wait," she said. "I don't want to forget this. I believe this is yours."

He looked down at the folded bill for a moment, then looked up at her and hunched his shoulders. He shook his head, frowned, his face wearing a puzzled look.

"That isn't mine," he said.

Big Mama finds her purse in the kitchen. She pulls out a chair and sits down at the big oak table, opens her wallet, and pulls out four crisp two-dollar bills. She spreads them in front of her one by one over the varnished oak, examines them, then puts them all back in her wallet. Yes, she used the right one. The others look just too new. It had taken her an hour on the bus, and thank God First Kansas City Trust was on the Eighteenth Street line. The woman at the teller's window looked at her like she was crazy, asking for "the oldest looking two-dollar bills you got." And even then she'd had to doctor it up plenty, using soap, a dab of bleach in hot water, and finally, when it was dry, what dust she could scoop up from the back of the cupboard. Anybody looking at it too hard would have known something was up. But just as she knew would happen, Olivia hadn't even looked at it; it served its purpose perfectly.

Two weeks she figures, more or less, is how long they'll be gone. That is, if L.J. is as determined as he seems, and she's sure he is. She likes that man, always has. She'd liked him even before she learned he was the one who hand-delivered her life's greatest blessing. He was strong, a fighter. Shoot, the boy pulled himself up half-dead out of a river, kept himself alive on the streets of New York, and he was still awful good-looking and strong. Now that was something. From what she's heard, just staying alive *indoors* in that city is a miracle. If he did all that and lived to tell, surely he wouldn't pass up a second chance to convince his own wife to take a little trip.

As Big Mama reaches to put her wallet back in her purse, she sees a hint of color buried deep in the well of leather; she brought something else from home to give to Olivia, then thought better of it. The timing was not just right, she told herself, but maybe *she* just needed more time, because she could not yet bear to part with it.

Folded over into a ten-inch square and wrapped in box tissue, the blue and green baby quilt is frayed and yellowed with years. She pulls it out, unfolds it, and holds it against her face. She breathes in; it smells of new life and old regrets, of joy and grief and time itself. She runs her fingers along the neatly sewn stitches, the multicolored patches of fabric. Cotton plaids mostly, some denim, even a little seersucker. Unlikely patterns, haphazard pieces joined together in the way that creates perfection. She imagines her daughter's hands, delicate and small, or maybe like hers, strong and ample, patiently quilting a coverlet of love. Against her skin she can almost feel the impression of three lives—a newborn infant, a frightened but determined boy, a heartbroken mother—all there in the worn fabric, threaded together into an inseparable weave. One day she'll give the quilt to Olivia, and she'll see it as the precious thing it is. But for now Big Mama's fingers savor the texture, the feel of worn cloth and each stitch her daughter's hands have made. It's all she has of her now, and all she'll ever have (that much she knows). Olivia, she has that voice.

Big Mama puts the quilt away. She washes the breakfast dishes and wipes the kitchen counter of biscuit flour and looks at her watch. Soon, the three of them will be on their way, Marcus singing and bouncing in the back of the car. That little boy—she wonders how he'll figure in, just how and when and in what way it will all work out. God never made a sweeter child. Given time, she believes the three of them could piece together a family just as strong as one made from whole cloth. Stronger even, since there's such a *need* in each one of them to do so. It just might take a while, is all.

Sometimes the road ain't so hard as it is just plain long, she thinks. But if you're willing to do the waiting, something good might just show up at your door.

She steps out onto the porch, looks up through the leaves of maple and oak that shade the eaves of the house. Translucent clouds veil a climbing sun along the eastern edge of the sky. Across the street, Imogene Jenson sweeps her porch in her red housecoat. "How you doin', Big Mama?" she says, waving. "Thanks for that sweet-potato pie you sent over yesterday for Sharita. Delicious."

Big Mama waves, one hand on her hip. "You welcome, child. How you feeling this morning?"

"Not too good. Got me a little cold I'm trying to get rid of."

"Well, I'll fix you some of my head-cold tea. I put sassafras and ginger root in it…and uh, couple other things." Big Mama stops herself. She's never been one to give away the secrets of her remedies. "Don't taste too good, but it'll knock that cold right outta you. Be good as new, come tomorrow, guaranteed."

"Sure it's no trouble?"

"None at all."

"Be right over after I get dressed."

"That's fine." Big Mama smiles as Imogene goes back inside her house. Big Mama folds her arms and sucks in the morning air, then lifts her arms and stretches wide. There are some days she feels every minute of her nearly ninety years, and some days, like today, when she feels as eternally young as the woman who's on her mind.

All things in time, she thinks. All things in their own rhythm.

Mother-of-pearl clouds break and scatter, no longer shielding the May sun's light. All around her, spring blooms unsheath and wrest free from secret night-beds of winter. May breezes circle the green-shuttered house, singing earth songs in measured time (old harmonies and new ones), while songbirds chorus in flight, full of knowing.

Truth, too, circles like easy winds, dancing, playing, before finding its place and time. Love finds love; somehow a child finds home, and a woman finds peace. And lives begin again.

Rest easy, Vaughn, your work's done, your life and death worth all the trouble.

Big Mama takes a long, calming breath. She looks again at the oversized watch face leather-strapped to her wrist. She needs to hurry up and fix that tea, and then get busy. Olivia's house sure could use a good cleaning. But she remembers last night, and begins to hum. She feels like singing. That's a joke. She's never been good at singing. Tone-deaf, truth be told. But she still knows good music when she hears it. Just knows when it is right, when all the little notes fit together, like something that's just meant to be. How did that one song go? She can't think it out. So she lets the pieces of it dance into the distant regions of her mind, and with a last look at the climbing sun, turns and goes back inside the house.